Me & Georgette

D.B. Schaefer

Author's Note:

This is a work of fiction. Names, characters, places, and incidents are the product of the author's imagination, and any resemblance to actual persons, living or dead, is entirely coincidental.

*This book is dedicated to the memory of
British author Georgette Heyer
(August 16, 1902 - July 4, 1974).*

Acknowledgments

I am indebted to a number of people without whom this book would never have become a reality. Long-time friend Nancy Ogle introduced me to my first Regency novel; friend and author Janice Young Brooks (also known as mystery writer Jill Churchill) introduced me to *The Grand Sophy* and the world of Georgette Heyer. BFF and author Libi Astaire provided endless encouragement, as well as countless hours of mentoring on the intricacies of independent and digital publishing. Many thanks, also, to my editor Avigail S., to Tana Frij for her amazing cover, friend Avigail Frij for general encouragement and technical assistance, and Heron Enterprises for graciously allowing me to quote Miss Heyer and use her name in the book title.

A special debt of gratitude is owed to early Internet pioneers Robert Kahn and Vinton Cerf, and to the United States Department of Defense Advanced Research Projects Agency (DARPA), which funded their work. The invention of the Internet, and the explosion of information it has made available with the click of a button, is nothing short of miraculous to those of us who remember spending hours at libraries juggling periodical indexes, card catalogues, microfiche and heavy reference books. The websites I visited while researching *Me & Georgette* are too numerous to mention, even if I were to remember them all, but two sites in particular deserve acknowledgment: Kathryn Kane's www.regencyredingote.wordpress.com, and Vic Sanborn's www.janeaustensworld.wordpress.com. Miss Kane also took time from her busy schedule to patiently answer many questions regarding Regency England.

Finally, no acknowledgment would be complete without a special thanks to my long-suffering husband and children, who set aside many of their own demands so that I could write.

Prologue

*E*ven to the most unimpassioned observer, the tableau in the elegant Blue Drawing Room at Silverleaves must have appeared excessively charged with tension on that unusually sunny day in March. One of the scene's two participants, a slight young man whose yellow pantaloons, intricately arranged neckcloth, and dark hair swept into a Brutus proclaimed him a pink of the ton, had flung one carefully manicured, aristocratic hand against the Italian marble fireplace and now appeared to be clinging mercilessly to the mantel of that appendage.

"Dash it, Dev," he exclaimed with much emotion to the raven-haired beauty facing him. "I'm asking you to marry me, to share my life with me. I'm laying my heart and my life at your feet."

"Well, then pick them up again," the beauty replied ruthlessly. "I have no intention of marrying you, now or ever."

"Dev, you cannot mean that. Is it my expectations? You shouldn't worry about that. I have—"

"Yes, I know, Jeremy," Devorah interrupted impatiently, slapping her lavender kid gloves against the skirt of her blue-and-white striped muslin half dress. "You have Great Expectations. They mean nothing to me, however. As I've told you about one hundred—a thousand—times, if you'd only care to listen, I don't want to marry you. I won't marry you."

The disappointed lover removed his hand from the mantel and pressed it to his breast with an anguished groan. A heartfelt sigh escaping him, he knelt upon the blue-and-gold Axminster carpet covering the room's parquet floor, his right hand still positioned somewhere in the region of his heart.

"Dev, please marry me. Without you I have nothing to live for. I may as well enlist as a common foot soldier (though now that Napoleon's been brought to bay there's not much action these days on the Continent). I may as well destroy myself with Blue Ruin in some gaming hell. I may as well ... as well kill myself."

He shook his head mournfully. "Perhaps, yet, I shall."

Devorah snorted in a most unladylike manner. "Doing it just a little too brown, Jeremy. Now, quit acting like an idiot and pick yourself up from the floor like a good boy."

Jeremy flushed and rose angrily to his feet. "Even in my despair you torment and tease me. If only you knew... How my arms ache for you at night. How I yearn to hold you, to kiss you. To make you mine. I'm a man, damn it, and I want you, need you."

Grabbing her ruthlessly by the arms, he yanked her to him and pressed his mouth against her own for a brief instance, then thrust her violently away. Devorah screamed faintly as she fell against one of the velvet armchairs that flanked the fireplace.

"You—you brute. You animal. Get away from me. Get out!"

But instead of obeying, Jeremy stared at her in horror, momentarily stunned by his own actions. As he came to his senses, a look of abject remorse spread across his handsome features. "Oh no, Dev! What have I done? What have I done? I would die rather than harm you. Please forgive me, my darling."

The beauty trembled with rage and helplessness as she struggled to pull herself upright. But her face softened and, as she mastered control over herself, her voice held a note of forgiveness. "Oh, Jeremy. It was probably partially my fault, as well. I'm very sorry if I've misled you in any way. I certainly didn't mean to. If any kindness on my part has been misinterpreted, please forgive *me*. You must understand, however, that we would never suit. Our backgrounds are too disparate."

Jeremy plucked a Dresden figurine from the mantel and began toying with the pink-and-gold porcelain flounces on the tiny shepherdess's skirt. "If it doesn't matter to me, Dev, I don't understand why it should matter to you. It won't be the first time the lower orders married into the peerage. Once my Uncle Elmore dies—Lord Edgemore, you know—he's nearly eighty and could pop off any day now—and I inherit the title and property and you become Lady Edgemore, all of the London ton will open its arms to you. As for my mother and all her stuffy old sisters, for that matter, they'll love you once they meet you. Besides, they've been after me for years to settle down."

"No, Jeremy, there's more to it than that. There are things about myself I've kept secret from you. But now, it seems, I must tell you. You see, I'm... I'm...."

Jeremy's eyebrows shot up. "Yes?"

Devorah's voice faltered. Reaching unconsciously for the gold filigree, six-pointed star that hung from a delicate chain beneath the high-necked bodice of her dress, she took a deep breath before plunging into her revelation. But the bracing breath was unnecessary. The doorbell at Silverleaves suddenly began ringing loudly and relentlessly to the accompaniment of frantic knocking on the front door. As the noise continued unabated, footsteps could be heard in the far regions of the great house. First the dignified step of the ancient butler, Grayton, and the decisive click of James the footman, then the hurried steps of the housekeeper, and finally the varied taps and shuffles of lesser household servants.

"I'm...." Devorah intoned softly. But seeing that he was no longer listening, she shrugged her shoulders and followed Jeremy out of the room to discover, along with everyone else, just what the commotion was all about.

Chapter 1

*D*evorah Asher swam toward wakefulness from the cushioned ocean of her sleep. Breaking through the barrier between half dreams and reality, she groaned, turned over and reached for the radio alarm on the rosewood nightstand beside her bed. Eight o'clock on a Sunday morning. Strange. She thought she had set the alarm for nine.

As her dreams receded further and further into the background, she realized that the ringing and pounding that had awakened her continued even with the alarm turned off. The sounds emanated from downstairs—more specifically from the heavy oak front door. Who, she wondered, would be breaking down her door at eight o'clock on a Sunday morning? She rolled back over on her pillow and shut her eyes. Perhaps if she ignored the knocking, the perpetrator would go away.

The knocking became more frantic. "Devorah, *Devorah,*" a female voice with a pronounced Brooklyn accent made itself heard clearly through the door. "Are you in there? Are you all right? *Devorah,* open up!"

"Okay, okay, I'm coming," Devorah muttered, throwing off the bedcovers and reaching for her robe. "Just quit knocking, whoever you are, though it sounds suspiciously like you, Gitty, and if so you are in Big Trouble. Let me get decent and wash my hands. I'm coming."

The golden light of dreams was totally obliterated by the tepid reality of an overcast New York March morning as Devorah recited the blessing upon awakening and padded over to the small, decorative sink opposite her bed. Whoever was at the door—and she was now positive it was Gitty—was obviously ignoring the necessity of performing morning ablutions before she traipsed downstairs.

"Well, let her wait," she thought rebelliously, peering into the mirror above the sink and examining her appearance. Disheveled black hair, ivory skin with a minute sprinkling of freckles on a delicately sculpted nose, and large blue-gray eyes framed by a thick fringe of black lashes were reflected back at her. To the disinterested observer, she would have presented a picture of rare beauty. To Devorah, the mirror was ruthless, accentuating faint blue-black circles under her eyes, the result of a near-sleepless night, and miniscule lines beginning to form at their corners. She washed her hands, rinsed her mouth and face, dragged a brush through her hair and, tying her robe more tightly around her, headed toward the stairs.

"Devorah, *Devorah Asher!* Open up this instant, or I'll call the police. Your mother said you would be home this morning," the voice behind the door commanded.

Devorah pulled back the dead bolt and yanked open the door. Gitty halted mid-knock and stared blankly for a split second. Quickly recovering herself, she examined Devorah critically. "You look lousy this morning. Are you feeling okay?"

"I'm feeling great. I *love* being rudely awaked at eight o'clock on a Sunday morning. Maybe you could come back at ten, when I've had my morning coffee?"

"Maybe," Gitty said, propelling her seven-month-pregnant bulk past Devorah. "But I need to see you now. I'm in a big hurry. I can only stay a few minutes."

"By all means," Devorah replied sarcastically.

"I need a book. A good book."

"A book? You woke me up to get a *book*?"

Gitty turned to the mirror on the wall next to the door and adjusted her immaculately styled, dark-blond wig. "It's an emergency. I have an appointment with Dr. Rosenzweig at 8:45. He's gotten so popular that he's now taking patients on

Sunday mornings—*early* Sunday mornings—and even though *I* have to be there on time, *he's* always late. And I'm so tired of reading the back copies of *Family First* that he keeps in his waiting room."

Married more than a decade before to Yitzhak Klein and already the mother of six, Gitty had used Dr. Rosenzweig during all of her previous pregnancies. But something about her excuse sounded false. "I've known you all my life, Gitty. Why did you really knock on my door at the crack of dawn?" Devorah asked suspiciously.

Gitty turned away from the mirror with an expression that nicely combined innocence and indignation. "Why, only to get a book. What can you loan me that's fun? Maybe one by that authoress, the one you are always trilling on about. What do you call her—Georgette?"

"*Heyer.* You want a Georgette Heyer. I'll loan you my entire collection, if it will get you out of here. Come on upstairs and I'll find you something. But I warn you—you will probably have to wrap it in a brown paper bag because the cover will be too much for a Boro Park doctor's office."

Gitty groaned. "Don't you have any of your Georgette Heyers downstairs?"

Devorah eyed Gitty wickedly. "Too early for exercise? Okay, go pour yourself a glass of milk or juice and put your feet up. I'll be right back."

Devorah returned within minutes and dumped an armful of paperbacks on the glass-topped breakfast table. "Behold, the world of Georgette Heyer," she said, spreading her arms wide. "I brought you a selection of the best, though best is relative, because I have about ten different favorites. Here, take this one with you. It's great. I just stayed up till three a.m. rereading it for probably the tenth time."

"*Sylvester or the Wicked Uncle?* If you say so." Gitty looked doubtfully at the cover before stuffing the book in her purse and hoisting herself to her feet. "Looks clean enough even for Dr. Rosenzweig's office. I'll let you know how I like it. Gotta hurry now."

7

Midway to the front door, she halted. "By the way," she said, her voice flattening to a monotone, "are you interested in joining us for the Purim festivities this year? We'd love to have you. The kids keep asking when they're going to see Aunt Devori."

Devorah's eyes narrowed. "What's the catch? You know that I go to my parents or brother's every year."

"What would you say if I already got you released from your family obligations? I spoke to your mother and told her we'd especially love to have you with us."

"Can't be. Spending Purim with my family is Holy." For Gitty to have gotten her out of going to her family for the mandatory festive meal on the Jewish holiday of Purim was something indeed. Her life-long friend must be hatching a plot—with her mother's acquiescence.

Gitty smoothed the rounded stomach of her mock-tweed maternity jacket and stared down at the sport shoes she always wore in the more advanced stages of her pregnancies. "I, er.... I presented your mother with a compelling reason for releasing you from your family obligations this year."

"Such as?"

"Such as something very compelling. Think, Devori. What could be the most compelling reason for anything where you are concerned?"

"Oh, Gitty, you didn't! Who is he?"

"Don't worry so much! He's a nice guy."

"They're all nice guys. Who *is* he?" Devorah repeated, recalling a succession of unsuccessful and often embarrassing matchmaking attempts. Though lately, any kind of attempted match was rare.

"You've never heard of him. He's a first cousin of Yitzhak's, a professor of Jewish history at McGill University. He's going to be in New York for a conference right before Purim, and Yitzhak has convinced him to stay with us a few extra days. So what could be more natural than having him join us? It's not like you think," Gitty added quickly. "I've figured out by now that I have no idea what you are looking for in a husband, so before you meet for a date, you get to approve him. He doesn't know he's meeting you. Yitzhak hasn't even mentioned you. You get to look at him over at the meal and decide whether you're interested. Then Yitzhak will jog his memory as to who you are and ask whether he wants to be introduced."

"What important detail about this male aren't you telling me? And why wasn't I informed of his existence until now?"

"Nothing; don't worry. He's a good guy, *very* okay. Yitz will tell you all about him," Gitty said airily, moving toward the front door and making a speedy exit. "Call him between seven and eight this evening and he'll tell you everything."

With a sigh, Devorah watched Gitty propel her bulky form down the front walk, then closed the front door behind her and headed back to the kitchen for a cup of coffee.

Sunday morning coffee had been a ritual for years, ever since she landed her first job with a Wall Street brokerage firm—a part-time internship while she was working on her master's degree in business administration at Columbia University. To celebrate, she had purchased an inexpensive, hand-crank coffee grinder and a small sack of gourmet coffee beans. She discovered that grinding the beans and steeping the grounds in her coffee press was a soothing antidote to the rigors of juggling a fledgling, high-pressure career with the intense hours of study required to hold her own in a highly competitive business school atmosphere.

After graduating business school with top honors, Devorah was offered a lucrative, full-time position with the same Wall Street firm where she had interned. Soon she had a reputation as a shrewd investment advisor and was building a solid clientele from all over the city. She bought a house not far from her parents' Boro Park home, and—to the surprise of many in her community—moved out on her own.

As Devorah's career blossomed, the original, budget coffee grinder gave out and she replaced it with a more upscale, electric model. But the Sunday morning ritual of grinding the beans, steeping the grounds, and sitting down to relax with a fresh, aromatic cup of coffee remained the same.

This Sunday, however, the ritual of coffee failed to relax her. As she spooned the beans into her high-tech grinder, Devorah was reminded of her humble first machine. She had purchased it seven years before, when she was twenty-three and still cherished some illusions that, gifted with brains and beauty, as well as good family and character traits, she could be one of the few lucky ones who had it all. Back then, she still believed that even though she had "bucked the system," so to speak, by going to university and then to graduate school, she would nonetheless meet and marry a fine man and raise a family while maintaining a career.

Devorah, like her friends, had been educated at an Orthodox Jewish girls' school, and the majority had continued on to seminary in Israel for a year or to a Jewish teachers college. Many, like her friend Gitty, had married at nineteen or twenty and now had large families. Others had delayed marriage for a few years until they had obtained their teaching degree or some type of minor career training. Of her high school graduating class, all the others were married now; most had children, and most of those who worked outside the home were teachers, secretaries, bookkeepers or, if they were ambitious, business owners or accountants.

Only Devorah remained single. But why?

It wasn't because of her background, which was perfectly ordinary for someone from her community. The middle of five siblings, she was the child of immigrants who had lost extensive family in the Holocaust and whose remaining family were scattered throughout Europe, Israel and the Americas. Like many of her classmates' fathers, Devorah's, a successful diamond dealer from Antwerp, was a Torah scholar as well as a businessman; her mother, born in England, was a teacher.

And it wasn't for lack of matchmaking efforts on the part of family and friends. As she neared her last few years at the local Bais Yaakov high school, Devorah had been packed off to England to an elderly grandmother and a myriad of aunts and uncles in London for a brief vacation, then shipped north to Gateshead to attend seminary. As her years there neared their end, the aunts and uncles began recalling her to London to propel her into a flurried round of matchmaking with the carefully selected sons of friends and friends of friends. None of the staid young Englishmen of suitable background duly presented to her caught her interest; after graduation, Devorah was sent on to Belgium, where the diamond-dealing branch of the family tried its hand at *shidduchim*—matchmaking—from a continental pool of prospective matches.

The relatives shook their head in wonderment that such a beautiful, intelligent, charming girl could fail to make a match quickly. But, as Devorah had learned in one of her classes in seminary, a *shidduch* wasn't necessarily a *zivug*. A *shidduch* was merely a match, the putting together of two people of common goals and similar backgrounds; a *zivug* was one's life partner—one's soulmate, one's other half, predetermined before birth by the Holy One, Blessed Be He.

Returning from her relatives in Europe with no wedding on her horizon, Devorah had rocked her parents' household by applying to various universities. She was accepted by several and settled on Columbia University. It was, perhaps, not the most suitable for a nice Orthodox Jewish girl who had been gently, conservatively reared in Boro Park, but it was the most prestigious of the lot and she was able to live at home while completing a degree in mathematics. When she graduated *summa cum laude* and her *zivug* had still failed to appear on the scene, she stayed at Columbia, continuing on for her MBA.

In the meantime, all the decent, eligible young men were being married off quickly. Soon there would be no one left except for the rejects—the ones with blemishes on their person, background or family tree, and the recycles—the ones who had been married already.

As Devorah passed her landmark twenty-fifth birthday, attempts at *shidduchim* grew fewer and farther between. Of the men she did meet, most of them were clearly unsuitable, but a few did actually appeal to her in intellect, personal attraction and personality. However, none of the latter possessed the courage—or so she told herself—to pursue a lasting relationship with an intelligent young woman with one foot firmly planted in the secular career world. As she approached her thirtieth birthday, the prospects dribbled down to practically nothing, except for the occasional, problematic divorcé or the middle-aged widower with a daunting number of young children.

Despite her desire to work out in the big, wide world, Devorah remained a traditional "girl" at heart, and as the prospect of spinsterhood became more realistic, it was difficult to keep up her spirits. She tried to remain optimistic. "He isn't available yet; perhaps he's still meeting all the wrong women," she told herself of the soulmate who had yet to make an appearance. Or, "He isn't in the country right now, but is spending a year in Jerusalem before settling in New York."

Gitty, however, had a different explanation for Devorah's continued state of singlehood. "You're chicken," she said succinctly. "Afraid of getting married and sharing your life with someone else, afraid of ever having to make your ego subservient to that of a man. So, you deliberately scare them off before they start thinking seriously about marrying you."

"Not true, Gitty," Devorah had protested when first presented with her closest friend's explanation.

"Yes true," Gitty had retorted. "I've known you since we were toddlers. I may even know you better than you know yourself. The problem with you is that you are too smart for your own good. So, you want a brilliant man. But if he's more brilliant than you are you'll feel threatened, and if he is your mental equal you'll feel that he's inferior. On top of which, you expect your husband to be perfect in every other way, and you know, realistically, that such perfection is impossible to achieve. So, you set yourself up for failure at the outset of every match."

Devorah had glared at Gitty and rapidly changed the subject. Still, she had to admit that Gitty's words contained a great deal of truth. She was afraid—afraid that the man she wanted did not exist—or that if she thought she had found him, her respect would rapidly turn into disillusionment.

As she set the aromatic cup of coffee down on her breakfast table that Sunday morning in March and settled into a chair, Devorah sighed what could be construed as the tragic sigh of a heroine in a Regency romance novel. Twelve years after graduating from Gateshead, her soulmate remained as elusive as ever. And now, nearly half a year after her last, disastrous date, when her hopes of meeting someone were at their lowest ebb and she had started to feel the cold hand of fear creeping down her back, warning her that time was running out, her friend Gitty was willing to try again to introduce her to someone—Yitzhak Klein's cousin from Montreal. In the nearly eleven years that her best friend had been married to Yitzhak, she had never mentioned an unmarried male cousin in Montreal. If he were available, there must be something wrong with him.

Most of the community had given her up as nearly a lost cause. They considered her one of the difficult, special cases, the type from which professional matchmakers made thousands of dollars—if they could contrive a match at all. Even Gitty had appeared somewhat evasive when broaching the subject to Devorah. She brought it up, then fled as quickly as possible. Still, Devorah felt a faint spark of hope flicker within her, which she tried quickly to suppress. It wouldn't do to get her hopes up again, only to have them dashed like all the times past.

"Control yourself," she scolded herself as she sipped her coffee and thumbed absently through one of the Georgette novels still scattered across the table. "There's no reason to be too hopeful. All of this will probably come to nothing, even at first glance."

13

Chapter 2

Devorah Asher would have been superhuman not to dwell occasionally on the prospect of meeting Yitzhak Klein's cousin. A woman who has reached the age of thirty years, two months and twelve days, who has not yet been under the marriage canopy, and who openly admits her desire to wed, would be a strange being indeed if a tiny spark of hope didn't flicker up in her breast upon hearing of a potential match; she would be exceptional if her thoughts did not fan that tiny spark into a small flame that hissed, on occasion, *Maybe this time*.

Devorah was not superhuman, no strange or exceptional being, but instead was warm flesh and blood, with the dreams and desires of mortal females.

Thus, even before she called Gitty to confirm that she would attend the Kleins' festive Purim meal, even before Gitty handed the telephone to Yitzhak so that he could give her some details of the nameless cousin's background, she pondered what kind of man this cousin would be. Had he ever been married? If so, was he widowed or divorced, and did he have children? Though Devorah had plenty of nieces and nephews with whom she was a definite favorite, she had a morbid fear of inheriting a ready-made family and its incumbent responsibilities, even if the offspring of a previous marriage came to visit only on weekends or holidays. Was he intelligent? Obviously, yes, to be a professor at McGill University—though Devorah had met some dolts of university professors in her day. Would he be a decent person? She had liked Yitzhak the moment she met him during his engagement to Gitty, and over the ensuing years she had come to strongly respect his integrity and judgment. She doubted that Yitzhak would attempt to match her up with someone whose character traits were deficient or who had other serious issues.

Lastly, would he be what she liked to term "streetable"? Physical beauty in and of itself was unimportant to Devorah; it was important, however, that she be strongly attracted, both mentally and physically, to any potential mate, and that he be refined of person as well as of spirit. In the past, well-meaning persons (as she generously described them) had attempted to match her up with men who, no matter how mentally agile or spiritual they might be, were boorish, hideously unattractive or unkempt, or for some other reason types with whom she was ashamed to be seen in public.

While Devorah was thus occupied with her ponderings, the object of her musings was some three hundred and thirty miles away, comfortably settled in a well-worn wingchair inherited from his Great-Aunt Faigie—a chair admirably stereotypic of the furniture one might expect to find in the home of a tweedy professor type.

It was a chilly March evening in the city of Montreal, and Jonathan Weisman had wrapped a suitably tweedy sweater, purchased at Marks & Spencer during a research trip to London the previous year, around his shoulders. His left hand held an open volume pertinent to his profession as a Jewish historian: Samuel Usque's sixteenth century classic, *Consolation for the Tribulations of Israel,* printed in its original Portuguese. But his eyes were not on the book, and to an impartial observer, his thoughts would appear to be far, far away.

However, Jonathan Weisman's thought processes were not running particularly deep that Sunday evening. He was contemplating what to eat for dinner. The choices were limited and somewhat unappealing: leftover baked chicken from Friday evening's Sabbath dinner (purchased already oven browned from the nearby kosher market), leftover *cholent* from Sabbath lunch (purchased by the quart from the same kosher market), or leftover tuna salad (his own concoction). For variety, Jonathan thought, he could always whip himself up an omelet. Or, better yet, he could call his mother and see whether his parents had already sat down to eat before he invited himself over for dinner.

He snapped his book shut and reached for the phone, but his fingers hovered over the buttons. He checked himself just before dialing. "Face it, Jonathan, you're lonely," he told himself. "You want company with your food. But is it right for a grown man to continually foist himself upon his parents?"

With great mental effort, he hoisted himself out of the wingchair and headed for the kitchen. As he delved into his aging refrigerator and searched among its contents for the carton of eggs he knew was in there somewhere, faint memories of many years before assailed him. Memories of happier times at the beginning of a marriage, when meals had been prepared regularly for him and served with a smile. But that time, so full of hope and anticipation, had been all too brief; the smile had been the first to go, then the regularity of the meals, and finally he had been left to fend for himself.

The omelet, Jonathan's only culinary achievement in nearly a decade of singlehood, was almost cooked when the doorbell rang. He lifted the omelet pan off the gas range and set it on the adjacent burner, then went to answer the door. It was his older sister Rachel, holding her six-year-old son, Reuven, by the hand.

"Ah, Rachel, Reuven," he said, his eyes lighting up. "You're just in time to keep me company while I eat."

Rachel stepped over the threshold and sniffed. "Evening, Jonathan. Smells like gas."

"I'm making an omelet. Come on in the kitchen."

Rachel and Reuven dutifully followed him through the family room and into the maple-paneled kitchen at the back of the house. "Forget your omelet. I've brought you

16

leftovers," Rachel said, setting a large bag on the kitchen table.

"But it's cooked already. It'd be a shame to waste it. What did you bring that I can eat with it?"

Rachel began emptying the contents of the bag onto the table. "How about some homemade challah rolls? I also have some carrot salad and Waldorf salad, which you can eat with anything. You can save the green bean casserole and the brisket for tomorrow."

Jonathan reached for the carrot salad and forked a healthy portion onto a plate. "To what do I owe this singular honor, Rachel? If my memory is correct, the only time you ever brought me food was when I was nursing a broken foot."

"Don't thank me, thank Mom," she said, carrying the containers of green beans and brisket over to the refrigerator. She opened the door and began scrutinizing its dismal contents. "She called me this afternoon, worried about what you'd eat tonight because they were at that bar mitzvah in Toronto over the Sabbath and were invited out to dinner tonight. You know Mom; she was afraid you would starve. So she asked me to bring you some leftovers. I can see why."

Reuven, busy playing with refrigerator magnets on the floor, looked up. "Not the chocolate cake, though. You didn't bring the chocolate cake, did you? You promised you'd save it for me."

Rachel reached down to smooth two fine locks of brown hair back behind her son's ears. "Don't worry, Reuvie. There's plenty of chocolate cake left at home. I just brought Uncle Jonathan one piece."

"You can share it with me for dessert," Jonathan promised, moving toward the sink to wash his hands.

"Delicious challah, Rachel. You bake these?" he asked, as he savored his first bite.

"Of course. I always bake my own challahs."

"Funny, I tend to forget these things," Jonathan murmured, his voice deceptively soft. "But you didn't come here to discuss challahs with me."

Rachel extracted a bottle of diet cola from the back of the refrigerator and set it on the counter. "What makes you think I came for a specific purpose?" she asked in a carefully casual voice as she searched through the over-crowded dish drainer for a glass.

"Call it my professorial antennae. Besides, you've been a study in nonchalance since you stepped over my threshold. That's always been a dead give-away. Admit it, you're about to spring something unsavory on me." He watched with some amusement as Rachel tested a wobbly kitchen chair for stability. "Go ahead and sit. They're all like that; the screws just need tightening. Don't worry, it won't collapse under you."

Rachel sat down gingerly. She slowly drew the chair to the table and, placing her elbows on the orange-and-yellow flowered plastic tablecloth, rested her face thoughtfully in her hands. "Very perceptive, Jonathan."

"Well, out with it."

Rachel took a long sip and set her half-empty glass on the table. "Quite frankly," she said, looking her brother steadily in the eyes, "I've been doing some thinking, and I've decided it's time for you to remarry. It's over time, actually. Something should have been done about you already years ago."

"Well, well, well. Ever since Shira and I divorced, you've managed to hold your tongue and refrain from joining the general Weisman chorus of 'Jonathan Must Get Remarried.' What suddenly has inspired you to chime in, as well? Were you visited by divine inspiration? Or, did someone approach you with a suitable candidate for the next Mrs. Weisman?"

Rachel cast a meaningful look in Reuven's direction. "Oh hush, Jonathan; keep your voice down. It isn't like that at all."

"It's a little late to be thinking about Reuvie," Jonathan told her. "But I wouldn't worry about him. He appears to be totally engrossed in the kitchen magnets and probably hasn't heard a word we've said."

Reuven looked up on cue. "Are you getting married? Do I get to come?"

"Of course you get to come, darling," Rachel reassured him.

"Whoa, not so fast. First you have to find me someone to marry," Jonathan objected.

"Oh, Mommy and Aunt Sara already have," Reuven said blithely. "They were talking on the phone about it this morning—a lot!"

Rachel flushed slightly. "Reuvie, dear, this is a conversation for big people. Play with your magnets while I talk to Uncle Jonathan."

"If you didn't want me to talk, you shouldn't have brought me along," Reuvie pointed out. "Besides, they aren't my magnets, they're Uncle Jonathan's."

"I'm glad your mother brought you along," the owner of the magnets declared stoutly. "I have no doubt that your comments will add immeasurably to the conversation your mother and I are about to have. And don't glare at me, big sister. Instead, tell me who she is. She must be quite a paragon to inspire you to confer on the telephone all morning, then rush over here laden with decoy foodstuffs.

"Or did a new face suddenly appear on the Montreal Jewish singles scene? I thought I'd already been introduced to every eligible woman from Toronto to Montreal. Or, more likely, what is her fatal flaw?"

Rachel smirked. Pulling her purse off the nearby countertop, she fished inside and produced an envelope. "See for yourself, smart guy," she said, holding it in the air with a triumphant flourish. She tossed the envelope across the table to Jonathan.

"A letter from Aunt Malka?"

"Exactly. Mom got it on Friday. Aunt Malka included pictures from Chanukah. There are several photos in there of a Chanukah party at Yitzhak and Gitty's house that you should look at."

Jonathan carefully withdrew the photographs from the envelope and glanced through them one by one until he came to a photograph of Gitty holding a toddler on her lap. To her right, a slender brunette sat with her arm around a chubby girl who appeared to be about nine or ten years old. "Gitty hasn't changed much since she got married," he commented wryly. "And I'm assuming that this little guy is her youngest, and the girl must be her oldest, because Yitzhak and Gitty were married not all that long before Shira and I. But who's the dusky beauty?"

"That," Rachel announced dramatically, "is Her."

"She," he corrected.

"She, her, what's the difference? She's a good friend of Gitty's, and according to Aunt Malka, she's bright, charming, thirtyish—and unattached."

"Sounds too good to be true. There's a catch here somewhere. Maybe it's merely an excruciatingly grating voice, or a Brooklyn accent that is too Brooklynese to be borne. But just perhaps Aunt Malka neglected to tell you that she's divorced or widowed and has a gaggle of kids. Or maybe she's really *fortyish*. It's okay to lie about your age a little bit, but I've noticed that lots of people have a tendency to totally alter reality where a potential partner is concerned."

"Men who wait until they are thirty-five to look for a wife can't expect to find someone cute, twenty, and perfect, no kids attached," Rachel retorted with some asperity. "Look, just listen to me for a minute, will you? You're going to be in New York for a conference right before Purim, right? Well, Aunt Malka heard about it from Mom, and she suddenly thought of Gitty's friend, that perhaps you would be perfect for each other. According to Auntie M, she's a very nice girl, and there is *absolutely* nothing wrong with her—and no, she's never been married. And, she doesn't even have a Brooklyn accent. She's Gitty's age—she and Gitty were classmates— and Aunt Malka has known her ever since Gitty married Yitzhak."

"How neat and clean. And this lovely friend just happened to materialize, unmarried, unspoken for, after all these years?"

Rachel sighed. "Jonathan, sometimes these things aren't obvious even when they are right in front of our noses. But listen, here's the plan: You stay on in New York for a few days after the conference as a guest of Yitzhak and Gitty. That way you'll be at the Kleins' house for Purim. What could be more natural than Gitty's good friend coming to the Kleins' Purim meal?"

"Do I sense a conspiracy in the making?"

"No, no—absolutely not!" Rachel protested hotly. "It's all very open and above board—well, at least on your part. Devorah—that's Gitty's friend—is to know nothing about this. You get to have a discreet look at Devorah across the table and decide whether you want to meet her officially. If you are interested, Gitty will mention it to her."

"Sounds like a conspiracy to me. I wonder which version of the story Devorah has been told."

Rachel had the grace to blush, but denied rather unconvincingly that Devorah had been told any story at all. "There is something else, however," she added, almost as an afterthought. "Well, two something elses, actually. The first is, we'd like you to extend your return ticket until a few days after Purim, just in case you want to meet her formally, spend some time with her."

"And the second?"

"The second—the second is that Sara, Mom and I have been talking."

"And?"

"And, we'd like to touch you up a bit. Groom you, I mean. Nothing much. A good barber, for a change, and maybe a new suit."

"A new suit?!" Jonathan thundered.

"Jonathan, Jonathan, when is the last time you purchased a new suit. For your wedding? Ten years and twenty pounds ago?"

"Something like that." He shrugged. "But what do a new suit and a haircut have to do with it?"

"You know as well as I do that prospective matches are getting fewer and farther between. This may be your last chance to meet someone normal and decent before you start making the rounds of professional matchmakers and have all the 'special cases,' as you call them, thrown in your face. Why not make that extra little effort now so that Potential Miss Perfect likes what she sees and decides that she wants to meet you, instead of giving her an eyeful of your lovable but slightly scruffy true self at first glance?"

"Okay, okay. I'll do it, if only to get you and Sara and Mom off my back. Tell me what, exactly, you want me to do."

Rachel carefully pushed her wobbly chair back from the table and stood up. "Nothing much," she said, smoothing down her black wool skirt and looking around for her car keys. "You don't have classes or office hours tomorrow afternoon, do you?"

Jonathan shook his head.

"Mom thought not. I'll call you in the morning before you leave to tell you when and where you are to meet us. Bring your credit cards. Come, Reuvie, say 'bye to Uncle Jonathan. We're leaving now."

Only a full half-hour later, as he was haphazardly sticking the magnets back on the door of his refrigerator, did Jonathan wonder why he had submitted so meekly to the women of his family. He glanced at the forlorn remains of his omelet on the table and thought of the long, chilly evening ahead of him, with only Samuel Usque in the original Portuguese to keep him company. A feeling of longing for gentle companionship and a real home suddenly enveloped him.

But just as suddenly, he was assailed by a vision of his sisters and his mother bearing down on him with a purposeful gleam in their collective eyes, and the longing for home and hearth was replaced by a subtle but ominous

22

feeling. The survival instinct in him told him that the easy life he heretofore had enjoyed was about to come to an end, to be replaced with one rendered hideous by all sorts of complications and obligations.

Unfortunately, Jonathan's survival instinct failed to transmit to him some very important additional information: where to run, and where to hide.

Chapter 3

*W*hile Jonathan fretted about just what specific tortures, besides having his hair and beard trimmed and a new suit purchased, his mother and sisters had in store for him that afternoon, Devorah was contemplating appropriate attire for Gitty's Purim dinner. She had no doubt that her most recent purchase, an elegant black silk suit with a contrasting silk blouse, would show her to her best advantage. Certainly, it was the type of outfit she would select immediately for an ordinary first meeting. It was cultured, classic, sophisticated and tasteful; expensive without being ostentatious; modest without being dowdy.

But this wasn't an ordinary meeting. Any cousin of Yitzhak's, put forward with Yitzhak's sanction, had true potential—unless Gitty and Yitzhak, like everyone else, were beginning to place her in that dreaded category where hopeless singles were matched up with one another by virtue of being...hopeless. Besides, it really wasn't a date at all, but rather a sort of embarrassing "Let's look each other over in front of everybody from across the room" situation. The worst kind. First impressions required further thought.

It was an especially slow day at work. As she sat doodling on her desk pad, Devorah had ample time to ponder the problem of proper dress. If she were the heroine of a Georgette Heyer novel, how would Georgette dress her to meet the potential hero? Would she deck Devorah out like the intrepid Sophia Stanton Lacy of *The Grand Sophy* fame, who donned a sophisticated, pale-green crêpe Parisian evening gown, with rich trimmings and a cord and tassel at the waist, for that first dinner with her cousin, Charles Rivenhall? Or would she take Devorah's vanity—possibly her greatest character flaw—to task and dress her *à la* Jenny Chawleigh of *A Civil Contract*, who was covered in too much lace and silk floss and too many pearls, rubies and diamonds when introduced to Lord Lynton?

Devorah tried to remember how other Georgette heroines had been robed when presented to their prospective mates, but could call to mind only poor little Phoebe Marlow in *Sylvester*, who had worn a singularly unbecoming white gown with short puffed sleeves when formally reintroduced to the Duke of Salford on a chilly winter's eve and had broken out in goose bumps.

From contemplation of Heyeresque heroines (who, even when they weren't suitably attired were inevitably introduced to The Ideal Man), it was just a short step to the happy thought that checking out Georgette on the Internet would be an amusing way of whiling away the time. At last count, more than a million matches had shown up when Devorah googled "Georgette Heyer."

Devorah soon discovered that not much had changed since her last search. She therefore occupied herself with reading quotes from her favorite Georgettes and was deep in a conversation between the intrepid Sophy and Charles Rivenhall of *The Grand Sophy* when a voice over her left shoulder made her jump.

"I shall be much obliged to you, cousin, if you will refrain from telling my sisters that she has a face like a horse!" "But, Charles, no blame attaches to Miss Wraxton! She cannot help it, and that, I assure you, I have always pointed out to your sisters!" the voice intoned. *"I consider Miss Wraxton's countenance particularly well-bred!" "Yes, indeed, but you have quite misunderstood the matter! I meant a particularly well-bred horse!"*

"Not bad. Not bad at all, Dev!" the voice said. "What are you reading, might I ask?"

Devorah blushed and turned to face the intruder. "Jeremy, do you think you could knock next time before entering my office?"

"I did knock," Jeremy said, flipping a shock of dark hair off his face. "You didn't answer. The door was wide open, so I took my chances and came in."

While Devorah turned back to the computer with as much dignity as she could muster and closed her browser, Jeremy moved aside some papers on the side table and settled himself into the vacant spot. A slightly built young man with a pale, sensitive face framed by dark hair that was just slightly too long, and large, silvery eyes fringed with dark lashes, he reminded Devorah in his moodier moments of the physical prototype for a nineteenth-century Byronic hero. Even elegantly dressed, as he now was, in an impeccably tailored gray silk suit, the jacket of which was casually draped over the shoulders of his beautifully cut, blue Pima cotton shirt, his red silk tie slightly askew, he presented to the unknowing observer a slightly rakish, romantic-looking figure. Indeed, even his very mannerisms seemed calculated to cultivate the romantic image: the occasional, subtle flick of the head to clear his hair from his eyes; the pensive manner in which he rested his bowed head on the tips of his long, slender fingers; the slight shrug with which he sloughed off annoying questions.

But Devorah knew better. Before he came to occupy the much more spacious office next to hers at Longren & Longren, commandeered for him by his Great-Uncle Elmore, the senior Longren of Longren & Longren, Jeremy had been in theater. And he had never forgotten those few, all-too-short years on the boards, in which he had featured in numerous tragic rôles, mostly Shakespearean, but ranging from early Greek to very modern, on off-off-Broadway.

The family had soon determined that a Longren—all the more so one who was A Harvard Graduate—should cease mingling with dramatic low-life and had whisked him back to the safe bosom of the ancient family firm as a management trainee. Even now, after three years on Wall Street, Jeremy retained prominent traces of his previous life, including the carefully cultivated mannerisms that gave him his slightly romantic image. Devorah, who had been responsible for much of his training—and who had not yet figured out whether his occasional flashes of brilliance (which generally surprised his uncle as much as less closely related members of the firm) were due to a hidden methodology or merely to good intuition—had a sneaking suspicion that the lingering dramatist sprang more from a desire to punish his family than from a continued longing for the stage.

Certainly, every effort had been made to ensure that he was made as comfortable as possible at Longren & Longren. Jeremy was given an enviable salary and commission that enabled him to afford the hand-tailored, silk designer suits he favored, as well an expensive collection of gold watches and daily six-pack of imported mineral water. A junior partner up for promotion had been unceremoniously moved from the spacious corner office to a much smaller one down the hall, and one of the most expensive decorators in town had been called in to "do" Jeremy's new working quarters.

Though this vast expanse of office space featured windows on two walls instead of one, affording a much better view of the Manhattan skyline than did Devorah's cubbyhole, the overall results of the lavish makeover, to Devorah's mind, had not been happy. Pale gray reigned supreme, from the nubby carpeting to the linen-upholstered sofas and armchairs, to the ultra-modern, Formica-finished desk and cabinets. The only splashes of color were the artwork, and these were mere dashes of color on white canvases, hung unframed over each sofa and behind Jeremy's desk. Even Jeremy said he found it depressing. But instead of redecorating his pale gray shrine, he took to lurking about Devorah's office.

"You busy tonight, Dev?" he asked when, after a pointed interlude of silence, she finally turned her attention back to him.

"Busy as in what?" she asked, reaching into her top desk drawer for a bottle of nail polish.

"Like to go with me to have a drink somewhere? What say, even right now? What do you say we knock off early today? Indications are that the market won't pick up on late trading. It's positively moribund; rigor mortis has probably already set in."

Devorah opened the bottle of nail polish and began to painstakingly touch up an infinitesimal chip on the nail of her right ring finger. "Are you asking me for business or for pleasure?"

"I say," protested Jeremy, who, after graduating Harvard had studied theater in London for two years at the Royal Academy of Dramatic Arts. "You know what my intentions are—entirely honorable, but nothing to do with business. I've been trying to get you to go out with me ever since Uncle El installed me in the Gray Room. Romance. A little candlelight, a little wine, a little whatever. We're the same age, two consenting adults. And, I positively adore you, as you well know. If the carpet in this closet of yours didn't need vacuuming so seriously, I think I would prostrate myself at your feet. For three years I've been asking you. Come out with me tonight. Please?"

Devorah raised her finger and blew on her nail. "Forget it."

"That's all? Just 'forget it'?"

"Yeah. What else is there to say? For three years it's always been the same thing: You've asked, and I've answered, 'Forget it.' "

Jeremy uncurled from the side table and, feet planted firmly on the dusty carpeting, slowly lifted one sculpted white hand and pushed a shock of dark hair away from his silvery eyes with all the drama he could muster. "Might I inquire why?"

"Yes, you certainly might," Devorah said, blowing again on her fingernail. "Where I come from, people don't go out on casual dates. It's not done."

"What does *It's not done* mean?"

"It's against my religion."

"But I've gone out with other women of your faith. *They've* never minded casual dating... and so on."

"Yes, but *they* don't come from Boro Park." Devorah blew one last tiny puff on her nail, placed the capped bottle back into the top drawer, and swiveled around to face Jeremy. "Look, let me try to explain something to you. In my community, boys and girls, men and women, don't date casually... and so on. Nor do they just meet by chance, fall in love and get married. We're matched up. Our parents or some interested relative or friend, or even a professional matchmaker, finds someone suitable based on our family background, common interests, personality, or whatever. They check the person out, and if it sounds like a good thing, then we meet. And if we hit it off, we get married. It's as simple as that."

For one historic moment, Jeremy slipped out of persona and gaped at her.

"Shut your mouth, Jeremy. The dust bunnies will get in."

Jeremy clamped his mouth shut, then opened it again. "But that's archaic!" he sputtered. "Like out of the Middle Ages."

"Yep, positively Gothic. But we people are, you know. Been around for millennia and still haven't changed our habits."

"Well," Jeremy said, rapidly recovering, "if it's that simple, why aren't you married yet?"

"*I* am an anomaly," Devorah explained affably.

"Meaning?"

"Meaning, I have a career. I have a high IQ, which I use out here in the big, wide world. In other words, I scare lots of men—at least, the men who are supposed to be interested in me. Also, I'm not interested in being a homebody; I don't think I *could* be a homebody, though I know how to cook and do laundry and keep a shining home and all that. So, I doubly scare the men I should be meeting. I scare their mothers and fathers, too. I am a dubious commodity."

"Not to me you aren't," Jeremy said, half-serious. "Marry me, Dev. Or, at least come grace my pleasure palace with your divine physical presence in an informal arrangement. You don't frighten me at all, and I can afford to hire you all the domestic help you need."

"No, Jeremy," Devorah said, coloring slightly. "I come with too many strings attached. Besides, if I actually accepted you—for marriage, that is, because I would only accept honorable intentions—your crafty mind would be working furiously within five minutes of my acceptance, trying to figure out how you could worm your way out of it. You don't really want me; you just like to *think* you want me."

Jeremy sighed. "I suppose you're right. You know, it's funny, Dev, but I have this sneaking feeling that I have a lot more fun haunting your cubbyhole and trying to lure you into a little illicit office romance than if we were to actually get involved. It's kind of like fox hunting. The heat of the chase and all that."

"As opposed to catching the poor little vixen."

"You said it, Dev. I didn't."

"Fox, Jeremy. I meant a female fox." Devorah turned back to her computer and shut down. "Do you think it's okay to cut out of here now? I've got some shopping to do."

"Want company? I'm totally bored and wouldn't mind tagging along. We could take in a bottle of mineral water and a corned beef sandwich at some kosher deli before you go home. That way you wouldn't have to cook."

"You never stop, do you?" Devorah reached into her bottom desk drawer for her purse. "Besides, you'd be even more bored by my shopping. I've got to buy something to wear to—" She stopped mid-motion, turned toward Jeremy and flashed him a blinding smile. "I have the most *brilliant* idea."

Jeremy backed away from her desk. "Why do I get the feeling that whatever it is you want from me is going to mean trouble?"

She shook her head. "No, no trouble at all. You know the theater scene, don't you? Do you also know costumes? Where to buy them, I mean? Because I need a costume for a party next week. You look puzzled. Let me explain. Next Tuesday is Purim, a Jewish holiday when, among other things, Members of the Tribe dress up in costume. Or, at least the kids dress up. I've been invited this year to my best friend's festive Purim meal, and instead of racking my brain for what to wear, I think I'll go in costume. It'll be perfect!"

"What kind of costume?" Jeremy asked suspiciously. "And why are my antennae receiving signals that you are telling me only half the story?"

"Oh, I am," Devorah admitted. "But you don't need to know the other half quite yet. All you have to know is that I need a costume. I've decided to go dressed as someone out of Regency England. If necessary, in Jane Austen-type garb, but preferably something a little more highbrow, like what the nobility and all the nabobs would wear. Please, Jeremy, say you'll help me."

"Well," he said thoughtfully, "I suppose I could take you to Franchot's. It certainly would be a great deal more amusing than eating kosher deli—which, by the way, I suggested merely for your sake. I never could stomach the stuff."

"Franchot's? Like in a Georgette Heyer novel?"

"Who is Georgette Heyer? Franchot's is Manhattan's answer to Angels, the famous cinema costumers in London where you can rent things that were actually worn on movie sets. Of course, Franchot's isn't quite the same. It's smaller, for one thing, and it only deals in period costumes. But you also can find costumes worn in theater productions, as well as original creations. My former colleague, Fred, who runs the place, can outfit you from head to toe."

A quarter of an hour later, Jeremy pushed open the solid wooden door of an unassuming shop on a fashionable side street whose window displayed only a single, antique ivory lace dress draped against peach satin. Devorah stepped over the threshold into an elegant salon of sorts, furnished in what appeared to be either well-preserved period pieces or excellent reproductions. Somewhere within the shop a bell tinkled. A tall, angular man dressed in an eighteenth-century French court costume, lace dripping from the collar and cuffs of his brocaded, skirted jacket, minced out from behind a heavy tapestry. He took one look at Jeremy, then at Devorah, swept his wide, feathered hat off his bewigged head, and executed a low bow, his long mustache sweeping the toes of his rhinestone-studded shoes. Righting himself again, he clapped his hands in glee.

"*What is she, Isaac?*" he quoted softly. "*Thy wife or thy daughter, that Eastern houri that thou lockest under thy arm as thou wouldst thy treasure casket?*"

"Wouldst that she but let me lock her under my arm," Jeremy answered. "This is Devorah, no Eastern houri, but equally as unapproachable as the exquisite Rebecca."

"Devorah," the French fop repeated dryly. "How biblical. You are, I take it, a Member of the Tribe?"

"Devorah Asher, meet Fred Rabinowitz, the brains and moving force behind Franchot's. Devorah is here to find a suitable costume for a Purim party. Do I have that right?"

"Excellent," Fred said, clapping his hands together again. "Did you have anything in mind? I envision you in Eastern garb, with a celestial-blue silk turban half-covering your raven tresses, such as was worn last year in that horrid Broadway production of *Ivanhoe*. Despite that ivory complexion, you *are* Rebecca, though you could tell everyone you are dressed as Queen Esther."

"Actually," Devorah said, recovering her voice after initially being rendered speechless, "I was thinking more along the lines of Regency England. The nobility, not the gentry."

"Ah, still, I see you in blue. Blue, and exotic. Give me a minute to think what I have in your size. We do alternations, of course, but a close fit is preferable." Fred motioned to a pair of velvet-covered Louis XVI chairs flanking a small table, and Devorah and Jeremy sank into them obediently. "In the meantime, I'll have Celeste bring you some drinks."

Not ten minutes later, as Devorah and Jeremy sat sipping their mineral water from Waterford goblets, Fred's pixie-like assistant ceremoniously pulled aside the tapestry. Fred appeared, reverently bearing several dresses that he hung on an ornate, gilded hook. "I think I have found it, the perfect robe for you. But, I have brought out other suitable dresses, just in case your taste and mine are *not* the same. Celeste, the accessories, if you please." Celeste nodded and disappeared again into Franchot's inner recesses.

Fred reached for a long, pelisse-style gown of pale, plum-colored silk, with a matching ruffled collar and flounces of the same material down the center front and sleeves. A contrasting border at the wrists and hem lent an unusual touch to the garment. "This is a copy of an actual dinner dress from an 1814 edition of *La Belle Assemblee*. Very few women can wear this color of plum, but you, fair Rebecca, could carry it off. In *La Belle Assemblee*, the model is shown wearing a feathered toque. However, I would suggest instead dressing your hair *à la grecque*. We'll show you how. Amethyst drops in your ears and a short rope of pearls around your neck would complete the ensemble. Not for you? No? Not my first choice, either."

A powder-blue, long-sleeve chemise, with lace flounces at the wrists and low-cut neckline was brought forth next for Devorah's inspection. "This one was actually worn in one of those innumerable productions of *Pride and Prejudice*," Fred explained. "I personally think it's a bit insipid, but then, most of Austen's characters were insipid, too. The Becky Sharps of literature are *much* more fun. But that's irrelevant. Here, I've saved the best for last." He reached for an azure-blue silk dress and spread it carefully out in front of him. The skirt fell in rich folds from a band of matching satin at the high waist, and a deep trim of ivory satin rosettes circled the hem. The long, fitted sleeves, gathered into a puff at the top, were banded at the wrists with the same trim. "One of my own creations. This, I think, is you."

Devorah nodded, awed. "It's beautiful," she whispered. "Exactly what I would choose, except for one problem. The neck is too low."

"Too low? This is high by Regency standards," Fred protested.

"Hey, you're talking to a woman who has never shown her collarbone in public," Jeremy chimed in. "Honest."

"He's right," Devorah said with some embarrassment. "I need a high neck."

"We can fix that by adding a *chemisette,* a kind of cloth dicky. I have a few in the shop. If Celeste ever finds her way out of the storeroom, I'll ask her to bring you one."

One of Celeste's tiny, black-booted feet could be seen just then, attempting to kick aside the tapestry, followed by her blue-jeaned knee, and finally the much tattooed and pierced Celeste herself, a stack of boxes clasped to the front of her burgundy velvet tunic.

"Celeste, go find the off-white *chemisette* to wear with the azure dinner dress," Fred ordered. He turned back to Devorah. "I presumed that you would choose the azure, so I asked Celeste to bring accessories to match. I'll show them to you when you've tried on the dress. Go on, get started. Celeste will be back in a minute to button you up."

Devorah was soon being propelled by a triumphant Celeste out of a dressing room hidden behind a pair of antique brocade curtains. Fred looked her over carefully and again clapped his hands in glee. "This," he repeated, "is you. Simply exquisite. It's nearly a perfect fit, too. All it needs is a bodice inset with a high neck, rather than that insipid *chemisette.* I envision ivory silk to match the rosettes—I believe we still have some of the original in stock—with the same rosettes banding the neck. It will be something not quite in the ordinary way. Celeste, load on the extras."

Celeste began opening boxes and drew out a strand of faux pearls, kid gloves, a mesh reticule and an elegant cashmere shawl in a creamy tone-on-tone design, which Fred draped casually over Devorah's shoulders. "Again, I can give you a bonnet to wear with this, but I recommend putting your hair up and threading it through with ropes of faux pearls," he advised. "You can hire Celeste to come dress you and your hair. A lady's maid for the evening is one of our services, and it's worth the additional cost to make sure you are turned out authentically. Last but not least, you need shoes. Give her the size six-and-a-half, Celeste; they should fit just about right."

Celeste helped Devorah place pale-blue, ballerina-style flats on her feet, and carefully tied their contrasting satin bows. Then she minutely adjusted the drape of Devorah's shawl and stood back to admire the effect.

"Perfect, just perfect," Fred murmured. "Fair Queen Esther, you are ready for the Purim bash."

Chapter 4

On a gloriously sunny afternoon in late March, when the crocuses and daffodils were just beginning to send forth their shoots, and the scent of hope and expectation was in the air, a figure out of time appeared at the Kleins' front door. Pausing to pull her shawl more closely around her shoulders and minutely adjust the hang of her reticule over her left wrist, she reached up and rang the bell, then stepped back to nervously await her welcome.

From somewhere within the house came the sound of laughter and clinking glasses, and an intelligent phrase could be deciphered here and there. "That must be Devorah," someone—it sounded like Gitty—called out. "Miri, will you please answer it?"

Footsteps could be heard, and the Kleins' faded green door was opened cautiously by a miniature bride. "*Purim Same'ach*! Happy Purim, Auntie Devorah!" The door opened wider, and the little bride's eyes grew round as she took in Devorah's costume. "Wow," she exhaled slowly.

"You like it, Miri?" Devorah asked, making her way into the Kleins' foyer.

"Yeah, it's great. Like something out of the movies."

Devorah laughed. She doubted that Miri had seen above half a dozen movies in her ten-year-old life. "Where's your mother?"

"Mommy's in the kitchen with Bubbe Klein. Our cousin Jonathan is here from Montreal. He's drinking with Tatte right now. He's Bubbe Klein's nephew, because she and

36

Jonathan's mommy are sisters. He's very nice, and he even brought us all presents."

Devorah followed Miri past the living room, where Yitzhak Klein and several male guests appeared to be well on their way to that deliciously intoxicated state where they could no longer distinguish between Mordechai, the hero of Purim, and Haman the villain. One of those guests would be Jonathan Weisman. She hoped he wasn't very drunk.

"Tatte's getting drunk already," Miri observed, wrinkling her nose in distaste. "He invited five boys from his yeshiva. I hope they don't get sick all over the place like they did last year. Cousin Jonathan is the only one who's still acting normal."

Gitty, a chef's apron around her bulging middle and hair straying from under her wig, was busy arranging hors d'oeuvres on paper plates. She looked up as Devorah entered the kitchen, a slightly harassed expression on her face. "Happy Purim. Devorah, what—?"

"You like it?" Devorah asked defensively, nervously readjusting her shawl. "Miri likes it."

"It's beautiful," Gitty said quickly. "It's just that..., just that...."

"That you weren't expecting me to come in costume," Devorah finished for her. "Well, surprise, surprise. I thought I'd add to the general fun." She had not failed to notice when she passed by the living room that at least two of the guests wore clown wigs, and Yitzhak himself was wearing Groucho Marx glasses and nose. "Here. Happy Purim." She pulled a plastic bag from under her shawl and extracted a bottle of wine and box of dried fruits.

"But, what will...." Gitty began, her voice trailing off as she reached for Devorah's offerings.

"It's lovely, simply lovely, the costume," chimed in a voice from a corner of the vast kitchen. Devorah recollected herself and went over to offer her hand to the elderly woman seated next to the sink, a toddler perched on her knee.

"Happy Purim, Mrs. Klein. It's good to see you again."

"Likewise. A Happy Purim to you, too, Devori. Turn around, turn around, and take off that shawl for a minute. I want to see the whole costume. It's wonderful! Tell me, dahlink, what exactly is it supposed to be?"

Devorah pirouetted. "Let me guess," Gitty said, placing forks in the hors d'oeuvres. "You are a character out of a Georgette novel."

"You got it."

"It's quite clever, Dev. However, I was expecting you to show up in something a little more, uh…."

"Mainstream?" Devorah suggested helpfully.

"Yes, mainstream. Not everyone here is familiar with Georgette Heyer. I don't know that you'll be properly appreciated."

"Nonsense, Gitty," retorted Yitzhak's mother. "A nice-looking girl like Devori will be appreciated just fine. Just one thing I was wondering, though. How did you get yourself dressed, with all those little buttons up the back?"

"No problem. I rented a professional dresser along with the dress. It's part of the service. She came a few hours early, buttoned me, draped me, styled my hair and even did my nails and picked out my jewelry. She's an expert in period costumes." Devorah held out one slender white hand, whose freshly filed nails were coated with translucent pearl polish, then reached up to pat the curls that cascaded down from a knot of hair at the top of her head. "And she's coming back later to help me take these things off."

"So much money, Devori, just for a Purim costume."

"But worth every penny," she asserted.

"We'll see," Gitty said, picking up the hors d'oeuvres tray and handing it to a waiting Miri. "Make yourself useful as long as you're in here, Devorah, and put a slice of fish on each of these plates, then place a cooked carrot and sprig of parsley next to it."

While Devorah busied herself with garnishing plates of gefilte fish, Jonathan was slowly sipping a Scotch and water, his mind seething with conjecture. From his corner of the

Kleins' living room, he had caught a glimpse of the dark, slender figure most recently arrived, and his worst fears appeared on their way to being confirmed. Yitzhak had assured him that Devorah was entirely normal, albeit a bit too brainy and self-confident for most men. She was also supposed to be a looker, although beauty didn't rate as high on Jonathan's list of requisites as many other qualities. But, as Devorah sailed through the entry hall, clutching one corner of a pale, fringed shawl, a string purse dangling from her uplifted wrist, and her silken skirts brushing the floor, Jonathan was reminded forcibly of a hideous episode in his childhood when his eccentric cousin Elka had come to visit.

Elka, who lived in a rural settlement in upstate New York with a group of similarly minded individuals, was a New Age Jew. She and her kindred spirits had forged a kind of cosmic Judaism that combined spirituality with biblical back-to-nature. Years later, when a mature Jonathan had visited Elka's small settlement, he could appreciate, if not embrace, many elements of his now-middle-aged cousin's lifestyle. True, the biblical garb was still a little difficult to assimilate, but the sunrise, outdoor prayer services on a hilltop overlooking green valleys were awe-inspiring, and organic farming and free-range kosher chickens were no longer ideas imported from Mars.

But to the ten-year-old child, the distant, mythical cousin in a long, flowing dress straight out of the Book of Genesis, her head covered with a white kerchief and circled by an embroidered band of cloth, her feet encased in thick socks and Israeli kibbutz sandals, made an odd impression. Equally odd was her young husband, Ephraim, who dressed in much the same mode, with a coarsely crocheted skullcap that nearly covered his entire head and ritual fringes hanging from the edges of a shirt that reminded Jonathan of Joseph's Coat of Many Colors, and who spent hours early each morning bobbing up and down in the Weismans' snow-covered backyard, praying to his Creator.

Jonathan and his siblings could have contented themselves with snickering privately at Elka and her soulmate's idiosyncrasies had the latter two not been in the throes of messianic nutritionism. Elka, who in upstate New York headed a thriving organic egg enterprise, had shuddered visibly when forced to consume her squash fritters across the table from Jonathan and Co.'s favorite hamburgers and mashed potatoes on the first memorable night of The Visit. She then proceeded to subject Jonathan's mother to thrice daily lectures on the evils of white sugar (and all cookies, candies and pastries quite obviously containing thereof), canned tuna, white bread, processed peanut butter and all other much-beloved staples of a normal, healthy child's diet.

Mrs. Weisman, rising nobly to the occasion and determined to keep the peace until the troublemakers left, gave in gracefully; for the remainder of the week she attempted to feed her recalcitrant children natural peanut butter-and-honey sandwiches on stone-ground whole wheat, sourdough bread.

Jonathan had never heard of Georgette Heyer, much less read any of her books. Therefore he could only, inevitably, associate Devorah's quickly glimpsed costume with his lingering memories of long biblical dresses, macramé purses and everything terrible they represented. Yitzhak, Gitty, his mother and his sister Rachel had lied to him, he realized morosely as he took a large swig of Scotch and water. And he, fool that he was, had allowed himself to be duped.

Alcohol breath swooshed into Jonathan's right ear as Yitzhak leaned over and slurred the dreaded words. "Well, Cousin, she's arrived. Come into the kitchen. You can get a better look at her, and I'll find some pretext for introducing you."

"I thought you said she was normal," Jonathan accused. "She's a reincarnation of Cousin Elka. Remember her—all that fringe and organic food?"

"She *is* normal—at least, she was until about fifteen minutes ago. She's always very well groomed. I've never seen her dressed like this before, even on Purim."

"At least now I know the answer to the riddle," Jonathan continued, peering dismally into his near-empty glass and wondering whether he should ask for a refill. Large quantities of alcohol did not agree with him, and as a general rule he did not get more than pleasantly tipsy on Purim. He wondered, however, whether it was time to break his self-imposed rule and drink himself into oblivion.

"What riddle?"

"The riddle of why Miss Perfect is not yet married."

"Who are you or I to question the ways of the One Above, Jonathan? Maybe she's your soulmate and has been waiting all these years for you to show up at the Kleins' Purim celebration so that you can be introduced."

"But now that I've seen her, I don't want to be introduced."

"Chicken?" Yitzhak asked ever so softly.

"No, I have a justifiable fear that a woman who dresses like that would condemn me to a life of brown rice and soy patties."

Never one to take on a losing battle without additional ammunition, Yitzhak patted his cousin on the shoulder and loped off toward the kitchen. Gitty, who had been checking the steaming contents of a voluminous pot sitting on a hotplate, turned as he reached the kitchen door. He shrugged and darted a look over his shoulder. Correctly interpreting this time-honored signal between husband and wife, Gitty nodded, placed the lid back on the pot, and followed Yitzhak into the adjoining family room.

"Things are not going well," Yitzhak explained in a low voice. "He doesn't like Devorah's outfit, so he doesn't want to meet her. What prompted her to wear such a getup?"

"I was afraid it might be a little off-putting the moment I saw it," Gitty admitted. "But you know Devorah; sometimes she gets these weird whims, and when she does there's no stopping her. Did you tell Jonathan it's just a Purim costume and she doesn't usually dress like this?"

"I tried, but Cousin Elka keeps intruding. Remember her—the one who dresses like one of the Matriarchs?"

"What does Cousin Elka have to do with anything?"

"Everything," Yitzhak explained. "Jonathan sees a long dress and fringed shawl, and he has visions of organic diets and strange religious customs."

Gitty burst out laughing. "Oh, now I see. Poor Jonathan! Please explain to your dear cousin that Devorah is dressed like a character out of a Regency romance novel. Considering that Jonathan is an historian, he should be able to appreciate the attention to detail that went into her costume."

"She's your friend; you tell him," Yitzhak said, turning on his heel.

Meanwhile, in the kitchen, the elder Mrs. Klein had moved her chair over to the table, where she sat at Devorah's elbow, watching her arrange gefilte fish on the salad plates. "Dahlink," she began, "did Gitty tell you that Yitzhak's cousin is visiting from Montreal? Mine own nephew. Such a nice boy, and smart, too. A professor. He'll make some lucky girl a very good husband; so kind and considerate, and a good earner, besides he learned in yeshiva in Jerusalem for five years before getting his doctorate. But he's shy. You know how men are when they get to be a certain age and they've been single for so long. They're scared of the girls, scared to take on all that responsibility. What he needs is someone like you, a bright, pretty girl from a good family. You want I should introduce you?"

Devorah looked up sharply. "Excuse me for asking, Mrs. Klein, but are you in on this too?"

Hurt and feigned ignorance warred briefly on Mrs. Klein's expressive face. Hurt won out. "You make it sound like I'm plotting against you. Heaven forbid! I love you like a daughter and I only want the best for you. A nice girl like you should be married by now. It's better to start young—for you, for the husband, for the *kinderlach*. I should know; I was no

42

spring chicken myself when I married Mr. Klein, may he rest in peace. By the time the rabbi introduced us, I was as old as you are. And believe me, to become a mother at the age of thirty-something wasn't so easy, not to mention that Mr. Klein and I were each settled in our ways and had to learn how to get along with each other."

Mrs. Klein sighed poignantly, as if remembering times better forgotten; the troubled look was quickly replaced by a faraway smile. "But we learned to live with each other and we learned to love each other. And now I want that my nephew Jonathan should have that too. You *must* meet. My heart will break if you don't."

It is inevitable; I am doomed, Devorah thought. She was being pulled inexorably toward her fate. And she had not yet even caught a glimpse of the man.

Yitzhak's mother, correctly interpreting the yielding expression on Devorah's face, leaned forward to take her hand in a brief, loving clasp. Then she stood up slowly, carefully smoothed her skirt, and walked soundlessly toward the living room, where Jonathan Weisman was indulging liberally in his second Scotch and water. Venturing into the all-male bastion where Yitzhak and his assembled guests were singing raucous renditions of well-known Purim songs, Mrs. Klein tapped her nephew resolutely on the shoulder. "Come," she commanded.

Jonathan stood obediently and, Scotch and water still in hand, followed her to the corner of the family room where Yitzhak and Gitty had gone tête-à-tête. "Enough with the drinking," Mrs. Klein said, taking the glass from his hand and setting it on a side table. "It's time to meet Devorah Asher."

"But I don't want to."

"Don't want to? You *have* to."

"Sorry, Aunt Malka, but I'm not required. That wasn't part of the agreement. The agreement was that I got to look the candidate over from afar. Well, from afar I saw enough to make me want to run even farther. There will be no meeting,

43

no staying over. I'm changing my ticket and going back to Montreal tomorrow."

"But dahlink," Mrs. Klein ventured tremulously, "she hasn't stepped foot in the same room as you. When did you even get a peek?"

"When she made her Grand Entrance, trailing skirts, fringes and all."

"Oh *that.*" Mrs. Klein dismissed Devorah's costume with a wave of the hand. "It's her Regency costume, whatever that means. With yards of buttons down the back, no less. A little joke on Gitty, who almost fainted, you should know, when Devori waltzed into the kitchen. Such a nice girl, but every once in a while her humor gets the better of her." She sadly scrutinized her nephew's belligerent face. "Not good timing, no?"

"No."

As a nephew, he was a dear, but he was also totally hopeless. Stronger measures were obviously required if Jonathan were ever to bless his mother, Malka Klein's younger sister and the most precious person in her life after her own family, with grandchildren. Mrs. Klein sucked in her breath and drew herself up to her full five-foot-one height. "Jonathan, dear," she said, her voice steely, "for shame, judging someone by their Purim costume. You are behaving like a child, an idiot. As your aunt, your elder, I am ordering you to come with me into the kitchen, where you will see that Devori is a perfectly normal, lovely young lady."

Meanwhile Gitty, having realized that her usually reliable spouse could not be depended to actually bring Jonathan and Devorah face-to-face, flounced angrily into the kitchen. Grabbing a gargantuan tray, she clumsily stacked it with plates of gefilte fish.

"Is something wrong?" Devorah asked innocently. "Can I help you do that?"

Gitty shook her head. "Aargh, men! Just keep the plates coming. I'll put them on the table."

"They're all done. Maybe I could put the horseradish and the mayonnaise in some kind of dish so that I can bring them in. Then we'll be ready to start the meal."

"You could, if there were any to be had," Gitty said. "The only relish dishes not already being used are up in the cabinet over the fridge. We'll have to ask Yitzhak to get them down. We need a salad bowl from up there anyway." She wedged the tray atop her stomach and marched out again.

Miri wandered in, a three-year-old soldier in her wake. "Aunt Devorah, where's Mommy? We're hungry; we want to eat."

"We're almost ready. Your mother's putting the fish on the table right now. Maybe you could find your father for me, though. I need him to get some dishes down for me from a high shelf."

"Forget Tatte; I think he's having trouble standing. He gets like this every year on Purim."

"Oh dear," Devorah murmured, dubiously scrutinizing the shelf high above the refrigerator. "I guess I'll have to get them down myself."

"You mean the good Lenox we keep up there?" Miri pointed. "Mommy said to use the good Lenox?"

"She didn't say specifically to use the Lenox," Devorah answered, dragging a chair to the refrigerator. "But she did say to use the relish dishes and salad bowl that she stores up there. Come here, Miri, so I can hand stuff down to you." Devorah hitched up her skirts, grabbed hold of the refrigerator door for support, and hoisted herself onto the chair.

Within seconds, the crystal relish dishes had been located and handed down to Miri, who placed them carefully on the table. Devorah turned back to the cabinet and was in the process of extracting a delicately patterned china bowl that appeared to be salad size when Mrs. Klein marched purposely into the kitchen with Jonathan.

"Devori," Mrs. Klein announced gaily, "I have someone for you to meet."

45

Startled, Devorah turned quickly. For one split second, time froze. Her blue-gray eyes met a pair of hazel ones framed by thick brown lashes. Jonathan, resigning himself to the inevitable, had schooled himself into a semblance of good humor; as he rapidly assimilated the details of Devorah's costume, good humor deepened to appreciation. He expertly recognized it as being historical; as a historian, he vaguely wondered which time period and which country it represented. Devorah was obviously no nature-loving prairie miss, but rather a woman of deeper attributes. His interest was piqued. Unaware of his reaction, he smiled up at her, the smile transforming his face.

It would be an overstatement to say that Devorah, like the heroine in a novel, fell in love with Jonathan at the sight of that smile. Rather, in the instant in which she turned and met his gaze, she suffered a slight jolt, as if she recognized someone she knew very well, who after traveling long and far had finally returned home. A brief look of curiosity quivered on Jonathan's face, to be replaced by a smile that bathed her in its warmth. She felt a tug in the region of her heart and a blush spreading across her cheeks. Confused, she attempted to turn back toward the cabinet.

But time resumed and reality intruded. "I have Yitzhak's cousin here, come from Montreal," Mrs. Klein said, stepping forward to where Devorah was perched on the chair. Jonathan moved toward her at the same time.

Devorah, the Lenox bowl in one hand, the other clutching the refrigerator, turned too swiftly and lost her balance. Jonathan's pace quickened as Devorah made a frantic grab for the handle of the freezer door. The freezer door swung open and Devorah swayed backward, catching her shoe in the hem of her dress and releasing her hold on the bowl. A stifled scream escaped her lips as she fell sideways off the chair, banging her head against Gitty's granite kitchen countertop. Jonathan, Mrs. Klein and a bewildered Miri watched helplessly as she crumpled gracefully to the kitchen floor, surrounded by the shards of a very expensive piece of Lenox china.

Chapter 5

The day already bid to be hot and sultry when the Duchess and her small procession set out from Ravenscourt to visit the Ardsleighs, recently arrived back in Gloucestershire after an extended visit to Lady Ardsleigh's failing mother in Scotland. As the ancient traveling coach in which she invariably traveled in state to visit her neighbors throughout the county sprang into motion, Augusta Melville, Duchess of Ravenscroft, smoothed her skirts against the faded velvet seat coverings, removed a yellowing ivory fan from her reticule, and began to fan herself vigorously. She was an imposing woman with high cheekbones and a great beak of a nose, who had been regarded as handsome, rather than beautiful, in her day; as she still favored the full, waisted skirts of an earlier era and towering feathered turbans, her ramrod-straight figure was vested with a regal appearance.

"It was all to secure the inheritance, you know," her grace explained knowingly to her two travelling companions, peering at them over the high bridge of her nose. "There had been some talk that Lady Glenbuck was to leave her entire fortune to her eldest son, Horace, who though being an entirely praiseworthy gentleman, stands to inherit the title and Lord Glenbuck's estates, besides being married to Lady Griselda Perry, who comes from one of the wealthiest families in England. An unexceptionable woman, I am sure, though her lineage isn't *nearly* equal to the Glenbucks' and *not* what I could wish for in a daughter-in-law."

"Not everyone, Duchess, has such delicacy of principal as Yourself, if I may be so bold as to say. For many of the Upper Ten Thousand, the lure of wealth offered by aligning with families of lesser breeding overcomes any revulsion they may feel by marrying beneath themselves," the Duchess's chaplain, the Reverend Lucas Duckwaithe, interjected sagely from the opposite seat.

The Lady Albinia Brinkburn, seated next to the Duchess and herself the daughter of an earl, nodded. "Too true, too true," she murmured knowingly, bringing one skinny, gloved hand to her sunken, maiden chest. "Breeding will out in the end."

"To continue," interrupted the Duchess, fanning herself ever more vigorously, "it would be *criminal* for Horace to Inherit All. When One considers how Aurelia has devoted herself to her mother for years, ever since Lady Glenbuck suffered her first stroke, and when One remembers that she has five daughters to establish creditably, One is horrified to think that Lady Glenbuck should have rewritten her will to leave her portion to Him—and just when her doctors warn that she may not last through the summer. She is a Mexworth, as you know, and they are nearly as well endowed as the Perrys, besides having been here since the Conquest. Her personal fortune, as I understand it, is considerable."

Momentarily overcome by the vision of fortune falling where it was least deserved, she relaxed her rigid perch on the seat and sank back against the faded squabs. "Ah, but it is hot today. If it had been anyone but my dear Aurelia, who only left Lady Glenbuck's bedside because she must organize Cressida's come-out this spring and will be spending only a few weeks at Ardsleigh Manor before traveling on to London, I would *not* have gone calling this morning. One can only hope that she will be able to present Cressida at Court before being forced to hurry back to Scotland for Lady Glenbuck's last days here on earth. It would be a tragedy if Lady Glenbuck were unable to hold on long enough to see Cressida creditably established."

"We must all of us pray for Lady Glenbuck's continuing health, so to speak, and for Miss Ardsleigh's timely success this season," said Mr. Duckwaithe.

"Yes," Lady Albinia, who had thus far passed her twentieth year without success and knew all too well what it meant to return for a repeat season, murmured in assent.

"And for your success, as well, Lady Albinia," the Duchess's chaplain added coyly. "I am in daily anticipation of that announcement which cannot fail to bring happiness to their graces and to your own esteemed family."

The Lady Albinia's pallid complexion flushed slightly beneath the shadow of her chip straw bonnet. "I hope I am not unaware of where my duty lies," she answered, preening herself ever so slightly. "To align oneself with a family so closely connected with one's own in rank, status and friendship is surely one of the highest services one can render one's King and country."

"Your sentiments do you honor," said Mr. Duckwaithe, who, most unfortunately, was only the younger son of the younger son of a viscount. "One must keep the nobility noble. To unite in Holy Matrimony with one beneath One's rank would undermine the foundations—indeed the very social fabric—on which our Great Empire is built."

"Nonsense," the Duchess interjected, briskly rapping her chaplain's knee with her fan. "Social fabric, indeed! It is my heart's desire that Albinia marry Adam only because her mother is my oldest friend and dear Albinia is like a daughter to me. How Sophia and I were used to plan when, all those years after Adam was born, she finally gave birth to a daughter. If I were to see you and Adam comfortably wed, my dear, I could die happy tomorrow."

Another maidenly blush spread across Albinia's pale face. "And it is *my* dearest wish, Godmama, to grant you that happiness you seek, though I hope you will continue to enjoy it for many a long year."

Mr. Duckwaithe, marveling privately at the Duchess's sagacious selection of a proper bride for her elder son, nodded again in approval, and in this manner the trio within the traveling coach happily—and optimistically—whiled away the first mile or two of the short journey to Ardsleigh Manor.

Not so the other two members of the procession, who were traveling leisurely on horseback a little way ahead. "What a prose!" Lord Robert exclaimed heatedly to his brother, Adam Melville, sixth Duke of Ravenscroft, as soon as they were out of earshot of the coach. "I can't believe that you agreed to let Mother talk us into accompanying them. To be forced to put up with Lucas for an entire day is more than any mortal should have to bear, not to mention that odious Albinia. It's just like Mother to invite her for a visit when she knows that neither of us can abide her."

"Oh she's harmless enough, Robert," the Duke said dispassionately. "And she does provide Mother with some welcome company. Bear up. In a few days or so you can come up with an unavoidable engagement and dash off to London."

"Yes, and leave you to do battle all on your own? I should think not!" Robert retorted. "Some brother I'd be. Mark my words, they're busy planning your nuptials right now, under cover of the ducal procession. Were I to shab off at a time like this, I'd return to find you fixing to become a tenant for life—or should I say in your case, a *prisoner* for life—and no way to wiggle out of the shackles. If I was you, I'd also start conjuring up some unavoidable engagements or pressing business in town, and disappear while the disappearing is good."

"I do, er, hope, dear brother, that things will not come to that pass," the Duke replied with an amused grin. "But I am reasonably sure that I am resourceful enough to keep myself out of any compromising situations of Mother's or Albinia's making. And if not, I believe that I can be creative enough to furnish Albinia with a dozen reasons to wish herself well rid of me."

"I doubt it. That woman lives and breathes strawberry leaves. She'd have you even if you were blind, lame and mentally defective, which the Lord knows you ain't none of them. It'll take divine providence to get you out of her clutches. Were I in your boots, I'd vanish tomorrow. Yesterday was none too soon in a case like this."

The Duke made no answer, and the brothers continued on in a comfortable silence for some minutes more. The sun, nearly at its zenith and beating down with an intensity unusual for a day in late March, made the going hot and uncomfortable, and the dust rising from a country road cracked and dried after an unusually prolonged late-winter dry spell cast a fine mist that blurred the brilliant green of the countryside. Adam, scanning the road ahead for particularly hazardous ruts and holes, was keeping his own counsel, but he also was calculating the best way to extricate Robert and himself from what he predicted would be a prolonged visit to the Ardsleighs once the Duchess and Aurelia Ardsleigh settled in for a comfortable cose, and one that was rife with potential complications.

Divine providence would indeed be needed to rescue Robert and him from what could develop into an awkward situation. It would be just like his mother, spreading her skirts over the stiff brocade upholstery of one of Lady Ardsleigh's rock-hard sofas for the duration, to send Robert and Lucas off on some transparently false errand and then command him to take Albinia for a turn in the rose garden. But to be forearmed was the best defense, and Adam was determined not to be tricked into spending any time alone with Lady Albinia, let alone wasting the entire day at Ardsleigh Manor.

He was chewing over the complexities of wiggling out of the situation without committing any irredeemable social solecism when he spied what appeared to be a curious mound of blue some way ahead at the side of the road. As the brothers rounded a bend and drew nearer, Adam perceived that the blue belonged to a dress—quite possibly silk, judging by the way it shimmered in the sunlight—and that rather than having been discarded at the roadside, it still very properly covered the body of a woman.

52

Robert's sharp intake of breath at that moment told Adam that he, too, had spied the body. "Divine providence appears to have come calling," the Duke commented, spurring his horse forward.

"I only hope that it isn't too gruesome," his brother answered, following fast behind.

"Don't be ridiculous," Adam said, dismounting and kneeling beside the inert form. "The bodice of a corpse doesn't rise and fall. She appears to be merely stunned." Setting aside his hat, he looked down at the pale face with its perfectly shaped features and the fringe of dark lashes on the closed eyelids. His keen gaze took in the diamond drops in her ears and the rope of pearls around her neck, and lastly took in her soft, slender hands with their curiously styled sapphire ring and the even more curious pearly glow of her shapely nails. "She appears to be gently reared, judging by her appearance. She's lovely."

"Beautiful, I'd say," Robert agreed. "I wonder who she is." He rubbed his hands together in glee. "Oh, Adam, this is beyond anything wonderful. I can see it now: Albinia's visit is about to be eclipsed!"

Chapter 6

Devorah returned slowly to consciousness. She became aware first of smells: the odor of fresh sweat, followed by the more subtle scents of earth and grass and wildflowers and, perhaps, weeds. Next came a feeling of extreme warmth, as if a ray of heat were pounding down, enveloping her. She was so hot, so very, very hot and thirsty. Then came the excruciating throbbing at the back of her head, as if she had been viciously battered by a sledgehammer. She moaned and tried to open her eyes, only to be blinded by a blaze of sunlight. She shut them again and tried to rest, to ignore the brutal pain in her head and the parchedness of her throat.

"Look, Adam, she's coming to," said a disembodied voice with a precise British accent.

"She appears to be slightly disoriented, as if she has a concussion. She must have sustained a blow to the head, though how the deuce—?" an older, more arrogant voice answered in the same, elegant Queen's English. *"Brandy is what's needed. Do you have any on you?"*

"No, but Mother, you know, always keeps a flask in the carriage for just such emergencies as may arise. I see the team rounding the bend now. Shall I signal John Coachman to spring 'em?"

"No need. Just go wait for them and explain what has happened. The lady—if I may call her that—appears to have gone off again. I'll see whether I can rouse her."

Devorah made a supreme effort to open her eyes and focus on the figure crouched before her. Dark, piercing eyes set in a harsh, unfamiliar face stared back at her. She took in the strange cut of their owner's black hair, then her gaze traveled wonderingly down to the white cloth tied at the stranger's neck, the uptilted points of his exaggerated shirt collar and the antiquated cut of his blue jacket. Involuntarily, her gaze traveled still further down, and she saw with some embarrassment that he was wearing tightly fitted buff breeches fastened with buttons.

"Oh!" she exclaimed, startled, as her eyes flew up quickly to meet the stranger's own.

"Come, that is better now," he said in a slightly amused voice. A smile flickered at the corners of his mouth.

Devorah struggled to raise herself, and he reached out to help pull her into a sitting position. "Much better," he said coaxingly. "How is your head?"

Devorah, still trying to assimilate the stranger's unusual costume, felt the back of her head at the exact spot where the sledgehammer was battering her and realized with some shock that a lump had sprouted there. "Better, I guess," she said. But where was she? Who was this man? If only she didn't feel so confused.

A coach and four came rushing into view and, obeying signals from the younger man, slowed to a halt. This latter person, too, was clothed in knee breeches and boots and an antiquated coat, and when he turned toward his companion, Devorah saw that he sported a similar neck cloth and shirt points. Where had she seen that dress style before? It was strange, but—at the same time—familiar. It looked like something out of Regency England, she realized, the thought coming to her out of nowhere.

"Oh, no!" she cried out, falling backward. She knew, then, what had come of reading too many Georgette Heyer novels.

★ ★

When Devorah again regained consciousness, she felt the cold, bitter metal of a flask against her lips and a fiery liquid being forced into her mouth. She choked, spat it out, and pushed the flask away. "Water," she whispered. "Just water."

"Water? Where the deuce are we going to find water, Adam?"

"If my memory serves me well, there's a small spring to the side of the road, just up ahead. It feeds into the brook that runs under the bridge. Here, take the flask and rinse it out. I doubt any brandy Mother puts in it is worth keeping."

Those voices—hadn't they been part of a dream, along with that clothing, those costumes? But the hard ground beneath her was very real, as were the pain at the back of her skull and the heat from the sun beating relentlessly down. Could it be—was it not a dream after all?

"Where am I?" Devorah asked, her head beginning to clear.

"Gloucestershire, Cotswold country," came the simple reply.

"Gloucestershire? In England?"

"The King's very own," said the man with the piercing dark eyes.

"What...what day is it?"

"Why, Monday, of course," came the answer. "What day did you think it to be?"

"I'm...I'm not sure. I'm very confused."

"Of course you are. You appear to have hit your head against something, perhaps in a fall. Please to lie here quietly. I see John Coachman coming round with my mother's smelling salts, and my brother should be returning with water any minute. Once you have drunk a little and got your bearings, we will bundle you into Mother's coach and take you home, where you will be more comfortable. You will have plenty of time when you feel better to explain how you came to be in this predicament."

Her unknown rescuer swiveled around on his haunches to await the coachman's arrival, and Devorah took the opportunity to survey him from under the thin veil of her eyelashes. His tanned face, beneath the dark, artfully careless crop of hair, was lean and chiseled, with a high-bridged nose and a slightly arrogant set to the mouth. With those cheekbones, the nose and the mouth, no wonder his face appeared harsh, Devorah thought. Then he turned back

56

toward her and smiled gently, asking in his peculiar, aristocratic accent whether she was any better, and she thought that the harshness may have been an optical illusion or due to the shadows cast by the sun.

But that still didn't explain the knee breaches, the cut-away top coat and elaborate neck cloth, all of which she had read about in novels. Had she landed in the England of nearly two hundred years ago, or on the full-dress, twenty-first-century movie set of some period drama? In either case, how did she get there? she asked herself in bewilderment. And how did it suddenly become Monday, when she distinctly remembered the day being a Sunday?

John Coachman arrived on the scene and handed his master a vial, which the latter waved in front of her nostrils. "Don't. It's disgusting." Devorah pushed the vial away and struggled back into a sitting position.

"Certainly," came the calm, assured rejoinder. "Here is Robert now with the water. Drink up, my dear girl, and we will be on our way."

Devorah looked uncertainly at the flask, appeared to make a mental calculation and took a few experimental sips. The water tasted unexceptionable. She drank deeply.

"Now, my girl, up with you," said her rescuer, holding out his hand to assist her.

"Adam, I would carry her if I were you," Robert warned. "You don't want her swooning off again halfway to the carriage. Mother will be having vapors over the entire affair as it is."

"Good thinking," said Adam. Ignoring Devorah's protests, he gathered her into his arms.

John Coachman opened the coach door with a flourish, and Adam deposited Devorah next to a tall, angular gentleman dressed in mournful colors. Across from her, a bony young woman with a sallow complexion regarded her entrance in much the same manner as she would have welcomed the appearance of a cockroach.

"I have instructed John Coachman to return immediately to Ravenscourt," Adam announced to the coach's occupants.

"But, the Ardsleighs!" a regal woman just past middle age exclaimed in affronted accents.

"They will have to wait until tomorrow," Adam said smoothly.

"Now, now, ma'am," interjected the angular man next to Devorah. "The Duke is correct. Certainly we cannot leave the young lady lying unattended by the side of the road. And equally, we cannot take her to the Ardsleighs, can we now? Just what would dear Lady Ardsleigh think of us, eh?"

"No, no. You are right, Lucas. Your good sense comes to our rescue, as usual," the regal one agreed. "As for you, miss," she said, glaring at Devorah, "I hope you have a good explanation for yourself."

"I hope I do, too," mumbled Devorah, sinking further back against the squabs. She closed her eyes in an attempt to blot out her surroundings. The situation threatened to be tricky. What had she gotten herself into?

"What was that you said?" the regal one demanded sharply.

"I believe she is delirious," said a supercilious voice, which must belong to the sallow young woman. "Who is she? There is something not quite right about this whole affair. One does not just come to be lying unconscious, all alone in a ditch. There is always a reason for one's being there. I, for one, would like to know what it is."

"My sentiments exactly," the regal one proclaimed.

"If I may interject, ma'am, I think it would be better if we postponed this discussion for later," Lucas said in placating tones.

Devorah squeezed her eyes tightly shut. She appeared to have landed in with a pack of Bedlamites; it would be best if she continued to feign unconsciousness.

"I say," Lucas continued, "it is extremely gracious of you, Duchess, to help the young lady in her present sad predicament. Your involvement lends a certain respectability to this mysterious affair."

"Consent!" The regal one, who must be the duchess, snorted. "She was *thrust* upon me."

"I am not in the usual habit of reading novels," the sallow one said, "but I am now reading Madame d'Arblay's latest work, *The Wanderer*. A most edifying and unexceptionable book. And, Godmama, I believe it is a warning to us all. One cannot be too friendly or too careful with Unknown Young Persons one happens to meet on the road. With that Corsican Monster on the loose again in Europe, she might even be a French Spy!"

"Nonsense, Albinia!" the Duchess retorted. "I give Adam credit for *some* common sense. Be that as it may, I would rather he had found another conveyance for the young person and packed her off to the authorities rather than bringing her back to Ravenscourt."

"She appears to be gently reared," Lucas said doubtfully.

"Yes, but perhaps you have not noticed. She's wearing diamond earrings. And pearls," Albinia pointed out. "No woman of quality would be caught wearing diamonds and pearls in the morning. And her head is uncovered. Where is her hat?"

The Duchess harumphed again in outraged agreement, and the trio lapsed into a stony silence that continued until, with a great jolt, the coach turned up the drive leading up to Ravenscourt. Some minutes later it stopped and the coach door was heard to open. Devorah was swept into strong arms and carried across a gravel drive and up a broad sweep of steps.

She opened her eyes ever so slightly and peered from under her lashes in order to determine who was carrying her into what appeared to be an ancient stone mansion. Noting her surreptitious glance, Adam grinned down at her. "Been feigning oblivion, have you? Good tactic. But chin up. If you survived the journey here with that lot, you will do just fine."

He continued onward, past the dignified butler who greeted him at the doorway, through a massive hall, and deposited Devorah on an uncomfortable sofa in an ornate drawing room with a highly decorated ceiling. "You can open your eyes now," he whispered. "I've managed to lose them. But just to be safe, please to lie there quietly for the meanwhile."

He turned to the butler, who had appeared silently at the doorway. "Spilsby, the young lady has taken a fall. Please bring her a reviving cordial."

"Just water, please."

Adam's eyebrows shot up. "Oh yes, I forgot. Just water."

"As you wish, your grace." Spilsby bowed himself out of the room, nearly colliding with the regal-looking woman and her sallow sidekick.

"Adam! Not in my best drawing room," the Duchess said in chilling tones. "Hand the young person over to the housekeeper. Have her taken to the servants' quarters."

"You forget yourself, Mother," Adam said sharply. "It is *my* drawing room."

The Duchess sank dramatically into a wingchair. "I feel one of my spasms coming on."

Albinia quickly retrieved the fan from her grace's drooping hand and began fanning her vigorously.

Spilsby reappeared, bearing a tray of drinks. "A glass of water for the young lady, as you requested, your grace. And," the butler paused and looked significantly at the grouping around the wingchair, "reviving cordials for the ladies. I am given to understand that it has been a trying journey."

"Not trying. Outrageous," her grace snapped.

"Hush, now. I believe the young lady is regaining consciousness," said Lucas, who had come soundlessly into the room.

Taking her cue, Devorah opened her eyes slowly and looked at the assembled company with convincing confusion. "Where...where am I? Who are you? What am I doing here?"

she asked, pointedly ignoring Adam's expression of amused appreciation.

The man in mournful colors turned and beamed upon her a benevolent smile displaying a mouth filled with rotting teeth. "My dear child, you have met with a deplorable, unexplained accident, but you are now safe," he explained in dramatic tones. "Fortunately, you have been rescued by his grace, the Duke of Ravenscroft. He has conveyed you back to his ducal seat at Ravenscourt, where you now find yourself. It is the Duke's intention, I believe, for you to remain here under his protection until you have recovered sufficiently to return to your own home."

"Perhaps introductions would be in order, Duckwaithe," Robert said from behind him. "I'll do the honors." Stepping forward, he turned and bowed to the noble inhabitants of the room. "May I present—" At this he stopped short and cast Devorah an imploring look.

"Do you have a name, my dear child?" Mr. Duckwaithe asked, coming to Robert's aid.

"Of course she has a name," the Duchess objected. "Everyone has a name, Lucas. Except for foundlings, of course."

"Devorah. Devorah Asher," Devorah said softly, ignoring the slur.

"Devorah. How lovely, how biblical," Mr. Duckwaithe trilled. "The Hebraic rendering of Deborah, I believe."

"The Hebrew original," she corrected him.

"Someone in your family is a Hebraic scholar?" he asked with great interest.

"My father is a great biblical scholar," she answered truthfully.

"Oxford or Cambridge?"

"Neither. He, ah, had private tutors."

"Never mind that for now," Robert interrupted impatiently. He turned and bowed to his mother, who had recovered sufficiently to sit up straight in her wingchair and glare at Devorah. "Miss Asher, my mother, her grace the

Duchess of Ravenscroft." Devorah raised herself up on one arm and dipped her head in the Duchess's direction in what she hoped would be interpreted as a creditable substitute for a curtsy.

"Next to my mother, Lady Albinia Brinkburn, my mother's goddaughter and family friend. My brother, his grace the Duke of Ravenscroft. My mother's chaplain, the Reverend Lucas Duckwaithe. And I am Lord Robert Melville, the Duke's younger brother," Robert continued.

Awed by so much nobility, Devorah merely nodded again in acknowledgement.

"Enough!" the Duchess said. "What I want to know is, where are you from? How did you get here?"

"I'm from…I'm from…."

Devorah thought quickly. Just how was she to explain who, what, when, where and how, especially when she wasn't sure herself? These people would think she was a total lunatic. There seemed to be only one solution to the problem. "Oh, my head, my head," she moaned, clapping her hand to her forehead in a sudden movement. "I feel that I am about to faint. Smelling salts. Does anyone have smelling salts?"

Then she collapsed back onto the brocade upholstery and was still, one arm hanging limply off the sofa.

"Gone off again, has she?" Robert marveled. "That must have been some fall."

"Perhaps it would be better if you were all to remove to the Green Room to partake of refreshments until she has regained consciousness," the Duke suggested, trying to still the tremor in his voice.

"Yes, but can she be trusted alone in here with all the antiques?" Lady Albinia asked, daring to hint at the unmentionable. "Who knows Who or What she is?"

"'Fraid she'll come to and run off with one of the mediæval chairs?" Robert asked. "Welcome to it, I say."

"I'll remain here with her, Mother," Adam said. "That way she'll have someone to tend to her, if need be. Go on, now; don't argue."

"Come, Albinia," the Duchess said, sweeping out of the room. "I say, it does not pay to be too careful about people nowadays. But, Certain People—whom I *shall not* name— never learn. I just hope things do not come to such a pass that They Are Sorry!"

Chapter 7

Silence descended on the room. The Duke settled himself comfortably into the wingchair vacated by his outraged parent, crossed one booted leg over the other, and sat steadily regarding his unexpected houseguest. "Well?" he said, drumming his fingers on the side of the chair. It was a command, not a question.

Feeling herself at a disadvantage while lying on the sofa, Devorah sat up and smoothed down her skirts. An explanation was in order, she knew; as Lady Albinia had stated all too plainly, one did not just come to be lying unconscious, all alone, in a ditch. There was always a reason for one's being there. Yet, giving a rational explanation—if a rational explanation were to be had—would be difficult, especially when she couldn't remember much of anything.

To be sure, she remembered who she was: Devorah Asher, most recently of the Brooklyn neighborhood of Boro Park in New York City. The rest, however, was hazy, if not a total blank. She had no idea where she was, how she came to be there, or why she was dressed in what struck her as strange clothing, although bits and pieces of recent events were coming back to her. She had a faint memory of being at her friend Gitty Klein's house; she seemed to remember climbing on a chair and reaching for something. Then she was falling in slow motion, like Alice going down the rabbit's hole. The next thing she remembered was being discovered on the ground by the side of a road in what this strange man claimed was the English countryside.

But was that reality, or was she still in the midst of one long dream, replete with Heyeresque characters from the British Regency? And if the latter were true, when would she ever wake up?

Adam, studying her curiously, noticed her hesitation. "Come, Miss Asher," he chided her. "I've banished the enemy, and you have nothing to fear from me. An explanation is in order."

She raised her chin defiantly. "I'm afraid, your grace, that that may prove to be a little difficult."

"A little difficult, or a little inadvisable?"

Devorah looked at him questioningly. "Whatever can you mean?"

"There is something strange going on here," he said. "An *elusive* something strange. Not only did we find you under unusual circumstances—all alone by the side of a largely deserted country road, possibly the victim of some form of violence—but there is something not quite right about you. Your dress, for instance, is very nearly English, but not quite English enough; and while it is certainly acceptable evening dress for a gently reared young woman, it is somewhat out of place in the middle of the day. Then there is your accent, which is somewhat foreign, though I cannot for the life of me determine its origin. You appear to be a woman of intelligence; perhaps you would be so obliging as to explain just who you are and how you came to be here."

"But, I don't know," she protested.

"Don't know? Come, come. I think you can do better than that. I *know* you can do better. I want the unvarnished truth."

The Duke, obviously, was a man who would accept no prevarication. So be it, thought Devorah; she would give him the truth—or, at least, the greater part of the truth as it appeared to be if taken at face value. If he didn't believe her, that was his problem. "Well, this is only conjecture," she said baldly, "but apparently I fell off a chair and landed in the wrong century."

Stunned silence reigned for half a minute or so. Then Adam slapped his knee and burst out laughing. "Oh, that is rich. Very, very rich. I've heard excuses for everything before—or so I thought. But this is truly one for the books. If only Lord Robert were here to share the joke."

"It is no joke, sir," Devorah said with quiet dignity. "And what's more, I told you that an explanation would prove difficult, but you didn't listen to me. But it *is* the truth—unless I'm in the middle of a weird dream or my imagination has run amok. Or, perhaps I am delirious. My head aches dreadfully and I have a bump on the back of it, so I could be suffering the effects of a concussion. Generally, I am considered very level-headed, so I see no reason otherwise to have entered into such vivid hallucinations."

"Perhaps there is another reason," the Duke insinuated.

"Another reason?" she asked angrily. "To have landed thousands of miles from my home, in what previous century I can only guess?" She paused and attempted to bring her voice under control. It was unfair to become angry merely out of frustration. If she were in the Duke's boots, she would think her explanation equally ridiculous. Obviously, some elaboration was needed.

"Sir, do you speak Spanish, by any chance?"

"What the deuce does Spanish have to do with this? Unless.... But we'll get to that with the *other* reason in a minute."

"There is a famous seventeenth-century Spanish poet, Calderón de la Barca, who wrote a poem titled *La Vida es Sueño—Life is Dream*," Devorah continued, ignoring him. "*What is life? An illusion, a shadow, a fiction. ...All of life is a dream, and the dreams are dreams.*" Her voice dropped to a dramatic whisper. "And this life, too, the one I inhabit now, may be a dream. Because, if it is real, it is truly, truly bizarre."

Adam signaled for her silence and reached for the bell-pull. "Bravo! I can see that you have a bit of the master raconteur in you and that I am in for quite a story—dream tale, or otherwise. Let me order some refreshments before we continue. Meanwhile, Spilsby, our butler, will direct one of the maids to escort you upstairs so that you can attend to your toilette."

Devorah nodded gratefully and was soon whisked away to be initiated into the intricacies of early nineteenth-century plumbing. Some quarter of an hour later, she had resumed her position on the drawing room sofa and accepted a picture-perfect red apple from a bowl of fruit brought in by Spilsby as part of a laden tray of refreshments.

"Some ratafia?" the Duke offered, raising an eyebrow as Devorah mumbled under her breath before biting into the apple. He had seen that surreptitious gesture made before, but where and by whom?

Devorah shook her head. "Just water, please."

"I can have Spilsby bring you some soda water, if you so desire. No? Please to try one of these macaroons. They are my mother's favorite, and I admit that, though I myself am not partial to sweets, these are particularly flavorful. No again? Well then, finish your apple and we can have our little chat."

Adam lounged in the wingchair, sipping abstractedly from a glass of port while studying Devorah from under fierce brows. Who was she? He guessed her to be in her early to mid-twenties rather than in the first blush of youth, and she was still quite beautiful, in a faintly exotic way. And she appeared to be quality, judging by her elegant but modest dress and the way that she carried herself with a certain dignity and self-assurance, even in such an undignified situation as she now found herself. Yet she was obviously unfamiliar with proper etiquette in the presence of a nobleman, especially a duke. Perhaps she had never rubbed up against the nobility before, though she seemed too indefinably polished to be a mere Cit.

Who is she? Adam asked himself again. A woman of gentle birth and family cast all alone upon the world was deserving of his protection and hospitality. But a member of the common masses, a nobody, with no acquaintances and no recommendations, could consider herself lucky to be treated with the slightest mercy by the servants.

But there was a third possibility, that *other* reason, he thought with an inward shudder. With Napoleon having escaped from Elba and marched into Paris, again casting his dark shadow over Europe, England was rife with unsavory characters sent from foreign parts to gather intelligence for his cause. Miss Asher's English was slightly accented and idiomatically different from his own, giving rise to the suspicion that the beautiful stranger in distress who had been admitted into the great house of Ravenscroft was a viper in disguise.

As quickly as the suspicion welled up, however, he shook it off. Looking at her, nibbling daintily at her apple, her lashes casting fine shadows over her delicately tinted cheeks, he found it too difficult to believe.

Devorah finished the apple and gently wiped her fingers on a damask napkin. Her lips moved briefly again, as if in silent supplication, before she settled herself more comfortably on the sofa and returned the Duke's scrutiny. "You look like a sensible man to me," she said at last.

His lips twitched. "I am thought to be by most people," he answered appreciatively. "And being sensible, I am not in the way of believing farradiddles."

"Certainly not. You don't appear to be that type of person."

"Then, Miss Asher, might I be so bold as to request you to refrain from telling me farradiddles."

"You might," Devorah said calmly, "but then again, anything I could reasonably tell you might be construed as a farradiddle."

"Try me."

"Very well. But, please fortify yourself first," she advised him, motioning to the crystal decanter of Madeira on the satinwood side table. She watched approvingly as he poured himself another glass and took a long swallow. "Now, you asked me how I came to be here and I told you. Of course you did not believe me. I, too, would not have believed my answer were someone else to say the same thing to me. But it is true, all the same. I asked you where I was and you told me Gloucestershire, which I presume is in England. Now I must ask you, what is today's date?"

Adam shrugged. "Monday the twenty-seventh of March, in the year 1815."

"More or less what I thought," Devorah said matter-of-factly. "I presumed I had landed somewhere in the Regency period. However, English history is not my long suit. I know only what I read in novels."

"Yes, and they appear to have affected your brain," his grace commented wryly.

"My fears exactly," she agreed amiably.

"Enough!" he snapped, suddenly irritated. "Just explain yourself, if you please, in plain English, with no more digressions. Who are you? From where are you? What are you doing here?"

Devorah's eyes flashed. "In plain English, your grace, my name—as I previously told you—is Devorah Asher. I live in New York City in the United States of America—what you Englishmen might call the former American colonies. As for how I came to be here, I already told you: I think I fell off a chair. I vaguely remember being at a friend's house and climbing on a chair to reach for something. I remember losing my balance and falling. And the next thing I know, here I am.

"Oh yes, one other thing: When I climbed on the chair, the year was 2014. I must have bumped my head when I fell, because aside from the fact that it still aches dreadfully, I keep wondering what is real and what is a dream—and when I will wake up from this dream-turned-nightmare. And now I understand why, all those years when I was growing up, my parents admonished me not to stuff my head with so many novels. They can be dangerous."

Adam reached for the Madeira on the side table and filled an empty goblet. "My sentiments exactly, Miss Asher. *Very* dangerous. I don't believe you for a single moment, but on the other hand, I have great difficulty thinking of you as a spy or other dangerous, villainous person. Your answer is too ingenious; someone with something to hide would think up a more credible story. I think, at best, your senses are still disordered from your fall. At worst, who knows?" He held a glass out to Devorah. "Please to drink this. It may help you recover your wits."

Devorah shook her head and pushed the glass away.

He raised his eyebrows. "A teetotaler?"

"Religiously," she replied.

"Is there any other kind?" He set the glass back on the table. "The question remains. What am I to do with you? It appears you are not one of us; nor, I presume, are you of the lower orders. From a practical point of view, you fit neither here nor there. However, unless I am led in some way to conclude that you are not worthy of it, I feel obligated, since I rescued you, to offer you my protection. But how to do so?" He knit his brows. "Though it is against my better instincts, I can turn you over to the housekeeper, as my mother suggested, and have you housed with the servants until some solution can be found. Or——"

His dark eyes lit up suddenly.

He had been facing a bleak month at Ravenscourt due to the Duchess's unfortunate choice of houseguests while pressing business matters tied him there. His sense of honor too refined, he had balked at forcibly and directly depressing Albinia's intentions and foiling his mother's schemes, and he was too much the gentleman to give Mr. Duckwaithe the set-down he usually deserved for making such stupid, pretentious conversation. But, to introduce a beautiful, mysterious female—and one of obvious gentility, albeit dubious lineage—into their midst was just what was needed to shake things up a bit. Gad, Robert would also love the joke—should Adam choose to let him in on it.

"I think, my dear Miss Asher, that you are about to render me a singular service."

"I beg your pardon?"

"The only puzzle is how to pass you off as possibly being one of us. Any suggestions, my dear girl? Any nobility run through your veins, or anything else that would place you in the upper orders?"

Only a second's thought was required for Devorah to recall the carefully documented family tree, written in exquisite Hebrew script on fine parchment, miraculously rescued from the hellish inferno of Europe some seventy-odd years ago, and now stored safely away in a locked cupboard in her father's book-lined study. Written more than two centuries before and carefully added to by each successive generation, it detailed her father's family in an unbroken lineage stretching back hundreds of years to Prague and the legendary Rabbi Yehudah Loewe, also known as the Maharal, who in turn was descended directly from the biblical King David.

"Will royalty do?" she asked with aplomb.

Adam raised his eyebrows in surprise. "More than do. Who on earth are you?"

"Nobody special. But I *am* a direct descendant of a well-known, ancient king. Quite watered down by now, of course, but we can directly trace our lineage all the way back."

"And the king?"

"That, your grace, I would prefer not to divulge at this time."

"How discreet," Adam murmured.

"Yes, one cannot be too careful. It would not do to go puffing myself off, would it?"

The Duke wagged an admonitory finger at her. "My dear Miss Asher, you are a complete hand. I perceive having you as a guest will keep me continually on my toes."

"That, sir, I would not want to happen. Having gone so far as to rescue me, you are now being more than kind, quite beyond the call of duty." The dazzling smile she had bestowed on him with that last encomium faded, to be replaced by a look of consternation. "Still, the problem remains. Having landed here, heavens knows how...how in the world am I going to return to my own century and my own home?"

"We shall ponder that problem once suitable accommodations have been made for you and you have had a chance to recover. I shall direct Spilsby to introduce you to Mrs. Wigmore, our good housekeeper, who will show you to one of the guest chambers. She can also provide you with an abigail for the duration of your stay here and make provisions for supplying you with a temporary wardrobe."

He reached for the bell-pull, but his hand was stayed by a sudden commotion outside the drawing room. "What the devil?" he asked, as the sounds of a scuffle grew more pronounced.

"In you go now," a male voice said firmly.

"I shan't, I shan't," protested a much younger voice that Adam knew all too well.

"Certainly you shall, Master Theo," the first voice said reasonably, "and you shall tell the Duke all about it and face your punishment like a man. I have the distinct feeling that his grace has commanded you in no uncertain terms to confine your antics to the home wood and the park, where you are less likely to cause damage."

This curious conversation was brought to an abrupt end by the entrance of Spilsby, followed by a pleasant-looking man of some thirty-odd years, half-pushing, half-dragging a disheveled youth of no more than ten summers who was burdened with a bow and quiver of arrows. The butler, assuming a wooden countenance that somehow managed at the same time to convey an expression of long suffering, announced in dignified accents, "Mr. Jonathan Whyteman." He coughed slightly into his sleeve. "Accompanied by Master Theodore."

"Cousin Ravenscroft!" said Master Theodore, turning defiantly to face the Duke. "I am blameless."

Adam ignored him, addressing himself instead to Mr. Whyteman. "What has the little varmint done now? No, no, don't mince words. Tell me the extent of the damage. My agent, of course, will make restitution, but I want the punishment to fit the crime."

"I think, your grace, that perhaps it would be better if young Master Theo told you all about it himself."

"Well, Theo?" the Duke asked, a look of amusement on his face.

Theo hoisted the quiver over his shoulder and grimly approached Adam's chair. He was a sturdy boy with shaggy blonde hair sticking out from under a large, floppy, green-felt hat adorned with a pheasant feather, and a square face in which large gray eyes and a prominent nose warred for domination.

"It was *not* my fault," he announced in embittered accents. "He *would* keep the windows to his book-room wide open so that the pigeons could fly in. When the Otleys were tenants there, nobody but nobody used the book-room on such a fine day, so naturally all the windows were kept closed. And besides, all they kept on the mantelpiece were some brass candlesticks."

"Naturally," Adam agreed. "Been playing Robin Hood again, Theo?"

"Sir! I was defending the rights of the common man."

"Slew the pigeon, did you?"

"Of course," Theo said scornfully.

Mr. Whyteman, deeming it necessary at this point to embellish upon Theo's explanation, stepped forward to add his piece. "There is no denying, Duke, that he is an excellent marksman. Felled the bird on his first try from outside on the carriage drive. Unfortunately, there were a few pieces of china located quite unnecessarily near the pigeon at the time of its demise."

"Anything valuable broken?" inquired the Duke.

"Only a particularly ugly Sèvres vase. Being bequeathed to me by my Great-Aunt Fanny of blessed memory, it held great sentimental value for my mother who, fortunately, visits only once or twice a year. I will endeavor to explain the circumstances of its disappearance upon her next visit."

"And I will endeavor to send Theo over to greet her," the Duke added. "It may render any explanation of yours unnecessary."

"Sir, you speak of me as if I was some kind of *monster*," Theo objected.

"No, not a monster," Adam said indulgently. "Only an overly active boy with too much time on his hands and not enough to do. But let us set aside the subject of your exploits for the moment. Whyteman, Theo, I would like to present our houseguest, Miss Devorah Asher. Miss Asher, please to meet Mr. Jonathan Whyteman, my very esteemed tenant and friend at Ten Oaks Manor just down the lane, and my young cousin, Theodore Allenby. Theo's parents, Sir Martin and Lady Desdemona Allenby, are currently at the Congress of Vienna, where Sir Martin is a member of our Diplomatic Corps. Theo has agreed to keep us company while his parents are otherwise occupied abroad."

Mr. Whyteman turned at the sound of Devorah's name and looked at her sharply. It was a piercing look, full of questions. Then, his attention turned swiftly back to Adam and Theo, and she was able to look him over at leisure.

Her initial impression of a pleasant-looking man, of medium height and build, was reinforced. She guessed him to be anywhere from thirty to forty years of age—probably somewhere halfway in-between, judging by the laugh lines forming at the corners of his hazel eyes. Whereas the Duke, Lord Robert and Mr. Duckwaithe were clean-shaven, he wore a neat beard and mustache. His brown hair, covered partially by a small cap, was brushed carefully into the style that Devorah would learn to identify as the Brutus, and he was dressed simply in a dark-blue jacket of excellent cut and buckskins tucked into highly glossed boots. Instead of the intricately wound neckcloth sported by the Duke and his brother, he wore a handkerchief knotted casually around his neck. Devorah liked what she saw; he looked kind and trustworthy—and familiar. She had a nagging impression that she had met him before.

"Madame, your servant." Mr. Whyteman bowed in her direction before lowering himself into the hideously carved Jacobean chair indicated by the Duke. He looked at her again, appreciatively, but speculatively. "You live in a near county? No? Interesting…. I had the distinct impression that we have met previously."

"Miss Asher lives nowhere near here," Adam explained hastily. "Quite, quite far away, in fact. Due to circumstances that are best left unexplained at present, she will be staying with us indefinitely."

"How fortunate for her grace and the Lady Albinia," Mr. Whyteman commented in deadpan tones. "I am sure they will find a female addition to their company extremely gratifying."

"You lie, Whyteman!" the Duke said brazenly.

Mr. Whyteman choked only slightly, and was saved from answering by the reappearance of Spilsby, bearing a tray laden with additional refreshments. "Sir, I assume you will partake of your usual soda water and fruit," he said, handing Mr. Whyteman a glass filled with clear liquid. "And for you, Master Theo, I have brought a pitcher of lemonade and your favorite pound cake."

Master Theo, having spent the morning expending a great deal of energy and working up a mammoth appetite, enthusiastically attacked the cake.

"What, a fresh pound cake today, Theo? I heard that you finished the last lot off for a snack last evening," the Duke quizzed him, observing the cake's rapid disappearance. "What a lucky circumstance that you have Cook wrapped around your little finger. When I request that she make *my* favorite sweets, she merely grumbles and sends word up that she has more important things to do."

"You should visit her in the kitchen sometimes," Theo advised, licking the crumbs from his fingers. "Cook says that when you were a little devil like me, you had plenty of time for the likes of her, but now that you are a grand duke, you can't be bothered to give her the time of day."

"She said that?" Adam asked, impressed. "I must go pay her my compliments. Cook has been with our family, you see, since I was younger than Theo," he explained to Devorah and Mr. Whyteman. "Worked her way up from a scullery maid, and now she rules the kitchen like a despot. But when she was younger, before she started queening it over the ovens and stoves, she was used to have a soft spot for me and would set aside all kinds of sugar plums and macaroons for me. I would sneak them up the stairs in my pockets and eat them in my bed at night."

He was recalled from his reveries by a discreet cough from Spilsby, who had exited the drawing room unnoticed and magically reappeared at his master's side. "If you please, her grace wishes me to inform you that a light repast will be served in half an hour in the Small Dining Room."

Adam nodded. "There will be two more of us at table. Whyteman, you will stay and take your meal with us. No, no protests from you now. They are quite unnecessary. Spilsby will direct Cook to bring out your special tin of biscuits, and we have plenty of smoked fish to offer you from that batch you sent over to us last month. Spilsby, see to it, if you please."

"Certainly, your grace. Will there be anything else?"

"Ah, yes. It slipped my mind with the, ah, appearance of Master Theodore. Miss Asher will be staying at Ravenscourt as our guest, possibly for several weeks. Please make her known to Mrs. Wigmore, who will show her to one of the guest chambers. Mrs. Wigmore should send a girl to assist Miss Asher before we eat; she can prepare Miss Asher's room fully after Miss Asher is escorted down to the dining room. Mrs. Wigmore should report to me for further instructions regarding Miss Asher's stay."

Devorah had temporarily forgotten her predicament while quietly observing the affectionate bantering between the Duke, Theo and Mr. Whyteman. But the announcement that she was to lunch with the family and be shown to a guest room forcibly recalled her to the seriousness of her situation. She looked up, stricken, first at the Duke and then at Mr. Whyteman, who was calmly finishing off an apple. The latter placed the fruit's core on the refreshment tray and discreetly mumbled something under his breath.

Feeling Devorah's eyes upon him, he glanced up. The stricken look was still on her face, but it was replaced quickly by one of confusion and then, perhaps, of dawning comprehension. Mr. Whyteman glanced over at the Duke and saw that Theo had engaged his attention. "Don't worry," he said in an undertone. "You will be all right, and you shall come about in the end."

"I beg your pardon?"

"Remember Queen Esther. So many years of eating chickpeas."

Devorah gasped.

"Exactly," he said, nodding in confirmation. "You have no need to worry. I will show you the way."

Before she could press the matter, Spilsby requested that she follow him. Devorah stood and straightened her skirts and, mustering up all her dignity and courage to face whatever lay ahead, stepped forward without a backward glance.

Chapter 8

Mrs. Wigmore, a stately, middle-aged woman with salt-and-pepper hair pulled into a tight knot under her cap, accepted Devorah's unheralded arrival without a blink and stated instantly that she should be placed in the Rose Room in the West Wing. She would be across the hall from Lady Albinia, who was staying in the Royal Bedchamber, Mrs. Wigmore told Devorah amiably as she led her through the massive Great Hall, past a suit of armour, and up a broad flight of steps to a landing opening onto the various wings built around a large court.

"Lady Albinia, being as she is her grace's goddaughter and a favorite of hers, always stays in the Royal Bedchamber, which is reserved for important guests," the housekeeper explained, turning into a long, green-carpeted corridor hung with numerous portraits in gilded frames. "It is documented in the family history that while on an extended visit to the region, Queen Elizabeth slept in the Royal Bedchamber, and ever since then the furnishings have been replaced only as necessary, and then with exact replicas of the original. Perhaps Lady Albinia will be so good as to show you the chamber after luncheon."

But something in Mrs. Wigmore's tone of voice gave Devorah to think that she doubted it.

At long last, a door was flung open and Devorah was shown into a room decorated in varying shades of rose. Early-afternoon sunlight filtered in through a window hung with heavy rose-velvet curtains and cream-colored sheers, casting a gentle illumination on cream wallpaper figured with tiny rosebuds and on a great, carved four-poster bed in the center of the room. The bed, covered in rose-colored damask and draped with velvet curtains matching those at the window, stood upon a Chinese carpet that reflected the same hues as the bed and draperies, while a plush-looking armchair next to the window was upholstered in a duskier pink.

"Oh, how beautiful!" Devorah exclaimed, looking around.

"You had best hurry, miss," Mrs. Wigmore reminded her. "The family sits down to luncheon in twenty minutes, and her grace does not take kindly to latecomers." She stooped and pulled an ornate, covered china pot out from under the bed. "The water closet is straight down the hall, the last door on your left, but there is this if you should be needing it, because I doubt you will have time otherwise. Betsy will be up directly to bring you hot water and straighten your hair; then James, the second footman, will be along in ten minutes to escort you downstairs."

She was gone an instant later. Alone at last, Devorah turned to the cheval glass next to the delicate satinwood dressing table and briefly inspected her appearance. In the words of Georgette Heyer, she looked a fright. Her hair was coming unpinned and her face was smudged, most probably from her fall. But Betsy would attend to that. Devorah needed to use the few precious minutes of solitude to collect her wits and consider her situation.

In the past, she had frequently encountered situations that conflicted drastically with her values and the religious restrictions under which she operated. Undaunted, she had managed to build a successful career without compromising these principles. But now, if this wasn't a dream, she was thousands of miles and nearly two hundred years from her home. And she was alone—without community, family or friends. She had no one to whom to turn, no available means of support. Worse yet, she was a guest in a strange nobleman's house, about to dine at his table—a table that would be laden with foods that her religion prohibited her from eating. It would be the greatest challenge of her life, maintaining the charade thrust upon her while adhering to her religion, and she questioned her ability to carry it off. Unless....

Unless Mr. Whyteman could help her.

Who was he, and what was he doing in the middle of Gloucestershire—the friend of a duke and honored guest at his dining table? He had recognized immediately that her oh-so-biblical name was due to more than a parent's fondness for biblical scholarship. Then there was the blessing—or so it appeared to be—recited secretly under his breath after eating an apple, just as she had done. *Was he a Member of the Tribe?*

Finally, there was the matter of Queen Esther.

Queen Esther, the lovely Jewess married to Ahasuerus, powerful king of Persia, who ruled over one hundred and twenty-seven provinces. For years Esther guarded the secret of her birthright, avoiding forbidden foods by eating only fruits and vegetables...and chickpeas. Then Ahasuerus's evil advisor, Haman, persuaded him to issue a decree that all the Jews of his kingdom be destroyed. Esther intervened on behalf of her fellow Jews, revealing her identity and successfully saving them from slaughter. Thereafter, every year on the anniversary of their salvation, for more than two millennia, the Jewish people throughout the world had celebrated Purim.

Purim! Devorah's memory was returning with surprising rapidity, although certain details still eluded her. On Purim, for reasons she still couldn't remember, she apparently had gone to her friend Gitty Klein for the mandatory festive meal. She remembered going into the kitchen to help Gitty and climbing up on a chair, and the next thing she knew she was falling, falling.

But why was she in Regency England? Why was she dressed in this clothing? And why she had gone to Gitty's instead of to her parents?

A gentle knock intruded upon Devorah's reveries, and a buxom young woman with straw-colored hair and a ruddy, freckled face entered the room. After setting a jug of warm water down on the washstand in the corner, she bobbed a curtsy in Devorah's direction and introduced herself as Betsy. She was, she explained, to be Devorah's personal maid for the duration of her stay.

"Mrs. Wigmore says as we should 'urry," Betsy added, holding out a fluffy towel as Devorah rinsed her face and hands. She extracted an ivory-inlaid comb and brush set from her voluminous pockets and motioned her temporary mistress to be seated on the velvet-upholstered stool in front of the dressing table.

"'Ere, Mrs. Wigmore says you should have this set. Mrs. Wigmore says being as you did not bring any luggage, being found as you was after that terrible accident, she will Supply All. 'Never you worry,' she says. 'Lady Felicity, his grace's sister, is much of a size as you and has plenty of castoffs that would fit you to a nicety.' While you are at luncheon, Mrs. Wigmore and I will Take Care of Everything."

Having removed the pins from Devorah's hair, she applied the brush with a vengeance. "Oh, you do have beautiful hair, miss. So soft, and so nice-smelling, too." She fell silent as she rolled Devorah's hair back up and pinned it into place. "Though if I may say so, a smart crop might be more like. And so much easier for you to keep. Mrs. Wigmore says as 'ow her grace's dresser might be got to crop it for you, 'an her grace permits."

"I'll think about it," Devorah told her, turning from side to side to inspect her refurbished hairdo in the mirror.

"Also, miss," Betsy added, "Mrs. Wigmore says as you being a furrinner and not quite up on what's what, maybe I can hint you away from wearing all that jewelry just now in the afternoon."

"Which jewelry?"

"Beg pardon, but Mrs. Wigmore says as diamonds and pearls are quite unexceptionable at night, but ladies do not wear them for day."

"It is true that I am not up on local customs," Devorah admitted, removing the diamond drops from her ear lobes and reaching behind her neck to unclasp her pearls. "Please thank Mrs. Wigmore for me. Is there somewhere safe to put these so they do not get lost?"

"I'll ask Mrs. Wigmore." Betsy bobbed another curtsy. "Oh, miss, you do look beautiful. Would it not be something wonderful if—" She clapped her hand suddenly to her mouth as if to keep the next words from falling out and began blushing furiously. "Oh, I do beg pardon."

"Never mind," Devorah said, standing and smoothing down her skirts just as a smart rap sounded on the door. "That must be James. Thank you, Betsy."

The Small Dining Room was, Devorah soon discovered, a large, pine-paneled room with tall, mullioned windows along one side that afforded a somewhat dissected view of the park beyond. It was dominated by a massive mahogany dining table that could easily have accommodated twenty without leaves, though only eight, including Theo, sat down to luncheon, and an elaborate sideboard that held a huge display of fruit in a heavy silver bowl and a crystal vase filled with fresh roses.

Robert, seated to Devorah's left, inched his chair closer and informed her that the room, like the West Wing in which she stayed, was part of the original court built some three hundred years before on the ruins of an ancient castle. The court had been added to and improved upon by subsequent generations of Melvilles to include a cavernous, formal dining room under the third duke. The Small Dining Room, however, remained the traditional gathering place for those members of the household who partook of the usual cold collation served for luncheon.

"With the exception of Adam, all the Melvilles have added their touch to the court in one way or the other, but I daresay he will also tack on a wing or two once he becomes leg-shackled, because women seem to like to leave their mark on a place," Robert added, spearing a large slice of ham from the serving plate set in front of him. He lowered his voice to a whisper. "Adam's nearing five-and-thirty now, and there's pressure being brought to bear on him to produce an heir. Lord knows, he can have his pick of the marriage mart, but he's difficult to please. He may decide to marry at this point to please my mother, though I ain't saying that is exactly to his taste."

He inclined his head in the direction of Lady Albinia, seated across the table on the Duke's right. "Lady Albinia, there—Binny—she's Mother's goddaughter and *her* choice for the post. She is nearly twenty-one now, been on the marriage market for three seasons, and has had nary an offer that *I* know of. She's an earl's daughter and pretty puffed up about it, and she would positively jump at an offer from the Duke, as he knows all too well. My sister, Lady Felicity, and I call her the Duchess Presumptive, but Adam has been weaseling out of making her an offer ever since her come-out, and I think he means to keep on doing it. That is, unless the pressure becomes too awful. Albinia ain't too popular around here, though."

At this point Mr. Duckwaithe intervened from across the table and admonished Robert to fill Miss Asher's plate.

"No, no, nothing for me," Devorah said, waving Robert's hand away. "I never eat meat. Just some fruit, if you please."

"Never?" Mr. Duckwaithe asked. "But this cold roast is delicious. Cook's specialty. And the ham was cured in his grace's own smokehouse. I am sure you never will find another quite as tasty as that cured at Ravenscourt."

"Never," Devorah said emphatically, turning slightly green.

"You must try some Stilton, then," Mr. Duckwaithe persisted. "Adam says you are visiting from the Americas. I am sure you do not have anything like our cheeses in America."

"I am quite sure not," Devorah said agreeably. "Your English cheeses are famous. However, I never eat cheese, either."

"I say, you wouldn't be a follower of Mr. Shelley, by any chance, would you?" Robert asked, suddenly struck by a thought.

"Mr. Shelley?"

Lady Albinia, encouraged by the informal tone being set, nodded knowingly. "Certainly. The poet, Percy Bysshe Shelley. In his pamphlet, *A Vindication of Natural Diet Based on a French Tract, The Return to Nature,* published a few years ago, he maintains that a vegetable diet and pure water will cure all the body's ills."

"My, my, you certainly impress me, Lady Albinia," the Duke commented dryly. "I had no idea you were so bookish."

Lady Albinia colored slightly. "I am not at all a bluestocking, you know. However, I pride myself that I am able to maintain a well-informed mind while not being out-of-the-ordinary studious."

Mr. Whyteman, who until that moment had been silently discussing a plate of smoked salmon and fruit, looked up and advised Devorah to forget her scruples and partake of the former food item. "The smoked salmon was sent to the Duke compliments of my brother in Glasgow and is *quite* unexceptionable. You have my word on it that you may safely eat it."

Unsure of the best course of action, Devorah shifted uncomfortably in her seat. Should she trust Mr. Whyteman regarding what foods she could eat? Would he have known about Queen Esther and the chickpeas if he were not... were not like her? But then, instinct told her that perhaps it was better not to trust anyone at all for the time being. How much did the Duke know about Mr. Whyteman? How much did any of the others know about him? If she followed his lead, eating only the same foods as he ate, the Duke—and others who might be privy to his secret, if her assumption was correct—would know that she, too...was a Jew.

And then, instead of being a welcomed guest in the Duke's house, she might become *persona non grata.* Devorah, too, had read Fanny Burney's *The Wanderer*, and she knew that she might be cast out onto the open fields, all alone, in a strange country, a strange century.

As Devorah was debating her best course of action, salvation came from an unexpected quarter. Hitherto, Theo, placed on the other side of Devorah, had also been quietly discussing his luncheon. He now jerked his head up from his plate and demanded to know why the assembled hosts were bothering their guest.

"It's enough that you natter me day in, day out, to eat what's put on the table and to finish my plate, but at least I'm under age and have to listen to you—maybe. But I don't see why you have to do the same to *her*. *She's* certainly old enough to decide if she wants to eat something or not!"

Lady Albinia gasped and Mr. Duckwaithe could be heard saying, "Now, now, Master Theo," in baby-soothing tones.

"That will be enough, Theo," the Duke commanded coldly. "More out of you and you will return to the practice of taking your luncheon in the schoolroom."

Theo grinned triumphantly and reapplied his energies to his plate, leaving Devorah with the distinct impression that the threatened punishment was more to his taste than the measure of respect accorded him by letting him eat with his elders.

The Duchess, regarding Theo with a disapproving eye, took a sip of soda water before inquiring of the Duke, "When did Sir Martin say that he and Lady Desdemona will be returning to England?"

"Not soon enough," Robert grumbled.

"I believe that recent events in Europe, especially Napoleon's march on Paris, have rendered it impossible for Sir Martin to return at this time," the Duke answered.

"Pity," the Duchess said pithily, returning to her food.

Mr. Whyteman, taking advantage of the ensuing gap in the conversation, smiled at Devorah. "Trust me," he repeated softly. "You will like the fish and eggs. Also, the salted biscuits sitting in the tin over by young Theo's elbow. They come from London, from a baker whose reliability I have checked into personally, and are quite tasty."

His grace, leaning around Theo, also smiled at Devorah. "He's right. Trust him," he said. "You cannot go wrong with the fish and crackers. Mr. Whyteman should know."

Reason and instinct began to war within Devorah, and reason, veering to the side of caution, won out. "Like Mr. Shelley, just vegetables and water—and fruit," she said, reaching for an apple from the plate that had been placed in front of her.

Fortunately, the principal occupants of the table showed no desire to linger over their meal, and luncheon was soon over. The Duchess, studiously avoiding speaking directly to Devorah, regally announced to the emptying room that it was her time-honored practice to partake of a regenerating nap in the afternoon; the female guests could either follow her lead or fend for themselves until it was time to dress for dinner. Lady Albinia was quick to add that she also took to her bed in the afternoon with an inspirational book for entertainment until such time as sleep overcame her.

The Duke, perhaps determining that a masterful hand was needed to steer Devorah until she could make her own way, suggested that she, too, retire to her room. Perhaps Mrs. Wigmore had finished making it up properly for her, in addition to finding her suitable raiment to wear to supplement what she had on her back.

Thus it came about that Devorah found herself tucked up between lavender-scented linen sheets for an afternoon nap while wrapped—upon orders of Mrs. Wigmore—in a lavishly beribboned silk-and-lace dressing gown that had previously belonged to Lady Felicity. Her own clothing, removed to Ravenscourt's netherworld for cleaning and pressing, became the subject of much conversation and wonderment in the servants' quarters.

Of especial curiosity was her half-corset, as Betsy and Tilstock, the Duchess' own lofty dresser, called it. It was the flimsiest of undergarments ostensibly used for that purpose and a strange contraption made of lace, wire and a stretchy material that was similar to, but not exactly like, rubber. Devorah's scandalous pantalettes (because, what self-respecting woman wore them?), made all the more shocking by their brevity and constructed of another stretchy, but more silk-like, material, also received a great deal of comment. Not even the great Tilstock herself, in all her years of serving great ladies and leaders of fashion, had ever seen the like, and she was forced to set down the pagan practice to strange colonial customs.

Tilstock, who had taken on the refurbishing of Devorah's garments against her mistress's will, also pointed out to Mrs. Wigmore the tiny, exacting stitches set to the seams of Devorah's dress—stitches so perfect and uniform in size that, she declared, "There is something uncanny about them, almost as if they were stitched by other than human hands."

Exhausted by the day's events and overwhelmed by the thoughts churning through her mind, Devorah slipped gratefully into sleep while below-stairs Ravenscourt buzzed with servants' intrigue and gossip rife with speculation. She would have been shocked had she known the honor and condescension accorded her by Tilstock's decision to take her clothing in hand. That venerable servant, who had her mistress's best interests at heart, knew that the Duchess was pouring her energies into promoting a match between the Duke and her goddaughter. But try as she would, Tilstock could not like the Lady Albinia, and she regarded Miss Asher's sudden appearance as being providential. Knowing too well that Betsy, in normal circumstances a mere upstairs maid, had no experience as a dresser, she had determined that a more experienced hand was needed for the care and selection of Devorah's garments.

That hand was now attempting to calculate the exact worth of those obviously expensive garments down to the final penny. Moreover, her diamonds and pearls, given over to Spilsby by Mrs. Wigmore for safekeeping, had undergone the butler's and Tilstock's expert scrutiny and were judged to be of the very first quality.

There was no doubt about it, Tilstock and Spilsby decided, Miss Asher dressed like quality. Then there was her faint reserve and lack of condescension (which Spilsby had been quick to detect during her initial interview with the Duke, and Mrs. Wigmore had confirmed), which was not unbecoming and spoke of good breeding. Finally, snatches of conversation overheard between his grace and Lord Robert indicated that a connection with royalty might exist.

Miss Asher might be a plain miss, but she was still a lady, the upper servants determined. True, she was a foreigner and spoke with a funny accent, but wasn't she from the Americas and therefore a former British subject, rendering her nearly unobjectionable? And, she appeared to be a kinder, better-humored lady than the Duchess Presumptive. Perhaps, they speculated, the Duchess Presumptive was about to be deposed.

Chapter 9

*D*evorah awoke late in the afternoon to the murky vision of Betsy draping a variety of garments over the dusky pink armchair. Though her head was throbbing, she submitted meekly as Betsy assisted her into one of Lady Felicity's cast-offs. This resulted in a stand-off of sorts.

Betsy assured her that the white worked-muslin evening dress with tiny puffed sleeves and a low, square neck was normal evening wear for a chilly evening in March. Devorah, however, unused to baring such a vast expanse of chest, insisted that where *she* came from, it was a dress suitable only for the height of summer. An additional covering must be found for her upper torso or she would be forced to stay in her room next to the fire.

Tilstock was consulted. To the great relief of all, she managed to unearth from the back of Felicity's overcrowded wardrobe a high-necked, faux pearl-embroidered sarsnet overdress, purchased a few years previously and cast off after only one wearing with the complaint that its pale blush color made the younger lady of the house look insipid. The overall effect on Devorah, Tilstock admitted, was original but striking.

Informed by the Duchess's dresser that it wanted still an hour until the family gathered in the Grand Drawing Room for dinner, Devorah requested to be shown down to the library. Half an hour later, the Duke, already in full evening dress and splendid to behold, came in search of a farm journal he had been studying and found her there, reading the opening chapter in the first volume of Miss Burney's *Evelina*. Surprise flickered in his eyes for a split second as he took in her unusual outfit.

"My compliments. To whom does one credit your ensemble?" his grace asked, taking his snuffbox from his pocket and delicately removing a pinch of its contents. "I am certain you will set a new style."

Devorah tugged at the tight sleeves of the blush overdress. "Does it look alright?" she asked anxiously. "You have been most generous to me, but the clothes I was given to choose from seemed so, so—"

"Bare?" the Duke finished helpfully.

"Yes," Devorah answered lamely, struggling to control the color rising to her face.

"I believe the fashion right now—as it has nearly always been—is to display an expanse of flesh during the evening hours," his grace explained with a deadpan expression. "Certainly, my mother, who is a high stickler, has found nothing exceptional in the cut of the dresses my sister, Lady Felicity, has been wont to wear since her come-out last year."

"All the same, it is not what I am used to," Devorah said stiffly.

"As I said, your dress is charming," the Duke assured her. "There are those great ladies, you must know, who, even though they are among the leaders of fashion, would do well to emulate your style. Sometimes women look the better for a little cover-up." He shuddered, as if recalling a particularly hideous display of flesh.

"Lady Felicity is here at Ravenscourt?"

"No, my sister is already resident in London. She has been staying with my Aunt Elisabeth until my mother is able to join her there. The season has already begun, though on a small scale. As my mother has, to some extent, an aversion to town life and its social exigencies, and I am unavoidably detained here at Ravenscourt due to pressing estate business, we felt it most beneficial to all if Lady Felicity were kept suitably occupied by the London social whirl. My aunt was most happy to take her in hand.

"My mother, meantime, is saved from loneliness by the visit of Lady Albinia, who is her goddaughter. I expect that our cozy little house party will break up, though, when my estate business is completed and I post off to London. Mother and Lady Albinia will no longer have any reason for staying here," the Duke concluded cryptically.

"I hope," he added as an afterthought, "that we will have your situation suitably taken care of by then."

The clock on the mantelpiece struck half past the hour. The Duke picked up the small periodical he had been seeking from one of the side tables, made his excuses, and exited the library. Devorah turned her attention back to *Evelina*, but her reading was again curtailed by Lady Albinia's dramatic entrance to the library.

"Oh, it's *you*," the latter uttered in accents of contempt, freezing in her tracks and drawing her hand to her chest. Scanning the room and perceiving that the object of her prey wasn't in residence, Albinia walked past Devorah as if she didn't exist and settled herself in an embroidered armchair by the fire.

Devorah turned back to *Evelina*; Albinia, undecided whether to continue ignoring Devorah or to make her own presence more pronounced, squirmed and sighed and pulled her Norwich silk shawl more tightly about her dotted muslin evening dress. The library was a traditionally cold room, and Lady Albinia began to regret her decision to dress early for dinner and camp out in the Duke's favorite haunt in the hope of luring him into a tête-à-tête.

But, when Albinia glanced up a third time to see whether she had yet succeeded in making Devorah uncomfortable by her presence, she espied the cover of the novel the strange new guest was reading. "Well," she huffed, rising livid with anger from her chair. "That is *my* book." She started toward Devorah, hand outstretched.

"I'm sorry. I didn't know," Devorah said, snapping closed the marbled cover and handing over the slim volume.

The Lady Albinia huffed again, her half-clad sunken chest rising preternaturally out of the soft folds of Norwich silk, leaving Devorah to wonder whether it was just such an expanse of flesh the Duke had envisioned when he shuddered and expressed his appreciation for less-revealing evening wear. But Devorah's musings were interrupted by the Duchess's grand entrance. Her grace, too, paused for a moment in the doorway, looking down her regal nose at the general contents of the room before pushing up her purple turban and sweeping past Devorah in the direction of the fireplace.

"My dear," the Duchess murmured, extending a bejeweled hand toward Albinia, who dutifully rose and curtsied.

Devorah, watching the spectacle out of the corner of her eye, was struck suddenly by the agony of realization that, if she were to make an extended stay in Regency England, she would have to learn how to dip in the presence of nobility without making a fool of herself. But meanwhile she was stuck in the library, bookless and blatantly ignored by its other two occupants. Noting from the clock on the mantelpiece that it still wanted a quarter of an hour until the family gathered for dinner, she gathered her courage and prepared to leave the room. Perhaps she could return briefly to her own room, or perhaps she could while away the time in the portrait gallery. Every great house in England had a portrait gallery, didn't it? Ravenscourt shouldn't be any exception. She walked stealthily toward the door and reached for the handle—just as it opened unexpectedly, knocking her back against the wall.

"Evening, Mother, Lady Albinia," Robert said from the other side of the carved oak door. "Seen Adam anywhere?"

Devorah, peering around the side of the door, saw the Duchess turn majestically in her seat. "He should have been here; it is his custom to dress early and enjoy a moment of solitude among his books before joining the family for dinner. Certainly, One could always rely on finding him here," her grace answered peevishly.

"Perhaps, finding his library already inhabited, he chose to enjoy his solitude elsewhere," Albinia suggested in an oblique reference to Devorah.

"Hey, don't complain to me if you ladies scared him off," Robert said defensively. "If I were to come in and find the two of you prosing head-to-head in front of the fire, I'd jump ship, too."

Albinia rose, dramatically wrapping the shawl around her heaving chest. Raising one thin white hand from among its fringes, she pointed her index finger in the direction of the chair that Devorah had occupied just minutes before. "Neither I nor the Duchess was first in this room. It was *she*." The finger wavered in mid-air. "But, where *is* she? She was here only a moment ago."

She turned to the Duchess. "I said before, and I will say it again, there is something Not Quite Right about her. One does not just suddenly appear by the side of the road in the English countryside—on the barren *ground*, no less—and one does not just suddenly vanish from a Duke's library into thin air."

"Lady Albinia, have you been drinking?" Robert asked with some astonishment.

"Robert, I will thank you to mind your tongue when speaking to a lady," his mother admonished. "I am mortified. Certainly, I have raised you better than that." She turned to Albinia. "Most disconcerting, however. Where *is* she?"

"Well, if you haven't set eyes on Adam, I'll be pushing off now," Robert said, bowing himself out of the room. He shut the door behind him, exposing Devorah to two horrified pairs of eyes.

Perceiving that, most fortunately, both her grace and the Lady Albinia were stunned into silence, Devorah executed what she hoped was a creditable curtsy and followed Robert from the room. Explanations might be required, but she certainly wasn't going to offer any without the supporting presence of Robert or the Duke. Lifting her skirts, she walked quickly in what she hoped was the direction of the Great Hall.

"There's no need to rush," a voice said from behind her. "In spite of all this business about dinner being served promptly at six, nobody but nobody gathers in the drawing room until six on the gong, and then they all drivel on until Her Majesty leads them into dinner twenty minutes later."

Devorah turned to face Theo, freshly scrubbed and dressed in clean clothing. "Are you eating dinner with us?"

"Dining. Are you dining with us?" Theo corrected her. "Take care what you are about. Her Majesty will correct you, seeing as you don't properly speak the King's English." He sighed with palpable relief. "No, thankfully, I am spared that ordeal. To have to sit with my back straight as a stick for hours at end and listen to my aunt and Duckwaithe and Binny babble on and on, when I could be entertaining myself better on my own, would be more than I could bear. It's enough that I have to be polite to them during daylight."

Devorah soon found herself sympathizing with Theo and wishing that she could join him wherever he took his meals, as dinner, by custom, was a rigidly formal and ponderous affair. It was served in the Grand Dining Room (she was learning quickly that nearly every important room in the Ravenscroft ducal seat was labeled Great or Grand), a cavernous apartment with elaborately carved paneling and a molded and gilded ceiling, which reminded her of an over-decorated commercial banquet hall. The room's enormity rendered the formal dining table miniscule by comparison, but so massive was this highly carved article of furniture that fully three additional people could have been seated comfortably between each of the diners in residence. Conversation, by necessity, was conducted in a stage whisper. This presented Devorah with an additional challenge—over and above that of tactfully declining to sample all the dishes served, while at the same time silencing her rumbling stomach—of speaking loudly enough to be heard by her near neighbors without shouting.

"Have some buttered prawns," Robert said, passing the dish in her direction.

"No thank you." She shuddered. "I never eat prawns."

Robert grinned. "Give you indigestion, do they? Did the same thing to my father. Come to think of it, everything gave him indigestion. Dyspeptic, that's what he was. Made him very irritable."

"Your father," the Duchess pronounced, "was a Saint."

Robert turned in his seat to face his mother, holding court at the foot of the table. "Just so, Mother. Just so." He slewed back around to Devorah, lowering his voice so that she was forced to lean forward to catch his words. "Funny how people only become saints after they are dead. To watch the way he and Mother went at it while he was alive, you'd never believe she would say something nice about him now."

"Robert," the Duchess said imperiously. "I have been waiting for the chickens with tongue these past five minutes. Pray serve yourself if you so desire, then see that our guests are amply provided for."

A voice somewhere in the direction of Devorah's other elbow drew her attention. "Finding enough to eat, Miss Asher?" Devorah turned. The Duke smiled at her across the empty expanse of table, but the look behind his eyes was inscrutable.

"I'm fine, thank you."

"The water is to your liking? How about the hothouse grapes? I ordered them at table especially for you."

"Excellent, quite excellent, your grace."

"Yes, everything is excellent, isn't it? Your compliments to Cook."

Devorah, unsure whether the Duke was laughing at her or at his mother, drew herself up to what she hoped was an accurate imitation of the Duchess's most regal posture. "Just so," she said in her best British accent.

"Bravo," the Duke approved. "You'll get along famously here, if we can manage to keep you from dwindling away to nothing. I will ask Spilsby to supplement the next course with fresh apples and pears."

Dinner was gotten through lightly enough after that. The Lady Albinia might glare at her from across the table, the Duchess might bestow upon her a perpetual look of disapproval, but Devorah was kept entertained by two male members of the company. Robert, finding Devorah a more sympathetic listener than his mother, kept up a steady flow of small talk. The Duke, picking up snatches of their conversation, occasionally interjected a witty remark calculated to bring the blush to Devorah's cheeks or throw her into confusion. But Devorah, well trained by the intrepid Jeremy, her co-worker at Longren & Longren, was able to deftly parry these remarks, bringing an appreciative gleam to his grace's eyes.

But, the moment of the evening that Devorah most dreaded finally arrived. The Duchess led the ladies into the Burgundy Drawing Room while the men nursed their after-dinner port. Settling her purple-clad form into a comfortable wingchair close to the fire, The Duchess patted its twin and invited her dear Albinia to join her for a chat. Quickly surveying the room, Devorah spied the wingchair's orphaned triplet in a far corner and settled in for the duration.

The Burgundy Drawing Room, which drew its title from the heavy, claret-colored curtains at the French windows and the red-and-black Aubusson carpet on the parquet floor, was lit by small clusters of candles in gilded sconces along the walls. Those nearest to Devorah gave off enough light that she was able to examine a book of drawings she found on a side table, but she was able to do little more than discern the silhouettes of her grace and the Lady Albinia, backlit as they were by the fire. Still, she knew they were discussing her. They might be too well bred to ever inquire as to why Devorah had hidden behind the library door, but that would not stop them from chewing over such particularly strange and interesting behavior and discussing it from every angle.

Devorah glanced up from the picture book from time to time to find hostess and goddaughter looking in her direction. The third time, she met gaze with gaze, directing wide, innocent eyes at the Duchess's angry ones. Their eyes locked for several seconds before her grace heaved her chest in indignation and turned back to her companion.

The men joined them soon afterwards. Mr. Duckwaithe, observing the expanse of room separating Ravenscourt's newest inmate from its veterans, exclaimed in dismay. "But what is this, that Miss Asher has chosen to sit over in the cold? We cannot have the guests freezing, can we?" The Duchess merely stared.

The Duke shot another of his inscrutable looks at Devorah. "Yes, Miss Asher, pray do come sit by the fire. Evening fashions are so—shall we say—bare, that you are in danger of contracting gooseflesh."

Devorah bit her quivering lip and trod silently across the carpet to the sofa the Duke had indicated. He patted the cushion next to his and invited her to take a seat. Only after she was perched gingerly on the edge of the sofa did she dare look up at him. His face was expressionless, but something about his rigidly controlled features made her giggle. She coughed and covered her mouth, but her indiscretion did not escape the Duke's notice.

"Just so," he said mildly. "Your percipience is exceptional."

"Percipience? Who is percipient?" her grace asked sharply.

"Did I say that?" Adam asked languidly. "I must have been rambling." Devorah's shoulders began to shake. "Cough again, and this time cover your mouth with the handkerchief from your reticule," the Duke suggested in a low voice. "Otherwise you'll have the Duchess and Lady Albinia demanding to know Just What Is the Meaning of All This?"

"I say," drawled the Lady Albinia, "perhaps, since we are so fortunate to have a new voice among us, Miss Asher will be so kind as to delight us with a song."

"Yes, yes, sing for your supper, so to say," Mr. Duckwaithe quipped.

"But I never sing," Devorah protested.

"Never?" asked the Duchess. "How queer."

"Never."

"Then, perhaps you will play for us," Albinia suggested slyly. "Ravenscourt, as you will discover, is endowed with the finest harp and pianoforte to be had. Which do you play, Miss Asher? You do play, do you not?"

Devorah had taken piano lessons from the time she was a child, and she owned a sleek, black baby grand at which she still practiced several evenings a week. While she could never aspire to concert status, mastery of the piano was one of the few accomplishments of any genteel nineteenth-century female to which she could lay claim. However, she looked dubiously at the antiquated, elongated instrument at the other end of the room.

"Yes, I play the piano," she said tentatively. "But as to whether I can play that—I don't know. I'm used to the American piano."

"That," Duchess interrupted imperiously, "is a Broadwood."

"The finest pianoforte we Englishmen have to offer," Robert added helpfully, quick to note her puzzled expression.

"I believe our English pianoforte is Ludwig von Beethoven's instrument of choice," Albinia said.

"Our English products are *always* the finest," the Duchess said, brooking no argument.

"Whatever," Robert said. "Go play. Otherwise Mother will be organizing a game of whist at a penny a point."

"If you don't feel up to it, Miss Asher, you can play for us another day," the Duke interjected in a bored tone. "Considering you sustained quite a bump on the head this morning, I think I can safely say that all of us will understand should you defer your performance for when you are feeling more the thing."

But a perverse wish to demonstrate that she wasn't totally devoid of social graces spurred Devorah forward. "I would delighted to play," she said, and made her way across the carpet to the ornately carved piano. Mentally calculating which of the pieces in her repertoire would best give the Lady Albinia a much-needed set-down, she seated herself carefully and tested the instrument's tone. Beethoven was a contemporary of theirs, was he? She would play the first movement of his *Moonlight Sonata*.

At first, Devorah's fingers were stiff. But she warmed quickly to the music, letting it surround and encompass her. For an all-too-brief interlude, she immersed herself in the sound, forgetting her surroundings and her predicament; England and Ravenscourt were two hundred years and a million miles away. The assembled company, too, forgot the murky background of the figure at the piano and maintained a respectful, almost reverential silence.

As the last chord died away, Lady Albinia was first to break the silence. "Ah, Beethoven's *Sonata quasi una fantasia* in C-sharp minor. One of his more elementary pieces, I believe."

"Elementary? You call that elementary, having to memorize all those notes?" Robert asked.

"I am mesmerized, Miss Asher, simply mesmerized," Mr. Duckwaithe trilled. "Biblical—and accomplished!"

"A little too flamboyant for my taste," commented the Duchess. "Albinia, dear, perhaps you will sing us one of the arias you were practicing so nicely last week."

Robert shuddered. "If it's Gluck, I'm leaving. Join me for a game of billiards, Adam?"

"Nonsense," the Duchess retorted. "Albinia sings beautifully. You would insult both her and me were you to leave now."

Devorah had remained seated at the piano during this interchange, unsure whether to rejoin the company by the fire or, as she really wanted, to conjure up an excuse for returning to her room. It had been a long day, she was tired, her head hurt, and she had no desire to listen to the odious Lady Albinia's singing. But how did one excuse oneself gracefully from after-dinner entertainment?

"Tired, Miss Asher?" the Duke asked, taking quick note of her drooping eyelids and the way she tried to prop herself upright on the piano seat. "I shouldn't wonder, considering what you have been through today. Mother will excuse you should you desire to wish us goodnight at this early hour. In fact, I will personally escort you to Mrs. Wigmore, who will show you up to your room and make sure that everything has been readied for your comfort."

The Duke offered Devorah his arm. Demurring only slightly, she placed her hand on it, releasing it quickly once they were safely away from the Burgundy Drawing Room. "You owe me no thanks for this evening's rescue," his grace said as she pulled away from him in some confusion. "You have no idea how indebted I am to you for—shall we say— dropping in on us so unexpectedly, as you have. It is fortuitous that I wasn't already situated in London for the season. I wouldn't have missed this for the world."

On which note he directed her toward the Great Hall where, seeing Mrs. Wigmore passing through that very moment, he hailed her and requested that she escort Devorah to her room.

Devorah gratefully accepted the housekeeper's offer of one of Lady Felicity's nightdresses and allowed Betsy to comb out her hair and tuck her into a warm bed. Too tired to even think about the trouble she was in or pay attention to the rumblings of her stomach, she sank immediately into sleep.

But the morning light brought with it the full realization of her terrible predicament, along with the full force of her hunger. Suddenly finding oneself in the wrong century and wrong country was hideous enough, but her first day at Ravenscourt had been filled with further agonies and presaged tough times, indeed, to come. And, she had gone most of a day without anything more sustaining than fruit and water, with no respite in sight. She wondered how long she would be able to survive on such meager fare.

Devorah knew that she would require all the heavenly assistance she could garner if she were to extricate herself out of the insupportable situation she was in. Thus her prayers that morning, despite a persistent knocking on her locked bedroom door, were unusually prolonged and intense.

The knocking finally ceased, and when Betsy returned some ten minutes later she found the door unlocked and Devorah seated in the armchair by the window, staring out at a rose-planted courtyard, one of Lady Felicity's frilled and beribboned dressing gowns knotted tightly around her waist.

"Good morning, Miss," Betsy said, dumping an armful of dresses on the disordered bedcovers and dipping into an awkward curtsy. "Mrs. Wigmore wants to know should I bring you chocolate and toast in bed or was you wishing to dress now and join the men in the breakfast parlor? Her grace and Lady Albinia do not usually come down until later."

"Just some fruit and water here in the room," Devorah said. She glanced at the pile of clothes on the bed. "What have you brought me? Half of Lady Felicity's wardrobe?"

"Mrs. Wigmore had your dress and undergarments cleaned and pressed, but she says as the dress, be it ever so beautiful, is not a fit garment for morning, so she begs you will choose from these clothes that Lady Felicity does not wear anymore. She also wants to know if you would be wishing to bathe before you dress. The hip bath is available."

To this Devorah readily assented. After she had consumed a breakfast of fruit and water, her flagging spirits began to revive. By the time she had immersed in a bath filled with luxuriously hot water and was scrubbed and rubbed dry with a fluffy white towel, she began to feel quite human. Once she was outfitted in a high-necked dress of jaconet muslin with lace insets in the body and sleeves, and a short pelisse of deep lilac, trimmed with Spanish buttons and a quantity of fur, her natural confidence and optimism had returned.

She felt prepared to confront whatever lay ahead.

Chapter 10

The Green Room, which served as an informal sitting room for those members of Ravenscourt who had no other plans for the morning, or for any other time of day, was a medium-sized apartment decorated in varying ugly shades of green that forcibly reminded Devorah of a hospital. Although she had expended a good deal of time bathing and preparing her morning toilette, and had afterwards taken a detour to the library to find something to read, the Green Room was still empty when Spilsby ushered her through its double-doors that late morning. The venerable butler mumbled something about her grace and Lady Albinia not being early risers, adjured her to choose any seat except the wingchair by the fire (which belonged to her grace), and shut the door firmly behind her.

Devorah located a massive, velvet-covered chair by the well-lit window and curled up with *Castle Rackrent*. If nothing else during her strange stay in Regency England, she told herself, she would round out her education in popular literature of the day. She had read nearly half of Maria Edgeworth's slim classic when the Duchess's chaplain strolled into the room. After dispensing with the usual pleasantries and expressing proper surprise that neither the Duchess nor Lady Albinia had yet favored the room with her presence, Mr. Duckwaithe placed a high-backed chair next to Devorah and bent over to see what she was reading.

"Ah, one of Miss Edgeworth's interesting novels," he said with a sigh. "Have you read *The Absentee*? I was most taken by it."

Devorah looked up, somewhat in surprise. "You read novels?"

"The clergy must be awake on all suits, Miss Asher, eh? How can one inveigh against the evils of the marbled press if one is not familiar with the lures set out for unsuspecting and misguided readers by those writers who grace our lending libraries today?"

"Good point," she admitted, turning her head slightly to avoid the onslaught of the chaplain's rancid breath.

"Tell me more about your father," Mr. Duckwaithe persisted, leaning closer. "One meets so few true biblical scholars these days. Is he fluent in ancient Hebrew?"

"Very."

"Ah, so he has studied the Scriptures in their original?"

"All of them."

Mr. Duckwaithe leaned even closer, his breath quickening. "And Josephus? He has read his *Antiquities*?"

"Of course." Devorah turned back to her book.

"Marvelous." The chaplain hiccupped and clapped his hands together, causing Devorah to look up nervously. "One meets so few true Hebraic scholars these days. The daughter of one—she must be a pearl beyond price. What about yourself, Miss Asher? Has your father transmitted his knowledge and love of the Hebrew classics to you?"

"He has done his utmost to instill his love and knowledge in all his offspring. Fortunately, he has succeeded to a great extent." She snapped the book closed and rose from her chair. "You must excuse me, Mr. Duckwaithe. I just remembered something that must be done before luncheon."

Mr. Duckwaithe likewise stood up and bowed deeply. "I must say, Miss Asher, it has been a rare pleasure. I am quite looking forward to resuming our little chat so that I can discover which of the Hebrew classics your father has taught you. And then, perhaps, you and I may enjoy some interesting biblical discussions."

Devorah smiled sickly. "Perhaps—if I am still here. You must excuse me now."

She left the room as quickly as she could without appearing to flee, and shut the door behind her. Leaning against its oaken panels, she attempted to gather her wits and consider her next move. Apparently, life at Ravenscourt was fraught with further unforeseen dangers. As if she didn't have enough to contend with, the mere mention of biblical scholarship was enough to make the Duchess's chaplain breathe heavily in her direction.

Devorah was still contemplating where best to seek refuge when Robert, resplendent in buckskin breeches and high-tops, broke upon her vision. "So there you've got to. I've been looking all over for you." He paused, frowning. "Are you coming or going? If you are about to enter the Green Dungeon—I wouldn't, if I was you. Not but what all the females seem to like to gather there to gab or do a little petit point. But it's boring, dead boring. And, you would have to do the pretty to my mother, though there ain't pleasing her unless you happen to be Albinia, besides which Lucas seems to have a thing about the place and is always parking his carcass by the fire. Try making interesting conversation with him. It's beyond me."

"I was just leaving," Devorah finally managed to interject in a small voice.

"Good thinking. Do you ride? It's as beautiful a day as you'd ever hope to see. My sister, Lady Felicity has the perfect little filly for you, and there is still time for you to throw on a riding costume and have a go with Butterfly before we all congregate for a noon-time snack."

Devorah shook her head, and Robert clucked in dismay. "Well, I guess it can't be helped. But you can come for a drive with me, at any rate. Curricle's free; show you around the estate. On second thought, perhaps it would be better to take a stroll. I can show you the ducal rose garden, so if anybody asks you can tell them you already saw it."

She thought for only a minute. It would be nice to escape the suffocating confines of Ravenscourt, if only for a short while. The fresh air would do her good, and surely a walk on the grounds, in full view of the building, would be unexceptionable. Besides, Lord Robert, in her estimation, was not a threatening character. While he seemed friendly enough, he appeared to be a disinterested party, which rendered him, like Theo, one of the more desirable people to associate with in her present situation.

"I'll need shoes," she said, looking down at the thin-soled slippers she was wearing. "And a shawl or something."

"It is warmer out than you think," Robert countered. "And the grass is softer than these floors. What you will be wanting is a sunhat. We can leave by the side entrance, where Felicity hangs the bonnet she keeps handy when she wants to slip away unnoticed. If you are to be with us for any extended length of time, you should be knowing all the best escape routes anyway." On which positive note he led Devorah through a maze of corridors, out into the spring sunshine and, through a series of complicated paths, round to the front of Ravenscourt.

The present house was an imposing gray stone structure built in the early seventeenth century on the ruins of its burnt-out predecessor. Successive generations had changed various aspects of its facade and added to it until it no longer could claim any particular style; however, the fourth duke's contribution had been to plow over the rigidly formal gardens in the French fashion that had been so popular in their time and allow Capability Brown to unleash his full genius on the rather extensive estates. The fruits of Capability's unbridled labors had resulted in a verdant, pastoral setting in which the mansion, situated on a slight rise, overlooked acres of emerald ground sprawling gently downward toward a large, manmade lake, with the gently undulating hills of the Cotswolds beyond. A small temple in the Ionic style jutted out into the water's west edge; to the east, the lake was bordered by a small wood, now thick with the growth of more than four decades, through which the main avenue threaded toward the house.

After the oppressive splendor of the house itself, the open landscape acted upon Devorah like an elixir. She had been barely aware of her surroundings upon being conveyed to Ravenscourt the previous day, noticing only the leafy green trees overhanging the avenue and the cold gray stone of the portico framing Ravenscourt's main entry. But, in less than twenty-four hours, she had become all too aware of the vaulted, frescoed and gold-leafed ceilings of the mansion's interior, and the intricately paneled, painted and tooled-leather walls. The massive, ornately carved fireplaces, the priceless antique furniture, and the plush, oversize carpets were all very well for a brief museum visit, but after a few hours their luxury began to sicken her, affecting her like too many rich Belgium chocolates.

She craved home, not only because it was home, but because her tastes ran more toward the starkness of her underfurnished Boro Park townhouse, with its sleek moldings and dearth of collectibles to dust and vacuum, than to nineteenth-century opulence.

"The lake is too far away to get to this morning. We would have to be turning back before we were even halfway there," Robert informed her, breaking in on her thoughts. "We can make a picnic of it, perhaps tomorrow, and send John Coachman ahead with a basket. You, me, Adam and, of course, Albinia. Lord knows, she's always looking for ways to hobnob with Adam outside the ducal mansion, but won't it spike her guns if Adam was to pay more attention to you than to her!"

It was a rhetorical statement, rather than a question, and Devorah didn't even venture a suitable reply. Instead, she inquired into the purpose for which the temple was built. Robert, who had no turn of mind for historical details, said that somewhere along the line the origins of the temple had become obscured in the annals of family history; she would have to apply to his mother or Albinia for more information.

"Which Albinia, being as she has memorized all the archives at Ravenscourt, might actually be happy to tell you more than you would ever want to know," he said. "Though," he added as an afterthought, "more likely she'll just curl her lip and look at you like you are a worm. Seems that Albinia's aristocratic nose has scented competition."

Again Devorah refrained from comment and, instead, clutching the strings of her sunhat with one lilac-gloved hand, tripped alongside Robert past a never-ending wing of the mansion. As they wended their way down a stone path planted on either side with newly budding daffodils and tulips, Robert pointed out the different French windows to their right: library, Adam's private study, the muniment room, which contained all the family's archives and records. They were headed, he explained, toward the formal rose garden, which could also be reached from some of the drawing rooms located at that end of the main wing.

"I call it the ducal rose garden because it's been here ever since Ravenscourt was rebuilt," he said. "Duchesses past counting have been painted sitting on the stone benches, and it's been mentioned in practically every diary we've found stashed in the muniment room. Mother seems to have taken it on as her personal hobby since my father, the fifth duke, died. To see her out there mornings with her old sunhat on, ordering the gardeners where to snip and where to plant, you would think she has been gardening all her life. But, truth be told, she's done a pretty good job of it. The rose garden has never looked so good since I can remember when, and besides, it keeps her too busy to order the rest of us about."

Robert opened a shiny green gate set in a wall as he uttered this last observation, and ushered Devorah into a large, square court that, at first glance, appeared to be a veritable mass of roses. The walls, built of the same gray stone as the house, were covered over with climbing roses in varying delicate shades of pink. A small pool with a Grecian urn, surrounded by stone benches, crowned the center of the garden. Branching out from it were six stone paths, arched over by slender, rose-covered hoops, dividing the garden into wedge-shaped beds of roses planted in shades of red, pink and white.

"Oh, it's the same garden I can see from my bedroom window!" Devorah exclaimed delightedly.

"All the back guest chambers look onto the rose garden. Can't have them looking onto the outbuildings, can we? Imagine waking up in the morning to a view of the servants doing laundry or some such muck. But the best view, you know, is from the balcony leading off from the Italian windows on the first floor." Robert pointed to a balcony tucked into an alcove lined with floor-to-ceiling leaded windows, located just over the garden. "The guest rooms overlook the rose garden from an angle, so you miss some of the best details that you can only see from the balcony.

"Let's sit over there," he suggested, steering Devorah onto the nearest path. "It's this guest business I'd like to talk to you about." Pulling a handkerchief from his coat pocket, he dusted off a bench and gestured for her to be seated. Seating himself next to her, he checked the dirt factor on the handkerchief, refolded it with the clean side facing out, and restored it to his pocket.

"Perhaps you have noticed by now that I'm not quite in the petticoat line," Robert said, looking at Devorah intently. "At least, you should have noticed," he hastened to add when she failed to reply. "I haven't been making up to you, even though there's nothing stopping me from doing so. Adam has flirted with you a little; Lucas has been making up to you in a big way. I'm a bit ahead of him in rank—after all, a duke's brother is better than the second son of the second son of a viscount—so if you really are what you say you are, there's no reason why I shouldn't be in the running. But I ain't. Not that I don't think you're very pretty and all, and that you'd be a lot more fun to be married to than someone like Albinia, but I'm not itching to get riveted just yet. I'll leave that to Adam and Felicity."

"Why are you telling me this?" Devorah asked warily.

"Thought you ought to know how the land lies. Have a lot of questions to ask you, and I wanted you to know that my intentions are purely altruistic. Hope you'll answer me."

"Your brother has already asked me any number of questions, all of which I have answered to the best of my ability." Devorah reached over and snapped off a bent cluster of roses hanging awkwardly into the path. "What an amazing garden," she commented, stroking the rich red velvet of a half-open bud. "How many varieties of roses do you have planted here?"

"I don't know. Maybe twenty or so, but you can ask Mother or Adam," Robert answered, refusing to be diverted. "It's Adam I wanted to talk to you about. He seems quite taken with you. Are you really descended from royalty?"

"I am, though the line is stretched quite thin by the time you get to my generation," Devorah admitted, a little amused.

"I don't suppose you'd care to tell me who the royalty is, would you?" Robert persisted. "No, I thought not, because Adam wasn't exactly forthcoming about it himself." He frowned as a terrible thought came upon him. "You wouldn't be descended on the wrong side of the blanket, would you? No, no, don't look at me like that—*I* have nothing against unnatural relations."

He stopped, floundering for a tactful way to extract himself from a potential social solecism. "Damn, Miss Asher, what I mean is, the Melvilles are littered with our predecessors' byblows and we think nothing of it—though I don't want you to interpret that to mean that Adam has any. I don't *think* he has. He would have acknowledged them and provided for them properly if he had. Very straight and honorable Adam is, though he don't live the life of a monk, you should know."

Realizing that he was digging himself in deeper with every word, Robert clamped his mouth abruptly shut. Heaving a sigh that Devorah accurately interpreted as one of resignation, he withdrew the soiled handkerchief from his pocket and wiped his sweaty brow. "Sorry," he said contritely. "I didn't mean to offend you."

But Devorah was not offended. Although she could cheerfully wring the Duke's neck for publicly setting it about that she was of royal lineage, she had only herself to blame. She had offered him that tantalizing morsel of information to convince him to welcome her to Ravenscourt as a guest. He had accepted her claim without a blink, but he obviously had his own agenda for doing so. In the less than twenty-four hours she had spent at Ravenscourt, it had taken her not even half that time to get the measure of its occupants. Devorah had no doubt that the Duke's hospitality was motivated not by concern for her plight, nor by respect for her lineage— which he probably doubted anyway—but by some nefarious plot for affording himself amusement at everyone else's expense.

Well, the Duke wasn't the only one who could amuse himself. And just now Devorah's ready sense of humor was tickled by Robert's attempts to extricate himself from the extremely delicate subject upon which he had embarked.

Stifling the laughter that threatened to overcome her, Devorah got up and dusted off the back of her skirt. "No offence taken," she said in a choked voice. "Shall we take a turn around the rose garden before returning to the house? That way I can truly say I saw it."

"You are quite as bad as Adam about turning off questions," Robert said baldly as they circled around the pool. "I haven't had a straight answer yet—except that you have a sprinkling of royal blood in you. I wonder whether it is enough to make you acceptable to Mother. She can trace her family tree back before the Conquest to Saxon, Norman *and* Gaelic nobility, but even she ain't related to a king. That's one up on her, so how could she object? But I doubt that she'd ever approve of anyone besides Albinia. Unless—you wouldn't happen to be an heiress, by any chance?"

"Are you suggesting that his grace and I make a match of it?" Devorah asked in amazement, turning toward the gate.

Robert shrugged. "I'm suggesting that you consider the possibility." He reached out to open the gate, but paused, suddenly serious. "Like I said, Adam seems taken with you, and the likelihood of his meeting any other acceptable women while holed up here in the country isn't very great. He's had his pick of all the debutantes on the market, as well as all the repeats, and nothing seems to have moved him yet in the direction of matrimony. If he stays here at Ravenscourt much longer, there's a good chance that between them, Albinia and my mother will wear him down. Or, Albinia will concoct some plot to trick him into marriage. He's almost doomed; he's nearly resigned to tying the knot with her, because he has yet to meet someone whom he actually can fancy, and I *know* he'll marry her if only to shut Mother up."

Robert broke off and reached for the handkerchief again. "You see, Miss Asher, my brother's case is quite desperate, and I'm hoping you'll help rescue him from the Duchess Presumptive."

"Your brother appears quite able to fend for himself."

"I'm not saying he's defenseless," Robert persisted, "but it would be a lot easier for him to shake off Albinia if there was someone around for him to shake her off for."

Perceiving that it was not in her best interest to disclaim any interest in the Duke, Devorah bit back the retort forming on her lips: that she had no desire to marry Robert's brother and rescue the family from Lady Albinia. Although she could hardly believe the turn of events that had catapulted her into Regency England, Devorah was a realist at heart. She had no way of knowing how long she would be forced to remain at Ravenscourt and to what subterfuge she would be forced to resort to stay in the Duke's good graces. Without those good graces, she knew, she would be consigned to the servants' quarters—or worse. So she merely smiled a smile as enigmatic as that of the Duke and said that what would be would be and that only time would tell.

With these platitudes Robert had to be content. Devoting himself to trivial conversation as he led Devorah back along the winding paths flanking Ravenscourt, he was describing the glorious rhododendrons that would bloom on either side of the main road the following month when the sound of a carriage on gravel made itself heard. Rounding the side of the building, Devorah saw a coach-and-four stop on the gravel drive out front. Robert, frowning in an effort to remember whether any guests were expected to arrive by post-chaise that particular morning, suddenly spied a dusky-haired figure in an outrageously beribboned and flowered bonnet peeping from the carriage's window.

"What the—" he exclaimed, running toward the coach. "Felicity?"

Chapter 11

"*I* had to flee," the Lady Felicity announced to her brother in dramatic accents as he nudged aside a footman and assisted her down the steps of the chaise. "Scarlet fever. *All* of them."

"All of whom?" Robert asked, swinging her onto the ground.

"All of my Aunt Bellingham's household. Or, at least half the servants quarters, and Cousin Emily was threatening to throw out a rash," Felicity amended, enveloping him in a painful hug. "So, I asked Uncle to send me back to Ravenscourt. Dear Helen Wickham and I put up at Ashbury for the night, and here I am."

"I don't believe you," Robert said, squeezing her in return. "But I'm glad you are here, very glad. Won't it put another spoke in Albinia's wheel when she sees you!"

"She's still here?" Felicity asked in a carefully casual tone. "I *thought* as much."

Having released her brother, she turned her attention to Devorah, who had progressed up the walk at a more seemly pace and now stood shyly to one side. Robert's raven-haired companion was unfamiliar, but Felicity quickly recognized the jaconet muslin and the lilac pelisse she was wearing, as well as her favorite, battered sunhat. The older girl—if she was still a girl—was certainly a beauty, in an exotic, subtly foreign way. Here, then, was an interesting development: Robert and a strange and lovely woman—dressed in Felicity's own clothing. Could it be that her errant sibling had fallen in love at last?

Robert, suddenly recalled to his sense of duty, motioned Devorah forward and made the appropriate introductions. "Miss Asher is our unexpected, and *most* welcome houseguest," he explained to Felicity. "She will be staying with us indefinitely, much to Adam's and my delight."

Despite the words, there was nothing of the lover in Robert's manner. In fact, Felicity thought she detected a note of glee. Clearly, a mystery was afoot. Perhaps Miss Asher was Adam's new love, instead? But why, then, would Lady Albinia continue to cool her heels at Ravenscourt while the London season was getting under way?

Devorah, murmuring a suitable reply to Robert's introduction, was able to examine the Lady Felicity at her leisure. This damsel, who looked to be nineteen or twenty, was a damask-cheeked beauty with dark curls and mischievous green eyes peeping from under a poke-front bonnet decorated with a large quantity of green grosgrain ribbons, knotted and topped off with a generous bouquet of flowers. Like Devorah, she was of medium height, small-boned and slender, though her figure was more rounded, signaling a tendency toward fat in her later years.

Green eyes met blue-gray ones as the two females sized each other up. Then Lady Felicity's bow mouth widened into a smile and two dimples deepened in her cheeks. She extended one gloved hand. "I am so very glad to meet you, Miss Asher. I *knew* there must be a reason why I had to hurry home, and now I am sure of it. When I've settled in, you will have to tell me all about yourself and how you come to be at Ravenscourt. I want to know *everything*!"

Robert, looking at his pocket watch, assured Felicity that soon everything would be known, then adjured her to make haste and go wash the dust from her person before she was obliged to sit down with the family in the Small Dining Room. "Because Spilsby will be calling us all to luncheon soon, and you know what Mother is if one of us is late—and there's no use trying to cry off, because she'll take it as a personal affront if you don't put in an appearance at table."

Felicity, recognizing the truth of this statement, excused herself and tripped up the broad stairs to the house, but not before telling Devorah meaningfully that she looked forward to spending a quiet afternoon in conversation with her.

"And you should go ready yourself, too," Robert admonished Devorah with some irritation. "You've got a smut on your cheek and your hair needs fixing."

It behooved him, he realized, to clear all females from his landscape, because immediate, unimpeded thought was required. If one were to ask Robert, he wouldn't be able to say exactly why, but Lady's Felicity's sudden arrival at Ravenscourt rendered him vaguely uneasy. Something in her story about scarlet fever rang false; obviously she had another reason for posting off to Gloucestershire. Perhaps she had come to rescue Adam from Albinia's grasp.

But Robert doubted that Felicity could rescue Adam from anything. On the contrary, his younger sister had a tendency to wreak havoc wherever she meddled. Left untrammeled, she had a remarkable ability to plunge everyone in her path into a bigger mess than ever. Clearly, offensive action would be required to rein her in before she managed to cause any damage.

Still pondering the problem of how to deal with Felicity, Robert was largely silent during the midday repast. He not only ignored Felicity's vivid account of the scarlet fever so rampant at Bellingham House, but neglected to pay proper attention to Devorah, seated again to his right, and failed to notice the absence of Theo until Mr. Duckwaithe inquired where the dear boy was.

"Theo has been invited to lunch today with my tenant, Jonathan Whyteman," the Duke answered casually, selecting a pear to offer to Devorah. "Mr. Whyteman noticed that Theo has been at loose ends since the tutor that Sir Martin engaged before returning to Vienna—ah—remembered quite suddenly last week that he had pressing family business awaiting him back in Lincolnshire. Mr. Whyteman, fortunately, seems to have a knack for managing young Theo."

Felicity, seated between the Duchess and Mr. Duckwaithe, had fallen silent when her dramatic tale of London illnesses had failed to elicit much interest. But she pricked up her ears at this morsel of information. "Mr. Whyteman is still situated in the neighborhood?"

"He intends to be here for some time," the Duke informed her. "The lease he took on Ten Oaks Manor was quite long term."

"*Such* an unfortunate circumstance," sighed the Duchess. "He seems perfectly genteel, but I am convinced that he is not quite the thing."

"Yes, some mystery appears to be attached to him," Lady Albinia chimed in. "He is related to no one—at least to no one that you or I or any person of quality would know. And just what is he doing here? Why has he selected to lease a house precisely so near to Ravenscourt and yet to keep so insidiously to himself?"

"I, for one, find him to be very gentlemanly, and so quick of understanding. *Quite* unexceptionable," Lady Felicity said in his defense.

The situation grew worse and worse, Robert thought morosely. So his idiotic sister was still sweet on their totally ineligible tenant, was she? He could only hope that she wouldn't do anything rash that would plunge the family into scandal.

His grace, noting Robert's failure to respond provocatively to Felicity's comments in Mr. Whyteman's defense, took his younger brother aside at the first opportunity after the meal and asked what was weighing on his mind. Upon hearing Robert express the certainty that Felicity had returned precipitously to her ancestral home, bent on queering Albinia's plans, Adam asked in some exasperation, "And what does she think she can do to queer them that would be any more effective than anything I can do?"

"That's what has me puzzled," Robert said, rubbing his chin reflectively. "I haven't an idea what she could do, but I know whatever it is, it will be awful."

"Scarlet fever wouldn't be part of the plan, would it?" the Duke asked helpfully.

"Scarlet fever?"

"The sudden flight from Bellingham House, the liberal references to scarlet fever at luncheon. But perhaps you were so deep in thought that you failed to notice."

"So that's it, is it?" Robert grinned up at the Duke. "Felicity's thinking to scare Albinia away from Ravenscourt? It'll never work, not even if Felicity herself throws out an actual rash. Albinia has remarkable staying power. But there's another thing that's got me worried. Adam, you know what our little sister is. Never had an ounce of brains when it comes to the male sex, and it's just too bad that Westbury didn't come up to scratch last season and make her an offer. *He* would have seen to it that she behaved properly and didn't forever keep falling for the most inappropriate men. Stands to reason; she would have been his wife and all."

"I presume you are thinking about our near neighbor and tenant, Mr. Whyteman," Adam said, returning Robert's grin. "Don't worry. Mr. Whyteman is a man of exceptional good sense and will know just how to handle Felicity should she attempt to make a fool of herself."

"He wouldn't by any chance be a man of such exceptional wealth that he is impervious to the lures of an heiress, would he?"

"I doubt his wealth is exceptional, but I doubt equally that he would be susceptible to any lures that Felicity might send out," Adam said gravely. "A match with her is as totally inappropriate to his mind as it is to ours."

Meanwhile, the object of this discussion, displaying the ruthless determination for which she was already famous, followed Devorah from the luncheon table with the intent of pulling her into one of the empty rooms that lined the passage to the Green Room and prizing her story from her. Judging by the way the other females had ignored her at table, Devorah's appearance on the scene had not found favor with either her mother or Albinia. Clearly Devorah was a stranger set adrift in the vast complexities of the Melville clan, and it behooved Felicity to befriend her early on.

But before Felicity could put her noble plan into action, she was waylaid by the Duchess, who commanded her daughter to come to her room immediately for an important discussion. Felicity, guessing correctly that the discussion would center on Ravenscourt's newest guest rather than on her own unexpected appearance, floundered unsuccessfully for an excuse to weasel out of obeying her mother. "Whatever you need to do can wait for later," her grace said dismissively, sweeping her up the stairs.

"I need your assistance," the Duchess said, turning to Felicity once she had securely locked the door behind her.

"Mine?" that damsel asked, surprised.

"Yes, yours," the Duchess said, pacing nervously over to the window and pulling open its heavy velvet draperies. "You have been properly introduced to our newest visitor, I presume. But I need not ask. I saw the two of you enter the court together. I should tell you that neither I nor any other member of this household was previously acquainted with her. Not only was she not invited, but her descent on Ravenscourt was totally unanticipated and unwelcome. She is a foreigner, you know, and I suspect that she is not quite the thing."

"A foreigner? Really?" Felicity's eyes widened. "That explains the accent, though I must say that it is so faint that I wasn't sure whether I was imagining it."

"Yes, well, she is from the former colonies, by her own admission, and she is unable to furnish us with any of the particulars of her background. Adam claims she is descended from ancient royalty, but I myself think that Adam fabricated that particular little tale to advance some private joke of his.

You must know what your brother is; his sense of humor has always appeared to me to be rather perverse. But be that as it may—"

"How came she to be here?" Felicity interrupted.

"That is the strangest part of all," the Duchess said in some exasperation. "She was *found* by the side of the road. Adam and Robert were escorting dearest Albinia and me to the Ardsleighs—Aurelia is enjoying a brief stay at Ardsleigh Manor before hurrying off to London for Cressida's come-out—and she was lying in some ditch or another, with no memory, she claims, of how she came to be there. Most unusual. Women of our class do not suddenly find themselves lying unattended in ditches."

"I should think not," Felicity said, awed. "So Adam rescued her, did he? How romantic!"

"Romantic?" her grace repeated, outraged. "Instead of continuing on to the Ardsleighs, your brother most deplorably told John Coachman to turn the carriage around. I have yet to visit poor Aurelia. And that is not all. I and Albinia are forced to be civil to that person because she is now staying here as a personal guest of Adam's. I need not hesitate to tell you, Felicity, that matters have reached a delicate stage between Adam and Albinia. I have entertained hopes that he will presently honor her with a proposal. But now all my efforts to advance such a desirable match may come to naught.

"Adam is positively *flirting* with Miss Asher—if that, indeed, is her name. Robert says she is amusing, and Lucas Duckwaithe, who I thought was my faithful chaplain these dozen years or so, finds her charming and does absolutely nothing to discourage such social intercourse. I have been grossly deceived by all those upon whom I thought I could depend, and now, Felicity, my whole reliance is on you."

Felicity dutifully told her mother that she would do what she could to help, though she failed to see what that could be. Exercising unusual self-control, she left unsaid what she really thought: that if Adam really loved Albinia (which she doubted) and really wanted to marry Albinia (which nobody besides the Duchess and Albinia herself desired in the least), the sudden appearance on the scene of an unknown foreigner would do little to spike Cupid's plans. Rather, Miss Asher may have been heaven-sent to rescue Adam and his fellow Melvilles from what was rapidly becoming a force majeure.

The Duchess had her own misgivings about Adam's intentions toward Albinia, but these she, too, kept to herself. She had no doubt that the force of her convictions would eventually bring him about, and that her wishes would prevail in the end. "You do not have to do very much," she assured Felicity. "Merely befriend Miss Asher and stick close to her side; ensure that she is never alone, especially with Adam. Encourage her to confide in you. Find out everything you can about her and her family. And, if you discover something to her discredit, convey your findings to me privately. I will do the rest."

As Felicity already had every intention of befriending Devorah and worming her way into that saving angel's confidence, she saw no difficulty in agreeing to these instructions. She need not tell her mother that her intentions were purely altruistic and that she had no intention of discrediting Miss Asher to her mother. Besides, if Miss Asher was truly of royal descent, it was worth determining whether she was a worthy match for her brother. While Adam might not marry Albinia to oblige his mother, he knew his true worth and would never marry beneath him.

But unbeknown to the Duchess, her worst immediate fears were being realized at that very moment. While the Duchess was attempting to engage Felicity's assistance in plotting Devorah's downfall, the Duke shook off an invitation from Mr. Duckwaithe to join him and the Lady Albinia in the Green Room and, pleading pressing estate business, went instead in search of Devorah. He found her in the library, rifling its shelves for something interesting to read now that she had finished *Castle Rackrent*. Startled, Devorah looked up and dropped the volume she was holding.

121

"All very boring. Don't bother," the Duke said, causing her to giggle. "We have three books in this library worth reading, all smuggled in by my sister Felicity. The rest have been censured and pronounced unexceptionable by my mother and the ghosts of dowagers past—which means that you will find them bland and improving beyond repair."

The Duke advanced into the library, saying in a much more serious tone, "I'd like to speak to you privately, if I may."

"Of course. Now?"

The Duke nodded. "I thought we might take a stroll. Robert tells me he showed you the rose garden this morning, so I will point out the more significant features of the west prospect. We will never be out of range of the curious eyes of my family, but we certainly will be out of earshot."

Devorah readily assented, but asked leave to run upstairs to retrieve the sunhat she had left on her bed before luncheon. This was quickly done, and she returned to find his grace chatting with his butler in the Great Hall. Spilsby bestowed a grandfatherly smile on her as she approached, then bowed majestically as he threw open the massive front doors.

"My, you certainly have my butler charmed. That was the smile he usually reserves for members of the family whom he has known since the cradle," the Duke commented as the doors closed behind them and they trod down the steps and across the gravel drive.

"He has been most kind and helpful in directing me about Ravenscourt. I am repeatedly losing my way." A pensive look crossed Devorah's face. "That is something I wanted to talk to you about. I have no idea how long I will be here, and while you also have been most kind and helpful, I hope through some miracle that I will be home soon—or that, perhaps, I am only in an extended dream from which I will soon wake up. However, as long as I am here, I'm afraid I will require some pocket money for my personal needs, and shouldn't I be bestowing vails on the servants when I leave?"

The Duke was silent for a few minutes as he led Devorah across the drive to a narrow dirt road that cut across the sloping estate grounds to the west. The gentle Cotswold Hills, crisscrossed by gray stone walls, lay beyond, and here and there, clusters of honey-colored buildings nestled among the hills signaled a village in the distance.

"I've given much thought to your predicament," the Duke said finally, his chiseled features appearing even harsher in the afternoon sunlight. "That is actually what I wanted to speak to you about. If I take your explanation of how you came to be here at face value—which is very difficult to do, considering your story, but I must say I have no reason to suspect you of making it up—you might be here for a very long time. You cannot continue to live off fruit and vegetables, and certainly some provision must be made for your long-term maintenance. I wish you would confide in me."

Devorah shook her head. "There is nothing to confide. I've told you everything, unbelievable as it may sound, and I have spent hours considering how to solve my dilemma. So far it seems hopeless, but I am one who never gives up hope. However, that doesn't solve the problem at hand, which is something you *can* help me with. There are several personal purchases I must make immediately, let alone any future gratuities for Betsy, Spilsby and Mrs. Wigmore."

"No, it wouldn't do for you to stay here penniless," the Duke said, resigning himself to her evasiveness. "I can, of course, give you any sums you might require, minimal as they would be, but for some reason I don't think you'd care to accept money from me."

"Certainly not," Devorah said indignantly, stopping to remove a stone from the sole of her fawn-colored half boot. "I am already dependent upon your hospitality, and to ask you to pay for my toothbrush and silk stockings—for, whatever else Lady Felicity has loaned me, that is going too far!—would be the height of *chutzpah*."

"Pardon?" the Duke asked, perplexed.

Devorah quickly corrected her slip of the tongue. "Excuse me. *Chutzpah* is a word we use a lot in New York. It means brazenness or effrontery."

"*Kutz-pah?* I like it; it very accurately describes—er, several people of my near acquaintance, some of whom are at this very minute residing at Ravenscourt. What is the origin of this word, might I ask?"

"Oh, Yi—German, I mean. The word comes from a German dialect."

"Interesting," the Duke said. "I speak a little German, and I've never heard this word. But you speak German, do you? Perhaps we can puff you off as a distant relation of all those Hanoverian princes running around."

"I speak only a little German," Devorah admitted, "but because my parents have let a great number of Yi—German expressions seep into their everyday language, I have picked up this deplorable habit of mine."

The Duke turned to her, the cynical amusement on his face giving him a slightly devilish look. "There it is again. Yi-German. Strange, I've never heard of this dialect. Where, exactly, in Germany are your parents from?"

"They are not from Germany," Devorah corrected him. "They just use a lot of these words, because everyone uses them where we live. My father is from Belgium and my mother was actually born here in England, athough her parents took her to America as a very young girl."

"But surely you still have relations here? Why don't you——?"

"I don't appeal to my relations to get me out of this bind, because my relations didn't come to live in this country until around nineteen hundred and ten!" Devorah interrupted with some asperity.

"My, my," the Duke murmured in a placating manner. "You certainly have a way of sticking to your story. One would almost believe you …unless you are totally delusional."

"In which case, like most lunatics, I must be humored," Devorah retorted. "But again, you are veering off the subject."

"Which is?"

"Which is that I am in need of immediate pocket money. Perhaps you would be so good as to sell my diamond earrings for me? Either your butler or your housekeeper has them in safekeeping. I believe the diamonds to be particularly fine, and they should be worth quite a bit, even here."

"As you wish." The Duke sighed in resignation. "You shall instruct Spilsby to hand them over to me when we return to the court, and I will take them to the City at the earliest opportunity. In the meantime, I shall be more than happy to advance you funds enough to purchase a toothbrush and stockings and even to escort you into Tetbury to do your shopping. Now, do you allow me to act the gentleman and link your arm through mine as we continue to stroll down this particularly rocky path? No, I thought not; I am always quick to pick up on my guests' idiosyncrasies, and it has not been lost on me that you have been playing the Brahmin here at Ravenscourt, while we, the natives, are the untouchables."

Devorah laughed outright and looked up to find his grace smiling indulgently down at her. It was a smile that transformed his face, softening its harsh planes and taking at least a decade off its four-and-thirty years. It was a smile calculated to make an ordinary woman's heart flutter. But Devorah was no ordinary woman, and she already had discerned that whatever the Duke felt toward her, it had nothing to do with romance. Rather, the indulgent look was akin to the expression on her parents' faces when she was a small child and had done something precocious. She thought, perhaps, that he was humoring her, and had the horrible, lurking suspicion that he was on to her secret and was secretly mocking her.

To Albinia, who had fled to her bedroom and its conveniently front-facing window the moment the Duke stepped out with Devorah, and who had been spying on the two ever since, that smile signaled otherwise. Adam was actually encouraging the colonial usurper to flirt wantonly with him, and even at such a distance she could see his responsive smile as Miss Asher turned a face toward him that was brimful of laughter. He was charmed, was in danger of being ensnared, and so far lost already as to be in danger of any minute disappearing altogether from view as the ill-suited couple wended their way down the road and into the gently rolling countryside.

Lady Albinia gnashed her teeth in impotent rage as her mind turned over plot after plot for eradicating at the root what was obviously a spring romance sprouting like a noxious weed. However, she was a lady and the product of a long line of earls; therefore, any battle must be conducted in the dignified manner suited to her station. The preferred mode of warfare must be subtle, even underhanded, if she were to wage it undetected. She thought briefly of enlisting the Duchess's aid, knowing that her dear godmama would do anything in her power to further her cause with Adam. But Albinia felt that her godmama had already done enough by inviting her to Ravenscourt and pushing her into Adam's company at every possible opportunity. To ask that venerable lady to do more would admit of a certain failure on Albinia's part to earn the grand prize on her own merit.

As Albinia's brain seethed with various plans, the Duke and Miss Asher turned back toward the house. Adam said something that made Miss Asher laugh; she tossed her head provocatively and ventured an equally successful sally in return. Clearly, Miss Asher must be fought on three fronts: looks, charm, and lineage.

She, Lady Albinia, would take great pains to dress her very finest for dinner that evening. She would wear her most elegant evening outfit, the pale-green crepe with the wide ruche around the collar, which so cleverly added to her bust line while seeming to nip in her waist. Perhaps, just this once, she would allow Martha to apply an ever-so-tiny amount of the rouge she was forever pushing on Albinia, as well. Before becoming lady's maid to the Lady Albinia Brinkburn, Martha had worked for a lively young widow who had lived in the East Indies, and Martha knew all manner of potions and arts with which to bring a sparkle to a dull eye, a subtle blush to a sallow cheek, and a bloom of delicate color to a pale lip.

Then she, the Lady Albinia, would just happen to take a peek into the library when she descended for dinner, and if her quarry were not there, she would track her to the Grand Drawing Room, where she would seat herself most surprisingly next to Miss Asher. Instead of joining the Duchess in an evening of looking daggers and emitting huffs and indignant puffs, she would feign a friendliness she was far from feeling; she would pretend to join Miss Asher's admiration society, and she would even try to draw the hoydenish Lady Felicity—who seemed to be much impressed by Miss Asher—into their cozy little circle.

She would gush and simper and be all that was kind and condescending, and even Adam would be struck by her graciousness, magnanimity and condescension as she made genteel conversation with the unexpected guest.

And all the while, she, Lady Albinia, would be spiking Miss Asher's guns—to borrow one of Lord Robert's vulgar phrases. Those in the upper circles of the glorious British Empire knew that the colonials were all savages. They might cover themselves with a veneer of respectability and civilization, they might even pass themselves off credibly for a brief while as a cultured, mannered people. But, in the end, geography would out in much the same manner as birth and breeding, and it would be borne forcibly in on Adam that however much Miss Asher might hint that she was actually of royal lineage, she was nothing but a vulgar, uncouth savage from the wilds of the Americas.

Four pairs of eyes watched from various windows at Ravenscourt as his grace, innocently bantering with Devorah all the while, led her back into his ancestral home and closer to her anticipated doom. Albinia, tearing her eyes painfully away from the vision of Adam's smile as he ascended the front steps with Miss Asher, turned from the window and tugged angrily at the bell-pull for Martha. Felicity, whose apartments were situated next to Albinia's, happened to glance up at that same moment from the marbled covers of the gothic novel she was reading and look dreamily out the window. The charming scene below caught her eye, and she was able to note with satisfaction that Adam seemed to be quite taken by the exotic visitor from the former colonies. Matters were progressing quite nicely without her help, but were Felicity to align herself with Miss Asher and—under the guise of carrying out her mother's instructions—also manage to allay the Duchess's suspicions about Devorah's base origins, the romance could progress that much more smoothly.

The Lady Felicity, whose stay in London had provided her with just a little too much knowledge for a gently reared lady of only nineteen years, knew that her brother, while in the metropolis, had danced attendance on quite a few beautiful women over the years, eligible or otherwise. But she had never known her brother to be in love. Nor, until she happened to glance out her window at Adam and Devorah walking up the steps, had she ever seen her brother smile at a woman in just that way. Yes, the Melvilles' fortunes were certainly looking up.

The Duchess's reaction, as she and her chaplain peered out the library window, trying to determine whether the east wind blowing up boded rain, was rather akin to Albinia's. While she didn't experience the searing jealousy that gripped the heart in Albinia's sunken chest, she did experience the uncomfortable feeling of being dispossessed. She had long regarded Albinia as her rightful daughter-in-law, and so convinced was she of this rightfulness that it had never occurred to her that Adam might never, ever be brought to see matters in the same way. The thought that she might be losing her control over matters of paramount importance at Ravenscourt flitted briefly across her mind; her rather prominent jaw jutted out more prominently in her displeasure, and the frown lines deepened above her upper lip.

Mr. Duckwaithe, observing the barely suppressed heave of the Duchess's chest and correctly interpreting it to mean that she was keeping her churning emotions to herself, was so moved that he nearly forgot himself and started to place a consoling hand on that great lady's arm. But he quickly remembered his spot in the Ravenscourt pecking order and turned with great dignity back to the window. Then he, too, felt a pain the region of his heart, and he realized with a start that the green monster against which he was forever inveighing in his sermons and homilies had him in its clutches. He was jealous—of the Duke, no less.

When had he, too, fallen victim to the oh-so-biblical Miss Asher's charms?

Chapter 12

Having submitted her person to the enthusiastic talents of Martha, Lady Albinia Brinkburn made her appearance downstairs at Ravenscourt that evening a different woman. Eyes gleaming and cheeks gently blushed, she paused dramatically at the doorway to the Grand Drawing Room and drew in a long breath of anticipation, causing the ruche on her pale-green gown to tremble slightly over her chest in a manner that was not unattractive.

As the hour was yet early and the Grand Drawing Room still thin of company, only Devorah and Mr. Duckwaithe were privileged to witness the remade Lady Albinia's debut. Albinia's efforts were not totally wasted, however. Lucas, who had been attempting to draw Devorah into a discussion on the unusual merits of biblical heroines, happened to glance up at the very moment that Albinia's ruche rose and fell. Something about the Lady Albinia looked subtly different, and while she no longer seemed to present a perfect portrait of the compleat English gentlewoman, the difference was so becoming that he was moved to compliment her on her fine looks that evening.

"It must be the green gown. You must always wear that shade of green, Lady Albinia," Lucas said enthusiastically, executing a bow as Albinia seated herself at Devorah's other elbow. "I was just discussing the early biblical heroines with Miss Asher. Perhaps you would care to contribute your mite? We English, with our long history of Church and Country, are particularly situated to make a significant contribution to the theology of women in religion."

"I always defer to the views of men in such matters," Albinia countered. "I believe, like the Bible, that women should lend their talents to the home and not to philosophical, theological and political matters such as those in which men indulge. Scholarship is the man's domain; the home and family is the woman's."

"Well spoken," applauded the Duchess, who had entered the room unnoticed. "No, no, don't get up for me. You all appear to be going on so comfortably. Albinia, my dear, you look becomingly this evening. That shade of green brings the shine to your eye and color to your cheek."

Adam, who entered the room just then with Robert and Felicity, instantly ascribed Albinia's heightened color to an expertly applied coating of Liquid Bloom of Roses and her sparkling eyes to Arabian kohl, rather than to the color of her gown. But, adroitly grasping the reason for her sudden turnout in cosmetics, he kept his tongue and instead complimented her on the style of her dress. "You should always wear high necks with ruffles," he told her, leaving her torn between gratification that her appearance had wrung praise from him and uncertainty lest the praise contained a hidden barb. Flustered, Albinia turned her attention toward her undeclared rival and attempted to draw her into a discussion about the various members of Britain's noble families now residing in America.

The Duke, seating himself at a distance from this interesting tableau, congratulated himself on his foresight in inviting Miss Asher to stay at Ravenscourt. Her unexpected appearance was affording him even more amusement than he had anticipated. He hoped, however, that he could come up with a plan for safely returning her whence she came or, failing that, permanently situating her in a more appropriate environment, before things actually became embarrassing. Because, if his suspicions were correct, embarrassing they would become as soon as Miss Asher's secret spilled out.

Hoping that he could convince Miss Asher to trust him enough to open up to him, his grace sought several opportunities during the following days to hold private conversation with her. But Devorah eluded his attempts at privacy, preferring to either keep the door to the room partially open or else stroll outside within full view of Ravenscourt's many windows. A heavy spring rain that lasted nearly two days precluded such a stroll, and Albinia suddenly seemed to develop a predilection for all of the Duke's favorite haunts. Adam was forced to give up immediate hopes for confidences and instead contented himself with attempting to flirt outrageously with Devorah, thereby evoking a startling range of emotions in his onlookers.

If it had been any other woman, the Duke would not have gone to such lengths to amuse himself. The rules of society dictated that a gentleman not raise false expectations in respectable women. However, even though Miss Asher appeared to be respectable, Adam did not doubt that she would no more wed him than he would choose to marry her; nor did he doubt that she was amusing herself at his mother's and Albinia's expense. She was no fool, Miss Asher, and she must have realized within minutes of being brought to Ravenscourt that those two worthies considered her on the level of a worm—if not lower. To be able to instill in both their noble chests the fear that she and his grace would make a match of it would be the most exquisite revenge on them that Miss Asher could exact.

But Devorah, ticking off the days of the week and nervously noting that Friday—and the eve of the Jewish Sabbath—was fast approaching, had no thought of revenge in mind. She had, quite rapidly, accurately guessed the game that the Duke was playing for his own amusement. Despite any religious objections she might have, the here and now was Regency England; she reciprocated his grace's casual flirtation only because it seemed to be a relatively harmless way to pass the time while simultaneously ingratiating herself with him in case he should discover her origins. As his grace had so shrewdly perceived, she had no designs on his person other than to use him to shield herself from the unknown masses and, possibly, to help extract her from the mess she had—quite literally—landed in.

Early Friday morning, Devorah awoke with a sense of impending doom. All would soon be discovered, because there was no way she could secretly keep the Jewish Sabbath. There were too many difficulties to overcome; too many explanations would be required. Her confidence returned, however, as she washed and prepared for her morning prayers. She had read dozens of true accounts over the years of those who had observed the Sabbath despite all adversity, even in the face of death. Surely she, who was comfortably situated in a household that tolerated her presence, could devise a plan to keep the Sabbath holy.

As it transpired, her dilemma was to be solved by the Duke himself, who—Devorah was fast learning—possessed an uncanny perspicacity. Overtaking her as she made her way down to the lower quarters to see what she could requisition in the way of the basic Sabbath requirements, his grace favored her with a long, measured look and commanded her to quickly fetch a bonnet and meet him in the Great Hall.

"I've some errands to execute today, and I'd like to take you with me," he explained in a manner that brooked no protest. Some twenty minutes later she was safely seated in the carriage, neatly arranging the sprig-muslin skirts of her morning dress about her.

"Normally, I would perform such duties as I have today on horseback," the Duke said conversationally as his groom jumped up behind and he spurred his horses forward. "Indeed, it's a pity, because it is such a fine day, though the ground is still a great deal damp from these rains we've been having. But something you let slip to Robert tells me that you don't ride. Or do you, Miss Asher?"

He cast a glance at Devorah, who was watching the scenery with interest as he navigated the long lane that cut through the woods to the entrance to the estate. The Duke, attuned to every nuance in others, was quick to note the slight tautness around her jaw line and the rigid set of her body, and correctly set it down to the uncomfortable feeling that she might topple off her perch at any moment.

"For that matter, have you ever ridden in a curricle, Miss Asher?" he asked softly, eliciting a shake of her head. "Do they even have curricles in New York?"

"I doubt it. I've certainly never seen one."

"Oh? Then what do all the sporting bloods drive?" the Duke asked with interest.

"Sporting bloods? Oh, not horses. We only have horses in Central Park, and in the country, for sport. Certainly not for driving us places." Devorah turned to him with a grin. "In America, we drive *horseless* carriages."

"Steam powered, I presume," the Duke countered, returning her grin.

"No, not steam. Gasoline."

"Gas-o-what?"

"Gasoline. From oil. You know, the stuff that comes from the ground."

"No, I don't know. Just how fast do these modern marvels travel?"

"It depends on the make. Some of them can go up to 260, 270 miles an hour. But they usually don't go more than eighty, ninety, one-hundred miles an hour on the highway, although in the city they are forced to travel at considerably less speed."

"Oh?" The Duke cocked an eyebrow. "Next you'll be telling me that in America they also send people to the moon."

"They do," Devorah answered simply, enjoying the Duke's momentary loss for words.

But he made a quick recovery. "Tell me, Miss Asher," he said, "is there an—ahem—Yi-German word for tall tale?"

For one split second, Devorah looked at the Duke with horrified eyes. But he had turned his attention back to the road, watching it with a bland expression, so perhaps she was mistaken and hadn't heard what she thought she had heard. "Certainly," she replied, her voice deceptively calm. "*Bubbe meise*. It actually means an 'Old wives tale,' but I'm certain that it captures the essence of what you meant to say."

"Exactly. Nobody can say that you aren't needle-witted. But I do wish you would overcome your one stupidity and trust me."

Devorah turned wide eyes on him. "Why, whatever do you mean? I do trust you."

"Yes, but not enough."

Having exited Ravenscourt's gates and turned his curricle into the narrow country lane, the Duke contented himself with concentrating on navigating a series of ruts in the road left by the ravages of winter, leaving Devorah silent prey to two very different threads of thought warring within her. On the one hand, perhaps the Duke really had caught on to her secret and was to be trusted. He certainly had given her enough hints to that effect. On the other hand, perhaps she was imagining his amused tolerance of her strange habits and she still had a great deal to fear.

Then a third, horrifying thought presented itself: What if she was going crazy? What if she wasn't really in nineteenth-century England, but was instead in the midst of some endless dream brought on by having read and reread a dozen times every Georgette Heyer Regency novel in existence? If so, why, oh why, didn't she wake up already?

"Are you not even going to ask me where I am taking you?"

Startled by the Duke's voice, Devorah jumped slightly and clutched the side of the curricle. "We are going to visit my tenant, Jonathan Whyteman," his grace continued smoothly. "As you may have noticed, he has wisely absented himself from Ravenscourt these past few days. An estimable man, Mr. Whyteman, but—alas—most unsuitable as a brother-in-law, as you will soon discover, though I must commend my sister on her excellent taste. I hope you learn to value him as I do. I think you will find our visit most illuminating."

Devorah remained silent, and instead attended to maintaining her perch as the Duke turned sharply into a shallow drive framed by tall oaks. A minute later he brought the horses to a halt in front of a mellow, red-brick house of some two stories in height, with tall, wide windows.

"Much more homey than Ravenscourt, isn't it?" the Duke quizzed her, tossing the reins to the groom and assisting Devorah down from the curricle. "We'll be here for some few hours, as I have business to attend to with Mr. Whyteman, but I think you will find Ten Oak's inhabitants much more welcoming than those at Ravenscourt."

Their visit found Mr. Whyteman from home. The young housemaid who answered the door looked dubiously at the Duke, bobbed a small curtsy and bid them make themselves comfortable in the drawing room while she went in search of Mrs. Fenton, the housekeeper. This afforded Devorah an opportunity to survey her surroundings in some detail. These, as the Duke had stated, were much homier than the quarters at Ravenscourt.

The room into which they had been ushered, while spacious, was of a smaller scale than the formal drawing rooms at Ravenscourt, and its furnishings much more modest. Small mahogany occasional tables flanked a scroll-armed satinwood sofa upholstered in faded gold brocade. Several well-worn Hepplewhite chairs were scattered casually around the room, and a mahogany secretaire, set in a corner, held a collection of gilded, leather-bound books. The furnishings, though old, were scrupulously clean and polished; the room had the appearance of being comfortably well used, rather than shabby.

Mrs. Fenton, a plump, comely woman of some thirty years, threw up her hands upon entering the room a few minutes later and offered profuse apologies for not being on hand to properly greet the esteemed visitors. She bid one maidservant to bring light refreshments and another to go instantly in search of Mr. Whyteman, while simultaneously ordering the unexpected guests to seat themselves in the most comfortable chairs the drawing room had to offer.

"One of the stable boys got himself into a spot of trouble with our coachman," she explained, "and Mr. Whyteman went to smooth things over and deal with the boy himself. He is not *bad*, as boys go, just in need of a little loving discipline."

"Like Theo," the Duke said.

"Yes, exactly," she agreed. "Such a nice boy. I wish your grace would let Mr. Whyteman have the tutoring of him while he is staying with you. Mr. Whyteman seems to know just how to handle active young boys like Theo."

"My dear Mrs. Fenton," the Duke said, helping himself to one of the pastries the maid placed next to him on a side table, "that is exactly one of the items of business that has brought me here today."

Mr. Whyteman, entering the room just as Devorah politely declined the pastries, was quick to register the regretful look in her eye, and he drew his own conclusions about her situation. It was an impossible situation, to be sure, but Miss Asher couldn't have "fallen" into friendlier hands. Still, drastic action would probably be required to convince her to reveal her secret. He wondered whether that was why the Duke brought her to Ten Oaks.

After a brief exchange of pleasantries, the Duke shrugged in Devorah's direction to indicate that private business was to be discussed and suggested that Miss Asher would like to see the impressive closed stove recently installed at Ten Oaks Manor. Feeling that she had no choice, Devorah dutifully followed Mrs. Fenton from the room. No sooner had the two women descended the steep stairs leading to the lower kitchen quarters than a maid, hovering over a bowl of bread dough, looked up and exclaimed, "It's ready to shape, Mrs. Fenton—nearly over-risen, the dough is."

Mrs. Fenton gave a soft cry and hurried over to the table upon which the bowl was placed. She gently punched down the dough with both fists, uttered something softly under her breath, and broke off a piece of dough, which she held triumphantly in the air. "Here, Fanny," she said, handing it to the kitchen maid. "Burn this while I start shaping the loaves."

Devorah watched, fascinated, and with growing suspicion. Had she just witnessed Mrs. Fenton separate and burn a small portion of dough to comply with ancient Jewish law? Was it possible that Mrs. Fenton was making challahs, the special braided Jewish bread eaten on the Sabbath?

Her suspicion grew to near-certainty as Mrs. Fenton rolled out six long strips of dough, which she deftly braided into a loaf. Another loaf was braided, and another, and soon six beautifully braided loaves lay side by side on the table—looking exactly like the loaves that Devorah's own mother braided in honor of the Sabbath.

"My grandmother, may she rest in peace, taught me how to braid bread like this," Mrs. Fenton explained casually to Devorah as she braided. "It is a tradition in our family, and seeing as how my own mother was once housekeeper to Mr. Whyteman's family and I am housekeeper to Mr. Whyteman himself, I brought the tradition with me. I think it is good to keep the traditions of the old country, do you not agree?"

"Where, exactly, is the old country?" Devorah asked, in apparent innocence.

But Mrs. Fenton didn't appear to be listening. Casting an experienced eye toward the stove, she noticed a pot whose contents were boiling a little too rapidly. "Fanny, the chicken soup is about to boil over," she admonished the kitchen maid.

Fanny hurried to the stove, grabbed a towel to protect her hands, and lifted the heavy pot away from the fire. "The potatoes look done," she said, checking another pot. "Should I take them off the stove now? And the compote is ready, too. I think the cooking is nearly finished."

Certainly the kitchen was redolent with wonderful aromas—aromas that reminded Devorah with heart-wrenching nostalgia of her mother's kitchen on a late Friday morning. The chicken soup smelled heavenly, and the mouth-watering fragrance of roasted chicken wafted from the stove and mingled with the cinnamon scent of the compote. The nostalgia, combined with her aching hunger, caused a wave of nausea to wash over Devorah. She paled suddenly and reached for the tabletop to steady herself.

"I do not know what I was thinking, not offering you a chair and a glass of water in this hot kitchen," Mrs. Fenton exclaimed, hurriedly drawing forward a chair and forcing Devorah into it. "Fanny, quick, some water."

Devorah drank gratefully, but her head still swam. "Perhaps we should take her upstairs where it is cooler?" Fanny suggested. Devorah, feeling unable to stand, shook her head. Painful as it was to stay in a kitchen that smelled of home, it would be more painful to navigate the stairs in her current state of hunger. But, she knew, she couldn't stay in the kitchen indefinitely.

A young servant girl, hardly more than a child, entered the kitchen and held up two gleaming silver candlesticks for Mrs. Fenton's inspection. "Very good, Goldie," the housekeeper said with a nod. "Mr. Whyteman's silver cup needs polishing, too."

"It is nearly noon," Fanny reminded Mrs. Fenton. "Perhaps we should set the table upstairs soon for Mr. Whyteman's luncheon?"

Mrs. Fenton shook her head. "Into the oven with the rolls, first. We will serve them with the noon meal. His grace and Miss Asher here will stay to dine with us, if you please." She looked Devorah over carefully, as if testing her reaction.

Gathering the last remaining lucid threads of her parched and starved mind, Devorah tried to assimilate what she had just witnessed and follow a vague and elusive reasoning to its logical conclusion. Was Mr. Whyteman's kitchen actually kosher, or was she indulging in wishful thinking? "Me? But I wouldn't dream of imposing," she protested weakly in confusion. "And I'm not hungry at all; just thirsty, in fact."

"Nonsense," the Duke's voice behind her protested sharply. "You will stay, and you will eat. If you don't get a decent meal inside you soon, you will starve."

Devorah started and turned swiftly in her seat. She hadn't heard the Duke or Mr. Whyteman enter the kitchen. The latter stood a little behind his grace, watching her as closely as had Mrs. Fenton just minutes before.

"It is true," Mrs. Fenton said, finally breaking the silence. "The poor dear nearly fainted a few minutes ago, and for all I thought it was the heat, I cannot forget the way she keeps looking over at the stove, like a starving dog waiting for a scrap of meat."

"Mrs. Fenton," her employer broke in impatiently, "we must eat soon. It is well past noon, and we have a great deal yet to do before the onset of the Sabbath." He turned to Devorah. "You will stay for the Holy Sabbath, will you not? The Duke and I have agreed that it is the best thing for you to do, under the circumstances. As you can see, you will not lack for a proper chaperone, and you can eat anything cooked in this house."

"I should think so," Mrs. Fenton commented in an injured voice. "I keep a proper kosher kitchen, I do, and I have yet for anyone to tell me otherwise!"

"We love to have guests," Mr. Whyteman added. "But alas, proper Sabbath guests are so few and far between. Do give us the honor."

"Still in a quandary, Miss Asher?" the Duke asked, intently studying the different expressions that flitted rapidly across her face. "I say it is time for you to 'fess up. You are here, among your own, as was my intent, and it is my wish that you will finally declare yourself to be what we know you are."

Devorah thought for a moment, but knew that she was losing the battle. Three expectant pairs of eyes were upon her: it was indeed the perfect time for her to 'fess up. She swallowed hard and turned to Mr. Whyteman. "Are you sure it will be no trouble?" she asked.

"We would be honored," Mr. Whyteman repeated solemnly.

"Honored? We would be *thrilled!*" Mrs. Fenton interjected. "Why, Mr. Whyteman, many is the time you have sighed over the challah board, saying was it not just a shame that we did not have some new faces at our Sabbath table, that we had no opportunity to bring guests into our home. Why, it would be just like back in London in your dear parents' home."

Extending her hands in a gesture of welcome, she moved toward Devorah. "Not only are you welcome here for the Sabbath, but I am sure that Mr. Whyteman will let you stay for as long as you wish." With that, the housekeeper enveloped Devorah in a hug. Kissing her on each cheek, she whispered softly in Devorah's ear, "He is not married, you know."

Chapter 13

*I*t soon became evident that the Duke and Mr. Whyteman had been busy plotting in the drawing room. Or rather, Devorah suspected, the Duke had plotted and Mr. Whyteman had acquiesced. At any rate, it was his grace who outlined the plan for the next few days of Devorah's life.

"The plan is thus," he explained in a rather high-handed manner. "You, Miss Asher, will be Mr. Whyteman's guest for the Sabbath and remain on until Monday, thereby avoiding the mandatory chapel services at Ravenscourt on Sunday morning. My mother is quite emphatic about chapel participation. I will explain at Ravenscourt that you accompanied me to Ten Oaks Manor, my intention—quite truthfully—being to discuss estate business with my tenant. Upon climbing down from the carriage at Ten Oaks, you fell and bumped your head, thereby suffering another concussion and necessitating your residence here for a few days while you recover your health."

"Oh, *must* I?" Devorah sighed.

"Must you what? Stay here?" the Duke retorted with some asperity. "My girl, you must be out of your mind if you wish to return to Ravenscourt rather than enjoy the Sabbath with your co-religionists."

"The plan sounds delightful," Devorah said. "But must I bump my head again? To lend credence to the tale of successive concussions, I might have to start acting somewhat strange."

"My mother and Lady Albinia already think you somewhat strange," the Duke said. "As for the others—well, Lucas can pine for a few days, and Felicity and Robert will have to batten onto each other for company, should they wish for companionship."

Devorah glanced over at Mr. Whyteman, who was solemnly following the Duke's explanations. She thought she saw the corners of his mouth twitch in amusement, but he regained control over his facial muscles so quickly and resumed such a stolid expression that she might have been mistaken. Certainly, he didn't look very excited at the prospect of hosting her for the next few days. In fact, so different was he from the subtly humorous person who had appeared at Ravenscourt on the day of her arrival that for one brief moment she entertained the idea that he was the identical twin of that other Mr. Whyteman.

Mrs. Fenton bade the assembled company to hurry upstairs for their midday repast. The Duke placed a hand on his host's shoulder and accompanied him toward the stairway, nearly colliding with a small figure rapidly descending to the kitchen quarters two steps at a time.

"Theo?" the Duke asked in some surprise.

"Cousin Ravenscroft!" Theo replied in equal surprise. His muddy feet having by now reached the firm stones of the flagged kitchen flooring, he swept a comprehensive glance around the kitchen. "And you, too, Miss Asher!"

"Is something troubling you?" the Duke asked casually, noting that Theo's shaggy blond hair appeared even shaggier and that his gray eyes were nearly lost in the dirt on his face.

"My business is with Mr. Whyteman," Theo said defiantly.

"Yes?" that worthy inquired, making a valiant effort to stifle an amused grin.

"Sir, I have come to seek asylum!"

Theo waited for a reaction to this dramatic announcement, but to his dismay, it failed to elicit a response. "They have threatened to lock me up!" he

143

continued in great agitation. "I am in danger of all manner of abuse. I must have refuge!"

Signaling the Duke to maintain his silence, Mr. Whyteman turned to Theo. "Easy now. Exactly who is threatening to lock you up—and why?"

"Jim Groom claims that I made Cousin Adam's new filly bolt, but I was just training her not to be so nervous about everything. And Aunt Augusta *would* be frightened when she charged up the stairs and into the Great Hall. It's not *my* fault that the footman forgot to shut the main doors when Binny went out to take a morning stroll—besides which, if my cousin had wanted Binny's company, he would have asked for it. But no-ooo, Binny had to go looking for Cousin Ravenscroft instead."

Incomprehensible as this disjointed explanation was to Devorah, neither the Duke nor Mr. Whyteman appeared to find anything lacking. "What exactly did you do to firm up the filly's nerves?" the latter inquired with admirable self-control.

"What should I have done? Popped an air bladder behind her. If Jim Groom had spoken to her properly, she wouldn't have taken fright the way she did."

"Quite so," Mr. Whyteman agreed wisely. "And now her grace wishes to lock you up as punishment?"

"She, and Jim Groom, and even Mr. Duckwaithe who, if he was ever a boy, I find it hard to believe."

"You have my full sympathy," Mr. Whyteman said, his eyes twinkling appreciatively. "Childhood can be so difficult when one views life through the eyes of an adult, as most adults are wont to do—his grace excepted, of course. But, unfortunately, it will present difficulties for you to stay here today."

"But why?"

"For shame, Theo. You are imposing on Mr. Whyteman."

"No imposition, and under any other circumstances I'd be glad to have him," Mr. Whyteman countered. "But Miss Asher suffered another unfortunate accident today, Theo, and must remain here for a few days in absolute quiet. And I have certain pressing matters of business that I must take care of. Not only do I not have the room for you, but I fear that you would not receive the attention you deserve."

"Sir, you have an empty barn that is begging to be used," Theo persisted. "Let me sleep there tonight. Mrs. Fenton can make me up a picnic dinner and breakfast, and it will be like sleeping in the wild."

"I have a better idea," his grace interjected. "You will return home with me, and *I* will impose the punishment—two days spent in the schoolroom, including all meals. Which," he added slyly, "I know will be more of a reward than a punishment to you. I have discussed your situation with Mr. Whyteman. He has agreed, as of Monday morning, to assume the tutoring of you. Mr. Duckwaithe, worthy as he is, would prove a totally unsuitable successor to the tutor you have recently dispatched."

"Oh, capital! Cousin Ravenscroft, you are a great gun!"

Quick to capitalize on Theo's acquiescence, the Duke propelled his young charge up the steep stairs, a grinning Mr. Whyteman following close behind. Mrs. Fenton turned to Devorah and looked her over carefully. Miss Asher's thoughts seemed a thousand miles away, giving the housekeeper fuel for a great deal of speculation.

"We had best make haste," she said. "It is wanting but five hours until we light the Sabbath candles, and after we finish our luncheon there is your room to be made up, a bath to take, and we must find you some suitable clothing."

Later that evening, Devorah, freshly bathed and dressed in Fanny's second-best holiday gown, a simple, high-necked creation of dark green twill with ruffles at the hem and sleeves, sat in silence at Mr. Whyteman's Sabbath table, savoring the atmosphere as much as the food. Nearly a dozen adults and children of all ages—apparently comprising the entire Ten Oaks household and staff—were gathered around. It was a Sabbath table much like that of Devorah's own family back in Boro Park, other than the antiquity of the tableware and furnishings—and except that instead of her own, familiar, graying father, the much younger Jonathan Whyteman sat at its head.

A many-branched candelabra dominated the center of the table, its soft light glinting off the gold and silver threads stitched into the fringed, blue-velvet cloth that covered the braided Sabbath loaves and lending a mellow glow to the silver cutlery.

The candlelight, coupled with the headiness of the sweet, heavy wine that Devorah had sipped and the unaccustomed richness of the soup and chicken that she had consumed after so many days of semi-starvation, worked on her like a powerful narcotic, turning her limbs to jelly and making her eyelids droop. Mr. Whyteman, casting a sweeping glance around the table, happened to look at her as her head nodded downward to toward her chest. "Tired, Miss Asher?" he had asked from across the table, smiling warmly at her.

Devorah's head had jerked upward in time for her to catch a glimpse of his smile, and she felt an unaccountable flutter in the region of her heart.

Chapter 14

The news that Devorah had met with another accident and was recuperating at Ten Oaks Manor elicited varying reactions among the inhabitants of Ravenscourt. The Duchess was relieved to be rid of her unwelcome guest, however temporarily. Albinia, who openly declared that Devorah's temporary absence brought a much-needed respite from enforced contact with undesirable individuals, was glad to have Miss Asher out of the competition for a spell.

At the same time, Albinia was secretly jealous that Miss Asher had been admitted to the Duke's inner circle. There was no denying that the Duke and the reprehensible Mr. Whyteman were bosom friends. Although Mr. Whyteman seldom visited Ravenscourt, perhaps out of deference to the Duchess's sensibilities, Adam seemed to spend a great deal of unnecessary time at Ten Oaks enjoying Mr. Whyteman's company.

Felicity, for her part, was also jealous of Devorah. For all her machinations, this enterprising damsel had been unable to devise a credible stratagem for spending as much as an hour alone at Ten Oaks, let alone an entire day or two.

Only Robert and Mr. Duckwaithe remained impassive regarding Miss Asher's predicament. Robert received Adam's explanation at face value and reasoned that if his brother were to visit Miss Asher during her stay at Ten Oaks Manor, it would effectively remove him from Binny's orbit for a while. Lucas, though he clucked over the news that Miss Asher had, alas, suffered another major blow to the head,

147

expressed his belief that she would comport herself with the dignity befitting her somewhat hazy station and keep a proper distance from the lower orders inhabiting the Duke's leased property on the edge of the estate.

By Saturday morning, Felicity, fastening upon an excuse for invading Jonathan Whyteman's hearth and home, announced that a visit to the invalid was in order. After a great deal of argument, she was able to persuade Robert to drive her over to Ten Oaks. Lucas, coming through the Great Hall just as Felicity was pulling on her lilac gloves, expressed an interest in joining the siblings.

The trio arrived at Ten Oaks just in time to watch Goldie serve the Sabbath morning *cholent*. Devorah, who joined Mrs. Fenton and Fanny in the kitchen after Sabbath prayers, had enjoyed a full hour of mouth-watering contemplation of this savory treat while waiting for the men. It wouldn't be the Sabbath without the special, slow-cooking stew traditionally served at the day meal, and Devorah had watched eagerly the afternoon before as Mrs. Fenton checked the beans and barley before tossing them into the pot with potatoes and choice cuts of meat. By morning, the aroma emanating from Mrs. Fenton's new closed stove promised a *cholent* worth waiting for.

But even before the *cholent* bowl reached the table, Isaac Fenton, who had risen from the meal to answer an insistent knock on Mr. Whyteman's front door, announced Lord Robert Melville, the Lady Felicity and Mr. Duckwaithe.

Fortunately for Devorah, the remains of the fish course had already been removed and new plates not yet placed on the table. She had the presence of mind to drop the slice of bread she was eating into the folds of her napkin and rise automatically to greet the arrivals. Jonathan, nodding subtly to Devorah to indicate that he would take command of the situation, executed a miniscule bow in the visitors' direction. Ten pairs of eyes, meanwhile, watched in various stages of astonishment and shock as Felicity, followed by her brother and the chaplain, advanced into the room.

Felicity had taken great pains to outfit herself for the visit. Her jonquil muslin morning dress, with its matching treble flounce at the hem, was clearly the creation of a modiste of the first order, and the sprigged lilac pelisse buttoned high to the neck against the wind lacked nothing in expense, despite its simplicity. Matching lilac kid half boots and reticule completed her ensemble. When Felicity took a final look in the mirror before leaving Ravenscourt, she was positive that the charming picture she presented could not fail to please.

But she had reckoned without confronting an entire household, employer and servants alike, seated around the dining table, and a carefully rehearsed speech about her concern for Devorah's welfare withered on her lips.

As Jonathan advanced toward the trio, murmuring the standard civilities, Robert waved off additional ceremonies. "No need to get up," his lordship said. "I told your man that we could as well wait in the drawing room until you finish your meal, but Felicity here would have us brought straight to the dining room."

Felicity glared at Robert, but quickly reassembled her expression along the lines of a smile. "We came to see how Miss Asher does," she explained to Mr. Whyteman. "I am happy to see that she is well enough to join you downstairs for a meal. My dear Miss Asher, please sit down. I have been told that you suffered another knock on the head, and I will *not* have your fainting on my conscience."

Jonathan announced quite wickedly that Miss Asher was coming along famously, and that if only she would agree to eat something besides raw fruits and vegetables she would recover much more quickly.

"But—" Goldie opened her mouth to protest.

"Goldie, I need your help bringing in the salads," Fanny quickly intervened, having been apprised the previous evening of Devorah's precarious situation at Ravenscourt.

At Mrs. Fenton's discreet behest, Isaac brought in additional chairs for the visitors, and soon all three were seated around the Sabbath table discussing their portions of *cholent*.

"It's delicious," Robert exclaimed.

"Yes, a stew quite like nothing I have ever eaten before," agreed Felicity. "If only Cook could be convinced to create a dish like this."

"Forget it," Robert said. "Not fancy and French enough for Mother. White beans, she would say, are *too* common and don't lend themselves to fancy sauces."

"The Duchess is all that is good breeding," Lucas commented. Then, realizing the potential slight he had just delivered to his hosts at Ten Oaks, he hastened to add, "Not but what beans are extremely healthy food in their own way, but they are not fare befitting a duchess of the realm."

The company let this comment pass unchallenged and concentrated instead on the contents of their plates. Devorah, for her part, stared dolefully at the *cholent* Fanny was silently consuming next to her and wondered whether she would have the opportunity to taste some yet that day. Feeling a pair of eyes upon her, she looked up and met Mr. Whyteman's amused glance. She colored slightly, but his eyes twinkled in a sympathetic manner that heartened her. She had brushed through nearly five days at Ravenscourt without mishap, they seemed to say; surely she could survive a short visit from its inhabitants while enjoying temporary sanctuary in an allied camp.

Lady Felicity, not one to waste her time, realized that no further purpose could be served by her invasion of Mr. Whyteman's inner sanctum. Having taken stock of his home and the overly friendly relations on which he stood with his servants, she decided that she had seen enough. As soon as the compote and cakes were served, she stood, brushed off her skirts, and announced that the little party, having intended only to make a short stay at Ten Oaks, should be returning home.

"For no doubt you must be wishing us at Jericho by now," she said, adding that her dear mother and brother

150

must also be wondering to where she and Robert had disappeared. Expressing, in very pretty terms, the wish that Miss Asher would soon be better and back among her dear friends at Ravenscourt, she promised to pay another visit on the morrow, shooting a meaningful glance at Mr. Whyteman in between sentences.

Jonathan was quick to recognize the hint and announced, to Felicity's satisfaction, that he would escort his noble guests to their coach. Smiling in triumph, Felicity tucked her small hand into the crook of his arm and propelled him out on an ingenuous flow of small talk. Throwing opening the door to Ten Oaks and handing her into the coach, he announced that he wouldn't detain her with further idle chat because he was sure that she and her brother wanted to hurry home and report on Miss Asher's condition to the interested parties at Ravenscourt. Lady Felicity's protest, which sounded false even to her ears, was swallowed up by the click of the coach door rapidly closing behind her. Mr. Whyteman turned back toward the house without even exerting himself to wave to her in farewell, leaving the daughter of the great house of Ravenscroft with a vague feeling that her visit hadn't gone exactly as planned.

Back in the dining room, Mrs. Fenton turned to Devorah. "*Cholent*, Miss Asher? I've saved some back for you."

The ducal coach was already clattering down the drive by the time Devorah took her first bite of the stew. As the Ravenscourt contingent sped along, the Duchess's chaplain finally gave vent to all the shocked indignation he was suffering over the strange goings-on at Ten Oaks Manor.

"Understand that I have the utmost admiration and respect for his grace," he stated to his unsympathetic companions. "However, I have been long unable to fathom his unfortunate predilection for Mr. Whyteman's company. Though his manners have always been pleasing—I speak of Mr. Whyteman, of course; not the Duke—I have always sensed something plebian about him. To the discerning person, he smells of the lower orders, and that he had the audacity—not to say, *vulgarity*—to invite his housekeeper and manservant to dine with him, let alone the lower servants—"

He broke off, choking on the idea of master and servant sitting down at table to dine together.

"Hey, don't let your bile overcome you, Duckwaithe," Robert interjected. "Whyteman is a gentleman. My brother would not associate with him otherwise."

Felicity, for her part, would have happily excoriated Devorah and every other member of Mr. Whyteman's household staff on the same account. However, even though her excursion into his inner sanctum had ended on a hollow note, she would not brook any criticism, no matter how justified, of Mr. Whyteman himself.

"If my brother, the Duke, sees nothing amiss in Mr. Whyteman's actions, I fail to discern any reason for your censure," she stated with uncharacteristic dignity. "Certainly, what is acceptable to a Melville should be acceptable to one who is only remotely in line for a viscountcy."

Mr. Duckwaithe merely sniffed in reply. A man with lesser brains would have condoned Mr. Whyteman's social solecisms no more than he, chaplain to the Duchess of Ravenscroft. But he also knew that the Lady Felicity's protestations stemmed from an unfortunate, and not entirely unguarded, secret affection for Mr. Whyteman. Therefore he wisely held his tongue and privately hoped that the Duke knew what he was about. This, the chaplain thought to himself, was not a sure bet. Although he held his grace's intelligence and common sense in high esteem, he had frequently deplored the Duke's unfortunate tendency toward levity and his propensity to hobnob with persons of the lowest orders.

By the time he had reached Ravenscourt, it was all too evident that Mr. Duckwaithe was in dire need of further venting his spleen. This he did freely to Lady Albinia, whom he found seated on the olive-green brocade sofa in the Green Room, setting stitches to a new altar cloth for the Ravenscourt chapel. Here his words found more fertile ground. Albinia, who greatly disliked embroidery work but considered it a necessary adjunct to any well-bred young lady, had spent a desolate morning what with the Duke disappeared on estate business and her godmama abed with an attack of the gout. She was therefore ripe for any censure of Ravenscourt's nearest neighbor. She clucked sympathetically and expressed the hope that Miss Asher would transfer her temporary home to Ten Oaks Manor, where the vulgar atmosphere was much more fitting to persons such as she.

"My dear Lady Albinia, you cannot be serious!" Mr. Duckwaithe gently chided her, much shocked.

"Oh, can I not be?" Albinia retorted, picking up her embroidery frame and setting another stitch in a particularly beautiful shade of crimson. "When all is said and done, we know nothing about her save what she has told us herself and whatever ridiculous tales his grace has chosen to spread among us. For, while the Duke is, for the most part, a virtual paragon, you cannot deny that his aberrant sense of the ridiculous could lead him to so unwisely thrust a lowly individual—or worse—into the thick of Society. She is a *foreigner*, as we have previously noted, and while she herself claims that she is from America, how do we know that she is not from the Continent—not one of *them*?"

"You mean a—a French spy?" the chaplain asked in a whisper. "Can it be? I cannot believe it!" he exclaimed, seating himself next to Albinia and agitatedly taking her hand in his. The gesture was meant in all innocence, but it was not without ramification, as the needle the Lady Albinia was clutching punctured his skin.

"My dear sir," she said, coloring slightly, "you have injured yourself."

"Oh, it is nothing," he answered, pulling his pricked finger from her grasp and wiping it on his handkerchief. He rose and strode over to the white-painted fireplace and leaned against the mantel, his heart, for some unaccountable reason, pounding wildly. "Miss Asher is all that is gentle and cultured," he gently chided Lady Albinia when he was able to still the shaking in his voice. "And, the Duke has confirmed that she is descended from royalty. He would not otherwise shelter her here. I refuse to hear ill about her."

He hurriedly excused himself to prepare the next day's sermon, leaving Albinia to lament that the worthy Lucas, who in his agitation had displayed a heretofore-unrevealed manliness, was also caught in Miss Asher's toils.

The Duke received a different account from Robert and Felicity of the morning spent at Ravenscroft. Still satiated hours later due to the large quantities of *cholent* they had consumed, both his siblings were eager to obtain the recipe for this apparently French dish—called *chaud-lent*, which meant "hot slow" in that language, because it was left to simmer overnight—so that Cook could introduce it into the Melville household.

"It was nothing like," Robert recalled, "and Devorah— Miss Asher—missed it all because she is still subsisting on fruits and vegetables. Imagine, Whyteman invited all the servants to partake of it. He explained that it is a tradition in his family that whenever this particular stew is served, everyone from master to the lowliest servant sits down to dine together."

"I must contrive to visit Ten Oaks in time for dinner to see whether there is any left," Adam commented with a quiver in his voice. "Cook has been put to bed with an onion in her ear for a putrid infection, and I have been given to understand that dinner at Ravenscourt will consist of nothing but cold leftovers."

The *cholent* that so impressed the Ravenscourt visitors triggered an acute desire in Devorah for an afternoon nap. Bowing to a time-honored Sabbath tradition, she headed straight for her room and bed immediately after reciting the grace after meals, leaving Mrs. Fenton to postpone a planned tête-à-tête until later in the afternoon. When she awoke some two hours later, she found Mr. Whyteman and Isaac Fenton in the dining room, bent over a massive Hebrew tome, and

Mrs. Fenton quietly reciting Psalms in the drawing room. Otherwise, the house was silent.

Mrs. Fenton looked up to see Devorah framed in the entrance to the drawing room, an expression of inquiry on her face. Setting aside her Book of Psalms, the housekeeper gestured toward the sofa and invited Devorah to seat herself. "Now we can be private," she said comfortably. "Fanny and Goldie are entertaining the children in the schoolroom, and the men are so deep in their studies that they would not notice were the house to come crashing down about their ears. I do think that it is so much nicer to chat without men and children constantly interrupting. Do you not, as well?"

Devorah nodded in agreement, even though her sixth sense, finely honed from years of attempted matchmaking, told her that Mrs. Fenton's chat would more likely be an intensive interrogation. She arranged her full skirts around her and awaited the inevitable questions.

But Mrs. Fenton, perhaps being of a different era and country, or perhaps because she was merely wise, took a different approach. "I do not know whether his grace has told you much about Mr. Whyteman," she said in an entirely conversational manner. "They are great friends, and the queer thing about it is that for all their backgrounds are so different, they are similar in many ways."

She shook her head in wonderment. "I have the greatest regard for the Duke. For all his elevated position, he is not one to squander his fortune on play, like so many of the nobility, or ignore the plight of his fellow man. He has actually founded two orphanages for London urchins and a school for homeless girls, the likes of which are rarely seen here in England! I am sure that for the sake of peace he has kept the Duchess, herself being so tight and so full of her title, ignorant of the full extent of his societal commitments. But I digress. I meant to speak of Mr. Whyteman, not the Duke, who, for all he is everything of the most admirable, is not meant for one such as you."

"You think I would...that I actually had thought—?" Devorah broke off, flustered.

"There are rumors," Mrs. Fenton said gently, correctly interpreting Devorah's confusion. "It is well known that her grace has planned a match between the Duke and her goddaughter. And while the match is looked upon favorably by the Duchess's closest friends and her chaplain, it has not met with universal approval at Ravenscourt itself. Lady Albinia Brinkburn is not very popular in these parts, and there are those who had hoped, upon your arrival, that you would be more to his grace's taste. By the way, what is this about your being related to ancient royalty?"

Devorah blushed. "Oh, *that.*" She waved her hand airily. "Direct descendent of King David. Well, I had to tell the Duke *something*. He needed an excuse for allowing me to stay at Ravenscourt because, after all, he couldn't just thrust me onto his family without a character reference. Even I know that."

"Then Mr. Whyteman was right," the other woman said with a smile. "He usually is, you know. His grace, for some strange reason, has been totally silent on the subject of who you are and where you come from, for all that he was so certain that you are one of us. When this rumor circulated and Mr. Whyteman questioned him about it, his grace just chuckled and ignored him. Mr. Whyteman guessed that, if the rumor was true, you were speaking of lineage that goes all the way back to King David. He thought it was a great joke on the Duchess, who would *never* have that type of royalty in mind.

"Just as," Mrs. Fenton added, carefully weighing her words, "his grace would *never* consider taking you or me for a bride. He may be one for hobnobbing with Jews such as Mr. Whyteman, but it is one thing to befriend them and quite another to marry them. Quite right, you know. Nor is he the proper husband for you. You should marry only among your own."

"I have no intention of marrying the Duke," Devorah said stiffly. "I am fully aware that he has allowed me to stay at Ravenscourt merely to provide himself with a private sort of amusement while suffering through Lady Albinia's visit. And, for my part, I would certainly rather stay in a household where I can at least drink the tea, not to mention be able to eat a proper meal. His grace and I tolerate each other because it is to both our advantages."

Mrs. Fenton exhaled slowly in relief. She leaned toward Devorah and pressed her hand affectionately. "Mr. Whyteman is a great judge of character and he said he just *knew* by the way you comported yourself that first afternoon at Ravenscourt that you are a proper daughter of Israel!"

Jonathan Whyteman, for his part, felt no need to delve deeply into the interaction between Devorah and her noble host. He was far more interested in those of Miss Asher's personal details that she had declined to give the Duke. It would be no exaggeration to say that Jonathan was extremely interested in Miss Asher, though he was careful not to show it; he wanted to know everything about her up until the time the Duke and Lord Robert had discovered her unconscious by the side of the road. Thus, he felt himself fortunate when he chanced upon her alone in the library later that afternoon, studying the titles in one of the bookshelves.

"Do you read Hebrew, Queen Esther?" he asked conversationally, coming up behind her.

Devorah started and whirled around, eyes flashing. "You knew. You knew all along!" she said accusingly.

"Of course I knew. Only an idiot would have failed to pick up on the signs. The blessings muttered softly under your breath before you ate your fruit; your refusal to eat anything but raw fruits and vegetables. By the way, you really should peel your fruits before eating them, as is done in polite society."

Devorah sighed. "It is truly hopeless. I've tried so hard to pretend, to fit in, but none of the books I've read goes into explicit details about how I am supposed to behave in the nineteenth century. Between bowing and curtsying and *my lords* and *your graces*, and trying to distinguish between the butler and the lady's dresser and the resident nobility, I am thoroughly confused."

Jonathan grinned down at her. She did not appear to be confused in the least, but rather to be making a game of them all.

"Tell me, Miss Asher," he said, seating himself in one of the chairs flanking the fireplace and indicating that Devorah should do the same. "Have you always lived in America? Or, perhaps you spent some time in London before your precipitous fall into Gloucestershire? I have the strangest feeling that I have met you before."

So he also had that strange feeling, Devorah told herself wonderingly. But it wouldn't do to let him know that it was the same with her. "Couldn't be," she answered slowly. "As far as I know, I never laid eyes on you before I met you at the Duke's. How could I? I came straight from America. And besides—"

"Besides what?" Jonathan prodded.

"Besides... Besides, I can't remember everything from before the fall."

"But that was not what you were going to say, was it?" he asked.

"No, it wasn't," she retorted. "But I have it on good authority that you are a gentleman, and a gentleman respects a lady's secrets."

"But I am not really a gentleman," Jonathan said. "I am just a Jew."

Chapter 15

Mr. Whyteman's conversation with Devorah was cut short by the chiming of the clock on the library mantelpiece, reminding him that it was time for afternoon prayers. He found no further opportunity for a tête-à-tête during Devorah's stay, but in the event, the need to speak with her privately proved unnecessary. Instead, Mrs. Fenton and Fanny, both viewing Devorah as a heaven-sent match for their recalcitrant employer, became his willing, if unsolicited, assistants in the campaign to extract all pertinent information from her.

This was easily accomplished. Devorah, having little to occupy her, accompanied one or the other woman during the execution of their duties the following day, and Mrs. Fenton was able to acquire all the essential details regarding Miss Asher's family during a cozy chat in the kitchen.

Devorah, homesick for Boro Park and her parents, was only too glad to help check dried peas while talking about her gentle, scholarly father; her British-born mother; and her four brothers and sisters, and their various offspring. She made no mention of a fiancé, the housekeeper noted with satisfaction. But Mrs. Fenton wisely refrained from asking any pointed questions about why Miss Asher was still single and whether she had any desire for a home and hearth of her own. Instead, she steered the conversation toward recipes for sweet horseradish and sponge cakes in an attempt to determine whether Devorah's education had included any of the housewifely arts.

Fanny, on the other hand, broached the subject of The Ideal Husband when Devorah accompanied her to the deserted schoolroom to prepare it for Theo's lessons with Mr. Whyteman. "I do think that Mr. Whyteman is the most perfect man," she said with a sigh while polishing the brass base of a beautiful antique globe. "He is ever so gentlemanly and scholarly and wonderful with children. If only he was younger and not so much above my touch…."

Devorah, who had been roaming the schoolroom, gleefully discovering long-unused treasures, declined to take the bait. But Fanny, who hadn't expected Miss Asher to confide her own vision of the perfect man, was able to use this comment as a launching point for enumerating Mr. Whyteman's many virtues and to inform Devorah as to what he was doing in the wilds of Gloucestershire. This, Devorah learned, was somewhat convoluted and complicated and owed a great deal to the Duke.

His grace was a close friend of Prince Adolphus, the Duke of Cambridge, who became sympathetic toward England's Jews following a visit to London's Great Synagogue in 1809. Prince Adolphus had been sent to Hanover to represent the Regent more than a year previously, but word reached him of a London educator—a Jew—who had formed the novel goal of founding an orphanage-school for Jewish waifs from London's slums. That educator, naturally, was Jonathan Whyteman, who had decided to shelter and educate "strays" on a grand scale. The Duke of Cambridge applauded the idea and mentioned it in a subsequent letter to his friend, the Duke of Ravenscroft.

The letter reached fertile ground. The Duke of Ravenscroft, a progressive and enlightened man, had long been concerned with the problem of rising crime and poverty in London. He might live in luxury in Grosvenor Square, but he was not blind to what went on in the streets around him, and he had already established his own orphanage for waifs.

The Duke felt, however, that his own efforts were but a small dam against the rising tide of misery and hunger that threatened to engulf England as more and more soldiers trickled home from the Continent. Napoleon's escape from Elba and the subsequent remobilization of Europe's and England's armies to rout the Corsican once and for all were still in the future, but had his grace seen into the future he would have said that the flood had merely been delayed. Thus, when the Royal Duke's letter reached him, his interest was piqued. A Jew, planning to do something for those of his Hebrew brethren who formed part of the multitude of human refuse littering London's streets!

The Duke of Ravenscroft invited Mr. Whyteman to meet with him at his London townhouse. The two men, though moving in different worlds, discovered an instant rapport, and his grace, impressed by both Mr. Whyteman's refined demeanor and quick wit and erudition, thought that he might be able to help the latter find a suitable property for his project. The Whyteman household was soon packing to remove to Gloucestershire, where they had taken up residence in late November in an empty manor on the edge of the Duke's estate.

"And here we stay until Mr. Whyteman and the Duke find just the place for an orphanage," Fanny said. "I do think it is wonderful here. No noise, no smells, though Mrs. Fenton says that there is a great deal more to do in a larger house such as this than in London, and that if only Mr. Whyteman would remarry, it would take a great burden off her overworked shoulders."

"Oh, Mr. Whyteman has been married before?" Devorah asked casually.

"Yes, it is a sad story, his being widowed. More than ten years have passed since his wife died while giving birth to their first. And oh, miss, would it not be something wonderful if you and he was to wed!"

Fanny made a show of wrestling with the sash of a south-facing window, which she said she wanted to let open to the spring breeze. This afforded her a glance at Devorah, who appeared to be lost in confused contemplation of a picture book, her face bearing traces of a fiery blush. Satisfied that she had perhaps planted in the visitor the seed of an idea, if not an emotion, the housemaid announced that she had finished with the schoolroom and was ready to join Mrs. Fenton downstairs for further orders.

There she faithfully related the details of the schoolroom conversation to Mrs. Fenton, along with a description of Devorah's blush. Mrs. Fenton made a show of brushing off her domestic inferior's interest in her employer's affairs, but she secretly thought the maid was rather clever for having edged in so much information about Mr. Whyteman while plying her feather duster. That night, when the house was finally quiet, Mrs. Fenton sat her other half down for an informative chat about Mr. Whyteman and his lovely guest.

"You certainly have been busy, my dear," Isaac said when his wife paused for breath. "But I fail to see what I can do to advance your cause. True, Mr. Whyteman needs a helpmate for this huge project of his and—well, it stands to reason that no man should spend his life alone. It's time he remarried, I agree, and I shouldn't wonder if Miss Asher was sent here by the One Above just for that purpose. But mix in his private affairs I won't. If you want to play matchmaker, go ahead. A woman's touch is what's needed here. As a man, I'd only make a mull of things."

★ ★

When the Duke brought Theo over to Ten Oaks on Monday morning for his first lesson, he was met with the news that Mr. Whyteman was away from Ten Oaks for the day. "Your grace can leave Theo here all the same," Mrs. Fenton offered. "He can help Isaac, who has plenty of work to do, believe me, what with trying to put up a new hot house and fixing and cleaning around here before the Passover holiday. Isaac has taken a real shine to the boy, just like Mr. Whyteman. Seeming they find a bit of charm in all his mischief."

162

"And Passover, when might that be?" asked Devorah, who had been waiting with Mrs. Fenton for the Duke's arrival.

"Why, just three weeks from tonight!" Mrs. Fenton exclaimed with some surprise. "But, I suppose that your suddenly being took from home like that, you haven't been able to keep up with the calendar."

"Is there some problem?" the Duke interjected in response to the shocked look on Devorah's face.

"Nothing, I hope, that cannot be resolved," Devorah answered quickly.

"Well, if that is so, we'll take our leave. Theo is busy in the barn, so will you please make my goodbyes to him, Mrs. Fenton, and tell him to behave himself just a little until I come to see how he is going on here? No—tell him that I expect him to be on his *best* behavior so that we have no more broken vases."

Turning toward the door, his grace watched Devorah pick up a large parcel done up in a faded tablecloth. "Is that yours, Miss Asher? Give it to me, please. Good gad, what do you have in here? Rocks?"

"Provisions. Enough for an army, or at least for several days, should I not be able to get back to Ten Oaks for a meal."

"Nonsense," Mrs. Fenton countered, accompanying them outside. "A pot for boiling some eggs, and a kettle that Miss Asher can place on the fire in her room, and a teapot and cup, and some tea and sugar."

"And half a cake and some biscuits and a loaf of bread, and some cheese and even cheesecakes," Devorah added gaily. "Never fear. I shall not starve."

But when suitable goodbyes and thank-yous were said and the Duke had driven the staid carriage he was using that day a little down the lane, he turned to Devorah, his brow slightly furrowed, and asked her to please answer him truthfully. "Because now that Mrs. Fenton has outfitted your larder quite nicely, you are not afraid of not being able to eat anything when you return to us; that I know. And you are hardy enough to survive us all at Ravenscourt. It is my own opinion that you are secretly laughing up your sleeve at the lot of us. But something else is worrying you. Is it—how did Mrs. Fenton call it—the Passover holiday?"

"I did not know it was so close. I did not think—I don't know what I thought! I forgot all about it!" Devorah exclaimed, releasing her stranglehold on the door of the carriage and throwing her hands up. "Just three weeks away! Am I going to be able to get back home in three weeks?"

"What's the problem? If you cannot get home by then, you will spend the holiday at Ten Oaks. Or, if that is not possible, we will find you a family in London."

"But I wanted to spend it with my *own* family." A small sniffle escaped Devorah, and she fumbled in her reticule for a handkerchief.

In true Regency fashion, the Duke whipped his own out before she could find the small wisp of lace that had been allotted her upon her arrival at Ravenscourt. "Here, have one of mine," he said, handing it over to her. "Don't worry, it's clean."

"I was not worried about that. But what if—what if I can't get home? What I mean is, what if I can't get home *ever*? Or, at least not for Passover? My life is there, in America, in the twenty-first century. My family is there; they must be missing me. Besides, I cannot impose on your hospitality forever. I am *not* blind. Your mother and Albinia hate me, Lucas gives me the creeps, and it is only a matter of time before I am found out."

"I hope before that unfortunate happenstance occurs we will either have gotten you back to where you belong or else have you settled in comfortably elsewhere. In fact, I have already set my contingency plan into motion."

But what the plan was, the Duke refused to disclose. He merely looked at Devorah in a manner that raised acute foreboding in her mind and strengthened certain nebulous suspicions about his motive for settling her at Ten Oaks for the Sabbath.

They arrived at Ravenscourt to find the great house in turmoil. Cook, dragging herself from her sickbed in order to provide the household with a hot meal and suffering a severe bout of vertigo on the kitchen stairwell, had fallen down the stairs, taking the kitchen maid with her. It appeared that Cook had broken her leg and the kitchen maid had broken her arm and sustained a severe concussion, and Dr. Barrie was still dealing with the two of them.

"And what's to be done and how we will manage, I have no idea," the Duchess said, having collared Adam as soon as he entered Ravenscourt's portals and dragged him off to the Green Room to expand on her tale of woe. "I would have us remove to Melville House until Cook is back on her feet, despite the season's having just started. However, next week is dear Aurelia's dinner party, and I daren't miss it—especially as I have *yet* to make up our visit to the Ardsleighs that was so cruelly aborted last week.

"And, to add insult to injury, Spilsby informs me that he has just received communication from Melville House that Antoine is *leaving* us, so bringing him down to Ravenscourt for the interval is clearly ineligible. Adam, this family has been beset by nothing but bad luck since you took up that *foreigner* in your carriage. It is high time you got rid of her."

"Nonsense!" Adam said bracingly, and proceeded to add to the Duchess's spleen by turning abruptly on his heels and exiting the room without so much as an adieu.

The Duke, who had long anticipated the discontented Antoine's imminent departure from the kitchens at Melville House, was little surprised by his mother's news. If only his mother had taken his advice and ordered one of those new closed stoves that the French chef had long coveted and that even Mr. Whyteman had installed at Ten Oaks Manor. Of course, knowing how set the Duchess was in her old-fashioned ways, he should have overridden her and the

London housekeeper's objections and ordered the cursed stove himself. A pity he hadn't; Antoine's pastries and way of serving turbot were legendary and would be dearly missed, and his departure couldn't have come at a worse time. Clearly an immediate solution, however temporary, must be found.

Returning to the Great Hall, the Duke found Spilsby disconsolately flicking an infinitesimal speck of dust from an ivory-inlaid ebony side table with his handkerchief. "Your Grace, we are in a Situation," the elderly butler announced in sepulchral accents. "Dr. Barrie says it will be weeks and weeks before Cook and Eliza are back on their feet. And there is *worse*. Mrs. Wigmore informs me that the junior kitchen maid, upon learning of Cook's condition, has succumbed to hysterics, rendering her incapable of carrying out her duties. And as for the scullery maid—it appears that she has Abandoned Her Post. Your grace, the kitchen is Empty!"

"This does, indeed, present a problem," Adam agreed.

"What we are to do, I have no idea," the butler continued. "Be that as it may, we must take Immediate Action. May I suggest that we post word to your man of business to place an advertisement at the receiving office in London for a temporary replacement for Cook."

"Good idea," the Duke said, and directed Spilsby to write to Mr. Webster and request that he put the job search in train immediately. At that moment, however, the glimmer of an idea began to germinate in Adam's mind. If he was correct in his assumptions, all would soon be well—or at least, he would manage to stave off the starvation of Ravenscourt's inhabitants until a temporary replacement for Cook could be found.

"Of course," Spilsby added, "it could take weeks to find a candidate suited to Ravenscourt. Cooks as are used to the ways of the nobler households do not grow on trees. And Mrs. Wigmore says that if she finds a suitable kitchen maid amongst all the young persons looking for employment hereabouts, it is more than she expects."

"Chin up, Spilsby. We shall come about. Just you wait and see."

"You were forgetting, your grace, that we are expecting an important visitor next week," Spilsby pressed on triumphantly, eliciting a look of surprise from his master. "Yes, Mr. Coke of Norfolk. Perhaps Mr. Coke, being as he is a retiring sort of country gentleman, will not mind our dinners being somewhat plain and simple. But, it would not be fitting to your station if we were to cut our table to fewer than ten dishes a course. That is, if we were to find a body or two to populate our kitchens. As matters at Ravenscourt stand now, even a single course is beyond our capability."

"Drat it! I totally forgot about Mr. Coke's visit," the Duke exclaimed. "Oh, well, it can't be helped. And, as I said, we shall come about. So please to cheer up and send word to London immediately. Tell Webster that he must search for two cooks—one for here and one for Melville House. And, he should find the best place to procure a closed stove. That we must also have as soon as possible. And, please send for Miss Asher. I will be waiting for her in the library."

Unfortunately, Adam found his sister and Albinia already inhabiting the library when he entered that normally underutilized chamber to wait for Devorah. "Turning bookish all of a sudden, Sis?" he asked Felicity in a deceptively innocent voice. "And you, Albinia, camping out here for the second time since you've been visiting? Soon we will be calling you a bluestocking."

Felicity, who had been sitting side by side with Albinia on the sofa, whispering excitedly to her legendary enemy, turned and started and dropped the book she had been clutching. "We were just about to leave," she said guiltily.

"No, we were not," Albinia countered, setting her own book down on the sofa's leather surface and smoothing her skirts as she rose. "We were discussing the state of Ravenscourt. Oh, Duke, what is to be done?"

"To be done with what?" Adam asked, bewildered.

"The state of this household," Albinia announced. "I have always admired its tone. So, so—so distinguished. So discriminating. And now…."

"And now? Continue, please."

"A *foreigner* in this house. An *unknown* foreigner. And Cook sustaining a broken leg, and the kitchen maid a broken head. Who *is* this unknown person? What is this evil influence she is wreaking on your home?"

Felicity, to Adam's amazement, nodded in agreement.

"You've been speaking with my mother," Adam accused his guest. "And you, Felicity," he said in a menacing voice, "have been listening to both their nonsense."

"The Duchess and I are in accord more often than not," Albinia said defensively.

"Whatever," Adam said lamely, struggling mightily to keep from either rolling his eyes or bursting into laughter. Exiting the library and closing the door behind him, he paused for a moment to enjoy his private joke. Felicity and Albinia, united through jealousy in mutual dislike of Miss Asher! Whoever would have thought that he would enjoy himself so immensely during his dreaded stay in the country?

Meeting up with Devorah and Spilsby on the grand staircase, he suggested that Miss Asher put on a sunhat for a stroll in the garden. "The library, where I wanted to speak with you privately, is already occupied," he explained. "And I entertain fears that the company there will drift over to the Green Room, which would be our next logical choice for a conversation."

"If I may be so bold," the butler interjected, "Miss Asher has not yet seen the portrait gallery on the first floor, nor the Italian windows that lead onto its balcony overlooking the rose garden."

"An excellent suggestion," Adam said gratefully, and led his guest up the broad staircase to the next floor.

The Italian windows, a set of six wonderfully carved and gilded floor-to-ceiling frames inset with leaded glass, and so named because they had been salvaged off a crumbling Italian villa, formed a light-filled alcove off to one side of the portrait gallery. A set of upholstered benches flanked the two center windows that led out to the balcony. It was to one of these benches that the Duke led Devorah and bade her be seated. "For we are in a bind here at Ravenscourt and I am hoping that you will be able to help rescue us," he told her. "Forgive me for asking, but can you cook?"

Devorah, who hadn't been quite sure what she had been expecting the Duke to ask her, burst out laughing.

"It is no laughing matter," his grace said severely. "Cook is expected to be laid up for weeks, and the kitchen maid can hardly do the trick with her broken arm—not to mention that first her head needs to mend. And, to top off matters, Spilsby reliably informs me that we also have neither junior kitchen nor scullery maid. We are truly in a pickle here, as we have no one to direct the kitchens—or even to staff them—until we find suitable replacements, and we are expecting an important guest next week."

"You want me to take charge of the kitchens? To cook?" Devorah asked incredulously.

"If you know anything at all about cooking," the Duke pleaded, "please help me devise a plan. I would ask Mr. Whyteman to lend me Mrs. Fenton and Fanny, but they, too, have a household to feed. Please, if you know anything at all, I am begging for your help."

Devorah thought for a minute. "You have seen the kitchens at Ten Oaks. Are those at Ravenscourt anything like them?"

"I do not know," the Duke admitted with some embarrassment. "I have never been down to the kitchens here."

"I know recipes," Devorah said, her mind starting to churn with ideas. "But I do not know how many of the ingredients are available to you at Ravenscourt. And I know nothing about how to work your stoves and ovens. And… and…"—here she shuddered—"I do not think I could bring myself to cook rabbit or pork or beef in cream sauce, even if

I knew how. I mostly know how to make popular American foods and traditional Jewish dishes. They are not at all what you and your family are used to."

"So what's the problem?" the Duke asked. "We'll serve everyone Jewish food. And, even better yet, we will tell them that this new style of cooking is all the crack!"

Chapter 16

Devorah stared at him, her breath taken nearly away by such an audacious suggestion. "Do we *dare*, your grace?" she whispered in awe. "Will they not become suspicious?"

"We dare, yes. But possible? Of that I have no idea until we've explored the kitchen chambers. Do you come downstairs with me now to check them over."

When the unlikely pair went in search of Mrs. Wigmore to accompany them on a tour of the kitchen, they were informed that she had already descended into Ravenscourt's culinary netherworld in order to determine just how meals might be supplied to the great house's residents and army of servants until such time as kitchen staff could be found. They found her inspecting the ovens with Betsy and two of the lower maids. The sound of the Duke's boots on the stone kitchen floor caused her to look up. Directing the maids to inspect the scullery, she waited until they were out of earshot before plunging into speech.

"There is Betsy, as was a kitchen maid before we elevated her upstairs, and if Miss Asher would be pleased to loan her to the kitchen, she can supervise whichever lower staff we can spare to assist her. As you know, your grace, I have worked in great houses since I was a girl of twelve, but *never* have I worked in the kitchens. To ask me to step in temporarily to supervise would be a *disaster*, besides rendering me incapable of carrying out such duties as are attached to my position as housekeeper." At this she paused and directed a speaking look at Devorah and the Duke.

It was a calculated pause. The Duke understood quite quickly that it would be unbefitting for his housekeeper to temporarily assume command of the kitchen, even if she were capable. And capable she was not. He knew as well as the Duchess that Mrs. Wigmore had only too gladly handed over the housekeeper's task of concocting the household preserves to Cook and her minions. Indeed, it was a common joke in the upper servants' quarters, and one that had made its way to the Duke's ears, that Mrs. Wigmore was a heavy-handed cook who was prone to render even the simplest dish inedible. To hand the kitchen over to her would be disastrous—and possibly even fatal!

Devorah, meanwhile, squirmed in the Lady Felicity's second-best half boots. The housekeeper's speech had, she thought, been subtly nuanced. If Betsy did have past kitchen experience, it made her a suitable candidate for temporary cook; but the logic carried with it the inference that Miss Asher, being a foreigner and an unknown, was undeserving of a personal maid and that Betsy was the upper servant who could best be spared.

But Devorah had no way of knowing that she had found favor in the upper servants' hall just by merit of being an apparent—and much more likeable—rival to Lady Albinia. She was stunned when Mrs. Wigmore, sensing her indecision, announced that not only had suitable arrangements been made for someone else to assist her until such time as Betsy could resume the post, but that the great Tilstock herself had offered to dress Miss Asher's hair every evening for dinner. "That bit of information, however, your grace, I beg you will please to keep to yourself, being as Miss Tilstock has not requested her grace's permission to do so."

"My lips are sealed," the Duke said, drawing an imaginary line across his mouth with his index finger. He turned to Devorah. "Well, Miss Asher, what say you? Can you spare Betsy? Indeed, it is quite an honor that has been accorded you. In the thirty years that she has been my mother's dresser, I have never heard of Miss Tilstock's condescending to perform a favor for anyone except the Duchess herself!"

Devorah rapidly assessed the kitchen, from the old-fashioned brick ovens and well-worn wooden kitchen table to the brightly polished copper pots and molds that lined a sideboard next to the large window with a view of the kitchen gardens. She knew nothing about baking in a brick oven, let alone boiling puddings and soups over an open fire. Still, she felt that she owed her host something for rescuing her and providing sanctuary. She had relatively little to do at Ravenscourt until she could find her way home, so the least she could do was help ensure that Ravenscourt's inhabitants had something palatable to eat until temporary replacements for Cook and Eliza could be found.

"I can do one better," she heard herself answering the Duke's query. "I can devote several hours for the next few days to supervising Betsy and the other kitchen maids. Even though I am unfamiliar with your typical dishes and have absolutely no idea how to use your ovens, I can show Betsy how to make many of my family's favorite recipes. I am sure that everyone at Ravenscourt will enjoy them too. After all, it is only for a few days, until a temporary cook can be found, is it not?"

Thus Devorah found herself that very afternoon explaining to Betsy—after unearthing a large container of Spanish olive oil hidden behind a pile of crockery and discovering a beautifully large whole salmon, delivered just that morning, in the larder—how to make mayonnaise, and from there a mayonnaise dill sauce in which to cook the salmon. From salmon it was a short step to roasted pigeons with mushrooms, rich chicken soup with vermicelli noodles and carrots, and a boiled potato pudding that closely resembled what, in Miss Asher's family, was known as a *kugel*.

The Duke, who descended the treacherous back stairs several times to be entertained by the strange goings-on in his kitchen, came up with the idea of sending poultry raised on the Ravenscourt home farm over to Ten Oaks for slaughter.

None of the currently able-bodied servants at Ravenscourt was willing to take on the task of wringing a chicken's neck, he explained. "This way," he added, "Mrs. Fenton will have the opportunity of sending cooked food back for you along with the slaughtered chickens."

Meanwhile Robert, upon being let in on the secret that the American guest was lording it over the kitchen, sent down a request for *chaud-lent*. Devorah instructed the puzzled scullery maid, who had returned to her post, to institute a brief search for dried white beans and barley, and a large store of each was found in the pantry. She directed the much-harried Betsy to soak the beans overnight so that they could be placed over a low flame with meat and barley the following afternoon, and was thus able to whisper to Robert before going into dinner that evening that preparation of the slow-cooking *chaud-lent* was in progress; he could look forward to eating the treat in a few days.

A scant hour before dinner, Mrs. Wigmore summoned Devorah back upstairs to dress. The grateful housekeeper, correctly anticipating that Ravenscourt's heaven-sent guest would require a thorough scrubbing before she could be made presentable, had a hip bath and a replacement maid ready and waiting. Mrs. Wigmore, who had astutely picked up the undercurrents roiling through the other young ladies present at Ravenscourt, had also conferred with Tilstock; the latter formally requested Lady Felicity's permission to supply reinforcements to Miss Asher's wardrobe. Tilstock explained, in no uncertain terms, that to fail to do so would greatly incur his grace's displeasure.

"And, if I might be so bold as to point out to my lady, seeing as Miss Asher does not own a stitch to her name other than the silk dress in which she was carried here, to have her show up at dinner in a lesser person's castoffs would be just as fatal as if she were to wear that same silk dress night after night, beautiful though it may be. His grace, as you are well aware, is far from blind to the finer details of feminine attire; Lady Albinia would shine Miss Asher down if you was to seat both of them at the same dinner table without clothing Miss Asher as is her due—which might make her grace happy, but might not take as well with others here at Ravenscourt who Shall Not Be Named!"

Lady Felicity was shocked by both her mother's dresser's outspokenness and the fact that she not only knew what matchmaking plans her mistress was promoting, but was hell-bent on foiling them. But, after the pause of a heartbeat and a few feeble protestations, she plunged into the spirit of things and spent an enjoyable half hour with Tilstock, coming up with an evening ensemble for Miss Asher that would do any society damsel proud. The happy result was that when a well-dressed and well-scented Devorah was at last seated at table, no one but the Duke, Robert and Spilsby, hovering benevolently nearby, was any wiser about the role Miss Asher had played in supplying the evening's meal. And only Tilstock and Mrs. Wigmore knew what stratagems had been employed to ensure that Miss Asher was in her best looks.

Even the Duchess could not find fault with dinner that evening. Though the selection of dishes in each course was by necessity few in number, the menu included—in addition to the soup, dilled salmon and roasted pigeons—stuffed pheasant, haricots verts with onions and almonds, a glazed ham, some potted meats, apple crisp, preserved compote and lemon sponge cake.

Devorah's stomach had churned a little at the sight of the mangled pheasant when Robert brought it in from the home woods, but she realized reluctantly that she would have to accept its appearance—as well as that of the huge ham that Mrs. Wigmore unearthed from the larder—if she wanted to avoid any suspicion. Betsy had known exactly how to remove any remaining shot from the pheasant and had, with great resolution, thrust the mess into a vat of boiling water as she had seen done once before so that she could more easily remove the feathers. As to the cooking of the ham, Devorah at first declined to supervise, pleading ignorance as to how to best bring out its flavor. But then she remembered reading in some childhood novel that the holiday ham had been glazed with honey and riddled with cloves, so she suggested this cooking method to Betsy, with the rider that she had no other helpful information to add to this suggestion except to perhaps stick in some cloves of garlic, as well. The method apparently was successful, as the ham received rave reviews from Lucas and Robert, who voiced the happy expectation of being able to finish it off the following morning.

While the rest of the evening party oohed and aahed over the dilled salmon and the roasted pigeons and marveled over the lemon sponge cake, Devorah toyed with her apple and ransacked her brain for ideas of what fine dishes to prepare on the morrow. Mrs. Wigmore had informed her that they must meet even before breakfast to plan the day's meals, so great ideas were needed As Soon As Possible!

Devorah was just settling on the possibility of placing chicken cutlet and Italian meatballs on the next day's menu— perhaps oregano and tomatoes could be found in the kitchen garden—when the ladies adjourned to the Burgundy Drawing Room. Once again she was banished to the chair farthest from the fire. However, this time she had the luxury of a heavy Norwich silk shawl, courtesy of Lady Felicity. And Lady Felicity, perhaps because her temporary alliance with Albinia was wearing thin, sat herself down in the chair opposite Miss Asher's for a comfortable prose.

This, as both young women discovered, was rough going. Aside from their chilly spot away from the fire, they had little in common, and Devorah had no desire to address the great number of pointed questions that Lady Felicity, burning with curiosity regarding the Real Story, asked. The two ladies finally settled on the relatively safe topic of Miss Asher's family. But, after minutely discussing the number of Devorah's siblings at home or married, and the number of dear nieces and nephews she could claim, the subject was soon exhausted. Fortunately, the men joined them just as conversation was beginning to lag.

Lady Albinia, who had been discussing Lady Ardsleigh's upcoming dinner party with the Duchess, saw with consternation that the Duke immediately took a seat next to his sister and Miss Asher. Hampered by her conversation with her hostess from going over and breaking up what appeared to be a cozy little chat, she instead maliciously suggested a repeat of Miss Asher's delightful performance on the pianoforte the week before. "You enthralled us, Miss Asher, with Beethoven's *Sonata quasi una fantasia* last time you played. Surely you have mastered another piece that you can perform for us."

"Yes, do," Mr. Duckwaithe chimed in, clapping his hands together. "Such a delightful example of the feminine arts as you displayed for us before."

Devorah was exhausted from her day in the kitchen, but she was prepared. In fact, one might say that she was *armed*. She had spent several hours the previous day practicing on the piano at Ten Oaks and had polished her performance of an extremely difficult piano concerto. Positioning herself on the crimson-brocaded stool of the pianoforte, she turned and announced to her noble audience that she would be performing a piece by a German composer, Johannes Brahms: the second movement from his Piano Concerto No.2, arranged for solo piano.

"Mr. Brahms is one of the greatest composers in history. However, his works are not yet known here in England," she explained, neglecting to mention that Johannes Brahms's birth still lay eighteen years in the future and that the arrangement for solo piano did not make its debut until more than a century and a half later yet. "Therefore, you are in for a rare treat," she added before turning in her seat and plunging into the scherzo's dramatic opening.

Devorah's performance made the intended impression on her audience. As the final chords died away, Lucas and Robert broke into spontaneous applause. "Bravo! Bravo!" Mr. Duckwaithe cried. Even the Duchess, who was tone deaf, nodded her approbation.

Lady Albinia, who had anticipated something much more pedestrian, such as a Bach minuet, was rendered temporarily speechless. But she made a quick recovery and chimed in with her own left-handed compliment. "Such verve. Such style. But surely, Miss Asher, just a little too dramatic and complex for mere females such as ourselves to master."

"Seems to me she mastered it just fine," Robert retorted.

Albinia answered slowly, searching for just the right combination of words to indicate that Miss Asher's performance was indeed talented but somewhat lacking in femininity. "Indeed, Miss Asher's performance is to be commended. I merely meant to say that an *ordinary* female might find execution of Mr. Brahms's beautiful piece to require too much *exertion* at the keyboard. For myself, I will stick with my gentle Beethoven and my Bach."

"Most impressive," the Duke broke in. "Please, Miss Asher, impress us with something else. Perhaps another unknown piece up your sleeve?"

Enjoying her private joke, Devorah decided to entertain her audience with a composition that was more modern yet. "This is by an obscure French composer," she announced, launching into the piano variation from a movie soundtrack circa 1970.

"My dear Miss Asher, that was beautiful," Lucas exclaimed when she had finished.

"I for one am quite content to forgo hearing music by a Frenchman, no matter how beautiful. Britannia is suffering quite enough right now from a surfeit of Frenchmen, without having to hear them on the pianoforte," Albinia said.

Adam grinned and cocked an eyebrow at Devorah. "Well, Miss Asher, what is the obscure Frenchman's name? Have you forgotten?"

"Certainly not. However, I fail to see how it can be of any interest to you, as I doubt you will have any occasion to hear his compositions again."

"But surely you can teach us, Miss Asher. With your new compositions you can show us all the way."

Her grace, feeling that she had heard quite enough, rose majestically from her chair by the fire and rang for tea. "Well, I would say that we have been entertained most pleasantly this evening. Miss Asher, you must be exhausted after your musical excursions. Please feel free to excuse yourself instead of waiting for tea."

The Duke and Robert, appalled by their parent's rudeness, exchanged speaking glances and stood up in unison. "It's been an extremely long and wearying day. Please accept my apologies, but my brother and I will also bid you good night. There is no need to ring for Spilsby to show Miss Asher the way. Robert and I will escort her up the stairs," Adam said, heading for the door with Robert and Miss Asher in his wake.

"Well, if that doesn't beat all!" Robert expostulated once the trio was safely out of earshot. "If only my mother knew how you saved our groats, Miss Asher. It was only thanks to you that we ate more than a baked egg and a Gunter's tea biscuit for dinner. Well, not even a baked egg," he amended, "because that would have been cooked, too. Which reminds me, Miss Asher, I forgot to tell you how capital the dinner was that you prepared for us. Or, at least I didn't forget to tell you, but I wasn't able to because that would have spilled all the beans."

"Yes, my compliments, too," Adam said, pushing his brother toward the stairs. "I was about to pay them to you earlier, but you were called upon at that very moment to play for us. A breathtaking performance, Miss Asher, and one that has cast the other females in this household quite in the shade. But why does my instinct tell me that there is a private joke in there somewhere? In any case, come, the both of you. Miss Asher must be falling over with sleep by now."

The following morning, Devorah confirmed the presence of oregano and tomatoes in the kitchen garden and set in train the preparation of Italian meatballs as a central dish in the first course. These, served with long, thin noodles, were an unqualified success at dinner that night, as were the sweet-and-sour brisket, pumpkin soup with dumplings, country-style fried chicken, stuffed cabbage rolls, marinated beet salad, chocolate brownies and apple strudel. Devorah, whose list of unused recipes was growing thin, uttered a silent prayer that Mrs. Wigmore find a substitute cook before many more days, then set the *cholent* on to cook. She had decided to save the chicken cutlets to serve with it.

Wednesday morning, four slaughtered chickens arrived at Ravenscourt from Ten Oaks Manor, along with a package for Miss Asher and a personal note for his grace. The package, which Devorah opened in the privacy of her room, contained various foodstuffs to tide her over for the next few days, along with a scrawled message from Mrs. Fenton that she hoped to send additional provisions in time for Devorah to properly observe the Sabbath. The Duke's note was from Mr. Whyteman, who begged leave to visit sometime in the early afternoon as he desired private conversion with both his grace and Miss Asher.

Mr. Whyteman arrived just as the inhabitants of Ravenscourt were finishing a light luncheon and was shown into the library to await his grace's pleasure. This was not long in coming. He had time only to study a shelf devoted to histories and select a title before Adam entered the room with Devorah. Turning at the sound of their entrance, he snapped the book shut and settled himself in the nearest chair at the Duke's request.

"Before we get started, you must tell me how your new charge is comporting himself," the Duke said conversationally, crossing one booted leg over another in preparation for a long recitation of the havoc Theo had wreaked on Ten Oaks Manor.

Mr. Whyteman grinned. "Theo is amazing. He is determined to replace the Sèvres vase which he destroyed last week and has, in the absence of clay and kiln, taken up papier-mâché. I believe that Mrs. Fenton initiated him into the craft to keep him occupied—and out of the kitchen and out of trouble. Imagine! Discovering that he was still feeling remorseful about having shot the vase off the mantelpiece in my library, and also that he had nothing to do on Monday, being that I was attending to business elsewhere, she had the happy thought of supplying him with newspapers and flour, and water and paints. He has spent the last few days destroying the schoolroom with the mess from making his creations."

Seeing the Duke's look of disbelief, Mr. Whyteman paused and nodded in confirmation. "Seriously, your grace, I lie not. I understand that our enterprising houseguest has created, in addition to a creditable vase or two, some monster masks. When I left Ten Oaks today, he was terrorizing the hens and horses—not to mention the scullery maid—with these masks. He is now plotting life-size creatures, such as unicorns and dragons, and has requested that Isaac cut him suitably sized sticks on which to mold his creations. We have discovered within him heretofore unrevealed artistic talents and I, for one, intend to capitalize on them during our lessons."

"How?" the Duke asked, genuinely curious.

"As to that, I know not. I am waiting for divine inspiration," Mr. Whyteman said airily. "But, I digress from the true purpose of my visit.

"You will be interested in hearing that I have enlisted two more candidates for my project. Recent orphans whom my colleagues have rescued from lives of thievery, or worse. They are currently staying at my mother's house in London, as I have judged it inadvisable to bring them to Ten Oaks Manor just yet. I also have heard on credible authority that Lord Bromley's estate, some forty miles south of here, is for long-term let and might be suitable for my purposes. Are you familiar with it?"

His grace extracted a small, gold filigree box from his pocket and took a pinch of snuff. "I believe so. Would you like me to look into it for you?"

"Yes, please. You would be able to negotiate far better terms than I," Mr. Whyteman said gratefully. "Which leaves my other reason for coming here today. Miss Asher, I have written to London to both a rabbinical and medical authority regarding your situation, and have now received their replies. They are in agreement that you may be suffering from delusions brought on by a blow to your head, possibly received when you fell."

"There are no delusions!" Devorah interrupted hotly.

"Please, if I may speak candidly without interruption. Not knowing the best course of action under the circumstances, and knowing the difficulties placed on both you and his grace, I decided to seek wiser counsel." Mr. Whyteman, who had been studying Devorah intently, shifted his gaze to the Duke. "I have been advised that the best course of action for the time being, if your grace will agree, is for Miss Asher to continue her stay here at Ravenscourt. If, as is possible, Miss Asher fell off some conveyance here in the countryside and sustained a blow that caused her to lose her memory, it is best for her to remain nearby so that her near relations can more easily find her. On the other hand, if she was deliberately pushed off a conveyance, with the intent of injuring her, she is safest here at Ravenscourt under your grace's protection."

"What about taking her to Ten Oaks?" asked the Duke.

"To place an unmarried woman such as Miss Asher at Ten Oaks would not be suitable—at least not while I, as an unmarried man, am present. I am afraid, therefore, that spending another Sabbath at Ten Oaks is out of the question. We need to devise an alternate plan here at Ravenscourt for the duration of Miss Asher's stay."

"And I? What do I have to say to all of this?" Devorah asked.

"You? You have nothing to say to this," said the Duke. "You are my guest, on my sufferance. You are lucky that both Mr. Whyteman and I have your welfare uppermost in our minds. Do calm yourself, Miss Asher. I am not trying to be callous. I have nothing but the highest regard for you, as my tenant, Mr. Whyteman, well knows, and I am truly honored that you are my temporary guest. Mr. Whyteman and I will continue to explore all avenues for your rescue."

"And," Mr. Whyteman added, "if we are unable to reunite you with your family before Passover, which is in less than three weeks' time, I will convey you to London, where you have an invitation to spend the holiday with British Chief Rabbi Solomon Hirschell and his family. It is a most honorable and coveted invitation."

The honorable and coveted invitation, however, did nothing to recommend itself to Devorah; it was a mere sop to the insult she had just been served. To make plans for her keep without consulting her, to discuss her as though she were a child, and—worst of all—to patently disbelieve her! Every fiber revolted; she was most offended. And yet, her safety and security depended for the time being on these same two callous men. To display her anger would be counterproductive, so Devorah maintained her silence.

"By the way, sir, I received an item of news from London that will interest you deeply," Mr. Whyteman said. "As you know, the outlaw Bonaparte re-entered Paris on the twentieth this month and reassumed the throne. The United Kingdom and its allies, Austria, Prussia and Russia, have committed to restoring the throne to its rightful heir, Louis XVIII, and to routing Bonaparte once and for all. They have begun amassing troops—some say as many as one hundred and fifty thousand men each ally. Four days ago, on the Jewish Sabbath, the Allied troops commenced their march on Paris."

"Six hundred thousand men, you say? Quite a large army, if they have already gathered in their entirety, which I doubt. But Bonaparte has proved himself to be a formidable opponent in the past. One wonders who will be the victor in the end."

"The Allies will be the victors," Devorah interjected, to her own astonishment. "This June, the Allies will go against Napoleon on the battlefield near a small Flemish village called Waterloo. They will prevail. It will be recorded as one of the bloodiest—and most famous—battles in history."

"How come you to know these things?" the Duke asked cynically. "Are you a seer, Miss Asher? Or a witch? Or a spy?"

"You forget that I have fallen here from the twenty-first century," she answered lightly, inwardly chiding herself for speaking impulsively. "So, I have the gift of hindsight. Please believe me when I tell you that I have hidden nothing from you."

But she saw that his grace, who heretofore viewed himself as the slightly amused protector of a female anomaly who had landed nearly at his feet, was now regarding Devorah as something of a lunatic. Devorah looked from the Duke to Mr. Whyteman, who was regarding her with an expression of amusement, and back again. Clearly, neither of these men believed her or could be depended upon to help her return to where she belonged.

The question was, could she solve her dilemma by herself?

Chapter 17

Lucas Duckwaithe, scion of a noble line of viscounts dating back two centuries, was deeply in love. Thirty-two years old and in need of a helpmate, he had long despaired of ever finding the woman of his dreams: beautiful, talented, cultured, of good family and, above all else, sharing his interest in biblical literature. He had come to believe that his ideal did not exist—that is, until he met the lovely, biblical Devorah Asher. She was everything he yearned for, and more. But did he dare reveal his innermost feelings? Did she reciprocate his affections? She was modest and favored no one man at Ravenscourt more than another, although she seemed to laugh frequently at his grace's deplorable humor, most likely in an attempt to curry favor with the Duke, and she always responded kindly to Lord Robert when he bestowed his attentions on her.

The male inhabitants of Ravenscourt in general seemed to like Miss Asher, which would make it much easier for her to settle into her role as wife and helpmate of the Ravenscourt chaplain once they married. It was a pity that the Duchess did not seem to favor her, although Lucas knew that she would come to love Miss Asher once everything was official; he also knew that their marriage would set to rest the Duchess's suspicions about Miss Asher's background, as he was equally as meticulous about lineage as her grace. Nor, to Lucas's chagrin, did Lady Albinia seem to like Miss Asher—but that, the chaplain knew, was because she viewed Miss Asher, quite erroneously, as a rival candidate for the Duke's hand. Lucas had the highest regard for Lady Albinia; in fact, until Miss Asher had fallen so suddenly on the scene, he had entertained fantasies of taking her to wife, although he knew that due to Lady Albinia's station in life and her destined betrothal to the Duke, such a match could never be.

A pity, he often thought. Even though the Lady Albinia, though well enough in looks, paled in comparison to Miss Asher's beauty and intelligence, her thoughts and opinions were so much in accord with Lucas's own that sometimes when speaking with Lady Albinia it was as if he were speaking with the other half of himself.

"She is, indeed, too good for the Duke," Mr. Duckwaithe had on more than one occasion whispered to himself about the Lady Albinia. "Not that I don't value the Duke highly, but he does not share that elevation of character and purity of mind that so characterizes his intended bride."

Now, however, Lucas had cast aside thoughts of Albinia's elevation of character and purity of mind. Instead, he prayed fervently that the Duke would soon ask the Lady Albinia for the honor of becoming his wife. This would make his own proposal to Miss Asher so much more unexceptionable. But when to propose? And how? Devorah—dare he call his beloved by her so beautiful and so biblical name?—had been closeted for the past hour with the Duke and that atrocious tenant of his, Jonathan Whyteman. This would never do. They were probably arranging how to remove Miss Asher from the orbit of Ravenscourt. Lucas resolved to propose to Devorah as soon as possible. Indeed, he would waylay her as soon as she left the room. He headed in the direction of the library where the trio were closeted, and prepared to lay siege.

★ ★

"Tilstock," her grace said imperiously as her lady's maid loosened her gown in preparation for a light afternoon nap. "You have taken charge of the dressing of Miss Asher's hair for dinner, is that not so?"

"Yes, your grace. I apologize for not asking your grace's permission, but with Cook laid up with a broken leg and

Betsy taking over in the kitchens, we were left in a sudden bind. There was no time to ask whether your grace would consent to such a scheme, and as the Duke was so pleased with the results of my handiwork and I was able to do up Miss Asher's hair in a trice after making sure that you were properly turned out for dinner, to ask permission completely slipped my mind. Should I tell Mrs. Wigmore to find someone else to do Miss Asher's hair?"

"No, please continue," the Duchess said, removing her turban and handing it to her maid before reposing herself between the fine linen sheets of her bed. "I add only one qualification: in the future, please see to it that Miss Asher's hair does not look its best. We do not want her to outshine those who are her betters."

★ ★

Lady Felicity was in a quandary. Only consider: letters from Ravenscourt had delivered two cataclysmic pieces of news to her while she was staying at her aunt's house in London, the first being that her mother had invited Albinia for a visit to Ravenscourt. No genius was required to put the correct interpretation on the Duchess's actions; it had long been her dream that Binny and Adam make a match of it, and Binny, being Binny, cherished similar fantasies. While in the past Felicity had placed deep confidence in Adam's abilities to fend off Binny's advances, she was unsure of what the combined assault of the Duchess's promptings and a month's worth of Binny would do to wear down his defenses, especially when he was tied to Ravenscourt due to estate business and unable to flee. He might—although Felicity was not quite sure of this—pop the question just to buy himself some peace and quiet, even though in her opinion it would be far better for him to just cock up his toes and consign himself to a premature death.

And then, secondly, was the casual comment in Adam's last letter that his tenant, Jonathan Whyteman, had arrived back at Ten Oaks for what appeared to be an extended stay. The Lady Felicity had thought that her normally astute brother was aware of her interest in Mr. Whyteman, but clearly he was blind; otherwise he wouldn't have divulged such stirring information. At any rate, Felicity, who was prone to act quickly on her frequent snap decisions, had hurried home from London with the dual intent of conquering Jonathan Whyteman and dividing her brother and the Lady Albinia.

She had reckoned, however, without the mysterious appearance of Miss Asher.

This, then, was the source of the Lady Felicity's quandary. Miss Asher was beautiful and intelligent, well-born and talented—though Felicity entertained doubts about that German fellow—what was his name? Brahms?—whose scandalously dramatic piano concerto Devorah had played the previous evening. In all the years that Felicity had had the pianoforte drummed into her, she had never heard of him. That, though, was neither here nor there. What was more to the point was that dear Adam appeared to be somewhat smitten with his unexpected guest; or, at least, he was enjoying a light flirtation with her at Albinia's expense. In either case, that was a good thing, because it meant that Adam wasn't caught irrevocably between the Duchess and Albinia's machinations, as Felicity worried that he would be.

Miss Asher's providential appearance on the scene most certainly would have tipped Felicity in her favor were in not for the fact that the mysterious guest seemed to have cozened her way into Jonathan Whyteman's favor, as well, thereby presenting herself as a serious rival. The moment that Felicity clapped eyes on Mr. Whyteman upon his assuming tenancy at Ten Oaks several months before, Felicity knew that she had met The One. All the unattached males who had previously come into her orbit, with the exception of Adam and Mr. Duckwaithe (who, as a man of the cloth didn't really count), were notable chiefly for their frivolity, their fashion and their horses. Felicity herself was an intellectual lightweight, but she idolized her elder brother and hoped subconsciously to make a match with someone who, like Adam, combined a sense of humor with a deep sense of responsibility and seriousness of purpose. Felicity recognized instinctively these same qualities in Jonathan; once he unbent sufficiently to allow her a glimpse of his charming smile and a bit of his humor, she was thoroughly captivated. No matter that Adam, who frequently expressed his great regard for his tenant, for some reason apparently did not consider him a suitable candidate for her hand. She would bring her brother around eventually—and if not, well, she would just have to devise a scheme to force matters to their desired conclusion. In this case, Felicity knew well, the Duchess would fall in line with whatever Adam decided.

But all of Felicity's dreams for the future seemed to be crumbling into nothingness. It was Miss Asher, not Felicity, who had accompanied Adam to Ten Oaks. And, she had *stayed there* for the weekend. And now, she was closeted with Jonathan and Adam in the library, to what purpose one could only guess. Indeed, ever since Miss Asher's arrival, there appeared to be something strange going on at Ravenscourt and its surrounding estates; Felicity could not quite put her finger on it, but while Miss Asher appeared on the surface to be perfectly acceptable, the undercurrents suggested something about her not quite *comme il faut*.

How, then, should Felicity regard Miss Asher? Was she a heaven-sent angel, intended to save Ravenscourt from the throes of Albinia, or was she an evil seductress, intent upon spiking Felicity's plans to marry Mr. Whyteman?

★ ★

A murmur of voices still came from the library. Miss Asher had been closeted with the Duke and Mr. Whyteman for the better part of an hour. Certainly their conference should soon come to an end. But Lucas was becoming impatient. If Miss Asher didn't come out soon, he decided, he would break up the cozy little chat by entering and ostensibly searching for the copy of Gibbon's *Roman Empire* that he kept in the library just for those occasions when he found himself stranded at Ravenscourt with nothing to do.

Meanwhile, Felicity, pondering the conundrum of Miss Asher while heading toward the Green Room to attend to some long-neglected needlework, abruptly changed her destination for the library. She would accidentally interrupt the private conference going on inside so that she could search for her marbled copy of Mrs. Radcliffe's *The Italian,* which she had been panting to get back to ever since her return to Ravenscourt.

"Lady Felicity!" Mr. Duckwaithe, his hand already on the door handle, exclaimed in surprise as the daughter of the house materialized at his side.

"Mr. Duckwaithe! But what are you doing here?"

At that exact moment, the door to the library opened, causing Lucas to nearly fall inside. The Duke, who had been escorting his guests out, studied the newcomers with some amusement.

"I beg your pardon, Duke," the chaplain apologized. "I have forgotten my Gibbons here and, thinking the room empty, came to retrieve it."

"By all means," Adam said, ushering the chaplain in with a broad sweep of his arm. "And you, Felicity, have you also forgotten a book here?"

"*The Italian.* Mrs. Radcliffe, you know. I thought to read it during the afternoon."

"Don't let me detain either of you. If you will excuse us, Mr. Whyteman is needed back at Ten Oaks and Miss Asher has some urgent matters to attend to," Adam said in that slightly sardonic voice that never failed to irritate his sister, no matter how much she idolized him.

Finding themselves alone in the library, Lady Felicity and her mother's chaplain glared at each other before turning away to hunt for their respective volumes. It was a fruitless search for both—Felicity's because the Duchess, judging Mrs. Radcliffe's Gothic thriller to be objectionable, had tossed it on the fire one evening while Felicity was in London; Lucas's because that particular volume of *The Decline and Fall of the Roman Empire* now lay on the Lady Albinia's bedside table alongside a book of improving sermons. Felicity, after searching all the usual places in which she hid her objectionable novels, as well as all of the improbable places she could think of where she might have left her current forbidden tome, gave up the search and was debating whether social niceties dictated that she must bid the chaplain farewell before leaving the library, when a piercing scream erupted upstairs from the direction of the West Wing.

Neither Felicity nor the chaplain gave the other a passing glance as they turned as one and ran toward the grand staircase and the source of that blood-curdling cry. To the uninformed ear, it seemed to transform rapidly into a series of non-stop screams that were the work of two people rather than one. As she reached the second floor and raced toward the West Wing, Felicity correctly determined, with great astonishment, that the screams originated in either the Rose Room allotted to Miss Asher or the Royal Bedchamber in which Lady Albinia stayed. But Devorah appeared to have preceded Felicity up the stairs by mere seconds and was now entering Albinia's room. Felicity, hard on her heels, with a puffing Lucas Duckwaithe close behind, entered the Royal Bedchamber just in time to see Jonathan Whyteman rip the antique embroidered bed cover from the Elizabethan bed and throw it around Albinia's maid, Martha, who was engulfed in flames. As Albinia stood screaming in a corner, Jonathan pushed the maid to the floor and rolled her in the antique Persian carpet, badly scorching both the carpet and his shirtsleeves in the process, but succeeding in extinguishing any remaining fire.

"How badly burnt is she?" asked Adam, holding the empty washbasin, the contents of which he had tossed on the maid in an ineffectual attempt to staunch the fire.

"Bad enough," Jonathan said. "We need to place her in cool water. Immediately."

"Mrs. Wigmore has some excellent ointment for burns. I will run downstairs to get it," offered a much-shaken Felicity.

"No! No ointment. We need water, now!"

Devorah, casting an eye about the room, saw that Albinia, clothed in a cotton wrapper similar to that placed about her own person after her pre-dinner hip bath, was cowering next to a screen. Commanding her ladyship, who was now crying hysterically, to move aside, she strode over to the screen and looked behind it. "There is a hip bath here, still filled with water," she announced, pushing Albinia out of the way.

"I would remove her clothing first," Adam advised as Jonathan carefully deposited the maid in the bath. "You will want the water to reach as many of her burns as possible."

Jonathan shook her head. "No. Removing them may take off her skin."

"Why, Mr. Whyteman, you are also burnt!" Devorah exclaimed, espying his charred shirtsleeves.

"It is nothing," he said, dismissing his wounds. "If you will please to keep an eye on our patient and make sure that she does not drown—for she may pass out from her ordeal and you do not want her head sliding under the water—his grace and I will run to procure ice. I want to keep the water cool—not frigid, mind you, but cooler than it is now—and we will need to keep her in the bath for several hours until her skin cools down completely. Meanwhile, you may try to remove some of her outer clothing if you are able, but please make sure that you leave on any clothing that touches the skin."

Devorah turned back to the maid and, enlisting Felicity's help, set about removing as many of the charred upper garments as she could without inflicting additional pain. This was nearly impossible, as any little movement caused Martha to writhe in agony. Finally Devorah gave up and devoted herself to murmuring soothing phrases while blocking out Albinia's hysterics.

Mr. Duckwaithe, much shocked by the afternoon's events, determined that he could best help by calming Lady Albinia's overwrought nerves. "There, there, Lady Albinia. She is going to be all right," he said. But his efforts, rather than calming Albinia, only intensified her sobs.

"I don't know why *she's* crying," Felicity muttered viciously under her breath. "She's not the one nearly burnt to a crisp here. And she's done *nothing* to help."

After what seemed to be an eternity, Adam and Jonathan returned, accompanied by Robert and Mrs. Wigmore, and carrying a large wooden crate of ice. "What's she crying for?" Robert asked, jerking his chin in Albinia's direction. "*She* isn't hurt."

"She's been going on like this for nearly an hour," Felicity announced. "I never would have believed it if I hadn't been subjected to it personally."

"There, there. Lady Albinia has suffered a severe shock," Lucas remonstrated. "It is too much for one of her gentle breeding."

"Nonsense!" Jonathan answered, setting down his end of the crate and striding over to Albinia. "Quiet!" he ordered. "You, with your hysterics, are impeding the recovery of a severely injured person. Either dry your tears or please to remove yourself from this room immediately."

"How dare you?" asked Albinia, shocked out of her tears.

Mr. Whyteman turned to the Duchess's chaplain. "Mr. Duckwaithe, how would you like to earn your portion in the world to come within a single moment? You may do so by removing Lady Albinia from our orbit immediately."

Mr. Duckwaithe, divining from this that he and Albinia were very much *de trop*, cast about for a heavier robe to place over Albinia's thin wrapper. Mrs. Wigmore, who had been taking in the scene with arms akimbo, extracted a very ugly, brown-spotted dressing gown from a mahogany armoire, helped Albinia into it, and pushed her toward the door. "Here, my poor dear," she said with very little sympathy to match her words, "you run along with Mr. Duckwaithe. He will know what to do for you. I will just check how Martha here is going on, pop in on her grace to tell her what is afoot, and make arrangements for someone else to attend you until Martha is better." She paused and looked critically at Albinia. "Been curling your hair, have you? Managed to do only one

193

side before the accident? Well, I will tell her grace and Miss Tilstock about it and they will set all to rights."

Indeed, the astute Mrs. Wigmore had caught the nub of the matter. Albinia, noting with growing alarm how cozy Adam and Miss Asher had become over the past few days, had decided to curl and dress her hair à la Sappho in a desperate attempt to capture Adam's attention. Retiring to her room immediately after luncheon with the intent of devoting the entire afternoon to a beauty ritual that would have put Ahasuerus's harem to shame, she had taken an early bath, then subjected her mousy blond tresses to a vigorous brushing and the ministrations of Martha's curling tongs. All was well in train, with the locks on her right side already curled and ready to wind halfway around her head, when Martha's skirt caught a stray spark from the hearth as she was reheating the tongs. Within seconds the maid's clothing was aflame, and the Lady Albinia, whose domestic education did not include how to deal with life-threatening fires, launched into a series of screams whose intensity eclipsed those of the one who actually stood in mortal danger.

Her nerves had been overset; she doubted she would ever recover. By rights, her host should have applied himself immediately to calming her. But instead of doing so, he and that encroaching Mr. Whyteman had ignored her and devoted all their attention to Martha who, truth be known, had probably initiated that stirring little drama as payback for the slap Albinia had given her minutes earlier for singeing a lock of hair. The ploy had worked only too well. Mr. Whyteman had actually raked her—Albinia—down, and Adam was regarding Miss Asher—who had shoved her mercilessly aside—with warm approval. Even Felicity had realigned herself to Miss Asher's side.

Only the Duchess's dear chaplain understood the depth to which Albinia's sensibilities were lacerated. "Come, Lady Albinia," he said, gently taking her arm and escorting her to the very same Italian windows where his grace had conferred privately with Devorah about kitchen duties only days before.

194

Albinia was still sobbing quietly; thus it was that, after he took his seat beside her, it seemed only natural that he should place his arm around her and draw her closer so that she could have a good cry on his shoulder. It was a very masculine shoulder, Albinia noticed between tears.

Her sobs gradually faded away, but Lucas continued to hold her. "My dear Lady Albinia," he whispered in a voice that was unusually husky. He cleared his throat and searched his pockets with his free hand for a handkerchief. "Here, my lady. It is freshly washed."

Albinia, managing a watery smile, gratefully accepted the embroidered bit of muslin that the chaplain offered her and blotted her nose. "I am being a fool, I know. But it was horrible. Horrible! Martha was on fire! She could have set the entire room ablaze. I could have died!"

"Hush, it is over now." Despite the brave facade she always assumed, she was so delicate and defenseless, Lucas realized. She required protection from the harsher vicissitudes of life. An overwhelming feeling washed over him that he could be her gallant protector. Fighting his better instincts, he drew her a little closer.

Chapter 18

Several hours later, an extremely exhausted Devorah entrusted her patient to Mrs. Wigmore's care so that she could ready herself for dinner. By some miracle, Martha's burns weren't as severe as anticipated; and while the maid still moaned here and there in her sleep despite being heavily doused with laudanum, Mrs. Wigmore informed Devorah before sending her on her way that the cool water seemed to have done the trick and that no lasting scars should be anticipated.

"Though it will be weeks before her hands and legs are healed enough to do any work, and between having to find Lady Albinia a new lady's maid for the duration and having to explain to her grace just how it is that the counterpane that Queen Elizabeth herself slept under has been burnt to a crisp, I do not doubt that my nerves will be giving out long before Martha is back to her normal post!" the housekeeper declared.

She pulled back the light sheet covering Martha and studied the newly laundered gauze loosely wrapped around the worst of the maid's burns. "At any rate, there is a silver lining to all this," she continued. "Actually, two silver linings—and just maybe one more if we should be so blessed." Seeing Devorah's puzzlement, she hastened to enlighten her. "Is it not wonderful the way you and Mr. Whyteman knew exactly what to do to treat Martha's burns? I myself would have used a thick paste of whipped egg whites to keep the skin from blistering, but the cool water appears to work just as well; and, if Mr. Whyteman is to be believed, the egg whites could cause a putrid infection to set in, besides causing a big mess and being a waste of precious eggs. So, that is one silver lining. What with kitchen burns being a fact of life here at Ravenscourt—though heaven forbid usually not as serious as what befell Martha here—I will know for the next time exactly how to go on."

The housekeeper paused to wipe her perspiring brow with the edge of her apron before plunging into the second, and better, of the silver linings. "And Betsy, who I had no doubt would be totally at loose ends what with you kept busy upstairs with Martha, has distinguished herself beyond all expectations! Imagine. I thought tonight we would be serving only the *chaud-lent*, as Lord Robert calls it—though it looks to me just like a pot of peasant's pottage that has been kept cooking overnight. But Betsy has surprised us all and has prepared quite a number of dishes which she claims she learned at her mother's knee. It is not French food, which is just as well, because Lady Albinia has taken an aversion to all things French. But it is good, plain British cooking and plenty of it, with some herbs dredged over the top to make it fancy enough for her grace's table. Indeed, Betsy will do quite well until we find someone permanent to replace her."

Mrs. Wigmore seemed disinclined to reveal what the third possible silver lining might be, so Devorah turned to make her way to her room to freshen up. She was nearly out the door when Mrs. Wigmore laid a hand on her arm to halt her progress. "I am speaking out of turn, so please forgive me," the housekeeper whispered in her ear. "But it appears that this afternoon's near-tragedy has brought together two persons in this household for which it would be truly wonderful, besides preventing a great deal of annoyance for the rest of us, if they was to make a match of it. Of course, her ladyship still has his grace in her eye, and the match with the Duke has her grace's blessing. But, The Ways of the Lord are Mysterious, and it seems to me that if, by some miracle, we can bring about a match between those two instead, it will be a match made in heaven, as well as the answer to the entire household's prayers—her grace's excepted, of course."

Having exhausted her volubility, the housekeeper declined to elaborate further on this cryptic subject. Instead she apologized for her presumption and sped Miss Asher on her way, admonishing her to make herself more presentable before dinner was announced.

As it was, Devorah had just enough time to splash water on her face before Tilstock came in to dress her hair and help her into the same gown she wore her first evening at Ravenscourt. Nor was she afforded time to assimilate the afternoon's adventures or turn her thoughts toward the actions of the other dramatis personae. Of these, Mr. Whyteman figured most prominently, and Devorah was vaguely aware that her perception of him had subtly shifted after seeing him take charge of a situation that might otherwise have ended in tragedy. But dinner was called immediately upon her belated entrance to the Grand Drawing Room, and she had no time then or for the remainder of the evening to analyze just how her perception had changed.

Lady Albinia studiously ignored Devorah during dinner, affording Devorah some relief and the Duke much amusement. Indeed, the table that evening was divided on clearly delineated lines between two opposing factions: those who assisted in Martha's rescue or admired the heroic actions, and those who felt honor-bound to side with Lady Albinia. The latter was the smaller of the two camps and, besides Albinia herself, consisted of the Duchess, who hated Mr. Whyteman and anyone (Adam excepted) associated with him, and Lucas, who had discovered to his amazement that his infatuation with Miss Asher was rapidly undergoing a reversal. She was, he had realized with a startling clarity, quite a bold young woman and apt to make decisions that were better left to the hardier sex.

Conversation, quite naturally, was stilted until Robert had the happy idea of describing his descent into the kitchen quarters late in the day, whereupon he discovered young

Betsy, who had been a third maid until pressed into service as Devorah's handmaid, ominously waving a rolling pin as she lorded it over her small army of kitchen servants as a general born to command.

"And a pretty credible meal she's turned out, with none to guide her," he concluded. "Which just goes to show, when a challenge is placed in front of an ordinary person, no matter his walk in life, he—or she, as the case may be—is given the opportunity to rise to the challenge and show his true talents."

"But Betsy has been lording over the kitchen for the past three days, ever since Cook broke her leg," Felicity protested, grossly overlooking the fact that Robert, for perhaps the first time in his life, had uttered a profound statement.

"Yes, but—" Robert was brought up short. How was Felicity to know that Devorah's had been the guiding hand in the lower quarters the two previous days, and that Betsy's challenge had arisen only because Devorah was occupied upstairs with Martha?

"What Robert is referring to is Mrs. Wigmore's absence from the kitchen this afternoon due to events upstairs," Adam interjected smoothly, coming to his rescue. "Yesterday and the day before that, Betsy was able to rely on Mrs. Wigmore's guidance, both in terms of recipes and the best manner in which to present these dishes."

"An excellent dinner," the Duchess said, wiping her mouth and folding her linen napkin next to her plate. "The *chaud-lent* was especially tasty. I am happy, my dear Robert, that you insisted that I try it."

"Yes, despite having tasted it at Mr. Whyteman's, my initial reaction was that this is not a dish to grace a ducal table," the Duchess's chaplain chimed in. "But, the Duchess has led the way and, having pronounced her satisfaction, induced me to sample Ravenscourt's recipe for *chaud-lent*, as well. A most unusual dish, but one that I look forward to tasting frequently at table next winter."

★ ★

So exhausted was she by the time she was tucked into bed that night that Devorah dropped off to sleep almost as soon as her head hit the pillow. She awoke bright and early to what promised to be a beautiful spring day, and was not at all surprised to receive a missive from the Duke that the Duchess planned to pay a morning visit to Ardsleigh Manor. His grace would appreciate it if she would make up one of the party; to fail to do so, as an honored guest at Ravenscourt, would give rise to speculation such as he was certain she would wish to avoid.

By ten o'clock, Devorah was very prettily attired for the visit in a pale pink-and-white striped muslin dress patterned with sprigs and trailing flowers in a darker pink. However, she was soon to learn that the term "morning visit" was relative and that the visit was actually planned for closer to noon. Finding herself at loose ends, she headed for the library to see whether she could find anything interesting to read. The hall, with the exception of the unobtrusive presence of some upper servants, was quiet at that time of morning, and she would have been able to devote her uninterrupted attention to an unexceptionable novel, *Sense and Sensibility*, by An Unknown Lady—had she chosen to do so.

Instead, Devorah found herself preoccupied with her predicament and the cast of characters who shaped her life at Ravenscourt. Chief among these were the Duke and his tenant, Jonathan Whyteman. It was obvious that neither of these gentlemen believed her story of accidental time travel. No wonder. She herself had difficulty believing that she was actually living in the world of Jane Austen and Heyeresque heroes, instead of two centuries later in Boro Park. Fortunately, the Duke, for reasons of his own, had offered her his protection and the shelter of his home. This was no small gesture, Devorah realized. To be a woman alone and unknown in Regency England—and a foreigner, at that— would consign her under most circumstances to the harshest of fates.

Devorah had no illusions about the Duke's caprice. Altruistic he might be when it came to orphans, but her own position in his household was a different story. He would shelter her as long as it amused him and served his own purposes. But, if he became convinced that she had wormed her way into his household for nefarious purposes, he would cast her out onto the elements.

If the Duke cast her out, Jonathan Whyteman might rescue her—but to what end? Certainly, if she became *persona non grata* at Ravenscourt, Mr. Whyteman couldn't shelter her at Ten Oaks. But he might whisk her off to London or Manchester and deposit her on the Jewish community there, with the explanation that she had taken a serious fall, suffered a concussion, and was now suffering from all kinds of delusions. Then, who knew what her fate would be? Would some altruistic community member offer her a position as a servant, or would she be doomed to become an indigent member of the community, believed to be crazed and living off charity?

It was, strangely enough, a small step from contemplating this gruesome possibility to thinking of Jonathan Whyteman himself. Devorah was coming to appreciate him more every day. Much could be forgiven a man who had actually ordered Albinia to be quiet! Also, one had to admit that his quick thinking and actions had eclipsed the Duke's. Mr. Whyteman had assumed command and saved the day; despite having ruined the Duchess's heirloom bedcover, he was the hero of the entire saga rather than his grace, who had stood by ineffectively, holding an empty basin of water.

Devorah was given little time to consider the matter further, as Spilsby came to announce that the assembled company were waiting for her so that they could set out in good time for Ardsleigh Manor. With the addition of Felicity and Devorah to the party, this consisted of two carriages instead of only the one used on that fateful day a week and a half before when Devorah was discovered by the side of the road. Had it really been so long ago?

Fortunately, the Duchess and her chaplain occupied the ancient traveling coach, while Robert tooled Felicity, Albinia and Devorah in the barouche, leaving the Duke to escort the party on his mount at his own leisure. The day being particularly fine and sunny, Lady Albinia insisted on sitting under the hood with Felicity to protect her complexion, leaving Devorah to sit backward. But Devorah didn't mind. She was seldom travel sick and welcomed the sun on her face; she also enjoyed the green vistas that the open seat afforded her.

Lady Albinia, still smarting from the events of the previous day, felt that she had a score to settle with Devorah and pointedly excluded her from the conversation. This, however, was a tactical error. The incident of the fire was, apparently, a pivotal moment for many of the inhabitants at Ravenscourt due to Lady Albinia's unthinkable behavior throughout. The Duchess and Mr. Duckwaithe might attribute Albinia's hysterics to heightened sensibilities due to her exalted social station, but everyone else—from Robert and Felicity to Spilsby and Mrs. Wigmore, on down the line—attributed it to just plain, ordinary self-centeredness and a callous disregard for life or limb of anyone from the lower classes. Martha could have burnt to death for all Lady Albinia cared, and all her ladyship would have done was bemoan the charred odor that lingered in her bedchamber and the need to find a new lady's maid. Thus, unbeknown to Albinia, Miss Asher's star was again rising in Lady Felicity's orbit due to her quick thinking and willingness to assist in saving the maid.

Besides, Felicity had watched Devorah closely and had detected no lover-like looks between her and Mr. Whyteman. Even though she remained wary that Devorah was her rival for Mr. Whyteman's affections, she decided for the meantime to give Miss Asher the benefit of the doubt and, having a dozen of her own scores to pay off with Albinia, ranged herself on Devorah's side for the duration of the drive by maliciously rehashing the stirring events in Albinia's room and recalling Jonathan's and Devorah's heroic actions.

"And what's interesting," Lady Felicity commented to Devorah, seated opposite, "is that you seemed to know *exactly* what Mr. Whyteman intended to do."

Devorah cast around for a credible response. "Mr. Whyteman and I appear to have read the same scholarly article on the latest treatment of severe burns," she answered lamely, knowing full well that Lady Felicity wasn't in the least interested in scholarly reports.

"I, for one, do not believe for a *minute* that cool water is efficacious in healing burns," Albinia chimed in. "At Feldenham, we use a salve whose receipt has been handed down for centuries. My own dear mother and her housekeeper have been quite satisfied with it. While I am a great believer in modern medicine and in reading scholarly articles, one cannot be too careful with experimental treatments. Besides, it is not for us mere females to experiment."

Both Lady Felicity and Devorah chose to ignore these comments. Instead, Felicity pointed out a particularly fine copse of trees that signaled the approach to Ardsleigh Manor. "Their gardens are famous," she commented. "While Ardsleigh Manor is a relatively small estate by today's standards, the Ardsleighs are one of our oldest families. The previous baron was an avid gardener, and he, like my grandfather, the fourth duke, enlisted Capability Brown to design the landscape at Ardsleigh."

"Mr. Brown's contribution to the English garden has been reassessed since his death," pronounced Albinia, not to be outdone. "While Mr. Walpole allowed him to be 'a very able master,' many of those who understand gardening now consider his work but a feeble imitation of nature."

"Well," Devorah said, peering out the side of the carriage to better glimpse the prospect as they made their way up a lane bordered by low shrubbery to Ardsleigh Manor, "I am most impressed. I find your English landscapes to be quite beautiful, and I have heard a great deal about Capability Brown. If this is another example of his work, *I* would label him a genius."

The carriage rounded a bend in the lane, and a stately Elizabethan mansion faced in mellow Bath stone and lined with tall, mullioned windows came into view. A few minutes later, Robert reined in before a set of broad, shallow steps and sprang down from the box. A tall butler in livery threw open the manor doors and bowed in the Duchess and Lucas, who had arrived a few moments before, with a stateliness that made Ravenscourt's own Spilsby pale by comparison. "Forgot to tell you, the Ardsleighs like pomp. Lots of it," Robert whispered to Devorah as he offered her a hand to alight from the barouche. "That's why my mother and Lady Ardsleigh are such bosom bows. They're mutually stiff-rumped."

Declining Robert's support, Devorah grabbed ahold of the side of the carriage and jumped down to the graveled drive, wrenching her ankle in the process. "It is nothing," she told Robert, waving away his help and hobbling up the shallow stairs.

Cressida Ardsleigh, a very pretty blond in the classic peaches-and-cream mold, and Felicity fell into each other's arms upon the visitors entering the manor. Proper introductions were made and, after a suitable pause, Miss Ardsleigh invited Felicity and Miss Asher upstairs to see the wardrobe she was assembling for her launch into society. "For, one thing I must say about Mother," the eldest Ardsleigh daughter told Felicity as she escorted her up an ornately carved staircase while Devorah limped behind, "she has the most excellent taste. Imagine, she discovered this French modiste who was practically starving in some garret up in Glasgow, of all places, and has brought her home with us and installed her here at Ardsleigh until we go up to London after our dinner party on Monday next. She means to take Giselle with us, as my wardrobe isn't *nearly* complete, though she has only a few finishing touches to put on the gown I am to wear to be presented at court. Of course, once we get to London I still have to be outfitted with shoes and hats and *dozens* of other things that can't be got here in the countryside. Which reminds me, Felicity—I positively *adore* the slippers you are wearing."

Felicity lifted her skirts and peered down at her red morocco leather slippers with their ruby-beaded bows. "Aren't these wonderful?" she asked. "I purchased them just before leaving London."

Cressida's first stop was a large, oak-paneled guest chamber that had been converted into Giselle's workroom for the duration. While the ornate furniture, cheval glass and velvet curtains remained in what, apparently, had once been a beautiful room, the interior was otherwise stripped of ornamentation. Dresses were piled everywhere on the high, linen-draped bed and brocaded love seat, and a large, scarred oak worktable had been set up in one corner. In another corner, a dressmaker's dummy displayed the court dress in its full glory. Truly, Devorah thought, she was looking at a gown fitting for a fairy princess. Cut in the high-waisted empire fashion, with a low neck and short sleeves, the gown was made of sheer white gauze over an ivory satin underdress, with an ivory satin train. The voluminous skirt, so cut to accommodate the hoops required at court, was edged in an intricate design of pearl beading.

Both Felicity and Devorah displayed suitable raptures over the court dress and the procession of morning dresses, walking dresses, evening dresses, spencers, wraps, redingotes and tippets that Cressida displayed for them. "Look at this material," she said, picking up an especially elegant evening gown of white muslin with a jonquil underdress. The muslin was shot through with gold and silver threads that shimmered in the sunlight shining through two large windows. "This is from a sari that my Uncle Henry brought back from India for Mother years ago. He is her youngest brother, you know, and he was sent there after Eton in the hope that it would settle him down. We found the sari and all kinds of wonderful fabrics and old gowns packed away in trunks. Just *begging* to be used, Mother said!"

Additional suitable raptures were uttered, then Cressida bade Felicity and Miss Asher to come to her room for a coze.

"Should we ask Lady Albinia?" Felicity ventured doubtfully.

"Of course not!" was her hostess's instant reply. "The whole idea of visiting up here is to get away from Albinia—and our mothers, of course."

Recognizing the wisdom of Miss Ardsleigh's reasoning, her guests followed her into a cavernous room draped in pink and white and papered in a matching stripe, the entire effect of which set off Cressida's English beauty to perfection. Cressida offered them comfortable seats in chintz-covered chairs flanking the fireplace and reposed herself on her enormous bed's embroidered silk counterpane. All was in train for an animated discussion regarding Miss Ardsleigh's upcoming season, which was to commence immediately upon their arriving in London—that was, of course, if Lady Glenbuck didn't released her tenuous hold on life before then—when a knock on the door interrupted Felicity's reminiscences about her first waltz during her first season the previous year. In response to Cressida's command to enter, the door opened to admit Albinia.

"I hope I am not intruding," she said, as she looked around for an unoccupied chair. Finding none, she perched herself on the edge of Cressida's bed.

"Well, you are, Albinia," Felicity said crossly. "I don't see why you can't stay downstairs with Mother and Mr. Duckwaithe."

"Dear Mr. Duckwaithe has gone off with Lord Robert and the Duke to view some improvements Sir William made recently to the north side of the estate. And the Duchess, who is tired from the ride, and Lady Ardsleigh, who is worn down from planning Cressida's come-out while worrying at the same time about her mother's ill health, have decided to take a brief rest. And I, therefore, am free to join you in your comfortable little gossip!" Albinia explained triumphantly.

Ignoring Albinia, Felicity continued her description of her first waltz, the refreshments offered at Almack's, and the general delightfulness of an evening spent in that London social club's hallowed halls.

"I myself am not a supporter of the waltz. In this I share the view of my dear mother, who has pronounced such close dancing by couples to be indecent," Albinia interjected.

"Ah, but the waltz is a most beautiful dance!" Cressida protested vigorously, clapping her hands together. "Such synchronization is required, such a meeting of the minds as to when to turn, and in which direction, and when to continue forward. In preparation for my season, Mother hired a dancing master to teach the waltz when last we were in London, and I attended a few morning parties with my friends, here and there, so that we could practice in the privacy of our homes. Truly, I have never seen anything so delightful as a well-synchronized couple who move in perfect unison to the music."

"Do you waltz, Miss Asher?" Lady Felicity asked suddenly, turning to her guest.

Taken by surprise, Devorah repeated the question aloud. "No, I don't waltz," she answered after a few moments' pause. "I am more partial to other types of ... to folk dances."

"A pity. My brother Adam doesn't like to waltz, either. Nor does he like any other form of dancing. They dislike him immensely, I am sure, at Almack's."

"Your brother, the Duke, distinguishes himself such that I am sure any hostess may welcome him into her social circle," Lady Albinia objected.

"I see that your ankle is paining you, Miss Asher," Lady Felicity said, steering the conversation in a different direction. "Did you wrench it badly? You must ask Mrs. Wigmore for some ice for it when we return to Ravenscourt." She proceeded to launch into a description of the previous day's drama and Miss Asher's own supporting role in it. "And after such heroic actions—it is so anticlimactic that she should twist her ankle getting down from the carriage, when she escaped all injury—not even scorched sleeves—while saving Martha."

"I did not save Martha," Devorah corrected her. "Mr. Whyteman saved Martha with his quick thinking. All I did was place her in cool water. How fortunate, Lady Albinia, that you still had a full hip bath sitting behind that screen." But it was clear from the look Lady Albinia shot Miss Asher that she didn't think it at all fortunate. Devorah, cowed for the moment, lapsed into silence and spent the rest of the visit contemplating how she could turn a twisted ankle to good account.

It was only after she returned to Ravenscourt, however, that an idea regarding her ankle burst upon her in full brilliance.

Later that afternoon, she hobbled down to the library at his grace's summons and discovered the Duke and Mr. Whyteman in close conference regarding how to handle the upcoming Sabbath. "Mr. Whyteman will be sending over cold provisions so that you won't starve, but we are trying to find an excuse for you to keep to your room until Monday morning," the Duke said. Observing her puzzled look, he reminded her that while the Duchess was fairly liberal regarding participation in evening prayers in her private chapel, she was a stickler for attendance at chapel on Sunday mornings. "She also frowns on Sabbath travel, which is why I didn't bring you back to Ravenscourt on Sunday, and both luncheon and dinner are a cold, dismal affair. So even though I know you must stay isolated from the rest of us on Saturday so that you can properly observe *your* Sabbath, you must also stay out of my mother's sight through Sunday so that you don't observe *our* Sabbath."

At that moment, Devorah involuntarily shifted her weight to her twisted right ankle, bringing on a twinge of pain. It was then that her brilliant idea was born. "I know!" she

208

exclaimed. "As Felicity and Robert are both aware, I twisted my ankle jumping down from the carriage at Ardsleigh Manor earlier today. Even they know it is difficult for me to walk on it. I think it can become much worse."

"And because you find it difficult to walk up and down the stairs, you are confined to your room for the next few days until your ankle is better," Mr. Whyteman continued. "And, because it has become extremely swollen, you must keep it raised. Excellent! Even our esteemed Duke here, famous for his subterfuge, couldn't have come up with a better excuse."

Chapter 19

Staying in her room over the Sabbath and the following day was much easier than Devorah had anticipated. By the time she hobbled back upstairs following her interview with his grace and Mr. Whyteman, her ankle was seriously throbbing and starting to swell—so much so that she sent her new maid, Lucy, off in search of ice and some sort of bandage. The unintended result was that Mrs. Wigmore herself—who had privately sworn eternal gratitude to Devorah for services rendered to the household staff—came to inspect Devorah's ankle and promptly ordered her to rest comfortably in her room, with an ice pack on her ankle and a pillow to elevate it, for the next few days. All her meals would be brought to her, which would be no problem at all considering that Devorah ate nothing but fresh fruit and water, the housekeeper declared.

"And," Mrs. Wigmore continued, pausing to adjust her mob cap, "there is no need for you to be worrying yourself about the kitchens ever again. Betsy has proved herself more than capable to manage things until a substitute cook is found"

Fortunately, Mrs. Fenton had sent over both a prayer book and Book of Psalms from Ten Oaks, along with such miscellaneous provisions as a knife, fresh lemons and another small package of fine sugar. Once Lucy placed the kettle on the hob and steeped a pot of tea, Devorah found herself very well satisfied. She had, besides the tea and lemons for fresh lemonade, ample food provided by Mrs. Fenton and two novels that she had brought up the day before from the library, and the Duke had thoughtfully sent up a number of candles and a tinder box, along with instructions that Lucy should take care to keep Devorah's chamber well lit. Devorah's Sabbath vacation was assured.

When Felicity came to visit later that evening instead of joining the family in the Burgundy Drawing Room, she found Miss Asher propped up in bed, several pillows at her back, reading *The Mysteries of Udolpho*. For someone unused to literature of the late eighteenth century, Mrs. Radcliffe's Gothic novel, which had been spared the same fiery fate as that other popular work, *The Italian*, was best read at intervals rather than in a single effort, and its novelty was beginning to wane. Devorah, therefore, welcomed her visitor gladly, gestured toward the plush armchair by the window and bade her to pull up a seat and make herself comfortable so that they could enjoy a little chat.

Felicity's visit was not entirely altruistic. Two opposing sentiments still warred in her breast. On the one hand, she was drawn to Miss Asher and would much prefer to see her, rather than the Lady Albinia, married to Adam. Whereas Duchess Albinia would be insufferable, Duchess Devorah had a decidedly better ring. On the other hand, signs continued to point toward a growing interest between Miss Asher and Mr. Whyteman. Certainly, they had spent a great deal of time closeted together in the library, today being no exception, and Adam seemed to be positively encouraging it.

In keeping with the ostensible purpose of her visit, Lady Felicity asked all that was proper about Devorah's ankle before deftly steering the conversation in a direction intended to discover the general gist of Devorah's feelings. Didn't Miss Asher think the Duke all that was most desirable in a match? Such looks—such address—such intelligence. Coupled with his title and his fortune, why, he could have his pick of any of the eligible young ladies of England, his younger sister declared. Yet, for some unfathomable reason, none had as yet to catch his fancy.

211

As Devorah must know by now, Lady Albinia—who had arrived at Ravenscourt not so long before Miss Asher herself—was hopeful that she would be the lucky winner of the Duke's hand. The Duchess, as Albinia's godmother, had also set her sights on the match, Felicity continued, but she had good reason to believe that both their hopes were in vain. Instead, Adam seemed to be somewhat taken with Miss Asher herself. Why, hadn't Miss Asher—and might Lady Felicity call her Devorah?—noticed his attentions toward her?

"His grace's attentions toward me are not serious in the least," Devorah hastened to inform Felicity. "He is merely having some fun at my—and, possibly, others'—expense."

"But my dear Miss Asher—Devorah, I mean. Could you not find it in your heart to love my brother?" Felicity countered, her green eyes wide with disbelief.

"Your brother—his grace—and I are totally unsuited in both background and disposition. He knows that I know it, too. And knowing that I am not in the least danger of losing my heart to him, he continues his flirtation, which succeeds in rousing various responses he thinks amusing in other members of the house party."

"You mean that he flirts with you to *spite* Albinia? And my mother?" Lady Felicity clapped her small, elegant hands in glee. "How totally amusing. I will have to make a point of watching when next you two are together, to see how Albinia and Mother react." But, having ascertained Miss Asher's true sentiments toward her brother, she now probed the state of the invalid's feelings toward one less near, but more dear to her heart. "And Mr. Whyteman, my brother's tenant. What of him?" she asked, trembling inwardly. "He seems to be paying you an undue amount of attention. Is he a more suitable match for you? Could you find it in your heart to love him, instead?"

Devorah, who had watched Lady Felicity's eager attempts to earn Mr. Whyteman's attention and the warm looks that damsel cast his way when she thought she was unobserved,

212

knew that she must answer carefully. "My dear Lady Felicity," she answered lightly. "While Mr. Whyteman appears to have many excellent qualities and, I am sure, would make some lucky woman an excellent spouse, I am more interested in returning to my own home as soon as possible than I am in finding a spouse."

The answer appeared to be straightforward, but Felicity felt instinctively that Devorah was being evasive. Even so, she very much preferred to be allied with Miss Asher, rather than with the odious Albinia, who seemed to hate Devorah with a passion. Therefore, against her better instincts, she accepted Devorah's answer at face value. "And when you succeed in attaining that goal, you will have left a string of broken hearts behind," she teased with a nervous laugh. "Why, even Mr. Duckwaithe seems to be taken with you. And Robert, who never seems to even notice women, is forever praising your *chaud-lent.*"

"Mr. Duckwaithe was taken with my biblical knowledge," Devorah retorted. "If my observations are correct, he has since determined correctly that *that* match would never do. Is it not a shame, though, that he is not higher up in the nobility? In my opinion, he and Lady Albinia are perfect for one another, and they are not exactly indifferent to one another, either."

Felicity mentally chided herself on her blindness and stupidity. But of course! Albinia and Lucas would be perfect together. "Mr. Duckwaithe's lineage is excellent," she said slowly, mentally exploring various ideas for bringing two such equally tiresome individuals together for eternity. "His grandfather is a viscount, which is almost as good as an earl, and his mother is the daughter of a baron, so his blood is blue enough. But he himself is without possibilities. His father is the younger of the two brothers, you see. And, even if his father stood in line to inherit directly, there is Lucas's older brother, Harold, to consider. It's impossible, unless there is a miracle. Albinia would never marry someone who wasn't next in line to the peerage."

"Well then, we will just have to pray for a miracle," Devorah advised her visitor.

★ ★

Lady Felicity paid Devorah another visit the following morning and confided that she had included a special supplication for Mr. Duckwaithe in her evening prayers. "I hope I am not so unfeeling as to wish his family members dead, but it would be quite wonderful if a miracle did indeed happen and Lucas acquired the viscountcy. It would solve *all* our problems."

Robert also came to visit, bringing Theo with him. "Normally, I would not visit a lady's bedchamber," he explained. "But Theo insisted on seeing you, and *someone* must keep this youngster in check."

Theo grinned hugely and held out a misshapen, painted object that he had been hiding behind his back. "For you. I made it at Ten Oaks."

Devorah picked up the unidentifiable object and examined it. "Thank you so much, Theo. It's beautiful, but what is it?"

"It's a papier-mâché vase with wire and felt flowers. See, these are roses. And if you will notice, I painted the vase to match the color of your chamber."

Upon closer inspection, Devorah had to admit that the creation did indeed resemble some type of modernistic rose vase. She thanked Theo properly and suggested he put his gift on the mantel where she could better view it.

"Mrs. Fenton and Fanny would like you to come visit once your ankle is more the thing," Theo told Devorah. "And maybe you can explain to me why I am not allowed to go to Ten Oaks until Monday morning. It's boring here. At Ten Oaks, Isaac lets me hang around the stables when I am not having my lessons. And Mrs. Fenton doesn't mind if I make messes with my papier-mâché and my paints. Here at Ravenscourt, when I am kept inside, Aunt Augusta and Albinia keep telling me to quit fidgeting all the time, and if I spend time outdoors or with John Coachman or Jim Groom

214

in the stables, everyone from Spilsby down starts complaining, and then Aunt Augusta herself chimes in and starts complaining about how she is nursing a viper in her midst and wishes that my parents would hurry back from the Continent."

"Oh, you have totally mistaken the matter, Mr. Theodore," Robert said, clapping him on the back. "Jim Groom has had it in for you ever since you took Adam's new gray out for a ride without so much as a *by your leave*. As for my mother, she was merely taken aback for a moment when Lucas informed her that you had poured glue on his chair before your history lesson, which prevented him from getting up to whack you one when you got out of hand."

"That," Theo announced, "was Strategy. I had to do something to change the educational situation. Mr. Duckwaithe is a total bore. *You* try learning history from him. Besides, half the time he doesn't know what he's talking about."

"Well, yes, you have something there," Robert admitted. "Despite Mr. Whyteman's agreement to tutor Theo, Lucas has taken it upon himself to teach him our great British history. A challenging task, indeed, as our young genius here has learned history from the crib, so to speak," he explained to Miss Asher. "Theo's father, Sir Martin Allenby, is not only a senior member of the Foreign Office but also a noted expert on medieval and modern British history."

"You are forgetting my mother, Cousin Robert."

Robert cleared his throat with embarrassment. "Ah, yes. The Lady Desdemona is a bluestocking."

"Not a bluestocking. An intellectual and a feminist," Theo corrected him. "She is a great admirer of the teachings of Mary Wollstonecraft, who advocates for the education of women. My mother, who was carefully educated by my grandfather, Lord Pemstroke, has made European history her special area of expertise, and she has passed much of her knowledge on to me."

Devorah laughed. "Just how old are you Theo? Ten, or twenty? You are quite precocious for your age."

This elicited another huge grin from Theo, who launched into a detailed description of some of his more notable exploits at Ravenscourt. Eyes twinkling, he took great pains to explain to Miss Asher why many of those exploits could be considered in the realm of educational experiments instead of mere childhood pranks. "Why, even Sir Isaac Newton himself would have been blamed for tossing food about had Aunt Augusta been there when he performed his famous apple experiment."

"Clearly, only Mr. Whyteman has the mental capacity and the patience to handle him, which is why Monday morning can't come soon enough," Robert declared, grabbing Theo by the shirt sleeve and pulling him toward the door. "Come, young genius. You are starting to tire Miss Asher."

Still laughing, Devorah turned back to *The Mysteries of Udolpho,* which promised to keep her occupied for some time. The remainder of the day was uneventful, punctuated only by visits from Mrs. Wigmore and Betsy, both of whom managed to take time away from their duties to inquire after her ankle and report on Martha's progress. Albinia's lady's maid was still nursing her burns, which fortunately appeared be healing nicely, and the housekeeper would not allow her to return to her post quite so quickly.

In fact, Mrs. Wigmore so far forgot herself as to hint darkly to Miss Asher that, come what may, she would do her utmost to make sure that Martha remain at the much more benevolent Ravenscourt when Lady Albinia returned to her ancestral pile. "It may be what they countenance at Feldenham, for all I know, but here at Ravenscourt we treat our servants differently," she declared stoutly, her chest heaving with emotion. "It would not have made a mite of difference to her ladyship if poor Martha had been burnt to a crisp. And I will tell you something else. If her ladyship establishes herself as duchess here, which she has been designing to do ever since who knows when, that is when *I* give notice!"

Betsy, who still stood in awe of Devorah, was more circumspect. "Martha says she will never return to serving Lady Albinia. Never! Never! Mrs. Wigmore has sent to Bath for the agency there to supply her with a new lady's maid and, in the meantime, is keeping Martha abed," she confided in a whisper. "Martha is not to get up until Lady Albinia is gone."

"What does her grace have to say to all of this?" Devorah couldn't resist asking.

Betsy repressed a snort. "Her grace no longer takes a great interest in the domestic goings-on here at Ravenscourt—with the exception of Miss Tilstock, that is. It is the Duke himself what deals with Mrs. Wigmore."

Night fell quickly and was unrelieved by any additional visitors. Felicity did not return to visit until late morning on Sunday, when she announced that she had attended chapel *willingly* and had prayed and prayed for a miracle. "Because, if *you* aren't interested in Adam, then a different miracle is needed to save him from Albinia. And, for Binny to attach herself to Lucas instead, of course."

Devorah, who since her arrival at Ravenscourt had failed to observe his grace treat the Lady Albinia with anything but thinly concealed contempt, did not understand the source of Felicity's—or anyone else's—anxieties. Even so, she felt it incumbent upon herself to reassure Felicity on that head, and therefore repeated what she had already told Robert. "I would not worry about your brother. He seems perfectly able to watch out for his own interests."

Felicity felt anything but reassured, and said she would continue praying for a miracle. "Do *you* believe in miracles, Devorah?"

"Yes. But, even though in this case I don't think you need to worry that only a miracle can save his grace, in general I was taught not to rely on them."

217

Chapter 20

Devorah's ankle was well enough the following morning to allow her to go downstairs. She was enjoying a solitary breakfast of apples and the special soda biscuits with which Mrs. Fenton kept Ravenscourt generously supplied when Felicity burst into the breakfast parlor.

"The miracle! It has happened!" Felicity announced excitedly. Abandoning all inhibition, she began dancing happily around the breakfast table, clapping her hands together and giggling in unholy glee.

It was fortunate, Devorah reflected, that the Duchess was not present to witness the spectacle of Felicity's hoydenish behavior. "Lady Albinia has returned home?" she asked.

"No, no, something much, much better. You won't believe!"

"Be careful, then," Devorah advised. "Lady Albinia has yet to make an appearance. Think of the consequences were she to find you dancing around in circles."

"Really, Miss Asher. You are quite lowering today," Felicity accused her, sinking into a nearby chair. "Just when I have come to believe in chapel and prayers, too."

"Do my instincts tell me that this miracle has something to do with Mr. Duckwaithe then?"

"He is gone," Felicity said. "Posted north this morning to the family seat in Yorkshire to—to officiate at a *funeral*. At several funerals!"

Devorah's interest was finally piqued. She set down the soda biscuit that had been en route to her mouth and looked at Felicity in amazement. "Are you actually telling me that Mr. Duckwaithe is now heir to the viscountcy?"

"Better than that. He *is* the viscount. The most awful thing occurred, and while I dislike having it on my conscience and will have pangs of guilt for years to come, I can't help but feel it is the answer to my prayers. The miracle has happened! Food poisoning. Poisoned mushrooms. All of them."

"Why, Felicity, that's horrible. You say that he has lost his entire family? Poor, poor Mr. Duckwaithe."

"It is not as bad as you think. There is still Lucas's mother, who didn't eat the mushrooms, and his sister, Lady Eagleston, who wasn't even there. And besides, Lord Arkless, his grandfather, was a terrible old man, so nobody will miss *him*. Lucas hated him, though he was always too depressingly Christian to do more than sigh whenever Lord Arkless's name came up in conversation. But Lucas's father and uncle were visiting Hasborough Hall, along with his brother Harold and cousin Vincent, who was second in line to the viscountcy. It seems that Lord Arkless had requested everyone's presence for some great announcement, but Lucas begged off, pleading important matters here at Ravenscourt. I should tell you now that Lucas never got along with any of the Duckwaithes, except for his mother and sister. The family were never known for being amiable."

At that moment, Lady Albinia, dressed all in flowing white with a dove gray shawl trailing over her shoulder, entered the breakfast parlor. It was clear from her pallid complexion and reddened eyes, and from the much-used cambric handkerchief she was holding, that she was greatly affected by Mr. Duckwaithe's tragedy. "Have you heard the news?" she asked in a whisper. "So terrible. So pointless. Lord Arkless was such an esteemed person. He will be sadly missed by his peers." She gathered up her skirts and settled herself in a chair opposite Devorah's, assuming the pose of a tragic muse. "The Duchess succumbed to shock when the message arrived for Mr. Duckwaithe. She is even now laid up in her bed with palpitations."

Carefully schooling her face into utter blankness, Felicity offered to pass Albinia the tea pot and informed her that the toast was already cold.

Albinia waved her away. "No, nothing for me. I drank my morning tea in bed. And even if I had not, I could not now. Not when poor dear Mr. Duckwaithe is on his way to Yorkshire to officiate at the funerals of so many of his loved ones. Such a loss for Mr. Duckwaithe. *Such* a loss for England."

News of Mr. Duckwaithe's tragic trajectory into the peerage dominated the ladies' morning conversation in the Green Room. But it was not the only stirring news delivered to Ravenscourt that day. At luncheon, the Duke announced that Mr. Coke of Norfolk, whose visit to Ravenscourt was planned for the following day, had cancelled unexpectedly due to pressing estate matters. This, too, was much discussed when the ladies adjourned again to the Green Room following the cold repast.

"And, as he is the greatest gentleman farmer in England, I am sure that he would not have cancelled for just any reason," Felicity explained, looking up from the small needlepoint canvas she had started to work. "Adam says that he will have to go to Norfolk, instead, to ask Mr. Coke's advice about some of his crops."

"It is just as well, as it would not be fitting for Ravenscourt to be entertaining any visitors at present, considering that its chaplain has suffered a tragedy," Lady Albinia commented, deftly applying her own needle to a huge canvas printed with a hunting scene of hideous design. "Still, I truly feel for the Duke, to be required to trot off to Norfolk on farming business, of all things, when he is already totally consumed by the duties incumbent on his station here at Ravenscourt."

"Oh, don't feel bad for *him*. Adam is in his element. He loves farming. Oh drat! I've only just started, and already I've tangled up my stitches."

"Here, would you like me to help you sort it out?" Devorah offered. "I have become somewhat of an expert in this with my mother's own needlepoint."

"You needlepoint, Miss Asher?" Lady Albinia asked, a hint of accusation in her tone.

"A little, but not so well as yourself," Devorah replied, putting on her best false smile. "Your stitches are lovely. I could never aspire to such work."

Albinia's sunken chest puffed out a little. "Thank you. The Duchess has asked me to execute this new cover for the footrest in the Duke's study, now that I've finished the altar cloth. She has been meaning to replace the original brocade this age."

"It looks to be quite an undertaking. How long do you estimate it will take?"

"I expect the Duke to be able to enjoy his refurbished footrest before my visit is ended," Albinia said, coloring a little. "The present cover is *sadly* torn and the stuffing beneath it is starting to come out. It is my dear hope that by applying my modest talents with the needle, the Duke will be made somewhat more comfortable."

The afternoon passed pleasantly enough, with the daughter of the house and the noble visitor applying themselves vigorously to their needlework, while Miss Asher plowed her way through *The Mysteries of Udolpho* and untangled Lady Felicity's knots. Occasionally Devorah was called upon by one of the two needlewomen to select the better shade of two silks, and so unerring was her eye for color that even Lady Albinia was brought to exclaim that it was a waste that Miss Asher did not have some needlework of her own to execute.

"I know just the very thing!" Lady Felicity said, setting aside her canvas and excusing herself. She returned some quarter of an hour later pregnant with news, creating a welcome diversion from the awkward silence that settled between Lady Albinia and Miss Asher after she left.

"Mrs. Wigmore says that a new cook has been found for the London townhouse!" she announced with some excitement. "A French chef, in fact. And he has agreed to take up temporary residence here at Ravenscourt until Cook is back on her feet. He arrives tomorrow."

"A French chef! My dear godmama must be in raptures."

"Yes, or she would be if she weren't still so prostrate over the tragedy at Hasborough Hall. His name is Pierre or something French like that. Mrs. Wigmore says he has served years at Lord Alberstone's. But, owing to a disagreement with Lady Alberstone, he has given immediate notice and was snapped up by Adam's man of business."

Lady Albinia set down her needlework and gave a clap of delight. "Oh, if it is indeed the Alberstones' chef, he is famous for his sauces and veal dishes. Melville House's dinners will become the envy of all."

"There is More." Felicity paused for dramatic effect. "Adam has ordered a closed stove for both Melville House *and* Ravenscourt, and the one for Ravenscourt is arriving here tomorrow."

"Ravenscourt will be the envy of the neighborhood," Albinia said approvingly. "Even Ardsleigh Manor, which is known to have every modern convenience, cannot boast a closed stove."

Felicity nodded. "Exactly. Mother has *finally* one-upped Lady Ardsleigh. Won't *she* be all put out when she hears about the stove. Which reminds me, we are *not* going to dine at Ardsleigh Manor this evening. Mother says it is not proper for us to be indulging ourselves when her beloved chaplain has been plunged into deep mourning. Adam says it's just as well because there is no moon and getting back would be difficult.

"To think, I never thought I would *ever* be grateful to Lucas for anything, even if Cressida Ardsleigh *is* one of my oldest friends and I will miss her dearly when she goes off to

London tomorrow. But the thought of spending an entire evening in the company of Lady Ardsleigh herself was just too ominous to contemplate."

"No, it would not do for us to make up the better part of a dinner party under the circumstances," Albinia concurred, ignoring the latter part of Felicity's speech. "I wonder, would it be proper for us to put on black gloves in sympathy with Mr. Duckwaithe? As Ravenscourt's chaplain, he has become so very much part of your family over the years and has helped set the tone that I find so very elevating here at Ravenscourt."

Felicity rolled her eyes in Devorah's direction. But then she remembered that she had left the Green Room with the express purpose of bringing Miss Asher a small, painted canvas to work, with the intention of creating an elegant reticule. This she still held in her hand, and she offered it to Devorah, asking whether their American visitor knew the skill of petit point.

Devorah, whose Belgian and British grandmothers had both brought this skill over with them to America and had made sure that all their granddaughters were notable needlewomen, answered in the affirmative, but claimed that her needlework skills in general were very rusty. Thus the ladies subsided again into a cozy rhythm that kept them occupied for the better part of the next hour.

The time to dress for dinner drew near. Felicity was putting away her silks in preparation for going upstairs when Spilsby knocked and announced that Lady Ardsleigh was waiting in the Burgundy Drawing Room. Picking up her skirts, Felicity went off to greet her mother's bosom bow, with Lady Albinia following close behind. Devorah shrugged and set her own needlework aside. As she made her solitary way past the Burgundy Drawing Room toward the grand staircase, Lady Ardsleigh's shrill accents floated out to her, demanding that she be taken up to the Duchess's bedchamber immediately. "My dear Felicity, I *had* to come, to lend your mother my support, and I hope I am not to be put off by a surfeit of hartshorn and burnt feathers. So tragic, so shocking! Dear Augusta will now need to find a new chaplain."

Chapter 21

Robert was the first to witness the entrance upon the scene of Miss Chilvers and her brother.

Seeking respite after a long evening spent in the funereal company of the Duchess and Lady Albinia—an evening whose dispirited tone was encouraged, even amplified, by the presence of Lady Ardsleigh, who had stayed to dine now that her own dinner party was cancelled—he rose at a reasonable hour the following day, saddled his favorite mount and set off down the lane in the direction of Ravenscourt's main gates. It was a fine spring morning, with just the hint of a playful breeze in the air and cottony-white clouds contrasting vividly with the brilliant blue sky, and Robert was anticipating an enjoyable run across Gloucestershire's blooming countryside.

The remaining principals at Ravenscourt, perhaps dreading a breakfast as dreary as dinner the evening before, had either stayed in their rooms for the duration or else dawdled their way down to the breakfast parlor late in the morning and were still at table. The noble second son calculated that he had several hours in which to ride out the kinks and frustration engendered by being cooped up in the country with his mother and Lady Albinia.

The London season, moving into full whirl, beckoned, as did his good friends and old haunts. But Robert was not one to hedge off and leave his brother to face danger alone. Despite the unexpected arrival of Miss Asher some two weeks earlier, Robert felt that danger from Lady Albinia still existed. While she lived and breathed—and, judging by the longevity of his maternal grandparents, that would be for a good, long while—his mother would continue to promote a match between Adam and her goddaughter.

Like Felicity, Robert had started hoping for a miracle, something to save Ravenscourt from the eventuality of Albinia's assuming the rôle of ducal consort. While he knew that Adam could fend for himself, he still placed no reliance on his brother's holding out against the prolonged siege that was shaping against him at Ravenscourt. But whereas Felicity, believing in a Supreme Being who could not be so cruel as to saddle her with a sister-in-law such as Albinia, had turned to formal prayer, Robert's hopes manifested in the more physical realm. He was deep in a serious dialogue with himself as to be best method of dislodging Albinia from Ravenscourt and sending her back to Feldenham, when a circus spectacle taking place outside Ravenscourt's gates at that very moment brought him up short.

A dashing, high-perch phaeton, just such as Robert himself would like to own, lay half on its side in the shallow ditch immediately outside Ravenscourt's gate, its left wheel crushed. A London smart perhaps a few years younger than himself had hopped down from the wreckage and was attempting to direct two common service vehicles out of a tangle of horses and back onto the road. Judging by the mise-en-scène, one of these vehicles, a large, sturdy wagon, emblazed in bright green with the name of *Wallace Barton, Carriers*, had tried to turn in at the gate just as an oncoming coach from the opposite direction attempted to overtake the phaeton in order to make the same turn, and had crashed into the phaeton.

These stirring events, Robert noted with bitter irony, had occurred exactly on the day that Tom Badger, Ravenscourt's gatekeeper, was away visiting his ailing mother, leaving the lodge empty and Badger's strong pair of hands unavailable to assist. As a result, a voice of reason within the maelstrom was sadly lacking.

The fashionable gentleman's instructions regarding the best way to extricate the offending vehicles from the tangle were drowned out by a series of recriminations emanating from the coachman and the wagon driver. A much mustachioed man of middle age and broad, swarthy aspect, seated within the coach, uttered a fluid stream of curses in French, adding to the general racket. Not to be outdone, the carrier's assistant chimed in, using choice English expressions that made Robert blush.

From the recesses of the overturned phaeton, a dog barked, then a small, furry canine resembling a cross between a collie and a Pekingese, and displaying the worst features of both, scrambled over the side and hurled himself, yapping, at the fashionable gentleman's feet, causing one of the wagon's horses to rear up in fright.

"Confucius, dear, do shut up," a woman's voice commanded in cultured accents from within the phaeton. "William, dear," the woman added over the ever-increasing din. "I am terribly sorry, but I am unable to right myself. I seem to have done something to my arm."

William—if that were the name of the fashionable gentleman—ignored this comment and increased the volume of his own voice in an attempt to be heard.

"Oh, do shut up, William," the unseen female said calmly. "Don't you know it's useless to reason with these gentlemen? Do let them worry about this mess of their own making and come help me out of here, instead. My arm is starting to throb terribly, and I fear I have broken it."

Jolted out of his reverie by this bold statement, Robert slid from his horse and tied the reins to the gate. "*If* I may be of assistance," he offered, moving toward the phaeton.

Meanwhile, the coachman and wagon driver had ceased their curses and conferred briefly. The carrier's assistant jumped down and went to the head of the horses. Within a few minutes, both wagon and coach were backed safely away, allowing ample room for maneuvering the phaeton out of the ditch.

"If I hand my sister up to you, would you be able to lift her out of the carriage?" William asked. Not waiting for a reply, he climbed nimbly into the overturned phaeton and handed a tall, lanky woman tenderly into Robert's waiting arms. Soon she was standing on level ground, supporting her injured right arm awkwardly with her left hand.

Observing that her face was white as a sheet and fearing that she was about to faint, Robert quickly removed the light jacket he was wearing and spread it on the ground. "Here, sit on this until you feel more the thing," he told her.

"I am not such a poor thing that I am about to faint because of a little pain," she replied. She held out her left hand for him to shake. "By the way, I am Anne Chilvers, you know. And who are you?"

But Robert scarcely heard her, and instead lent an ear to the drama shaping up a few yards away. By this time, Robert had accurately guessed the purpose of the other two vehicles. Not so the occupant of the coach, who was still indulging in a stream of Gallic curses. Just then a few chance words dropped by the carrier exercised a powerful effect on the foreigner, who halted his curses midsentence and started exclaiming excitedly. The coachman and his foreign passenger joined the carrier and his assistant beside the wagon. Mr. Barton of *Wallace Barton, Carriers,* opened the heavy back doors of the wagon with a flourish, and the foreigner's Gallic exuberance transformed into a virtual flood of tears.

They were tears of happiness, however. Adam's new French chef had arrived at the same moment as the coveted closed stove.

★ ★

Despite Robert's well-founded suspicions that the coach transporting the Frenchman was not well sprung and would make for an uncomfortable ride, it was decided to bundle the

Chilvers siblings and Confucius in with Pierre for the short ride up to Ravenscourt. Robert rode on ahead to alert the staff, while the carrier's assistant stayed behind to guard William's team. The two service vehicles, arriving simultaneously at the impressive entrance to the ducal pile, came to a lumbering stop, and Spilsby, who had been keeping watch by a window, threw open the massive front doors and ordered an imposing-looking footman to assist Miss Chilvers to alight. The stately butler descended the broad, shallow steps and pointed off to the side of the sprawling building. "The service entrance is that way, if you please," he said, addressing the coachman and wagon driver.

William, clutching a struggling Confucius, followed Anne out of the coach. Bringing up the rear was a short, stocky man carrying an oversized carpetbag. Placing the carpetbag in the astonished butler's arms, the little Frenchman raised one hand to the collar of his brown serge suit and plucked off several dog hairs with some disgust before calmly following William and Anne inside.

Some minutes later, Miss Chilvers was firmly established in the Duchess's best drawing room on the same rock-hard sofa that Devorah had occupied only two weeks before, and proper introductions were in progress. William had been invited to seat himself in the wingchair that was the only comfortable chair in the room, while Robert made do with one of the priceless but unserviceable antiques that made up the bulk of the drawing room's furnishings.

Pierre was also present, through perseverance rather than by invitation. But, having correctly assessed the comfort level of the unoccupied chairs, he remained standing. At last, taking advantage of a pause in the formal introductions, he decided to present himself. "And *I* am Armand," he announced grandly.

"Armand? I thought you were Pierre," Robert said, puzzled.

"All zee English call *les chefs* Pierre or Antoine. *Moi*, I am Armand. I am zee best." Pierre-Armand executed a little bow.

229

Spilbsy reappeared, bearing a silver tray heavily laden with a decanter of sherry, several crystal glasses and a plate of macaroons, which he set on a lacquered table at Robert's elbow. The imposing footman followed close behind, carefully carrying a crystal bowl filled with water. "For the little doggie," he said, placing it on the floor next to Confucius, who was sprawled across William's feet.

Armand plucked a macaroon from the plate. Breaking off a small piece, he sniffed it contemptuously and tossed it over his shoulder. "Dry. And no water of oranges. Also zee desserts here Armand will now oversee."

Spilsby turned to the chef. "Mrs. Wigmore, our housekeeper, has been waiting with *much* anticipation for your arrival and wants to meet with you *immediately*. *If* you please, monsieur, I will show you to her now." Sweeping Armand out of the room with all the majesty of his station, the butler determined silently that after depositing the foreigner with Mrs. Wigmore, he would hurry upstairs to personally switch the new kitchen commander's carpetbag to the larger of the two rooms over which the housekeeper had been dithering. He would explain this unilateral move to Mrs. Wigmore later, but making Armand comfortable could *not* wait. Clearly, the Frenchman required preferential treatment if Ravenscourt were to enjoy any peace.

Now that the drawing room had been emptied of Armand's forceful presence, Robert took the opportunity to study Miss Chilvers and her brother. Overall, he liked what he saw.

Miss Chilvers, he judged, was a woman of some twenty-five to thirty summers who, at first glance, would be termed only passably handsome. Neither her light brown hair, though shining and fashionably cut despite its understandably disheveled appearance, nor her complexion, though clear, was particularly striking; she had a masterly nose and a mouth that was just a bit too large for her face. But her eyes, her best feature, were a wide, clear gray that held a twinkle as they watched him size her up, and her mouth widened frequently into a particularly appealing smile. Not Adam's style at all, Robert thought, but having her recuperate at Ravenscourt would certainly liven things up a bit. Wouldn't Binny be rabid as a dog over the appearance of yet another eligible female!

William, who appeared to be just a year or two younger than Robert's own twenty-four years, was a male likeness of his sister, although the nose and mouth sat better on his face and his own wide, gray eyes were more serious than twinkling. His manners, like those of his sister, were easy and unaffected. Better yet, judging by the phaeton and team that was pulling it, he was an expert in matters of horseflesh and could be expected to provide Robert with many hours of enjoyable conversation regarding a subject that was sadly ignored at Ravenscourt only because Adam was strangely uninterested in making a splash with the Corinthian set.

Miss Chilvers, slowly sipping her glass of sherry, had again turned pale with pain. Robert hastened to reassure her that a servant had been sent to fetch Dr. Barrie, who should be arriving within the hour, if she could just hang on until then. He launched into a series of profuse apologies for the accident that had occurred outside Ravenscourt's gates, but the invalid cut him off with protestations.

"Not only was it *not* your fault, but I would not have missed it for the world," she declared. "Armand has considerably enriched my French vocabulary, for which I will be forever grateful. I expect further entertainment from him before we are through."

William launched into a spirited description of just how the accident occurred. The siblings were staying with relatives near Bath and decided to visit their aunt, who had returned unexpectedly to her country estate due to their uncle's sudden ill health. This, he hastened to add, explained the phaeton, which was the only vehicle they had at hand. They were enjoying the fine weather and the beautiful countryside when all of a sudden, apparently out of nowhere, a heavy coach driven by a ham-fisted driver had overtaken them. They had heard the coachman declare to his passenger that he would attempt to break past the phaeton and take the turn before the approaching carrier's wagon came upon them. The next thing they knew there was a great crash, accompanied by a strong jolt, and their wagon had overturned into the ditch.

It was then, Miss Chilvers added, that Armand's full mastery of the intricacies of the French language were revealed. "But he cannot be taking over your kitchen, can he? He will soon overtake all of you, as well. He will be positively *ruling* Ravenscourt. I can envision it already. Even your butler has been seen to cower before him."

Robert grinned and assured her that Armand's reign at Ravenscourt was purely temporary. The little Frenchman was actually hired for the Duke's townhouse, Melville House, and was just filling in here in the country while Cook recovered from her broken leg.

"You do, I hope, spend a great deal of time entertaining at Melville House," Miss Chilvers commented. "Otherwise Armand will be positively *wasted.*"

The comment should have amused Robert, but he suddenly wasn't attending. Instead, he was assailed by the realization that Ravenscourt, of late, had been plagued by too many falling women and too many broken bones. First Miss Asher, who had fallen mysteriously at the side of the road, in broad daylight, in full evening dress. Fortunately, she had not broken her head, but she had sustained a serious-enough blow that it seemed to have driven important knowledge of her past from of her memory. Then there was Cook, who had broken her leg, and the kitchen maid, who had broken her arm and head, all in one go. Then Miss Asher had managed to wrench her ankle. It wasn't a broken bone, but it had certainly hobbled her for a few days. And now Miss Chilvers with her broken arm.

There was, also, the problem of so many strange women ending up at Ravenscourt. Miss Asher seemed entirely unexceptionable and not the least interested in Adam, if Robert interpreted the situation correctly, and Miss Chilvers had a plausible-enough excuse for meeting with an accident next to Ravenscourt's gates. But, Robert hadn't been born yesterday, and he had heard several stories in the past of eligible but unattainable noble bachelors ensnared by designing women who had concocted all sorts of accidents next to the nobleman's house. They had been taken in to recuperate, and next thing you knew, the noblemen themselves had been taken in. Caught, ensnared, riveted! And that was the end of that.

Robert was still pondering the probability of Miss Chilvers and her brother not being what they seemed when a discreet knock on the drawing room door heralded the entrance of Spilsby, announcing his grace.

"But what is all this?" the Duke asked, casually entering the room. "My dear Robert, *another* accident? Why, Ravenscourt will become positively infamous. So many unsuspecting persons meeting their doom within our environs!" He paused and waited expectantly for Robert to formally introduce him to the latest invalid and her brother. Robert said all that was proper, and Miss Chilvers struggled to rise from the sofa. Seeing the effort it cost her, the Duke motioned her back down.

It was at that moment that the world appeared to shift slightly on its axis. It happened so fast that Robert wasn't sure afterwards whether he had fleetingly imagined it. Adam, for perhaps the first time in his life, had been rendered speechless. Noticing the awkward angle of Miss Chilver's right arm, he had reached out and taken her left hand reverently in his own, bent over and brushed it with his lips.

"Charmed," he had uttered finally, then cleared his throat awkwardly.

The snare has been set and the hare has been caught. A crazed laughter rose in Robert's throat as the thought coursed through his mind, but he choked the laughter back. Wouldn't Binny be more than rabid! Well, well, well. Who would ever have thought his staid ancestral home would afford him so much entertainment?

★ ★

The Duchess bestowed her unexpected approval on the newcomers. She declared them quite unexceptionable and prettily behaved. It helped, Robert thought irreverently, that the aunt whom they were on their way to visit in Gloucestershire was Lady Loughborough, another of his mother's bosom bows.

"I had thought that Georgina was established in London for the season," the Duchess said upon hearing the details of the siblings' accident and arrival at Ravenscourt. "I wonder what brought her back to Ellsworth Hall." Her curiosity whetted, she yanked the bell-pull for Tilstock and roused herself from the daybed upon which she was still prostrated. Some half an hour later, attired entirely in floating layers of dove gray, she entered the Lavender Room, so named for the color of its paper and upholsteries, where Miss Chilvers now lay recuperating from the ministrations of Dr. Barrie.

Miss Chilvers had been doused heavily with laudanum only hours before in order to cushion the ordeal of having her arm set. Even so, recognizing this ghostly apparition as the formidable duchess about whom she had heard so much from her aunt, she rose from her sickbed with great pain and effort and executed a small curtsy. The action found immediate favor in the Duchess's eyes. "My poor dear," her grace said, commanding Miss Chilvers to return to her bed. She turned her steely eyes to William, who had just entered the room to see how his sister went on. William's bow, too, was all that was desired. It was then that the Duchess hit upon the very idea:

Robert would marry Miss Chilvers.

The idea sent shivers down the Duchess's spine. Never, since her pact twenty years ago with Albinia's mother, Sophia Brinkburn, to make a match between their eldest children, had she had such a brilliant notion.

It was high time that both of her sons settled down. Adam, of course, would soon be brought to realize that Albinia was the perfect wife for him in rank, family and fortune. Why, he probably recognized the wisdom of the

234

match already and was still opposing it just to be perverse, as usual.

Miss Chilvers, with her lineage and fortune, would do equally well for Robert. If the Duchess understood the connection correctly, Miss Chilver's maternal grandfather had been Lord Hashinger, one of the wealthiest men in the realm in his day, even wealthier than the famed Mexworth and Perry families. He was rumored to have settled the staggering sum of two hundred thousand pounds on his daughter upon her marriage to Charles Chilvers, Lady Loughborough's brother. Charles and Georgina's mother was Francesca Oliver, a fabled heiress in her own right. The Duchess knew for a fact that she had created substantial trusts for her children and grandchildren, and they had each come into quite a respectable sum upon her death some five years previous. Miss Chilvers was already wealthy in her own right; she would someday be even wealthier. Yes, she would do quite well for the younger brother of the sixth Duke of Ravenscroft.

And what of Felicity? The Duchess was determined that her recalcitrant daughter marry titled nobility. But which title? What nobleman? Dear Lucas, now that he had come into the title, was the most accessible prey to come to the Duchess's mind. This, too, would be just the thing, because already the Duchess had come to think of him as quite part of the family. But Felicity, who seemed to dislike the former chaplain, might prove to be sadly reluctant. If only she could be persuaded to appreciate his finer qualities.

Engrossed in these matchmaking schemes, the Duchess absently patted Miss Chilver's bandaged arm, causing her to wince, and hurried from the room. She *must* send a message to Georgina Loughborough immediately, requesting her assistance in setting her machinations in motion.

Chapter 22

Jonathan Whyteman discovered that a number of things were distinctly different when he visited Ravenscourt on Wednesday. Among these was the absence of the omnipresent chaplain, who wasn't expected to return to Ravenscourt until at least the following week. The Duke ushered Mr. Whyteman into the library, where he offered him an apple and regaled him with the terrible tale of the poisonous mushrooms and Mr. Duckwaithe's unexpected elevation into the peerage. "This is indeed a tragic story," Mr. Whyteman agreed. "But perhaps it will prove to be the *deus ex machina* that solves at least one of your more annoying problems."

In the past his grace, who had a quick mind, would have raised a sardonic eyebrow and asked "Whatever do you mean?" while knowing exactly what Jonathan meant. But the Duke, for some reason, appeared distracted. Mr. Whyteman did not take it personally, but thought that it was rather out of character. That, then, was the second difference at Ravenscourt.

Third was Felicity, who came in search of a book while Mr. Whyteman was finishing off his apple. She gave him a friendly greeting but left immediately after finding the book. This, too, was a major change from Felicity's unwelcome tendency to linger. What was happening at Ravenscourt? Was Mr. Whyteman falling out of favor?

The answer was soon supplied unintentionally by Miss Asher, whom the Duke summoned to the library before excusing himself to attend to pressing business. "We have new visitors," she announced, launching into a description of Anne and William Chilvers' descent on Ravenscourt. "They are proving to be extremely popular. Even the Duchess likes them, possibly because their aunt is one of her oldest friends, besides the fact that they are extremely wealthy."

"An accomplishment indeed, if they have found favor in her grace's eyes. Her taste in people is extremely fastidious."

"Yes, they have made a conquest of us all." Miss Asher paused for a pregnant moment, then added almost as an afterthought. "I believe her grace hopes that Lord Robert and Miss Chilvers will make a match of it."

"And will they?"

"I doubt it. She is not at all his type, besides being much too old for him. In my opinion, she is much more suitable for the Duke. She isn't at all beautiful, but she is very quick and has a good sense of humor."

Well, well, well, thought Mr. Whyteman. "And how does his grace appear to regard her?"

"I am not sure. He is being careful. There are other houseguests he must not offend, you know, not to mention his mother." Miss Asher paused again. "Also, since the Chilverses' arrival, there has been a change in Lady Felicity. She is more quiet and thoughtful and appears to have matured overnight."

Mr. Whyteman let this bit of information digest. "And Lady Albinia? How does she regard the newcomers?"

Devorah cast a wary eye toward the open door. "She takes her lead from the Duchess and generally tries to be amiable. I think she is also hoping for a match between Lord Robert and Miss Chilvers. It would take Miss Chilvers out of the competition. Even so, I have high hopes that everything will work out nicely before we are done. I believe we may truly witness a miracle."

This last comment elicited a quizzical look from Mr. Whyteman. But Miss Asher merely smiled cryptically and refused to be drawn.

"And how do you go on?" Mr. Whyteman asked, changing the subject. "Your ankle is fully healed?"

"It still hurts occasionally, but nothing like before. Besides, I am grateful that I wrenched it, because it gave me an excuse to hole up in my room this past Sabbath. I should only be so lucky this Sabbath, which is fast approaching. However, I still haven't found a way out of my larger problem. Passover is also fast approaching, and I want to be *home.*"

Rubbing his jaw thoughtfully, Mr. Whyteman agreed that if only home back in Boro Park would do for Miss Asher for the Passover holiday, she was indeed in a predicament. "And we don't have much time to get you there," he reminded her. "The new month was yesterday, which means that Passover is in less than two weeks."

"Yesterday? I totally forgot about it!"

"Understandable, considering the stirring events that have been going on here."

"Not stirring in the least. I missed out on the Chilverses' carriage accident and their arrival at Ravenscourt and only met William at dinner. I met Anne—Miss Chilvers, that is—this morning when I paid her a sickroom visit. I haven't laid eyes on Armand yet. Which reminds me, did the Duke tell you that the new French chef has arrived?"

Mr. Whyteman was forced to admit that he hadn't yet heard this major news, either, so Devorah launched into a description of Armand's Grand Entrance, as heard from Robert and William at table the evening before. Mr. Whyteman's lively sense of humor, quite as deplorable as the Duke's, was greatly tickled, and Adam returned to the library to be met by shouts of laughter. Satisfied that his tenant and Miss Asher were going on greatly, the ice between them finally broken, he stopped short before reaching the open door and retreated back down the hall.

★ ★

Mr. Whyteman had a chance to observe both the new chef and the Chilvers siblings when he stayed to a luncheon of cold meats and fruits and day-old bread. This, the Duke warned, was also likely to be the dinner menu due to the installation that day of the new closed stove.

Armand had taken command of the kitchen the afternoon before, just in time to throw a béchamel sauce over a dish of baked pheasants that he labeled otherwise inedible and to harass Betsy and her assistants into tears. He now felt it incumbent upon his honor to make an appearance and beg forgiveness for a meal the evening before that not only did nothing to preserve his reputation, but that would be followed by Much Worse!

At least three persons at table—the Duke, Jonathan and Devorah—were secretly pleased with the chef's appearance as it afforded Mr. Whyteman the opportunity to actually view this personage in the flesh. The opportunity, Jonathan later decided, was priceless, as the little Frenchman was in full Gallic flower.

"I, Armand, do not like to complain. *Moi*, I make do. I add zee sauce to disguise what is impossible to digest, or I cut and chop and I make zee ragout to disguise *le répugnant*. *Moi*, I am zee chef for who *les miracles* are possible. But what can Armand do when zee kitchen is full of *imbéciles* wizout *l'imagination?*"

Armand took a deep breath and launched into his final indignities. "*Les imbéciles*, it is not enough zat I, Armand, am asked to send zee uncut fruit to table. *Moi*, who am famed zee whole of England for zee beautiful fruit platters I arrange. I know zat *les noblesse* zey have *les bizarreries*, and I send up fruit wizout zee slicing or zee arrangement so beautiful. But, *les imbéciles* in ze kitchen request also zat I accommodate zee little doggie. It is Too Much!"

Suppressing a smile, Adam shot a glance at Miss Chilvers, seated to Robert's right. Her own eyes twinkled appreciatively back at him. This silent exchange was not lost on either Devorah or Jonathan, who shared their own look of unholy amusement from across the table. The reactions of the others differed. Both her grace and Lady Albinia, similar in temperament and equally jealous of their stations, appeared offended; Lady Felicity looked horrified. William, suppressing a desire to slide under the table, smiled sympathetically at Felicity, who managed to give him a watery smile in return. Robert, who had been taking in the different undercurrents and mentally calculating their future ramifications with great satisfaction, rose magnificently to the occasion.

"Well, yes, I suppose it is a great inconvenience to arrive here and find everything in shambles. But I dare say, Monsieur Armand, you will have everything arranged just as it should be within a day or two. M'mother and the Duke expect great things from you, you know. But not overnight, when the place has been a wreck for weeks," he said, keeping the asperity from his voice with great effort.

Satisfied that he had been heard, Armand bowed repeatedly to both their graces and beat a dignified departure from the Small Dining Room. As soon as the heavy doors swung closed behind him, Robert let out a long sigh of relief. "I just hope he isn't going to go into histrionics on a daily basis. It's more than my digestive system can bear."

"Surely not," Felicity said, much shocked. "Shouldn't he be spending most of his time in the kitchen?"

"Yes, indeed," Adam said. "But, probably having been ordered out of there by the workmen installing the closed stove, he had nothing to do except come up here and defend his reputation." He shot another look of amusement at Miss Chilvers, who was clumsily attempting to cut some cold meat with her left hand. "But Robert, your manners have gone begging. Please assist Miss Chilvers in cutting her food. If you don't, I will."

"I have a better idea," the younger son said. "Miss Chilvers, if you please, I will spread some slices of bread with mustard and place this meat and cheese between them so that you can easily hold your meal in your left hand."

"An excellent idea," the Duke said. "Miss Chilvers, you will set a new style at Ravenscourt for our informal luncheon."

"Even though in general it is not done to eat with one's hands, I agree that allowances should be made in this instance," the Duchess said approvingly.

"Yes, I believe it was a Greek philosopher who said, 'Necessity is the mother of invention,'" Albinia added. "You have, in this manner, Robert, come up with quite a sensible way for Miss Chilvers to enjoy her meal."

"Thank you for the compliment, but the Earl of Sandwich was before me."

Lady Albinia had nothing to say to this and lapsed into temporary silence. But mention of the Earl of Sandwich led William to recall the sandwiches he and his cronies had often concocted at Almack's from the day-old bread and butter and the dry cakes served as refreshments, just so they could feel that they had actually put something more substantial in their mouths. This, in turn, sparked a lively conversation among the younger set about the refreshments in general dished up at that hallowed social institution and the more unfortunate, but hilarious, culinary choices served by some of London's leading hostesses at balls and rout parties during seasons past.

The meats and fruits and sugared almonds served in place of pastries had long been consumed when the Duchess placed her napkin next to her plate and rose from the table. "Well, that was quite pleasant," she said. "I daresay I have seldom seen so lively a luncheon here at Ravenscourt. Miss Chilvers, you will accompany me to the Green Room now and tell me how my dear friend Lady Loughborough goes on. And you, Robert, will come help me untangle my silks so that I can work on the new drawing room chairs while we speak."

Robert cast a desperate eye at Adam. "I have asked Robert to discharge a few important duties for me this afternoon," the Duke said, coming to his brother's rescue. "If you will recall, I have a special aptitude for untangling threads, so I will volunteer myself for the job instead."

"Yes, I promised Adam that I would discuss the new stalls we are building with Jim Groom. I had meant to do so this morning already," Robert said, bolting for the door.

The Duchess looked disappointed. But, as Robert had already escaped down the hall, she had little recourse but to accept Adam's offer gracefully. The Lady Albinia, not to be out-maneuvered, also offered her assistance, and the foursome headed toward the Green Room. Lady Felicity turned and shrugged her shoulders at Miss Asher, but the pleading look in her eye was unmistakable.

"You might want to take Mr. Chilvers on a tour of the portrait gallery. He will enjoy the Italian windows and their view of the rose garden," Devorah suggested helpfully.

"If you please, I would like to see Ravenscourt's picture gallery," Mr. Chilvers said. "I have heard quite a bit about it from my aunt."

"You children run along then," Mr. Whyteman told them. "I will enjoy a short chat with Miss Asher before I leave." He waited until their retreating forms disappeared from view before turning to Devorah. "Well, that takes care of that, and much more easily than I had thought. Would you care to take a stroll across the grounds? It is quite warm out today, so you don't even need to run upstairs for your pelisse."

Devorah nodded her assent, and they strolled companionably out to the gravel drive and set off toward the expanse of green that lay just beyond.

"Matters appear to be moving along quite quickly and satisfactorily now," Mr. Whyteman said once they were out of earshot.

"Felicity has been praying for a miracle. She told me she included it in her prayers, even in Sunday chapel." Devorah kicked at a bit of gravel with the toe of her kid boot. "If it weren't for the horrible poisoning of Mr. Duckwaithe's family, it would be truly gratifying to see prayers working so quickly. But I am anxious to see how things will fall out once Mr. Duckwaithe returns to Ravenscourt."

"I hope that may be soon. My heart quite aches for Lady Albinia. I fear that she is finding herself decidedly *de trop* in the Green Room just now. Mr. Duckwaithe's return will make for a much smoother transition."

"You are, I presume, referring to the Duke and Miss Chilvers."

"There is no presumption about it," Mr. Whyteman said. "He is flattened."

Devorah paused at a set of stone steps leading onto the grounds. "I only hope she may return his regard. It's not a sure thing, you know."

"My dear, women have been trying to capture the Duke these dozen years. If you only knew what a matrimonial prize he is. Of course, he will win Miss Chilvers. I would even go so far to say it is already done. And as for Felicity, she seems to have forgotten my existence overnight. I am quite crushed." He held aside a stray branch of the shrubbery bordering the steps and motioned Devorah on through.

"You are just as deplorable as his grace," she said, pausing to survey the vista.

"I could be childish and tell you that you are quite as bad as both of us together. You've been making a game of all of us since you've arrived."

"I'll ignore that comment, which you know is patently untrue, and ask you instead to be serious."

"I am being serious. Come, let us sit on that bench over there," he said, pointing to an elaborately carved stone bench located conveniently under a beech tree some distance away. "We can discuss what other matches can be created here at Ravenscourt."

Devorah looked up sharply.

"Exactly so. I have been waiting forever to speak about us," Jonathan said conversationally. "But, there always seems to be some kind of interruption. If not one thing, then another. Felicity searching for a book, Lady Albinia's maid all on fire, your twisted ankle—which, by the way, was a brilliant ruse." They had reached the bench by then. Jonathan waited until Devorah seated herself, then settled himself at the opposite end.

"You mistake the matter," Devorah told him. "Either that, or you still aren't serious."

"I am totally serious. I have given the matter a great deal of consideration. A good woman is difficult to find, and I think you would do admirably as my helpmate. I am in need of a spouse, and you are in need of a solution to your predicament. Also, I think you should consider that your usefulness to the Duke may be about to come to an end."

"This is a proposal?" Devorah asked, much shocked.

"Yes, a clumsy one, but I am asking you to marry me."

"But you don't even know me. And why should I marry you just because you need a wife?"

Jonathan pulled a leaf off a low-hanging branch and threaded it through his fingers. "I am expressing myself badly. It is true that I barely know you, but I am impressed by what I have seen. I've come to admire the courage and humor you have exhibited in what could have been a catastrophic situation. I like your intelligence. I like...you.

"Come, Miss Asher, excellent matches have been made with even less to go on. My own parents met but once and were betrothed that very same night. Can you not find it in your heart to even consider my proposal?"

To say that Devorah was at a loss for words was an understatement. A strange lassitude overcame her; she felt as though she were caught in an undertow and all her strength was giving way. She had been thrown into a foreign situation, a foreign country, a foreign century, and she was treading water for all she was worth, just to stay afloat. And now, someone—an extremely attractive someone, she admitted—was offering her a lifebuoy. All she had to do was reach out and accept and she would be lifted out of the Dukedom of Ravenscroft, out of a malevolent, scheming whirlpool of the Duchess's and Lady Albinia's and even the Duke's own machinations, away from the lies and the playacting and the pretending and the stratagems that she was forced to constantly devise. She was so tired, and it was so tempting.

But it was wrong. All wrong.

"Well, Miss Asher? Will you not even consider it?"

Devorah raised both hands to her burning cheeks. What was wrong with her? Was she developing a fever? Just an hour before she had been going on so well, and now she felt so shaky. "I don't know—I must think!" She gathered her skirts and rose from the bench and walked as quickly as she could, while still maintaining her dignity, over the emerald green lawn and back to the house.

Mr. Whyteman watched her retreating form until the great doors of Ravenscourt were thrown wide open and she disappeared, a pale-blue blur of muslin, into the Great Hall's gloom. Then he, too, rose from the bench—albeit with much more reluctance—and dusted himself off. And, as weary as if he had just swam the English Channel and back, he headed to the stables to retrieve his mount.

It was only on his way back to Ten Oaks that he ruefully admitted to himself that he had neglected, while proposing to Miss Asher, to tell her the most important consideration of all: that he loved her.

Chapter 23

Devorah—Miss Asher—wasn't herself this morning. That much was clear, Felicity thought, as she watched the American guest carefully from under her lashes while bent over her embroidery frame in the Green Room. Miss Asher was unusually pale and quiet, and merely picked at the canvas of the petit point reticule that Felicity had given her only days before.

It must still be the headache that had felled Miss Asher the previous afternoon, possibly on account of too much sun. She had stayed in her darkened room over the dinner hour. This was unfortunate, because dinner last evening had been even livelier than luncheon earlier in the day. Both Adam and Robert had been in high form, as had William; and even Mother, who did not approve of levity of any kind, entered into the spirit of the evening and ventured a few humorous offerings of her own. Alas, these had fallen sadly flat, as had Albinia's attempts to join the fun. But, Anne—Miss Chilvers, that is—had nipped in with a few droll comments that were so clever that even Mother was forced to acknowledge them as a hit.

It was amazing, Felicity considered, how much livelier Ravenscourt had become now that Lucas had posted north. If it were up to her, he wouldn't return for months and months. But, she reminded herself, that would never do, because Lucas still had a major role to play in rescuing Ravenscourt from Albinia. In fact, if Felicity's suspicions were correct, Lucas's services would be needed now more than ever. Adam was at this very moment out for a morning drive with Miss Chilvers, a treat he had *never*, to Felicity's knowledge, offered Albinia. Mother, meanwhile, was trying to play cupid between Robert and Anne, as had become patently clear the day before. Once again, Felicity thought, Mother appeared to be way off the mark.

Felicity wished that she were alone with Devorah, and that Devorah didn't look quite so pulled this morning, because she wanted to ask her what *she* thought of these stirring new events. Somebody at Ravenscourt, somewhere along the line, was headed for disappointment, and Felicity doubted that that someone would be Adam. The way things were shaping up, once both Mother and Albinia realized that their matrimonial schemes were dashed, only the delivery of Lucas into the hands and heart of Albinia could avert a scene at Ravenscourt of epic proportions.

Robert, thankfully, seemed oblivious to Anne's manifest charm. But just as thankfully, he seemed to get along quite well with Mr. Chilvers. Felicity really wanted to ask Devorah what she thought of William. Since meeting him, she had come to realize just how childish was her infatuation with Mr. Whyteman. They were totally unsuited in both temperament and social standing, while William and she inhabited the same world. And William was just intelligent enough, but not too clever—not like Jonathan, in whose company she was constantly re-examining the conversation to check for hidden meanings.

Of course, she had just met William, and once she became better acquainted with him she might discover that he was just as fatuous as the rest of the men to whom she had been introduced during her previous London season. But there would be time enough for that; he and Anne had been invited to stay at Ravenscourt for at least another fortnight, when Anne would be well-enough healed to withstand the pothole-riddled twenty miles of country road that led to Lady Loughborough and Ellsworth Hall.

Yes, it was a shame that Devorah's head still pained her. Felicity so very much wanted to speak to her. But perhaps it wasn't her head, and she only needed a distraction. "Does your head still ache, dear Miss Asher?" Felicity asked solicitously. "You look sadly out of sorts this morning."

Devorah looked up from her petit point and glanced around the Green Room. The Duchess was snoring softly in the overstuffed wingchair she usually commandeered, the open copy of *Gibbons Roman Empire* she had been reading spread across her breast; but Lady Albinia appeared to be quite alert and poised to listen. Indeed, under cover of her own embroidery, which didn't appear to be progressing much better than Devorah's, Albinia presented the appearance of being All Ears.

"It is nothing. It must be the weather," she told Felicity.

"Yes, I myself have felt it this morning," Albinia chimed in, proof that she would happily listen in on any conversation carried out by the other two conscious occupants of the room. "It is growing warmer and warmer out, but so heavy and closed. I feel it must rain."

"I certainly hope not! Adam and Miss Chilvers are at this very moment out driving around in the curricle, and they won't be back for several hours," Felicity declared, choosing her words to inflict maximum pain. "It would be terrible if they were caught in a downpour."

Albinia bit her lower lip and bent back over her embroidery, and the three young women each lapsed back into her own thoughts.

What will be with me? Albinia wondered. All the dreams and plans she shared with her mother and the Duchess, on which she had been nurtured from infancy, were proving more elusive than she ever could have thought. She had always known that dear Adam was fickle, that he would play with her feelings until the very end. But when, after all these years, the Duke had failed to find a different partner in life, and when dear godmama had extended the invitation to visit Ravenscourt, she had been sure that victory, that brilliant

248

matrimonial prize, was within her grasp at last. Surely she would return home triumphant, ready to assemble her bride clothes.

But, like those shimmering oases she had read about in oriental tales and accounts of Arabia, marriage to Adam was fast becoming a mirage: so close, so real, but only an illusion. First Miss Asher and now, her instincts told her, Miss Chilvers. Adam flitted from one to another, playing them off against each other, playing them both off against *her*. What should she do? Should she stay at Ravenscourt until that final, painful moment when the Duke chose his bride? Did she still stand a chance? Or, by staying at Ravenscourt, was she opening herself up to ignominy? Would she return home to face yet another unpromising London season and the growing realization that she was nearly on the shelf?

If only Mr. Duckwaithe were here. The Duchess's chaplain had provided her with sage counsel in the past. Surely his wisdom could be relied upon to steer her regarding the proper course of action in this case.

The Lady Albinia sighed and returned to her embroidery.

To hold a private conversation in the Green Room was patently impossible. Felicity wondered whether she should invite Miss Asher to her room on pretext of giving her the excellent headache remedy that she had stashed away in her wardrobe. Devorah was looking more miserable by the minute, but she seemed disinclined to talk. Felicity really didn't want to talk about Devorah at this point, however; she wanted a sounding board for her impressions of William, and of Adam and Anne's budding romance. Then she realized that discussing Adam and Anne with Miss Asher really wasn't appropriate, especially as until just a few days before Devorah had been a top contender for her brother's hand. Perhaps that was the reason that Miss Asher was looking so pulled.

Poor Miss Asher, Felicity thought. *Just when she was so close to winning the matrimonial prize of the year—the only eligible British duke who isn't fat, forty, or deaf.*

Felicity stabbed viciously at the bookmark she was needlepointing. Perhaps, if matters progressed as she hoped, she could present it to William when it was finished.

Devorah was indeed feeling miserable. She didn't love Mr. Whyteman, and he didn't love her. But, she had detected in him a kindred spirit; she felt she had known him forever. On paper, as well, the pluses were weighted in Mr. Whyteman's favor. He was attractive and intelligent, a man of good morals and principles; he had a sense of humor. These were all important qualities. He was unattached, and he liked her. What more could she ask?

The big drawback was time and space; she had traveled backwards through both. Given enough time, the family and century she had left behind would become only a memory. She would forget her exciting job on Wall Street, the memory and taste of which was already fading fast; she would forget her beautiful little Brooklyn townhouse, her sleek electric coffeemaker, her kosher delicatessens, and she would give thanks every day that she was no longer on the lists of the special matchmakers, the ones who dealt in difficult cases. She would no longer be subjected to her mother's dispirited sighs and the pitying looks of her friends because she had yet to find her match.

Even so, she wanted to return home.

Adam and Miss Chilvers did not return in time for the family's traditional noontime repast, an omission the Duchess commented on several times at table.

"But Mother," Robert finally protested, "Adam often doesn't return to Ravenscourt at noon."

"Yes, but that is because he is attending to estate business with Babcock," the Duchess kindly explained to her younger son. "He is *never* absent because he is with a woman. I wonder, could something have happened to them?"

This, of course, was unanswerable. But the Duchess's lack of sensitivity in pointing out Adam and Anne's joint absence in the presence of Albinia set the seal on that lady's already miserable existence. Coughing discreetly into her napkin to cover up a momentary tendency to tears, she determined to escape at the earliest possible moment and seek refuge in her room with the new, improving novel that she had placed on her bedside table the evening before.

The meal had been doomed from the outset due to a lack of cooked foods caused by ongoing difficulties in installing the new closed stove; it now dwindled rapidly into a dismal affair. It was no surprise, therefore, when the Duchess rose and announced that she would repose herself in her rooms for the afternoon, as usual, rather than accompanying the young people to the Green Room as she had done for the past few days.

"I say, Lady Felicity," William whispered as they exited the Small Dining Room. "Do you sketch? Lord Robert has been showing me some of Ravenscourt's better vistas, and I would like nothing better than to spend the afternoon attempting to capture the view of the Grecian temple across the lake from the high ground. You must see—I've brought my Claude mirror with me, to assist me with perspective and effect."

Felicity did not sketch, but she readily agreed to spend the afternoon with Mr. Chilvers and his Claude mirror, and she told him that she would bring her needlepoint instead.

"Well, it looks like it's just you and me this afternoon in the Green Room," Robert told Devorah. "And if I was you, I'd also get some rest. You're not looking so chipper, either. What is with all the women today at Ravenscourt?"

Some afternoons are marked for lethargy and depression. The day required only cold, dismal rain to create the proper accompanying atmosphere. But instead, the sun shone, and outdoors it was warm and breezy. This unhappy noncooperation between nature and state of mind only added to Devorah's misery. Taking Robert's advice, she returned to her room and *The Mysteries of Udolpho*, which was becoming quite an old friend of hers. But her thoughts strayed continually from Mrs. Radcliffe's words to those of Mr. Whyteman, who began to loom large in her mind. From Mr.

Whyteman it was but a short step to her predicament in general, and the need to find a way back to Boro Park within the next ten days specifically.

Her thoughts roiled, but no solution could be found—except, perhaps, to accept Mr. Whyteman's less-than-perfect proposal. After an hour of such mental agonies, the headache that had plagued her the evening before returned in full force. By the time Lucy came to dress her for dinner, Devorah felt so far from well that the maid whispered for her to stay in bed and fled to find Mrs. Wigmore.

The housekeeper was much shocked when she saw Devorah's appearance. "But it is no great wonder," she later declared to Spilsby. "Miss Asher is intended to be a guest, and she has worn herself to a frazzle doing for everyone else. Between helping Betsy out in the kitchen and saving Martha's life, and then to top it all, she has not put a morsel in her mouth since she has been here, excepting some raw fruits and biscuits from a tin, as was sent over from Ten Oaks. Not to mention water. Always water; never milk or wine or anything with a bit of nourishment. Lord knows, I have tried to keep boiled water ready and waiting for her, but who is to say that someone else has not given her that which is not fit to drink? Next thing we know, she will be heaving her innards out."

Devorah didn't retch, but the following morning she was running a fever, causing Adam and Felicity to insist on calling in Dr. Barrie.

This Devorah protested violently, but to no avail. Fortunately, the good doctor wasn't to be found, having left earlier that morning to attend a wide swath of patients throughout the parish who were suffering from the same complaint as Miss Asher. Thus, when Mr. Whyteman arrived late Friday morning to secretly deliver a Sabbath basket full of provisions into his grace's hands and was shown into the Green Room, he was accorded an unusually enthusiastic reception by two of those at Ravenscourt who usually wished him at perdition.

The first of these was the Duchess, whose glee at finding Miss Asher noticeably absent from dinner the evening before was tempered by the spectacle, at the same meal, of Miss Chilvers shamelessly making up to Adam, who did nothing to discourage her attentions. The Duchess, who had planned so carefully for the Duke's future and who had finally found a magically eligible *parti* for her second son as well, now discovered that those from whom she had every right to expect filial obedience were thwarting her wishes at every turn. She was, consequently, in a vile mood.

But she brightened visibly upon setting eyes on Jonathan. "Ah, Mr. Whyteman," she cried, descending upon him with an evil smile on her lips.

"Your grace." Mr. Whyteman executed a small bow. "At your service, as always."

The Duchess pulled a dog-eaten grisaille fan of ivory and paper from her reticule and began fanning herself vigorously. "I *hope* you may be of service to me. I rely wholly on you to rescue Ravenscourt from the plague."

"Pardon?"

The Lady Albinia, to whom the very mention of fever conjured up visions of whole villages across the entirety of England and the Continent rendered desolate, hurried eagerly to the Duchess's side. "Yes, a plague," she whispered urgently. "Miss Asher has a fever, and it has spread throughout the parish. And Dr. Barrie is not to be found."

"Miss Asher ill?" Jonathan paled. "But how can this be?"

"She has not been looking well for several days. And this morning she broke out in a high fever," Lady Albinia explained.

Here the Duchess interrupted. "It was my original idea, because Dr. Barrie is already stretched far beyond capacity with the fever sweeping the countryside, that perhaps dear Mrs. Fenton can send over one of her own remedies to cure Miss Asher's ills. But then I conceived of the plan of sending Miss Asher directly to Mrs. Fenton. Your housekeeper is an excellent nurse and she could better keep her eye on Miss Asher were you to move her to Ten Oaks."

"But, is Miss Asher in any condition to be moved?"

"Of course not!" the Duke exclaimed, entering the Green Room in search of Mr. Whyteman. "That is a crackbrained idea, and you know it."

"But she can infect the entire household," his mother protested.

"Nonsense," the unfilial son retorted. "Miss Asher will stay in her room for the next several days until her fever is gone. I have no doubt that plenty of rest and a warm fire will do wonders to cure her speedily. But, if you please, Mr. Whyteman, I agree that one of Mrs. Fenton's remedies would do more for Miss Asher than any of the concoctions that Dr. Barrie has in his arsenal. Would it be possible to have one sent over this afternoon?"

He turned to Mr. Whyteman and motioned toward the door. "By the by, Whyteman, would it be possible to speak with you privately in the library?" he asked in a low voice as they headed down the hallway. "I have heard more strange rumblings of pending war on the Continent."

"Yes, Napoleon ordered a general mobilization last Saturday."

"So I have been informed. I am worried about Theo's parents, who are still at the Congress of Vienna. Do you think there is any danger to them?"

"I am sure that all non-military personnel will be evacuated if danger appears imminent," Jonathan assured him. "But, why don't you ask Miss Asher that question? She claims to know the future."

"Yes, so I have noticed," his grace replied amiably. "Your Miss Asher is a veritable witch. Are you are so sure that you wish to marry her anyway?"

Chapter 24

Saturday came and went, as did Sunday. Devorah tossed and turned in her bed, unused to suffering a fever without so much as an aspirin. On Friday afternoon, Mrs. Fenton sent over a vile-looking saline draught of her own concoction, along with a jar of chicken soup and a pitcher of lemonade. Devorah, made nauseous by their odor, ordered both the draught and soup taken away. Lucy placed the lemonade on the small table next to the fireplace and came to the sickroom at intervals to check on Devorah and force her to take a sip or two of this sustaining liquid. Otherwise, she remained alone, swathed in a murky darkness during the day, and bathed in the light of a single candle and the small fire that burned in the grate by night.

Meanwhile, downstairs, the Duke and Miss Chilvers took long strolls in the rose garden and spent many enjoyable hours in conversation in the secluded alcove of the Italian windows, their privacy ensured by the benevolent but watchful eye of Spilsby, who employed a variety of stratagems to keep others away.

Meanwhile, Lady Felicity and Mr. Chilvers spent the better part of two afternoons sprawled on the newly scythed grass that spread for emerald eternity across the broad expanse of Ravenscourt's grounds, gazing at Capability Brown's genius through the distorted lens of the Claude mirror and discussing all the hopes, dreams and unwelcome responsibilities attendant upon being the younger sister of a wealthy duke and the untitled heir to one of the greatest fortunes in England. On Sunday after chapel, they enjoyed a fine long walk beyond Ravenscourt's gates in the general direction of Ardsleigh Manor.

The spring weather was fine, the days were blooming with promise and beauty, and the pending war on the Continent was not yet even a distant echo in the Gloucestershire countryside. Two of the scions of Ravenscourt were enjoying their halcyon days to the maximum.

Robert, who had a great regard for his own skin, was absent from Ravenscourt for much of the time that Devorah lay upstairs tossing and turning, but the Duchess and Lady Albinia spent many a grim hour alone together in the Green Room, laboriously complimenting each other's progress with their needlepoints and discussing the relative merits of a sprawling ducal seat such as Ravenscourt as opposed to a more compact, but no less impressive earl's residence such as Feldenham. The Duchess, feeling that Albinia was being shamefully neglected, stepped down from her dignity a little and favored her goddaughter with several choice anecdotes from childhood romps with Albinia's mother, Sophia. These brought a smile to Albinia's eyes and lips, but in her heart of hearts she still felt betrayed and destitute. She wished desperately that Mr. Duckwaithe were in residence so that she could unburden her tale of treachery upon his ecclesiastical shoulder.

On Sunday afternoon, Mrs. Fenton accompanied Jonathan to Ravenscourt to check on the invalid and was as shocked at her appearance as Mrs. Wigmore had been only days before. But she pronounced the fever to be abating and predicted that Devorah would be sitting up in bed the very next day. This proved to be true. Miss Asher awoke fever free the next morning and was able to sit up to read a page or two of *Udolpho* before resting her head back on her pillow. She was so weak and spent, however, that even the elusive thought that she ought to be searching urgently for a way to return home for the Passover holiday, now only a week away, failed to elicit any visceral response. She was too tired; she would worry about it on the morrow.

But Miss Asher's recovery was slower than she would have liked. Not until Wednesday afternoon did she venture an invalidish descent into the Green Room, looking pale and drawn, and inwardly fretting because she must find a way to leave Ravenscourt as soon as possible. Her appearance coincided with Mr. Duckwaithe's return to Ravenscourt as the Viscount Arkless.

Devorah had just settled herself on a chair in a far corner of the room when the new viscount was announced. Pausing wearily in the doorway, his somber clothes of mourning covered in the dust of a two-day journey, he invested his debut as a peer of the realm with a drama rivaling that of Edmund Kean at his greatest. "Duchess!" he ejaculated. "I hurried back as soon as was humanly possible!"

"My dear Lord Arkless, please have a seat," the Duchess said grandly, patting the comfortable wingchair next to hers. "You must be exhausted."

"Ma'am, I came directly to this parlor merely to inform you of my arrival. I must go now to wash the dust from my face and change into more suitable raiment."

"Oh, never mind that," the Duchess said, waving her hand dismissively. "Sit and tell me of everything happening at Hasborough Hall. How do you all go on there? *Such* a terrible tragedy. *Such* a sudden responsibility for you to assume."

Lucas seated himself gingerly on the edge of the indicated chair. "Yes, we are all in chaos at Hasborough Hall. The cook, of course, has been dismissed, bringing even further chaos to that unhappy home. There was some discussion that the local magistrate would press charges, but because my grandfather himself brought back the mushrooms for the fatal meal—and you know, ma'am, how determined he could be once he had his mind set on something—I have convinced those responsible for the rule of law that it was only a tragic mistake. Even so, I determined that I should not linger on, but should instead place estate matters in the hands of my grandfather's capable agent for the time being so that I could return here immediately and put matters in train to find you a new chaplain. I am afraid, Duchess, that my duties now lie elsewhere."

He turned to take a glass of sherry from Spilsby, who had appeared magically at his side. The butler cleared his throat. "May I be so bold, my lord, as to convey condolences on behalf of the upper servants and myself? We will be sorry to see you go." He cast a sidelong glance at Lady Albinia, who was quietly plying her embroidery needle by the window.

Lucas nodded graciously to the butler. His eyes swept the room, taking in William, holding the colored silks for the chair cover that Felicity was now embroidering. "I see you have a new visitor."

"Yes, there was an unfortunate carriage accident just outside our gates that involved Mr. Chilvers and his sister. She has broken her arm, and they are settled here until she is well enough to travel." The Duchess leaned forward until she was nearly nose-to-nose with his lordship. "I have the sister in my eye for Robert. She has one hundred thousand pounds," she whispered.

"I look forward to meeting her," Lucas said, visibly impressed. "Where is she now?"

"I believe that she is at present touring our lands with Robert. They are spending a great deal of time outdoors together. Robert has been at loose ends because Adam has been greatly tied up with estate business."

Lucas turned his attention toward the other females of the room. "Lady Felicity, Lady Albinia, it is a pleasure to see you again. I hope you go on well. And, Miss Asher, yourself as well." Felicity remained intent on her silks, but Albinia blushed and nodded and bent again over her needlework. Devorah shivered and pulled the ends of her shawl closer.

Spilsby returned to announce that Mr. Whyteman had arrived from Ten Oaks and was waiting in the library to speak privately with Miss Asher. "He is *forever* coming to Ravenscourt and asking for Miss Asher," the Duchess hissed to Lucas, forgetting that gentleman's previous infatuation. "It is most inappropriate."

"Perhaps Lady Albinia is correct after all," Lucas jested under his breath. "A foreigner and all that. Perhaps she and Mr. Whyteman are involved in clandestine affairs."

"That is not at all amusing," the Duchess declared. "It shall not happen under *my* roof."

But Miss Asher dragged herself up the stairs to the library, where the Duke was deep in discussion with Mr. Whyteman. "We have found an immediate solution for you," Adam announced. "It will do well, especially because you are still too weak to travel any long distance."

Mr. Whyteman explained that he no longer planned to travel to London to spend Passover with his family, but would stay at Ten Oaks instead. "I have received an express message from my parents. They are to come to *me* for the holiday, rather than my traveling to *them*. They did not state their reason, but it can only be a very good one. They will be arriving tomorrow with my brothers and sisters to spend the Great Sabbath before Passover with us, and I would like you to spend the Sabbath with us, as well. Because Passover is on Monday night, I am afraid you will not be able to travel on to spend Passover with the Chief Rabbi, but will remain instead at Ten Oaks."

"And after Passover?"

"After Passover, I would like you to return to London with my family. They would love to have you as their guest until suitable arrangements can be made for you. I think you will enjoy yourself greatly. Besides my parents, I have several brothers and sisters still at home."

"Come, Miss Asher," the Duke said gently in response to Devorah's crestfallen expression. "I know you are greatly disappointed at not being able to return to your family for the holidays. But this is the only solution."

Summoning all her self-control, Devorah pushed back the tears that threatened to overwhelm her and promised to be waiting just after luncheon on Friday, when Mr. Whyteman would call personally to take her to Ten Oaks. "Now, if you will excuse me, I am feeling ill again," she muttered as she ran from the room.

★ ★

"I feel like a traitor," Anne said as Adam helped her into the curricle.

"How so?"

"I understand that your brother Robert has been playing least-in-sight for the past several days. The Duchess apparently believes that he is spending his time with me, while you are out attending to your estates."

Adam raised his eyebrows. "Your information is interesting. Just how did you find this out?"

"Something your returning chaplain chanced to mention." Anne gasped and leaned over to clutch the side of the carriage with her good arm as the Duke sped over a pothole. "Adam, do be careful! I am here at Ravenscourt to heal, not to be killed!"

"Perhaps you would prefer that I return you to the Green Room to read poetry aloud to the needlepointing ladies until dinner?" the Duke suggested.

"Pooh! I would die of boredom, rather. My brother will tell you that I have always been an active, designing female, totally unfit to grace those salons in which females generally congregate to show off their feminine accomplishments."

"And your own accomplishments are?"

"My mother and I have established two soup kitchens in London," Anne said proudly. "And, we have just acquired property near Peckingham to establish a school for fallen women. We will teach them millinery arts and fine needlework, and all sorts of skills to return to respectability through reliable employers—all the skills, that is, that I myself disdain."

"Miss Chilvers," Adam said, stopping the carriage abruptly and taking her into his arms. "You are one woman in a million and exactly after my own heart. Will you marry me?"

"I think your mother may be becoming suspicious," William whispered to Felicity as they congregated in the drawing room before dinner. "Perhaps we shouldn't be so much together, at least until your mother is resigned to what appears to be happening between your brother and my sister. Just look at those two, casting such eyes at each other that it is enough to make one sick!"

"With whom should I speak instead?" Felicity asked wonderingly. "Albinia has cornered Lucas and appears to be pouring her heart out to him even now, over there by the fire, judging by the number of handkerchiefs she's managing to wet. It's a wonder that my mother hasn't become suspicious of *them*."

Mr. Chilvers cast a glance at the couple before the fireplace, but dismissed Felicity's suggestions with a gesture. "It appears to be nothing. Lord Arkless, after all, used to be your mother's chaplain. He is the natural address for Lady Albinia's confidences. But what about this Mr. Whyteman, about whom you are forever telling me? He was here earlier. Couldn't you contrive, next time he appears, to grab his notice, just to divert your mother's attention from myself?"

"He is hardly ever here now because he is tutoring my cousin Theo at Ten Oaks," Felicity explained. "Besides, I think that he has eyes only for Miss Asher. Fortunately, *she* won't be at dinner tonight as she is still feeling poorly. Her presence at table, sipping her water and picking at her fruits, is all that is needed when everyone else is in such a mood just now."

William shrugged. "Oh, here is the Duchess just entered. I'd better scoot on over and talk to Robert."

★ ★

When the men joined the ladies in the Burgundy Drawing Room after the meal that evening, the Duchess signaled to Lord Arkless to sit next to her by the fire so that they could enjoy a comfortable coze while the young people entertained themselves.

"I do believe that Robert and Miss Chilvers make a handsome couple," her grace said companionably to Lucas.

Lucas agreed that this was so, but it appeared to him that Miss Chilvers had eyes more for the Duke than for Robert or anyone else in the room. This, he thought, did not bode well for Lady Albinia.

"Now that you have become a member of the peerage, you ought to be thinking of taking a wife," the Duchess continued. "I already recommended marriage to you when you were a mere chaplain. But it is fortunate, after all, that you have not married until now. As a viscount, you require quite a different type of partner, someone along the lines of my own Felicity. She has a dowry of forty thousand pounds, you know."

Lord Arkless didn't know, though he had heard rumblings that Lady Felicity was well dowered. However, he had only to recall some of the more illustrious scrapes into which that intrepid damsel had entered during her childhood. She was somewhat more settled now, but even so, she was much too impulsive and headstrong for Lucas.

Feeling suddenly choked, he ran a finger around the inside of his shirt collar. He wondered whether he should return to Hasborough Hall sooner than he originally intended.

Chapter 25

Lucy pushed back the rose velvet curtains and accompanying sheers with a flourish, letting bright sunlight fill the room. "How are you feeling today, miss?" she asked solicitously, pushing aside the bed hangings. "His grace asked that I wake you early and find out, are you feeling better? He plans to take you for a ride today, his grace says, and he says that you will want to dress to go out."

Devorah stretched luxuriously. "Yes, I am feeling better," she admitted. "But I could do with a bath. I am positively crawling with dirt."

A few hours later, fashionably attired in a yellow-and-cream striped dress sprigged with tiny red flowers, her freshly washed and curled hair tied back from her forehead with a matching red ribbon, Devorah sat in the plush pink armchair, waiting for Lucy to return with a pair of shoes. "These are all I could find," the maid said apologetically, entering the room and setting a pair of shoes at Devorah's feet. "Lady Felicity and Miss Chilvers have *both* gone through near every pair in the house, between all their walks in the parks and down country lanes and who knows what else. Why, Lady Felicity's favorite green half boots are torn near through, and her blue embroidered kid slippers are caked with mud!"

"Those are Lady Felicity's new red slippers! She will never agree to let me wear them."

"Miss Tilstock said to take them, and she has already asked permission of Lady Felicity. So do you just lift your feet, miss, and let me slip these on you, and then you will be ready to go downstairs. See, it only wants the red spencer Miss Tilstock found in the back of Lady Felicity's wardrobe to complete the outfit."

Devorah rose and examined herself in the cheval glass while Lucy bustled about her, adjusting the ruff of her gown and the ribbon in her hair, adding pearl eardrops and a small cameo on a riband and, finally, placing the red spencer over all. The maid started for the door, but Devorah lingered by the glass, debating whether to let Lucy into her confidence. Finally, friendship won over prudence.

"You have been a loyal maid to me, Lucy," she said, causing the girl to blush with pleasure. "I have something to tell you. Can you keep a secret, even from the other servants for now? Yes—good, I think you can. This is my last day at Ravenscourt, you must know. I am leaving here, never to return."

"Oh, miss, you are going home?"

"Home? I wish I were going home," Devorah cried. "I am only traveling to London, in hopes of finding my way home from there. That's why I don't want to take Lady Felicity's new shoes with me. Tell her, please, that I will guard them carefully, and I will try to send them back to her as soon as possible."

She tripped over to the dressing table and grabbed the small embroidered reticule that she had nearly left behind. "Here, please take this for your kind services." She reached into the bag and brought out several coins, which she handed to Lucy. "And as for the others who have been so kind— Betsy, Mrs. Wigmore, Spilsby, even Tilstock, without whom I never could have been properly dressed!—I have not forgotten them, either. His grace has promised to relay my vails to them. He will inform all of you of my leaving when I am already gone—except, perhaps, Tilstock, who may already know of the plan. It is possible that his grace has asked her to pack my bags for me."

At the luncheon table that day, Devorah considered with wry amusement how fortunate it was that she customarily didn't eat the cold meats and cakes offered at midday. She had no appetite, but was instead growing steadily more nauseous from nerves. Finally, the family rose from the table. As she pondered whether to follow the Duchess and Lady Albinia upstairs or to linger near the front hall until Jonathan arrived, Spilsby materialized at her side to whisper that Mr.

Whyteman had been delayed and would not be able to come fetch her until later that afternoon, and that he had therefore taken the liberty of hiding the bandboxes containing her possessions in the Great Hall, behind the marble stand holding the suit of armour.

"And, may I say, it has been a pleasure to serve you during your brief stay here at Ravenscourt," the butler added, bowing majestically before turning quickly away.

The clock in the library, where Devorah was reading the final pages of *Udolpho*, struck four in the afternoon when the crunch of wheels was heard on the gravel drive outside. Devorah ran to the library window and saw Mr. Whyteman throw the reins of his carriage to a groom and head toward Ravenscourt's front steps. She took a deep breath and hurried downstairs.

When she reached the Great Hall, Jonathan was talking to the Duke; he urged her to hurry, as there was much to do and sunset wasn't far behind. Smiling weakly at the Duke, Devorah tried, with much emotion, to thank him. But he brushed off her thanks and admonished her to take her boxes and make haste. With no further ceremony, Jonathan grabbed the two bandboxes that the Duke was holding, nodded his own thanks, and hurried Devorah out the door.

Felicity, who had spent much of the afternoon with William and had experienced her first real disagreement with him, was resting in her room in an attempt to recover her emotional equilibrium. The sound of voices and the commotion below awoke her from the light sleep into which she had finally fallen after much tossing and turning. She ran to her window just in time to see Mr. Whyteman hand Devorah and two bandboxes up into his carriage. Clearly, an elopement was in progress!

Her curiosity piqued, Felicity shoved her feet into her pink kid slippers and ran down the stairs to the Great Hall just as Spilsby hurriedly turned away from one of the mullioned windows. "But what is going on, Spilsby? I thought I saw Miss Asher just now, driving off with Mr. Whyteman."

"I have no idea, my lady," Spilsby disclaimed calmly. "I only just this minute arrived in the hall."

Casting her glance around the hall, Felicity noticed a bit of color peeking out from behind the suit of armour's marble base. "But what is this?" she asked, extracting a pretty papered bandbox from a hidden niche. "Miss Asher must have left it behind. I saw Mr. Whyteman place two similar boxes in his carriage."

She quickly untied the string that held the box closed. Inside were the azure-blue silk dinner dress, white chemisette, and pale blue slippers in which Devorah was discovered only weeks before, along with a mesh reticule that contained Miss Asher's diamond eardrops and pearl necklace. "Her earrings and necklace! She will certainly want these. Spilsby, where is Adam? He must be informed immediately."

But Adam, having safely sent Miss Asher off to Ten Oaks, had slipped out the back door to take a brief stroll with Miss Chilvers and was nowhere to be found.

Now that she had met William, the thought that Devorah and Mr. Whyteman were eloping failed to cause Lady Felicity any major heartbreak. She did think it strange, however. If they wanted to marry, why didn't they do so openly, rather than driving off in that clandestine manner? But elopement or no elopement, she was positive that Devorah would want the diamond eardrops and pearl necklace she had left behind. Undeterred by Adam's absence, she went in search of Robert, without any real expectation of finding him. Her brother, she had noticed on more than one occasion, was disappearing with greater and greater frequency now that the Chilvers siblings were staying at Ravenscourt, and her mother was becoming more obtuse by the minute.

When her efforts to ferret out Robert failed, she had no other choice but to seek out William, apologize, and ask him to accompany her.

"We can take my phaeton now that I've fixed the wheel," William offered instantly, glad to have an excuse to make up with Felicity. Within minutes he was impressing the stable boy with the need to harness the horses quickly, and it wasn't long before the carriage was being tooled out of the yard. William pressed a coach wheel into the youth's hand and swore him to secrecy, offered Felicity a hand up into the high seat, and they dashed down the lane in pursuit of Miss Asher, pausing only at the lodge to ask Badger in which direction Mr. Whyteman's coach was headed.

"We should have taken the barouche. At least then, we could have asked one of the under-coachmen to drive us or have brought along a groom. But I don't understand. If they are eloping, it makes more sense to travel north," Felicity marveled. "If Badger is correct and they have turned south, they must be going to Ten Oaks Manor."

"I doubt we would have been given the barouche on either your or my authority," William countered. "But if it's propriety you are worried about, I wouldn't. I expect that we have only a very short journey ahead of us; nothing to raise the alarm with any of the dragons. It's a little late in the day to be traveling to the border; it wants but a little over an hour and a half until sunset. I expect they are spending the night at Ten Oaks under the chaperonage of Mr. Whyteman's housekeeper, with the intent of getting an early start in the morning. We will go to Ten Oaks. If they are not there, we will leave the bandbox with the housekeeper. Miss Asher's diamond eardrops will be waiting for her when she returns from her wedding trip."

Albinia also indulged in a late afternoon nap, but she slept through Miss Asher's stirring departure. She awoke some half an hour later, just in time to be drawn to the window to witness Lady Felicity speeding off with Mr. Chilvers, groomless, unchaperoned, with a bandbox tightly clutched in her hands.

Lady Albinia looked over at the small mother-of-pearl clock on the mantelpiece. It wanted but twenty-five minutes until five. If something wasn't done to catch up with Felicity and Mr. Chilvers before nightfall, Felicity would be compromised. Realizing that the honor of Ravenscourt rested on her thin shoulders, she reached for the bell-pull and rang for her maid.

★ ★

"Are you sure, Lady Albinia, that you want to go dashing after them?" Lord Arkless asked Albinia for the third time.

"We must follow as quickly as possible. Precious minutes have already been lost, and the Duke is nowhere to be found!"

"My dear Lady Albinia, it will be nightfall in another hour or so. I suggest we ask Miss Asher to accompany us, or at least your maid."

"My maid is useless. We can take the barouche and ask John Coachman to drive us. I only hope we may succeed in averting this terrible deed before the Duchess learns of it. I wish to spare her any worry. Oh, please hurry!"

Lucas raced to the stables and ordered the boy on duty to harness up the barouche as quickly as possible. "Do as I say, boy," the viscount commanded, and went in search of a coachman. After an agonizing passage of time, the stable boy pronounced the barouche ready to go. Lucas pressed a couple of coach wheels into his hand and swore him to secrecy, then ordered the puzzled under-coachman he had pressed into service to tool the carriage out of the yard. Within minutes, Lucas and Albinia were dashing down the lane in pursuit of Felicity and her swain. But unlike Felicity and William, Lucas failed to ask Badger at the lodge in which direction their carriage was headed. Instead, going on erroneous instinct, he ordered the coachman to turn north in the direction of a stretch of road that linked up with the post road.

Adam and Anne returned half an hour later to be met by Spilsby with the news that Lady Felicity had gone dashing off with William in the Chilverses' phaeton an hour previously, and that the Lady Albinia and Lord Arkless followed in the barouche not long after. Should dinner be set back, or should their places be removed from the table?

"Would this by any chance have anything to do with Miss Asher's departure from Ravenscourt?" the Duke wondered.

"I would not know, your grace."

Theo, who had been lurking next to the suit of armour, took the opportunity to intervene. "It most definitely would, sir. Miss Asher and Mr. Whyteman are eloping, aren't they? I know because I heard Cousin Felicity say so, but Felicity and William *aren't* eloping, but just chasing after Miss Asher to give her the bandbox with her diamonds."

Theo paused for breath, then asked the same question as Felicity. "But why would they need to go to the trouble to elope when they can just get married? And does this mean that Mr. Whyteman will be too busy to learn with me *every* day and not just today?"

"Mr. Whyteman and Miss Asher are *not* eloping," the Duke corrected him. "But that still doesn't explain why Lucas and Albinia raced off together."

"Yes it does," Theo said triumphantly. "Binny thinks that Felicity and William are eloping, too, and she has gone off to bring them back before nightfall."

"*Lady Albinia* to you, Theo. How do you know all this, you little scamp?"

"I've been listening. And my hiding place is a secret and I am not about to tell you, so don't even ask." Theo saluted and turned on his heels. "Now, if you will excuse me, I am wanted up in the schoolroom."

Anne laughed. "He certainly is an original."

"Yes, indeed," Adam concurred. "But I am afraid that we may have to drive over to Ten Oaks to try to avert a disaster of major proportions. Spilsby, if anyone asks, you know nothing. And especially if my mother asks, you know nothing. But please concoct an excuse that will be acceptable to both Mother and Monsieur Armand for pushing dinner back an hour."

Spilsby nodded majestically and suggested, as the evening was becoming cool, that Anne wait indoors until the Duke returned with a suitable vehicle. This was speedily accomplished, and soon Anne was being assisted up into the Duke's curricle.

"Should we not ask your groom to accompany us for propriety's sake?" Miss Chilvers suggested as Adam started down the lane. "It will soon become dark."

"Certainly not. We are already engaged, or, if you do not intend that we become engaged, I will be happy to compromise you." The Duke turned to Miss Chilvers. "You never gave me your answer, you know."

"You never asked me properly," Miss Chilvers replied. "You are a duke, the top of the pomp. I expect, at the very least, a balladeer under my window on a moonlit night—such as tonight will be, as it's nearly a full moon. Or, a violinist or two. And you, dear Duke, may accompany them, getting down on one knee and looking up at me as you present your pretty request."

"You are incorrigible, Anne."

Adam slowed as they approached the lodge and leaned over to ask Badger in which direction the previous carriages had turned at the gate. The gatekeeper, who had known the Duke from his infancy, bowed low and grinned widely at his grace's companion, and rattled off the various directions of the three previous vehicles.

"Excellent." Adam nodded to Badger and turned south out of the gate. "Felicity and William, who may or may not have consulted Badger, appear to have followed Miss Asher and Mr. Whyteman to Ten Oaks. Lady Albinia and Lucas, on

270

the other hand, appeared to have bought into the crackbrained idea that Felicity and William are headed toward the border, having started on their long journey a mere hour before nightfall."

"Should we instead try to overtake Lady Albinia and his lordship? Or, do you think they will turn back before dark?"

"I wish they may not. Then I can hire a dozen balladeers and two dozen violinists to make music under your window without the least worry of offending Lady Albinia. She and Lucas are positively meant for each other, you know."

"But what about your mother?" Anne asked. The country air was becoming chill, and she moved closer to Adam for warmth.

"My mother will be mollified by the size of your fortune, of which I have no need. And, she and Lady Loughborough can share their transports and tell everyone that it was their lifelong wish fulfilled. We must go and visit your aunt, by the way. I know that William trotted off to see her earlier this week, but in this advanced age of transportation, there is no need to stay home just because of a broken arm."

Adam pulled over to the side of the road, slipped an arm around her waist and pulled her closer to his side. "There, you see, the sun has not yet set, but in only an hour or so I will have compromised you, I hope. Unless, dear Anne, you will marry me."

Anne rested her head on his shoulder. "Do I have any choice in the matter? You are crushing my broken arm."

★ ★

Devorah set the bandboxes down on her bed at Ten Oaks. Tilstock had packed them on the Duke's instructions, and somewhere among the contents should be the ivory-inlaid comb and brush set that Mrs. Wigmore had given her when she first arrived at Ravenscourt. There wasn't much time to freshen up, but at the very least she could splash water on her face and brush her hair and teeth.

Shedding the red spencer that Lucy had brought her, she searched the bandboxes for the Norwich silk shawl that

Felicity had given her. It was a shame that she couldn't change her shoes, too; but Tilstock appeared to have forgotten to pack the pale blue slippers she was wearing when she landed in England, so she would have to make do with Felicity's red morocco slippers. A further search revealed that Tilstock had also forgotten to pack the blue silk dress and her jewelry from America. No matter; she would send to Ravenscourt for them on Sunday morning. Better to concentrate on freshening up, she thought, because soon it would be time to light candles and usher in the Sabbath.

★ ★

Albinia was still certain that Felicity and William were headed north for the border. But his lordship wasn't so sure. It had showered briefly only that morning, and the country lanes were still a bit damp. Lucas pointed out—quite reasonably, he thought—that if Lady Felicity and Mr. Chilvers had been headed north, fresh tracks from their carriage would appear to some degree in the road.

Eventually giving in to the superior male mind, Lady Albinia agreed that perhaps they should stop and ask the next person they encountered whether a phaeton carrying a young couple had passed that way any time in the previous half hour. The next person was a sturdy young farmhand who respectfully tugged at his forelock and bobbed his head, but denied all knowledge of any other passing vehicles.

"Could they have headed east toward London instead?" Albinia wondered.

"They could," his lordship said. "But to what purpose?"

"I don't know. I am asking that myself. Why did they elope in the first place? Although the Duchess has always aimed higher for Felicity, surely with time and in contemplation of Mr. Chilver's fortune, she would have come around."

Lucas cleared his throat. "My own fortune, now, you know, is not at all contemptible. I have inherited, in addition to the title, all the Arkless and Duckwaithe lands, and these are quite extensive."

272

Albinia nodded. "Yes, I think that now that you have been elevated to the peerage, the Duchess has thought of you for Lady Felicity."

"The Duchess," his lordship said somewhat savagely, "is all that is good, but sometimes she is clearly wide of the mark. But enough, time is short! I see a crossroads ahead, and I will ask the coachman to turn the horses there."

"But where are we going?" Albinia asked.

"We will backtrack in the direction of the London road and see whether we can pick up their carriage tracks on our way. If not, we will return to Ravenscourt. I cannot in good conscience keep you out any longer."

Lady Albinia agreed that this was a good plan, and the couple spent the next twenty minutes in careful travel along country byways in a south-easterly direction toward Ten Oaks Manor and the London road beyond. The lanes were still rutted from the winter cold, and the afternoon light was beginning to wane. About a mile from Ten Oaks, the driver failed to notice a particularly large rut in the road, and the occupants of the carriage suffered a surprise when it suffered a rough jolt and, with a loud crack, a wheel fell off.

★ ★

"Shall I go in with you?" William asked as he brought the carriage to a halt.

"Yes, if you please. There is a strange quiet here today."

William started to climb down from his high perch. "Felicity," he said, almost as an afterthought. "I am sorry about our disagreement earlier today. Please forgive me. I hope we will always go on in harmony together."

He said *always*, Felicity thought happily.

Slightly breathless, her heart beating rapidly, she said that of course she forgave him.

★ ★

There was nothing for it but for Lucas and Albinia to walk to Ten Oaks Manor and impose upon Mr. Whyteman's generosity. Hopefully, he would offer them a ride back to

Ravenscourt, but if not, surely he would give them shelter for the night.

"It is rapidly approaching sundown, Lady Albinia. I have put you in an untenable situation, and I apologize with all my heart," his lordship said, absently taking Albinia's arm to steady her over the stones and ruts and low-lying plants that made the rough countryside so difficult to navigate on foot. "I hope, when we return together to Ravenscourt, that the Duke, in his benevolence, will continue to believe in your purity and innocence."

Albinia flushed. "I have been disappointed in Adam of late," she admitted. "I know that it has always been our mothers' fondest wish that we join the two families through holy matrimony, but I am beginning to question whether we could ever be of one mind and one heart. We are so different, that the bliss one expects with married life might elude us."

She sighed significantly, then stumbled on a particularly large hole in the road. Lord Arkless latched on to her arm more firmly. "We are nearly there," he assured her.

They continued down the road in perfect amiability. As Ten Oaks came into sight, Lucas absently released his grip on Lady Albinia's arm and took her hand instead. "This is merely conjecture," he ventured, "but should the Duke decide to bestow his heart elsewhere, do you think that you could marry me instead?"

★ ★

"I see that Felicity and William have beaten us here," the Duke said as he drew his own curricle up in front of Ten Oaks Manor.

"Adam, can you please tell me what is going on?" Anne pleaded. "You have dragged me halfway across the countryside when I am wanting my dinner, and you haven't even let me in on the secret of why a disaster is about to occur."

"I only dragged you out so that I would have an excuse for proposing to you again," the Duke said reasonably. "But, in the few minutes before we go knocking on the door, I will give you a brief history of what has occurred at Ravenscourt since Miss Asher's arrival." This he did succinctly and rapidly, eliciting a raised eyebrow here and a small exclamation of shock there, but overall Miss Chilvers accepted his explanation in the same spirit as she accepted Adam's other idiosyncracies.

"Anne, you are a woman in two million," the Duke said, jumping down from his seat.

★ ★

"It is strange that they are not answering," Felicity said, plying the knocker again loudly.

"Perhaps they are busy and don't hear you. Wait a few minutes, and then try again," William advised. But footsteps could be heard approaching from within, and finally the door was opened by Isaac Fenton, Ten Oak's butler and man of all trades, dressed in his Sunday best.

"I am sorry, Lady Felicity. Mr. Whyteman isn't home to visitors this evening." The servant executed a small bow and started to shut the door.

But Felicity proved quicker than Isaac. Thrusting the bandbox she was carrying into the doorway, she said boldly, "I have brought Miss Asher some items she left behind at Ravenscourt. She will see *me*."

"I will see that they reach her." Isaac held out his hand to take the box.

"What is it, Isaac?" Jonathan's familiar voice sounded behind him. "Why, Lady Felicity, Mr. Chilvers. Please come in and have a seat. Miss Asher will be with you shortly. Isaac, please show them to the drawing room."

The knocker sounded again, and a minute later the Duke and Miss Chilvers entered the drawing room just as Felicity and William were arranging themselves on the sofa. "Adam, what are you doing here?" Felicity asked in surprise.

"I could ask you the same question, but I already know the answer. I hope you have managed to convey the missing bandbox to Miss Asher safe and sound."

"No, I have not seen her yet," Felicity replied.

"Trust me, you needn't have brought it to her at all," the Duke told her. "Your being here creates all kinds of complications. But what is that I hear? The knocker again? I expect it is Lord Arkless and Lady Albinia, come to put the finishing touch to this little comedy."

"What are *they* doing here?" his sister asked.

"Come to save you from an elopement."

"An elopement?" William sputtered. "We are not eloping."

"I know that, but Albinia and Lucas do not share my extensive mental capabilities."

"You!" Albinia shrieked from the doorway, pointing a finger at Felicity. "I have traveled half the countryside to rescue you from a terrible deed, and you have been entertaining yourselves here all the time? And what are *you* doing here, Adam? Does my godmother know that you are attending a dinner party at Ten Oaks this evening?"

"Now, now, Lady Albinia, I am sure there is a good explanation for everything," Lucas said soothingly.

At that moment, Devorah's voice floated musically out of the dining room. "I will just take this box to her now and be on my way," Felicity announced. "Come William." Bearing the box as reverently as she would a gift to the king, she marched from the drawing room, the others trailing behind her.

This time Isaac wasn't present to place any obstacles in the visitors' path; nor was Mr. Whyteman there to arrest their progress. And none of the women and girls already assembled in the dining room paid any attention to the door or noticed that several members of Ravenscourt had joined them. Instead, their eyes were all on Devorah as Mrs. Fenton passed her a thin taper in a long silver holder. Devorah ceremoniously held the taper first to one tall candle and then to another in a glowing silver candelabrum placed on the sideboard. And then she waved her hands three times in front of the lit candles in strange, semi-circular motions, placed her hands over her eyes, and recited a strange incantation.

There was silence as Devorah continued with a silent prayer.

A shriek shattered the serenity of the moment. "A witch! A witch!" Lady Albinia cried out. "I *knew* there was something wrong with her. She is a *witch*. They are *all* witches here." Spent from her outburst, she tottered backwards and slid to the floor.

Time shifted into slow motion for Devorah as she looked around the room, gauging the reactions of the witnesses to this spectacle. They turned as one and looked in horror at Lady Albinia, prostrate on the floor, then back at her in speechless wonder. Felicity and William gawked, grim-faced, at the glowing candles in their silver candelabras; Lucas went so far as to cross himself, then, recollecting himself with a start, knelt solicitously over Albinia's prone body. A muscle twitched in Adam's cheek as he struggled to suppress a smile, and Anne leaned over to whisper to him, "I supposed we didn't get here in time." Jonathan and Isaac, summoned by Albinia's outburst, stood frozen in the doorway.

It was too much!

"I—I want to go home," Devorah whispered. "I want to go home!"

"Do you really want to go home?" Jonathan asked, edging his way toward her through the crowded room. Devorah nodded. "Then close your eyes, click your heels together three times and say it again."

Devorah squeezed her eyes shut and clicked the heels of her ruby-bowed, red morocco slippers. "I want to go home. Please, please, I want to go home," she repeated, and clicked. "I want to go home."

And then, like the Lady Albinia, she slid gracefully to the floor.

Chapter 26

"Can someone please clear a space around her so that she has some air," a decisive male voice said from far away.

"Water, I still think we should pour water on her," said an older female voice with a Yiddish accent from another distance.

"And I still say we need to call first responders," a different female voice said. "She really banged herself on the head."

"Yes, go call first responders," the male voice said. "Wait, wait—I think she's coming to."

Devorah slowly opened her eyes. At first, everything was a blur. But gradually she became aware of faces all around her, looking down at her from every angle. Kneeling next to her was someone in huge black glasses and a bulbous plastic nose. Yitzhak, someone else called him. There were younger men, dressed in clown costumes, and an older lady with a gray wig, and a miniature bride whom everyone was calling Miri. It was all so confusing, and her head hurt terribly. Where was she? She closed her eyes again. It hurt less in oblivion.

"You'll be better in no time, dahlink," said the gray-wigged lady with the Yiddish accent.

"When will the first responders get here? Did you call them?" the younger female voice asked. "Yitzhak, I'm worried about her. We should have called them right away."

"Devorah, Devorah," called another voice, lifting her from the depths. She knew this voice from somewhere. Her eyes fluttered open again, and she saw a pleasant-looking man of medium height and build, with laugh lines forming at the corners of his hazel eyes. He looked familiar, like someone she had once known somewhere. Like Jonathan Whyteman.

"Come, that's better now," the man said. Someone had said that before, but who? And when?

Something was wrong. The man looked like Jonathan Whyteman, but didn't look like him. The clothing was wrong, and even the lighting was different. There had been an accident, someone explained to her, and she might be feeling a little disoriented, but an ambulance was on the way, and soon she would be better.

The Jonathan who wasn't Jonathan smiled at her. Somehow this reassured her. She closed her eyes, but only to rest this time; not to sink back down into the black. "Devorah," he reminded her. "You are home now."

Startled, she opened her eyes and looked at him.

Someone pounded on the front door, and soon two volunteer paramedics in neon yellow vests rushed into the kitchen. The younger woman, whom everyone called Gitty, explained about the accident.

"That's a nasty crack on the head you got there," one of the medics commented as he shined a light into her eyes. "It's a miracle that you didn't split your head open when you hit it on the kitchen counter."

"Blood pressure is normal," the other medic said. "How long was she out?"

"A minute or two," Gitty answered.

"Everything looks normal," the first medic said. "But I think she should go get checked out. We'll need for someone to escort her." He indicated that Gitty should help her sit up, and after a few minutes said that she appeared to be merely banged up from the fall, but that it was better to not take any chances. "Can you walk, miss?"

Gitty helped her to her feet. "I think I'm okay," Devorah said bravely. "Just a little woozy. I'm sure if I rest a little bit and put an ice pack where I banged my head, I'll be fine."

The elderly woman shook her head. "No, dahlink, it's to the hospital you should go. You want I should go with you?"

Jonathan, who had been watching Devorah intently, held up his hand at this. "I'll take her."

Memories, as if from another life, of a stately, ancient mansion set on a huge expanse of gently rolling parkland, green and lush and wooded, came flowing back to her. Memories also of an ornately paneled study, and of a long table set with silver that gleamed by candlelight and braided loaves peeking from under an antique embroidered cloth, and a man who looked like Jonathan, but wasn't this Jonathan, seated confidently at the head of the table. The nostalgia was so poignant that it caused her to tremble.

She turned to Jonathan. "Would you please?" she whispered.

Gitty wrung her hands together and looked at Yitzhak. "Is it proper? They've only just been introduced."

"No, don't answer that," Jonathan commanded, interrupting his cousin. "For years now you and Gitty and everyone else have hounded me unceasingly in your efforts to get me riveted again, and now that everything is going on swimmingly, you want to put a spoke in my wheel? You both must be touched in your upper works!"

Yitzhak looked at Gitty out of the corner of his eye. "What is he talking about?"

Gitty shrugged. "Beats me."

"Thank you, Jonathan!" Devorah smiled. "Exactly what I myself wanted to say. Well, then, shall we go?"

"Your barouche is waiting, ma'am," Jonathan said, indicating that they should follow the medics.

Halfway to the door, Devorah stopped and turned to her hosts. "Don't worry about me. Everything—*everything*—will be okay."

Jonathan smiled at her again. And he winked.

About the Author

D.B. Schaefer was born and raised in the American Midwest, but headed to more exotic locales after university. A former journalist and still an incurable bookworm, she lives with her husband, children, and a vast collection of Georgette Heyer novels and is currently working on a new historical romance. *Me & Georgette* is her first novel.

The author welcomes comments and questions. You can contact her at db@dbschaefer.com. To learn more about her, visit D.B. Schaefer's website at www.dbschaefer.com.

If you enjoyed *Me & Georgette,* please let others know by leaving a review on www.amazon.com.

Made in the USA
Las Vegas, NV
20 December 2021

38981486R00173